CITY
OF
STAIRS

ROBERT JACKSON BENNETT

Jo Fletcher
BOOKS

First published in Great Britain in 2014 by Jo Fletcher Books
This edition published in Great Britain in 2015 by

Jo Fletcher Books
an imprint of
Quercus Publishing Ltd
Carmelite House
50 Victoria Embankment
London EC4Y 0DZ

An Hachette UK company

The moral right of Robert Jackson Bennett to be
identified as the author of this work has been
asserted in accordance with the Copyright,
Designs and Patents Act, 1988.

A CIP catalogue record for this book is available
from the British Library.

PB ISBN 978 1 84866 798 3
EBOOK ISBN 978 1 84866 797 6

This book is a work of fiction. Names, characters,
businesses, organizations, places and events are
either the product of the author's imagination
or used fictitiously. Any resemblance to
actual persons, living or dead, events or
locales is entirely coincidental.

10 9 8 7 6 5 4 3 2 1

Typeset by Jouve (UK), Milton Keynes

Printed and bound in Great Britain by Clays Ltd, St Ives plc

For Ashlee
who helps me believe in a better tomorrow

And Olvos said to them: 'Why have you done this, my children? Why is the sky wreathed with smoke? Why have you made war in far places, and shed blood in strange lands?'

And they said to Her: 'You blessed us as Your people, and we rejoiced, and were happy. But we found those who were not Your people, and they would not become Your people, and they were wilful and ignorant of You. They would not open their ears to Your songs, or lay Your words upon their tongues. They would not listen. So we dashed them upon the rocks and threw down their houses and shed their blood and scattered them to the winds, and we were right to do so. For we are Your people. We carry Your blessings. We are Yours, and so we are right. Is this not what You said?'

And Olvos was silent.

Book of the Red Lotus, Part IV, *13.51 – 13.59*

Someone even worse

'I believe the question, then,' says Vasily Yaroslav, 'is one of *intent*. I am aware that the court might disagree with me – this court has always ruled on the side of effect rather than intent – but you cannot seriously fine an honest, modest businessman such a hefty fee for an unintentional damage, can you? Especially when the damage is, well, one of *abstraction*?'

A cough echoes in the courtroom, dashing the pregnant pause. Through the window the shadows of drifting clouds race across the walls of Bulikov.

Governor Turyin Mulaghesh suppresses a sigh and checks her watch. *If he goes on for six more minutes*, she thinks, *we'll have a new record*.

'And you have heard testimony from my friends,' says Yaroslav, 'my neighbours, my employees, my family, my . . . my *bankers*. People who know me well, people who have no reason to lie! They have told you again and again that this is all just an unfortunate coincidence!'

Mulaghesh glances to her right along the high court bench. Prosecutor Jindash, his face the very picture of concern, is carefully doodling a picture of his own hand on the official Ministry of Foreign Affairs letterhead. To her left, Chief Diplomat Troonyi is staring with unabashed interest at the well-endowed girl in the first row of the courtroom seats. Next to Troonyi, at the end of the high court bench, is an empty chair, normally occupied by the visiting professor Dr Efrem Pangyui, who has been more and more absent from these proceedings lately. But frankly, Mulaghesh is only too happy for his absence: his presence in the courtroom, let alone in this whole damn country, has caused enough headaches for her.

'The court' – Yaroslav pounds on the table twice – 'must see reason!'

I must find someone else, thinks Mulaghesh, *to come to these things in my place*. But this is wishful thinking: as the Polis Governor of Bulikov, the capital city of the Continent, it is her duty to preside over all trials, no matter how frivolous.

'So you all have heard, and you must understand, that I never *intended* the sign that stood outside my business to be . . . to be of the nature that it was!'

The crowd in the courtroom mutters as Yaroslav skirts this sensitive subject. Troonyi strokes his beard and leans forward as the girl in the front row crosses her legs. Jindash is colouring in the fingernails on his sketch. Mulaghesh finds herself wishing once again that the polis courtroom had a much different design. The room is spare and stern, more the setting of a military tribunal than a civil court, and it harshly divides the two audiences: the Bulikovians and other Continentals, being citizens of the occupied nation, are seated behind the railings; the Saypuris, being the occupying force, are all seated behind the high bench, towering above everyone. (*Though can we really call ourselves occupiers*, wonders Mulaghesh, *if we've been here for nearly seventy-five years? When do we graduate to residents?*) The whole place is so forbidding, she finds, that the Continentals must expect every sentence handed down to be death by execution. She once submitted a formal request asking the design be reconsidered – 'At least divide us less,' she told them, 'as we're so brown and the Continentals so pale, we hardly need to have a railing to tell us who is who' – but the Saypuri Ministry of Foreign Affairs only made one adjustment: they made the court benches three inches higher.

Yaroslav summons up his nerve.

Here it comes, thinks Mulaghesh.

'I never *intended*,' he says clearly, 'for my sign to reference any Divinity, any trace of the celestial, nor any god!'

A quiet hum as the courtroom fills with whispers. Mulaghesh and the rest of the Saypuris on the bench remain unimpressed by the dramatic nature of this claim. 'How do they not know,' mutters Jindash, 'that this happens at every single Worldly Regulations trial?'

'Quiet,' whispers Mulaghesh.

This public breach of the law emboldens Yaroslav. 'Yes, I . . . I never intended to show fealty to any Divinity! I know *nothing* of the Divinities, of what they were or who they were . . .'

Mulaghesh barely stops herself from rolling her eyes. Every Continental knows *something* about the Divinities: to claim otherwise would be akin to claiming ignorance that rain is wet.

'. . . and thus I could not have known that the sign I posted outside my millinery unfortunately, *coincidentally*, mimicked a Divinity's sigil!'

A pause. Mulaghesh glances up, realising Yaroslav has stopped speaking. 'Are you finished, Mr Yaroslav?' she asks.

Yaroslav hesitates. 'Yes? Yes. Yes, I believe so, yes.'

'Thank you. You may take your seat.'

Prosecutor Jindash stands, takes the floor and produces a large photograph of a painted sign which reads: YAROSLAV HATS. Below the letters on the sign is a largish symbol, a straight line ending in a curlicue pointing down, yet it has been altered slightly to suggest the outline of a hat's brim.

Jindash swivels on his heels to face the crowd. 'Would this be your sign, Mr Yaroslav?'

'Y-yes,' says Yaroslav.

'Thank you.' Jindash flourishes the photograph before the bench, the crowd, everyone. 'Let the court please see that Mr Yaroslav has confirmed this sign – yes, *this* sign – as his own.'

CD Troonyi nods as if having gained deeply perceptive insight. The crowd of Continentals mutters anxiously. Jindash walks to his briefcase with the air of a magician before a trick – *How I hate*, Mulaghesh thinks, *that this theatrical little shit got assigned to Bulikov* – and produces a large imprint of a similar symbol: a straight line ending in a curlicue. But in this instance, the symbol has been rendered to look like it is made of dense, twisting vines, even sporting tiny leaves at the curlicue.

The crowd gasps at the reveal of this sign. Some move to make holy gestures, but stop themselves when they realise where they are. Yaroslav himself flinches.

Troonyi snorts. 'Knows nothing of the Divinities *indeed*.'

'Were the estimable Dr Efrem Pangyui here' – Jindash gestures to the empty chair beside Troonyi – 'I have no doubt that he would quickly identify this as the holy sigil of the Divinity . . . I apologise, the *deceased* Divinity . . .'

The crowd mutters in outrage; Mulaghesh makes a note to reward Jindash's arrogance with a transfer to somewhere cold and inhospitable, with plenty of rats.

'. . . known as *Ahanas*,' Jindash finishes. 'This sigil, specifically, was believed by Continentals to imbue great fecundity, fertility and vigour. For a milliner it would suggest, however peripherally, that his hats imbued their wearers with these same properties. Though Mr Yaroslav may protest, we have heard from Mr Yaroslav's financiers that his business experienced a robust upturn after installing this sign outside his property! In fact, his quarterly revenue increased by *twenty-three per cent.*' Jindash sets down the imprint, and makes a two with the fingers of one hand and a three with the other. 'Twenty. Three. Per cent.'

'Oh my goodness,' says Troonyi.

Mulaghesh cannot bear it: she covers her eyes in embarrassment. *I should never have left the military*.

'How did you—' says Yaroslav.

'I'm sorry, Mr Yaroslav,' says Jindash. 'I believe I have the floor? Thank you. I will continue. The Worldly Regulations were passed by the Saypuri Parliament in 1650, outlawing *any* public acknowledgement of the Divine on the Continent, however peripheral. One may no more mutter the name of a Divinity on the Continent than write their name in bright red paint on the side of a mountain. One need only make any acknowledgement – *any* acknowledgement – of the Divine to be in violation of the Worldly Regulations, and thus incur punishment. The significant financial gain does suggest that Mr Yaroslav installed the sign with both knowledge and intent . . .'

'That's a lie!' cries Yaroslav.

'. . . of its Divine nature. It does not matter that the Divinity the sigil referenced is dead, and the sigil could not have bestowed any properties on anyone or anything. The acknowledgement is made. As such, Mr Yaroslav's actions incur the formal punishment of a fine of' – Jindash consults a note – 'fifteen thousand drekels.'

The crowd shifts and mutters until it is a low roar.

Yaroslav sputters. 'You can't . . . you can't possibly . . .'

Jindash retakes his seat at the bench. He gives Mulaghesh a proud smile; Mulaghesh strongly considers smashing it with her fist.

She wishes she could somehow bypass all this pomp and pageantry. Worldly Regulations cases usually only go to court every five months or so: the vast majority of all WR infractions are settled out of court, between Mulaghesh's office and the defendant. Very, very rarely does anyone feel confident or righteous enough to bring their case to court; and when they do, it's always a dramatic, ridiculous affair.

Mulaghesh looks out over the packed courthouse; there are people standing at the back, as if this dull municipal trial was grand theatre. *But they are not here to see the trial*, she thinks. She glances down the high court bench to Dr Efrem Pangyui's empty chair. *They're here to see the man who's caused me so many problems.*

However, whenever a WR case does go to trial, it's almost always a conviction. In fact, Mulaghesh believes she has acquitted only three people in her two decades as Polis Governor. *And we convict almost every case*, she thinks, *because the law requires us to prosecute them for living their way of life. How can they defend simply being who they are?*

She clears her throat. 'The prosecution has finished its case. You may now make your rebuttal, Mr Yaroslav.'

'But . . . but this isn't fair!' says Yaroslav. 'Why do *you* get to bandy about *our* sigils, *our* holy signs, but we can't?'

'The Polis Governor's quarters' – Jindash waves a hand at the walls – 'are technically Saypuri soil. We are not under the jurisdiction of the Worldly Regulations, which apply only to the Continent.'

'That's . . . that's ridiculous! No, it's not just ridiculous, it's . . . it's *heretical!*' He gets to his feet.

The courtroom is dead silent. Everyone stares at Yaroslav.

Oh, excellent, thinks Mulaghesh. *We have another protest.*

'You have no right to do these things to us,' says Yaroslav. 'You strip our buildings of their holy art, loot and pillage our libraries, arrest people for mentioning a *name*—'

'We are not here,' says Jindash, 'to debate the law, or history.'

'But we are! The Worldly Regulations *deny* us our history! I . . . I have never been able to see that sign you showed me, the sign of, of . . .'

'Of your Divinity,' says Jindash. 'Ahanas.'

Mulaghesh can see two City Fathers of Bulikov – their version of elected councillors – staring at Jindash with cold rage.

'Yes!' says Yaroslav. 'I was never allowed such a thing! And she was *our* god! Ours!'

The crowd looks back at the court guards, expecting them to charge forward and hack down Yaroslav where he stands.

'This is not exactly a rebuttal, is it?' asks Troonyi.

'And you . . . you let *that* man' – Yaroslav points a finger at Dr Efrem Pangyui's empty seat – 'come into our country, and read all of our histories, all of our stories, all of our legends that we ourselves do *not* know! That we ourselves are not *allowed* to know!'

Mulaghesh winces. She knew this would come up eventually.

Mulaghesh is sensitive to the fact that, in the full scope of history, Saypur's global hegemony is minutes old. For many hundreds of years before the Great War, Saypur was the Continent's colony – established and enforced, naturally, by the Continent's Divinities – and few have forgotten this in Bulikov: why else would the City Fathers call the current arrangement 'the masters serving the servants'? In private only, of course.

So it was a show of enormous negligence and stupidity on the part of the Ministry of Foreign Affairs to ignore these tensions, and allow the esteemed Dr Pangyui to travel here, to Bulikov, to study all the history of the Continent: history that the Continentals are legally prevented from studying themselves. Mulaghesh warned the Ministry it'd wreak havoc in Bulikov and, as she predicted, Dr Pangyui's time in Bulikov has not exemplified the mission of peace and understanding he supposedly arrived under: she has had to deal with protests, threats and, once, assault, when someone threw a stone at Dr Pangyui but accidentally struck a police officer on the chin.

'That man,' says Yaroslav, still pointing at the empty chair, 'is an insult to Bulikov and the entire Continent! That man is . . . is the manifestation of the utter contempt Saypur has for the Continent!'

'Oh, now,' says Troonyi, 'that's a bit much, isn't it?'

'He gets to read the things no one else can read!' says Yaroslav. 'He gets to read things written by our fathers, our grandfathers!'

'He is allowed to do so,' says Jindash, 'by the Ministry of Foreign Affairs. His mission here is of an ambassadorial nature. And this is not part of your tria—'

'Just because you won the War doesn't mean you can do whatever you like!' says Yaroslav. 'And just because we lost it doesn't mean you can strip us of everything we value!'

'You tell them, Vasily!' shouts someone at the back of the room.

Mulaghesh taps her gavel against her desk; immediately, the room falls silent.

'Would I be correct in thinking, Mr Yaroslav,' she says wearily, 'that your rebuttal is finished?'

'I . . . I reject the legitimacy of this court!' he says hoarsely.

'Duly noted. Chief Diplomat Troonyi – your verdict?'

'Oh, guilty,' says Troonyi. 'Very much guilty. Incredibly guilty.'

Eyes in the room shift to Mulaghesh. Yaroslav is shaking his head, mouthing 'no' at her.

I need a smoke, thinks Mulaghesh.

'Mr Yaroslav,' she says. 'If you had pleaded no contest when initially charged with the infraction, your fine would have been more lenient. However, against the recommendation of this court – and against my *personal advice* – you chose instead to bring it to trial. I believe you can understand that the evidence Prosecutor Jindash has brought against you is highly incriminating. As Prosecutor Jindash said, we do not debate history here: we merely deal with its effects. As such, it is with regret that I am forced to—'

The courtroom door bangs open. Seventy-two heads turn at once.

A small Saypuri official stands in the doorway, looking nervous and alarmed. Mulaghesh recognises him: Pitry something or other, from the embassy, one of Troonyi's lackeys.

Pitry swallows and totters down the aisle towards the bench.

'Yes?' says Mulaghesh. 'Is there a reason for this intrusion?'

Pitry does not answer. He extends a hand, holding a paper message. Mulaghesh takes it, unfolds it and reads:

The body of Efrem Pangyui has been discovered in his office at Bulikov University. Murder is suspected but unconfirmed..

Mulaghesh looks up, and realises everyone in the room is watching her. *This damned trial*, she thinks, *is now even less important than it was before.*

She clears her throat. 'Mr Yaroslav . . . In light of recent events, I am forced to reconsider the priority of your case.'

Jindash and Troonyi both say, 'What?'

Yaroslav frowns. 'What?'

'Would you say, Mr Yaroslav, that you have learned your lesson?' asks Mulaghesh.

Two Continentals creep in through the courtroom doors. They find friends in the crowd, and whisper in their ears. Soon word is spreading throughout the courtroom audience. '*Murdered*?' someone says loudly.

'My . . . lesson?' says Yaroslav.

'To put it bluntly, Mr Yaroslav,' says Mulaghesh, 'will you be stupid enough in the future to publicly display what is obviously a Divinity's sigil in the hope of drumming up more business?'

'What are you *doing*?' says Jindash. Mulaghesh hands him the message; he scans it and goes white. 'Oh, no . . . oh, by the seas . . .'

'Beaten to death!' someone says out in the audience.

The whole of Bulikov must know by now, thinks Mulaghesh.

'I . . . No,' says Yaroslav. 'No, I would . . . I would not?'

Troonyi has now read the message. He gasps and stares at Dr Pangyui's empty chair as if expecting to find it occupied by his dead body.

'Good answer,' says Mulaghesh. She taps her gavel. 'Then, as the authority in this courtroom, I will set aside CD Troonyi's estimable opinions and dismiss your case. You are free to leave.'

'I am? Really?' says Yaroslav.

'Yes,' says Mulaghesh. 'And I would advise you exercise your freedom to leave with all due haste.'

The crowd has devolved into shouts and cries. A voice bellows, 'He's dead! He's really dead! Victory, oh, glorious victory!'

Jindash slumps in his chair as if his spine has been pulled out.

'What are we going to *do*?' says Troonyi.

Someone in the crowd is crying, 'No. No! *Now* who will they send?'

Someone shouts back, 'Who cares who they send?'

'Don't you see?' cries the voice in the crowd. 'They will reinvade us, reoccupy! Now they will send someone even *worse!*'

Mulaghesh sets her gavel aside and gratefully lights a cigarillo.

How do they do it, Pitry wonders? How can anyone in Bulikov sit next to the city walls or even live with them in sight, peeking through the blinds and drapes of high windows, and feel in any way normal? Pitry tries to look at anything else: his watch, which is five minutes slow, and getting slower; his fingernails, which are quite fine except for the little finger, which remains irritatingly rippled; he even looks across at the train station porter, who keeps glaring at him. Yet eventually Pitry cannot resist, and he sneaks a glance to his left, to the east, where the crushing white walls wait.

They are smooth and blank as milk. After thousands of years, not a single crack shows. He does not even try to see the tops: seven hundred feet up or so they disappear behind a veil of grey smog.

There is always grey smog at the edge of the walls of Bulikov. They seem to collect it, as if they are not city walls but the walls of a vast tunnel extending down from the sky, and no air escapes in or out.

It comforts Pitry not one jot that he is, more or less, partly right.

He looks back at his watch, and does some calculations. Is the train late? Are such unusual trains late? Perhaps they come on their own time. Perhaps its engineer, whoever it might be, was never told of the telegram stating, quite clearly, '15:00' and does not know that very important official people are taking this secret appointment quite seriously. Or perhaps no one cares that the person waiting for this train might be cold, hungry, unnerved by these white walls and practically death-threatened by the milky blue gaze of the train station porter.

He sighs. If Pitry were to die and see all of his life flash before his eyes in his penultimate moment, he is fairly sure it would be a boring show. For though he thought a position in the Saypuri embassies would be an interesting and exotic job, taking him to new and exotic lands (and exposing him to new and exotic women), so far it has mostly consisted of waiting. As an assistant to the Associate Ambassadorial Administrator, Pitry has learned how to wait on new and unexciting things in new and unexciting ways: he is an intrepid explorer in the field of waiting, an expert at watching the second hand of a clock slowly crank out the hours. The purpose of an assistant, he has decided, is to have someone upon whom you can unload all the deadly little nothings that fill the bureaucratic day.

He checks his watch. Twenty minutes, maybe. His breath roils with steam. *By all the seas, what an awful job.*

Perhaps he can transfer out, he thinks. There are actually many opportunities for a Saypuri here: the Continent is divided into four regions, each of which has its own Regional Governor and accompanying staff office; in the next tier below, there are the Polis Governors, which regulate each major metropolitan area on the Continent; and in the next tier below that are the embassies, which regulate . . . well, culture. Which almost everyone has interpreted to mean nothing at all. Honestly, why establish an embassy in cities you effectively control?

The station porter strolls from his offices and stands at the edge of the platform. He glances back at Pitry, who nods and smiles. The porter looks at Pitry's headcloth and his short, dark beard, sniffs twice – *I smell a shally* – and then, with a lingering glare, turns and walks back to his office, as if saying, *I know you're there, so don't try and steal anything.* As if there is anything to steal in a deserted train station.

They hate us, thinks Pitry. But of course they do. It is something he has come to terms with during his short period at the embassy. *We tell them to forget, but can they? Can we? Can anyone?*

Yet Pitry underestimated the nature of their hatred. He had no understanding of it until he came here and saw the empty places on the walls and in the shop windows, the frames and facades shorn clean of any images or carvings; he saw how the people of Bulikov behaved at certain hours of the day, as if they knew this time was designated for some show of deference, yet they could not act, and instead simply milled about; and, in his walks throughout the city, he came upon the roundabouts and cul-de-sacs that had obviously once played host to something – some marvellous sculpture, or a shrine fogged with incense – but were now paved over, or held nothing more marvellous than a street lamp, or a bland municipal garden, or a lonely bench.

Saypur still celebrates the passage of the Worldly Regulations as if they were some martial victory, rather than a complicated piece of legislation. And in Saypur, the overwhelming feeling is that the Regulations have been a wild success, curbing and correcting the behaviour of the Continentals over the course of seventy-five years. But in his time in Bulikov, Pitry has begun to feel that, though the Regulations appear to have had some superficial success – for, true, no one in Bulikov praises, mentions or acknowledges any aspect of the Divine, at least not in public – in reality, the Regulations have failed.

The city knows. It remembers. Its past is written in its bones, though now the past speaks in silences.

Pitry shivers in the cold.

He is not sure if he would rather be at the office, so alight with concern and chaos in the wake of Dr Efrem Pangyui's murder. Telegraphs spitting out papers like drunks vomiting at closing time. The endless cranking of phones. Secretaries sprinting into offices, staking papers on to spikes with the viciousness of shrikes.

Yet then came the one telegram that silenced everyone:

C-AMB THIVANI TO BULIKOV MOROV STATION 15:00 <STOP> VTS512

And from the coding on the end it was clear this had not come from the Polis Governor's Office, but from the *Regional* Governor's Office, which is the only place on the Continent that has direct, immediate connection with Saypur . . . and so, the Comm Department secretary announced with terrible dread, the telegram might have been rerouted across the South Sea from the Ministry of Foreign Affairs itself.

There was a flurry of discussion as to who should meet this Thivani person, because he had doubtlessly been sent here in reaction to the professor's death, bringing swift and terrible retribution; for had not Dr Efrem Pangyui been one of Saypur's brightest and most favoured sons? Had his ambassadorial mission not been one of the greatest scholarly endeavours in history? Thus it was quickly decided that Pitry, being young, exuberant, cheerful – and not in the room at the time – would be the best man for the job.

But they did wonder at the coding, C-AMB, for 'Cultural Ambassador'. Why would they send one of *those*? Weren't CAs the lowest caste of the Ministry? Most of them were fresh-faced students, picked solely because they were bi- or tri- or quadrilingual, and often harboured a rather unhealthy interest in foreign cultures and histories, something metropolitan Saypuris found rather distasteful. Usually CAs served as ornamentation to frivolous receptions and galas, and little more. So why send a simple CA into the middle of one of the greatest diplomatic debacles of the past decade?

'Unless,' Pitry wondered aloud back at the embassy, 'it's not related at all. Maybe it's just coincidence.'

'Oh, it's related,' said Nidayin, who was Assistant Manager of the embassy Comm Department. 'The telegram came through just hours after we sent out the news. This is their reaction.'

'So why send a CA? They might as well have sent a plumber, or a harpist.'

'Unless,' said Nidayin, 'Mr Thivani is *not* a Cultural Ambassador. He might be something else entirely.'

'Are you saying,' Pitry asked, fingers reaching up into his headcloth to scratch his scalp, 'that the telegram lied?'

Nidayin simply shook his head. 'Oh, Pitry. How *did* you get yourself into the Ministry?'

Nidayin, thinks Pitry in the cold. *How I hate you. One day I will dance with your beautiful girlfriend, and she will fall helplessly in love with me, and you shall walk in upon us mussing your sheets and ice will pierce your muddy heart.*

But Pitry now sees he was a fool. Nidayin was suggesting this Thivani might be *travelling* as a CA, but he could in truth be some high-ranking secret operative, infiltrating enemy territories and toppling resistance to Saypur. Pitry imagines a burly, bearded man with bandoliers of explosives and a glimmering knife clutched in his teeth, a knife that's tasted blood in many shadows. The more he thinks on it, the more Pitry grows a little afraid of this Thivani person. *Perhaps he will emerge from the train car like a djinnifrit*, he thinks, *spouting flames from his eyes and black poison from his mouth*.

There is a rumbling in the east. Pitry looks to the city walls and the tiny aperture in the bottom. From here it looks like a hole gnawed by vermin, but if he were closer it'd be nearly thirty feet tall.

The dark little hole fills with light. There is a flash, a screech and the train pounds through.

It is not really a train: just a beaten, stained engine and a single sad little passenger car. It looks like something from coal country, a car the workers would ride in while being carted from mine to mine. Certainly nothing for an Ambassador – even a Cultural Ambassador.

The train thuds up to the platform. Pitry scurries over and stands before the doors, hands clasped behind him and chest thrown gallantly forward. Are his buttons set? Is his headcloth straight? Did he shine his epaulets? He cannot remember. He frantically licks a thumb, and begins rubbing at one. Then the doors scream open, and there is . . .

Red. No, not red – burgundy. A lot of burgundy, as if a drape has been hung across the door. Yet then the drape shifts, and Pitry sees it is split in the middle by a stripe of white cloth with buttons down the middle.

It is not a drape. It is the chest of a man in a dark burgundy coat. The biggest man Pitry has ever seen – a giant.

The giant unfolds himself and steps out of the car. His feet fall on the boards like millstones. Pitry stumbles back to allow him room. The giant's long red coat kisses the tops of immense black books, his shirt is open-throated with no scarf, and he wears a wide-brimmed grey hat at a piratical angle. On his right hand is a soft grey glove; his left is bare. He is well over six and a half feet tall, incredibly broad in the shoulders and back, but there is not an ounce of fat on him: his face has a lean, starved look, and it is a face Pitry never expected to see on a Saypuri Ambassador. The man's skin is pale with many pink scars, his beard and hair are blond-white and his eyes – or rather *eye*, for one eye is but a dark, hooded cavity – is so blue it is almost a whitish-grey.

He is a Dreyling, a North-man. The Ambassador, however impossible it seems, is one of the mountain savages, a foreigner to both the Continent and Saypur.

If this is their response, thinks Pitry, *then what an awful and terrible response it is.*

The giant stares at Pitry with a flat, passive gaze, as if wondering if this runty little Saypuri is worth stomping on.

Pitry attempts a bow. 'Greetings, Ambassador Thivani, to the w-wondrous city of B-Bulikov. I am Pitry Suturashni. I hope your journey was good?'

Silence.

Pitry, still bowed, tilts his head up. The giant is staring down at him, though one eyebrow rises just slightly in what could be a look of contemptuous bemusement.

From somewhere behind the giant comes the sound of a throat being politely cleared. The giant, without a word of greeting or goodbye, turns and walks towards the station manager's desk.

Pitry scratches his head and watches him go. The little cough sounds again, and he realises there is someone else standing in the doorway.

It is a small Saypuri woman, dark-skinned and even smaller than Pitry. She is dressed rather plainly – a blue robe that is noticeable only in its Saypuri cut – and she watches him from behind enormously thick eyeglasses. She wears a light grey trench coat and a short-brimmed blue hat with a paper orchid in its band. Pitry finds there is something off about her eyes. The giant's gaze was incredibly, lifelessly still, but this woman's eyes are the precise opposite: huge and soft and dark, like deep wells with many fish swimming in them.

The woman smiles. The smile is neither pleasant nor unpleasant: it is a smile like fine silver plate, used for one occasion and polished and put away once finished. 'I thank you for coming to meet us at such a late hour,' she says.

Pitry looks at her, then back at the giant, who is cramming his way into the station porter's office, much to the porter's concern. 'Am . . . Ambassador Thivani?'

She nods, and steps off the train.

A woman? Thivani is a *woman*? Why didn't they . . . ?

Oh, damn the Comm Department! Damn their gossip and their lies!

'I trust that Chief Diplomat Troonyi,' she says, 'is busy with the consequences of the murder. Otherwise he would be here himself?'

'Uh . . .' Pitry does not wish to admit that he knows no more of

CD Troonyi's intentions than he does of the movements of the stars in the sky.

She blinks at him from behind her eyeglasses. Silence swells to engulf Pitry like the tide. He scrambles for something to say, anything. He lands on, 'It's very nice to have you here in Bulikov.' No, no, absolutely *wrong*. Yet he continues, 'I hope your journey was . . . pleasant.' Wrong! Worse!

She looks at him a moment longer. 'Pitry, you said your name was?'

'Y-Yes.'

There is a shout from behind them. Pitry looks, but Thivani does not – she keeps watching Pitry as one would an interesting bug. Pitry sees that the giant is forcibly taking something from the station porter – some kind of clipboard – which makes the porter none too pleased. The giant stoops, removes the grey glove from his right hand and opens his fingers to show . . . something. The porter, whose face previously had been the colour of old beets, goes quite white. The giant tears out a sheet of paper from the clipboard, gives the clipboard back to the porter, and exits.

'Who is . . . ?'

'That is my secretary,' says Thivani. 'Sigrud. He assists me in my duties.'

The giant takes out a match, lights it on a thumbnail, and sets fire to the piece of paper.

'S-secretary?' says Pitry.

Flames lick the giant's fingers. If this pains him, he does not show it. After he deems the paper has sufficiently burned, he blows on it – *puff* – and embers dance across the station platform. He tugs the grey glove back on and surveys the station coldly.

'Yes,' she says. 'Now, if it does not trouble you, I believe I would like to go straight to the embassy. Has the embassy informed any of the officials of Bulikov about my arrival?'

'Well. Uh . . .'

'I see. Do we have possession of the professor's body?'

Pitry's mind whirls. He wonders, perhaps for the first time, what happens to a body after it dies – this suddenly seems much more perplexing than the whereabouts of its spirit.

'I see,' she says. 'Do you have a car with you?'

Pitry nods.

'If you would, please lead me to it.'

He nods again, perplexed, and takes her across the shadow-laden station to the car in the alleyway. He cannot stop glancing over his shoulder at her. *This* is who they send? This tiny, plain girl with the too-high voice? What could she possibly hope to accomplish in this endlessly hostile, endlessly suspicious place? Could she even last the night?

One of the most puzzling and fascinating obstacles in trying to understand the forces that governed so much of our past, and continue to affect our future, is that even today, after we have attempted so much research and recovered so many artefacts, we still have no visual concept of what they looked like. All the sculptures, paintings, murals, bas-reliefs and carvings render the figures either indistinct or incoherently. For in one depiction Kolkan appears as a smooth stone beneath a tree; and in another, a dark mountain against the bright sun; and in yet another, a man made of clay seated on a mountain. And these inconsistent portrayals are still a great improvement over others, which render their subjects as a vague pattern or colour hanging in the air, no more than the stroke of a brush: for example, if we are to take the Continent's ancient art at its word, the Divinity Jukov only ever appeared as a storm of starlings.

As in so many of these studies, it is difficult to conclude anything from such disparate scraps. One must wonder if the subjects of these works of art actually chose to present themselves in this way. Or, perhaps, the subjects were experienced in a manner that was impossible to translate into conventional art.

Perhaps no one on the Continent ever quite knew what they were seeing. And, now that the Divinities are gone, we might never know.

Time renders all people and all things silent. And gods, it seems, are no exception.

The Nature of Continental Art, *Dr Efrem Pangyui*

We must civilise them

Bulikov. City of Walls. Most Holy Mount. Seat of the World. The City of Stairs.

She'd never figured that last one out. Walls and mounts and seats of the world, that's something to brag about. But stairs? Why stairs?

Yet now Ashara — or just Shara, usually — finally sees. The stairs lead everywhere, nowhere: there are huge mountains of stairs, suddenly rising out of the curb to slash up the hillsides; then there will be a set of uneven stairs that wind down the slope like trickling creeks; and sometimes the stairs materialise before you like falls on white-water rapids, and you see a huge vista crack open mere yards ahead.

The name must be a new one. This could have only happened after the War. When everything . . . broke.

So this is what the Blink looks like, she thinks. *Or, rather, this is what it did to the city.*

She wonders where the stairs went before the War. Not to where they go now, that's for sure. She struggles with the reality of where she is, of how she came here, of how this could possibly really be happening.

Bulikov. The Divine City.

She stares out of the car window. Once the greatest city in the world, yet now one of the most ravaged places on Earth. Yet still the population clings to it: it remains the third or fourth most populated city in the world, though once it was much, much larger. Why do they stay here? What keeps these people in this half-city, vivisected and shadowy and cold?

'Do your eyes hurt?' asks Pitry.

'Pardon?' says Shara.

'Your eyes. Mine would swim sometimes, when I first came here. When you look at the city, in certain places, things aren't quite . . . right. They make you sick. It used to happen a lot more, I'm told, and it happens less and less these days.'

'What is it like, Pitry?' asks Shara, though she knows the answer: she has read and heard about this phenomenon for years.

'It's like . . . I don't know. Like looking into glass.'

'Glass?'

'Well, no, not glass. Like a window. But the window looks out on a place that isn't there any more. It's hard to explain. You'll know it when you see it.'

She does not think she can ever get used to the walls. It is a backdrop she has never, ever seen before: parts of the walls appear as a vast blankness, almost part of the night, and it is only at their farthest reaches, when the walls curve away, that you see light playing upon their bend, and realise the blankness is not flat but curved, and you are trapped within it.

The historian in her fights with her operative's instincts. *Look at the arched doorways, the street names, the ripples and dents in the city walls!* says one. *Look at the people, watch where they walk, see how they look over their shoulders*, says the other. There are only a few people on the streets; it is, after all, well after midnight. But those she sees are like most of the Continental sort: stocky, with heavy limbs and heavy features, dark hands and faces but pale arms and necks. The buildings all seem very small to her. When they crest a hill, she looks out and sees fields of low, flat structures, all the way across to the other side of the city walls. She is not used to such a barren skyline. Even in Kolkashtan and Ahanashtan the structures have begun the slow climb into the skies, and it *certainly* does not compare to Ghaladesh in Saypur. (*But*, she wonders, *whatever could?*) Perhaps it is because the city is so old, she thinks, predating the materials and techniques allowing such heights. But this is Bulikov, where those kinds of things didn't matter for thousands of years. Are such shows of glory outlawed? Is there something in the Worldly Regulations? These she knows backwards and forwards, so she's sure there isn't. Then why such small, bland structures? Why no towers or shows of architecture of any kind?

Perhaps they did have greater things, she thinks, *before the War. Could so much have suddenly vanished?*

'You probably know this,' says Pitry. 'But it's good to have a car in the neighbourhoods around the embassy. It's not quite in . . . a reputable part of town. When we established the embassy, they say, a lot of the good sorts moved out. Didn't want to be near the shallies.'

'Ah, yes,' says Shara. 'I'd forgotten they call us that here.' *Shally*, she remembers, inspired by the quantity of shallots Saypuris use in their food. Which is incorrect, as any sensible Saypuri prefers garlic.

She glances at Sigrud. He stares straight ahead – maybe. It is always difficult to tell what Sigrud is paying attention to. He sits so still, and seems so blithely indifferent to all around him, that you almost treat him like a statue. Either way, he seems neither impressed nor interested in the city around him: it is simply another event, neither threatening violence nor requiring it, and thus not worth attention.

She tries to save her thoughts for what is sure to be a difficult and tricky next few hours. And she tries to avoid the one thought that has been eating into her since yesterday, when the telegraph in Ahanashtan unspooled into her hands. But she cannot.

Oh, poor Efrem. How could this happen to you?

CD Troonyi's office is a perfect recreation of a stately office in Saypur, albeit a gaudy one: the dark wooden blinds, the red floral carpet, the soft blue walls, the copper lamps with beaded chimneys above the desk. An elephant's ear fern, indigenous to Saypur, blooms off one wall, its fragile, undulating leaves unfurling from its base of moss in a green-grey wave. Below it, a small pot of water bubbles on a tiny candle; a trickle of steam rises up, allowing the fern the copious humidity it needs to survive. None of this is at all, Shara notes, a melding of cultures, a show of learning and communication and post-regionalism unity, as all the ministerial committees claim back in Saypur.

But the decor does not even come *close* to the level of transgression of what hangs on the wall behind the desk chair.

Shara stares at it, incensed and morbidly fascinated. *How could he be such a fool?*

Troonyi bursts into his office with a face so theatrically grave it's like he's died rather than Efrem. 'Cultural Ambassador Thivani,' he says. He plants his left heel forward, hitches up his right shoulder and assumes the courtliest of courtly bows. 'It is an honour to have you here, even if it is under such sad circumstances.'

Immediately Shara wonders which preparatory school he attended in Saypur. She read his file before she came, of course, and it reinforced her conviction that the chaff of powerful families is all too often dumped into Saypur's embassies across the world. *And he thinks me to be from exactly such a family*, she reminds herself, *hence the show*. 'It is an honour to be here.'

'And for us, we . . .' Troonyi looks up and sees Sigrud slouched in a chair in the corner, idly stuffing his pipe. 'Ehm. Wh-who is that?'

'That is Sigrud,' says Shara. 'My secretary.'

'Must you have him here?'

'Sigrud assists me on all matters, confidential or otherwise.'

Troonyi peers at him. 'Is he deaf, or dumb?'

Sigrud's one eye flicks up for one moment, before returning to his pipe.

'Neither,' says Shara.

'Well,' says Troonyi. He mops his brow with a handkerchief, and recovers. 'Well, it is a testament to the good professor's memory,' he says as he sits behind his desk, 'that Minister Komayd sent someone so quickly to oversee the care of his remains. Have you travelled all night?'

Shara nods.

'My goodness gracious. How horrible. Tea!' he shouts suddenly, for no apparent reason. '*Tea!*' He grabs a bell on his desk and begins violently shaking it, then repeatedly slams it on the desk when it does not get the response he desires.

A girl no more than fifteen swivels into the room, bearing a battleship of a tea tray.

'What took you so long?' he snaps. 'I have a *guest*.'

The girl averts her eyes and pours.

Troonyi turns back to Shara, as if they are alone. 'I understand you were nearby in Ahanashtan? An awful polis, or so I think it. The seagulls, they are trained thieves, and the people have learned from the seagulls.' With a twitch of two fingers he waves the girl away, who bows low before exiting.

'We must civilise them, however – the people, I mean, not the birds.' He laughs. 'Would you care for a cup? It's our best sirlang.'

Shara shakes her head with the slightest of smiles. In truth Shara, a thorough caffeine addict, is in desperate need of a cup, but she'll be damned if she takes even one thing from CD Troonyi.

'Suit yourself. But Bulikov, as I'm sure you've heard, is quite different. It has structures that remain in place, inflexible to our influence. And I don't just mean the walls. Why, just three months ago the Polis Governor had to stop them from hanging a woman for taking up with another man . . . I am sorry to discuss such a thing before a young woman, but . . . for taking up with another man after her husband died. And the man had died *years* ago! The City Fathers would not listen to me, of course, but Mulaghesh . . .' He trails off. 'How odd it is that the city most decimated by the past is also the city most dead set against reform, don't you think?'

Shara smiles and nods. 'I agree entirely.' She tries very hard to avoid looking at the painting hanging over his shoulder. 'So you do possess Dr Pangyui's remains?'

'What? Oh, yes,' he says around a mouthful of biscuit. 'I apologise – yes, yes, we do have the body. Terrible thing. Tragedy.'

'Might I examine it before its transport?'

'You wish to see his *remains*? They are not . . . I am so sorry, but the man is *not* in a presentable state.'

'I am aware of how he died.'

'Are you? He died violently. *Violently*. It is abominable, my girl.'

My girl, thinks Shara. 'That has been communicated to me. But I must still ask to see them.'

'Are you so sure?'

'I am.'

'Well . . . hm.' He smears on his nicest smile. 'Let me give you a bit of advice, my girl. I once was in your shoes – a young CA, patriotic, going through the motions, all the dog and pony shows. You know, anything to make a bit of a name for myself. But, trust me, you can send all the messages you want, but there's no one on the other line. No one's *listening*. The

Ministry simply doesn't pay attention to Cultural Ambassadors. It's purgatory, my dear – you do your time until you can get out. But don't work up a sweat. Enjoy yourself. I'm sure they'll send someone serious on to handle it soon enough.'

Shara is not angry: her irritation has long since ebbed away into bemusement. As she thinks of a way to answer him, her eye wanders back up to the painting on the wall.

Troonyi catches her looking. 'Ah. I see you're taken with my beauty.' He gestures to the painting. '"The Night of the Red Sands", by Rishna. One of the great patriotic works. It's not an original, I'm sad to say, but a very old copy of the original. But it's close enough.'

Even though Shara has seen it many times before – it's quite popular in schools and city halls in Saypur – it still strikes her as a curious, disturbing painting. It depicts a battle taking place in a vast, sandy desert at night. On the closest wave of dunes there stands a small, threadbare army of Saypuris, staring across the desert at an immense opposing force of armoured swordsmen. The armour they wear is huge and thick and gleaming, protecting every inch of their bodies; their helmets depict the glinting visages of shrieking demons; their swords are utterly immense, nearly six feet in length, and they flicker with a cold fire. The painting makes it plain that these terrifying men of steel and blade will cleave the poor, ragged Saypuris in two. Yet the swordsmen are standing in a state of some shock. They stare at one Saypuri, who stands on the top of one tall dune at the back of his army, brave and resplendent in a fluttering coat: the general of this tattered force, surely. He is manipulating a strange weapon: a long, thin cannon, delicate as a horsefly, which is firing a flaming wad up over his army, over the heads of the opposing force, where it strikes . . .

Something. Perhaps a person: a huge person, rendered in shadow. It is difficult to see, or perhaps the painter never knew what this figure looked like.

Shara stares at the Saypuri general. She knows that the painting is historically inaccurate: the Kaj was actually stationed at the *front* of his army during the Night of the Red Sands, and did not personally fire the fatal shot, nor was he near the weaponry at all. Some historians, she recalls, claim this was due to his bravery as a leader; others contend that the Kaj, who after all had never used his experimental weaponry on this scale and had no idea if it would be a success or a disaster, chose to be far away if it proved to be the latter. But regardless of where he stood, that fatal shot was the exact moment when everything started.

Enough politeness.

'Do you meet with the City Fathers of Bulikov in this office, Ambassador?' asks Shara.

'Hm? Oh, yes. Of course.'

'And have they never . . . commented upon that painting?'

'Not that I can recall. They are sometimes struck quiet at the sight of it. A magnificent work, if I do say so myself.'

She smiles. 'Chief Diplomat Troonyi, you are aware of what the professor's purpose was in this city?'

'Mm? Of course I am. It kicked up quite a fuss. Digging through all their old museums, looking at all their old writings . . . I got a lot of letters about it. I have some of them here.' He shoves around some papers in a drawer.

'And you are aware that it was Minister of Foreign Affairs Vinya Komayd who approved his mission?'

'Yes?'

'So you must be aware that the jurisdiction of his death falls under neither the embassy, nor the Polis Governor, nor the Regional Governor, but the Ministry of Foreign Affairs *itself*?'

Troonyi's birdshit-coloured eyes dance as he thinks through the tiers. 'I believe . . . that makes sense . . .'

'Then perhaps what you do not know,' says Shara, 'is that I am given the title of Cultural Ambassador mostly as a *formality*.'

His moustache twitches. His eye flicks to Sigrud as if to confirm this, but Sigrud simply sits with his fingers threaded together in his lap. 'A formality?'

'Yes. Because while I do think you believe my appearance in Bulikov to *also* be a formality, you should be aware that I am here for other reasons.' She reaches into her robe, produces a small leather shield and slides it across the table for him to see the small, dry, neat insignia of Saypur in its centre and, written just below it, the small words: MINISTRY OF FOREIGN AFFAIRS.

It takes a while for this to fall into place within Troonyi's head. He manages a, 'Wha . . . Hm.'

'So yes,' says Shara. 'You are no longer the most senior official at this embassy.' She reaches forward, grabs the bell on his desk and rings it.

The tea girl enters, and is a little confused when Shara addresses her.

'Please fetch the maintenance staff to take down that painting.'

Troonyi practically begins to froth. 'What! What do you mean by—'

'What I mean to do,' says Shara, 'is to make this office look like a responsible representative of Saypur works here. And a good way to start is to take down *that* painting, which romanticises the *exact* moment when this Continent's history started to take a very, very bloody turn.'

'I say! It is a great moment for our people, miss—'

'Yes, for *our* people. Not for *theirs*. I will hazard a guess, Mr Troonyi, and say that the reason the City Fathers of Bulikov do not listen to you and do not *respect* you, and the reason your career has not been upwardly mobile for the past five years, is that you are willing to hang a painting on your office wall that must insult and *incense* the very peoples you were sent here to work with! Sigrud!'

The giant man stands.

'Since the maintenance staff respond so slowly to voices other than CD Troonyi's, please remove that painting and *break* it over your knee. And Troonyi, please sit down. We need to discuss the conditions of your retirement.'

Afterwards, when Troonyi is bustled away and gone, Shara returns to the desk, pours herself a generous cup of tea, and downs it. She is happy to see the painting gone, unpatriotic as these feelings may be: more and more in her service for the Ministry, vainglorious displays of jingoism put a bad taste in her mouth.

She looks over to Sigrud, who sits in the corner with his feet up on the desk, holding a scrap of the now demolished canvas. 'Well?' she says. 'Too much?'

He looks up at her – *what do you think?*

'Good,' says Shara. 'I'm pleased to hear it. It was quite enjoyable, I admit.'

Sigrud clears his throat and says in a voice made of smoke and mud, and an accent thicker than roofing tar, 'Who is Shara Thivani?'

'A Cultural Ambassador, of course. At least on paper, that is. She was a mildly unimportant CA in Jukoshtan about six years ago. She died in a boating accident, but she was rather surreally good at filing paperwork – everyone had records of her, and what she'd done. When it came time for her clearance to expire, and to purge her from the rolls, I opted to suspend her, and held on to her myself.'

'Because you both share the same first name?'

'Perhaps. But we have other similarities – do I not look the part of a drab, unimpressive little bureaucrat?'

Sigrud smirks. 'No one will believe you are just a CA, though. Not after firing Troonyi.'

'No, and I don't *want* them to. I want them worried. I want them upset. I want them to wonder if I am what I actually am.' She goes to the window and stares out at the smoke-smeared night sky. 'If you stir up a hornet's nest, all the hornets might come out and chase you, that's true – but at least then you can get a good, proper look at them.'

'If you *really* wanted to stir them up,' he says, 'you could just use your *real* name.'

'I want to stir them up, yes, but I don't want to *die*.'

Sigrud smiles wickedly and returns to the scrap of canvas in his hands.

'What are you looking at?' she asks.

He turns the scrap of canvas around for her to see. It is the piece of the painting with the Kaj on it, standing in profile, his stern, patrician face lit by the burst of light from his weaponry.

Sigrud turns it back around and holds it up so that Shara's face and the tiny painted face of the Kaj appear side by side from his perspective.

Sigrud says, 'I can definitely see the family resemblance.'

'Oh, be quiet,' snaps Shara. 'And put that away!'

Sigrud smiles, scrunches up the canvas and tosses it in a waste-paper basket.

'All right,' Shara says. She drinks the second cup of tea, and her body rejoices. 'I suppose we ought to move along, then. Please fetch Pitry for me.' Then, speaking more softly, 'We have a body to examine.'

The room is small, hot, bare and unventilated. Decay has not yet set in, so the tiny room is mercifully bereft of scent. Shara stares at the thing sitting on the trolley with one small, slender leg dangling over the side. *It's as if he lay down for a nap*, she thinks, *unaware he'd been hurt at all*.

She does not see her hero. Not the gentle little man she met. She sees only curled and crusted flesh arranged on what looks like a lump of white, knotted stone. It is connected, of course, to something quite familiar: the birdy little neck, the linen suit, the long, elegant arms and fingers and, yes, his ridiculous coloured socks. But it is not Efrem Pangyui. It cannot be.

She touches the lapels of his coat. They have been shredded like ribbons. 'What happened to his clothes?'

Pitry, Sigrud and the vault guard lean in to look. 'Sorry?' asks the vault guard; since the embassy has no funerary facilities, the mortal remains of Dr Efrem Pangyui have been stored in the embassy vault on a trolley, like a precious heirloom waiting for the red tape to clear so it can return home. *Which it is, a bit*, thinks Shara.

'Look at his clothes,' she says. 'All the seams and cuffs have been slit. Even the trouser cuffs. Everything.'

'So?'

'Did you receive the body in this state?'

The guard favours the body with a leery eye. 'Well, *we* didn't do that.'

'So would you say it was the Bulikov police?'

'I guess? I'm sorry, ma'am. I don't quite know.'

Shara is still. She has seen this before, of course, and even performed this procedure herself, once or twice – the more clothing one wears, with more pockets and linings and cuffs, the more places to hide highly sensitive material.

Which begs the question, she thinks, *why would anyone think a historian on a diplomatic mission would have something to hide?*

'You can go,' she says.

'What?'

'You can leave us.'

'Well . . . You're in the vault, ma'am. I can't just leave you in the—'

Shara looks up at him. Perhaps it is the fatigue from the trip or the grief now trickling into her face, or perhaps it is the generations of command reverberating through her bloodline, but the guard coughs, scratches his head and finds something to busy himself in the hall.

Pitry moves to follow, but she says, 'No, Pitry – not you. Please stay.'

'Are you sure?'

'Yes. I'd like to have some embassy input, however limited.' She looks to Sigrud. 'What do you think?'

Sigrud bends over the tiny body. He examines the skull quite carefully, like a painter trying to identify a forgery. To Pitry's evident disgust, he lifts one flap of skin and examines the indentations on the bone underneath. 'Tool,' he says. 'Wrench, probably. Something with teeth.'

'You're sure?'

He nods.

'So nothing useful there?'

He shrugs. *Maybe – maybe not.* 'Was first hit on the front.' He points to just above what was once the professor's left eyebrow. 'The marks are deep there. Others . . . not so deep.'

Any tool, thinks Shara. *Any weapon. Anybody could have done this.*

Shara keeps looking at the body. She tells herself for the second time this night – *Ignore the ornamentations.* But it is the ruined visage of her hero, his hands and neck and shirt and tie. Can she dismiss all these familiar sights as mere ornamentation?

Wait a minute. A tie?

'Pitry – did you see the professor much during his time here?' she asks.

'Um. Not really?'

'You didn't see him at all?'

'Well, I *saw* him, yes, but we weren't friends.'

'Then you don't remember,' she asks softly, 'if he developed the habit of wearing a tie?'

'A tie? I don't know, ma'am.'

Shara reaches over and plucks up the tie. It is striped, red and creamy white, made of exquisite silk. A northern affectation, and a recent one.

'The Efrem Pangyui *I* knew,' she says, 'always preferred scarves. It's a very academic look, I understand – scarves, usually orange or pink or red. School colours. But one thing I don't ever recall him wearing is a tie. Do you know much about ties, Pitry?'

'A little, I suppose. They're common here.'

'Yes. And not at all at home. And wouldn't you say that this tie is of an unusually fine make?' She turns it over to show him. 'Very fine, and very . . . thin?'

'Ahm. Yes?'

Without taking her eyes off the tie, she holds an open hand out to Sigrud. 'Knife, please.'

Instantly there is a tiny fragment of glittering metal in the big man's hand. He hands it to Shara – a scalpel of some kind. She pushes her glasses up on her nose and leans in low over his body. The faint smell of putrefaction comes leaking up out of his shirt. She tries to ignore it – another unpleasant ornamentation.

She looks closely at the white silk. *No, he wouldn't do it with white*, she thinks. *It'd be too noticeable*.

She spots a line of incredibly fine red threads going against the grain. She nicks each one with the scalpel. The threads form a little window to the inside of the tie, which she sees is like a pocket.

There is a strip of white cloth inside. Not the cloth of the tie – something else. She slides it out and holds it up to the light.

There are writings on one side of the white cloth, done in charcoal – a code of some kind.

'They would never have thought to look in the tie,' she says softly. 'Not if it was an especially *nice* tie. They wouldn't have expected that from a Saypuri, would they? And he would have known that.'

Pitry stares at the gutted tie. 'Wherever did he learn a trick like that?'

Shara hands the scalpel back to Sigrud. 'That,' she says, 'is a very good question.'

Dawn light crawls through her office window, creeping across the bare desk and the rug, which is riddled with indentations from the furniture she had them remove. She goes to the window. It is so strange: the city walls would normally prevent any light from entering the city unless the sun was directly above, yet she can see the sun cresting the horizon. Or she *thinks* she does. Perhaps a more apt way to put it is that she gets an *impression* of the sun rising, rather than seeing the actual sun itself.

What was the man's name, Shara thinks, *who wrote about this?* She snaps her fingers, trying to remember. 'Vochek,' she says. 'Anton Vochek. That's right.' A professor at Bulikov University. He'd theorised, however many dozens of years ago, that the fact that the Miracle of Light still functioned – one of Bulikov's oldest and most famous miraculous characteristics – was proof that one or several of the original Divinities still existed in some manner. Such an open violation of the WR meant he had to go into hiding immediately. But, regardless, the Continental populace did not much appreciate his theory: for if any of the Divinities still existed, where were they, and why did they not help their people?

This is the problem with the miraculous, she recalls Efrem saying. *It is so matter of fact. What it says it does, it does.*

It seems like only yesterday that she last spoke to him, when actually it was just over a year ago. When he first arrived on the Continent, Shara trained Efrem Pangyui in very basic tradecraft – simple things like exfiltration, evasion, how to work the various labyrinthine offices of authorities and, though she thought it'd be unlikely he'd ever use it, the creation and maintenance of dead drop sites. Mostly just safety precautions, for no place on the Continent is completely safe for Saypuris. As the most experienced active Continental operative, Shara was ridiculously overqualified for what any operative would normally consider babysitting duty, but Shara fought for the job, because there was no Saypuri she revered and respected more than Efrem Pangyui, reformist, lecturer and vaunted historian. He was the man who had single-handedly changed Saypur's concept of the past, the man who had resurrected the entire Saypuri judicial system, the man who had prised Saypuri schools from the hands of the wealthy and brought education to the slums. It had been so strange to have this great man sitting across the table from her in Ahanashtan, nodding patiently as she explained (hoping she did not sound too awed) that when a Bulikovian border agent asks for your papers, what they're *really* asking for are twenty-drekel notes. A surreal experience, to be sure, but one of Shara's most treasured memories.

She sent him off, wondering whether they'd ever meet again. And just yesterday she caught a telegram floating across her desk reporting he'd been found dead – no, not just dead, *murdered*. That was shock enough for Shara, but now to find secret messages sewn into his clothing, tradecraft *she* certainly didn't teach him.

I suddenly doubt, she thinks, *if his mission was truly one of historical understanding after all*.

She rubs her eyes. Her back is stiff from the train ride. But she looks at the time, and thinks.

Nearly eight in the morning in Saypur.

Shara does not wish to do this – she is too tired, too weak – but she knows she should. If she doesn't do it now, she'll pay for it later: so many simple oversights, like failing to communicate a jaunt to Bulikov, can be mistaken for treachery.

She opens the door to her new office and confirms there is no one outside. She shuts the door, locks it. She goes to the window and closes the shutters on the outside (which is a relief – she is tired of feeling the sun but never quite *seeing* it over the wall). Then she slides the window shut.

She sniffs, wriggles her fingers. Then she licks the tip of her index finger and begins writing on the top pane of glass in the window.

Shara often does illegal things in her trade, but that's business as usual: 'illegal', after all, is a subjective term, depending on where you are. But it's one thing to violate a country's law when you're actively working against that country, and it's another to do what Shara is doing right now, which is so horrendously dreaded in Saypur and so fervently outlawed and regulated and monitored on the Continent, the birthplace of this particular act.

Because right now, in CD Troonyi's office, Shara is about to perform a miracle.

As always, the change is quite imperceptible: there is a shift in the air, a coolness on the skin, as if someone has cracked a door somewhere. As she writes, the tip of her finger begins to feel that the glass's surface is softer and softer, until it is like she is writing on water.

The glass changes: it mists over, frost creeping across the pane; then the frost recedes, but the window no longer shows the shutter on the outside, as it should. Instead, it is like there's a hole in a wall, and on the other side is an office with a big teak desk, at which sits a tall, handsome woman reading a thick file.

How odd it feels, thinks Shara, *to literally change the world*.

Shara likes to think she is above such sentiments, though it does irk her that Saypur's considerable technological advances have yet to catch up to most of the Divine tricks. The Divinity Olvos originally created this little miracle hundreds or perhaps thousands of years ago, specifically so she could look into one frozen lake and see and communicate out of a different frozen lake of her choosing, miles away. Shara has never been quite sure why the miracle works on glass: the generally accepted theory is that the original Continental term for 'glass' was very similar to 'ice', so the miracle unintentionally overlaps – though the Divine were fond of using glass for many strange purposes, storing items and even people within a hair's breadth of glass like a sunbeam caught in a crystal.

The woman in the glass looks up. The perspective is a little peculiar: it is like peering through a porthole. But what is really on the other side of the glass, Shara knows, is the shutter on the embassy window, and after that a two-hundred-foot drop. It is all a play of images and sound: somewhere in Ghaladesh, across the Western Sea in Saypur, a single pane of glass in this woman's office is showing Shara herself, staring out from Troonyi's rooms.

The woman appears quite startled, and her mouth moves. A voice accompanies the movement of her lips, yet it is soft and tinny like it is echoing up a drainpipe, 'Oh! Oh.'

'You look like you expected someone else,' says Shara.

'No. I wondered if you'd call, but I didn't expect the *emergency* line.' Despite the distortion, her voice is quite low and husky, the voice of a chain-smoker.

'You'd prefer I didn't use the emergency line?'

'You so rarely use the tools I give you,' says the woman as she stands and walks over, 'for the purposes for which they are intended.'

'It is true that this is not . . . *quite* an emergency,' says Shara. 'I wanted to let you know that I have . . . I have picked up an operation in Bulikov.'

The woman in the glass smiles. Despite her mature age, she is quite striking: her coal-black hair falls in thick locks about her shoulders, the front forelock shot through with a streak of grey, and though she is at an age when most women begin to abandon any attempt at a fetching figure, she still retains nearly every curve, many more than Shara could ever aspire to. But Auntie Vinya's allure, Shara feels, has always gone beyond her beauty: it is something in her eyes, which are both wide and widely set, and deep brown. It is like Auntie Vinya is always half-remembering a long life most people would have killed to lead.

'Not an operation,' says Vinya. 'An outright diplomatic mission.'

'So you know.'

'My darling girl, once the professor's endeavour got approved, you couldn't think we wouldn't be hypersensitive to any sort of movement, could you?'

Shara sighs inwardly. 'What tipped you off?'

'The Thivani identity,' says Vinya. 'You've been sitting on it for years. I tend to notice things like that, when someone – how shall I say? – walks by the buffet and tucks a biscuit or two in their sleeve. Then suddenly the name gets activated the very night we hear about poor Efrem. There's only one thing you could be doing, isn't there?'

This was a mistake, thinks Shara. *I should not have done this when I'm so tired.*

'Shara, what *are* you doing?' says Vinya gently. 'You know I never would have approved this.'

'Why not? I was the closest agent, and the most qualified.'

'You are *not* the most qualified, because you were personally connected to Efrem. You are better used elsewhere. And you should have sent in a request first.'

'You might wish to check your post,' says Shara.

A shadow of irritation crosses Vinya's face. She walks to the letter box in her door, flips through the waiting bundle and takes out a small slip of paper. 'Four hours ago,' she says. 'Very timely.'

'Quite. So,' says Shara, 'I've made all the official overtures. I have violated no rules. I am the highest ranking agent. And I am an expert in this field. No one knows more about Bulikov's history than me.'

'Oh, yes,' says Vinya. She walks back to look into the glass. 'You are our most experienced agent in Continental history. I doubt if anyone in the world knows more about their dead gods than you, now that Efrem's gone.'

Shara looks away.

'I'm . . . sorry,' says Vinya. 'That was insensitive of me. You must understand. It's often a little hard for me to keep my sense of common compassion, even in this case.'

'I know,' says Shara. It has been a little over seven years since Auntie Vinya assumed the role of Minister of Foreign Affairs. She was always the powerhouse of the Ministry, the officer whom all the decisions wound up going through, one way or another; eventually it just became a matter of making it formal. In the time since her elevation, the boundaries of the Ministry have both grown, and grown permeable: it spills over into commerce, into industry, into political parties and environmental management. And now, whenever Shara gets close to Saypur – which is very rare – she hears whispers that Vinya Komayd, matriarch of the eminent Komayd family and one of the most high muck-a-mucks in Ghaladesh, is eyeing the next highest seat, that of Prime Minister. It is an idea that both unnerves and thrills Shara: perhaps if her aunt occupied the highest office in Saypur, in the *world*, she could finally come home. But what sort of home would she return to?

'If it had not been you who trained Efrem,' says Vinya, 'if you had not been the one to volunteer to put him through his paces, to spend so much time with him, you know I'd use you in a second, my love. But case officers are never allowed to react to the death of one of their operatives, you know that.'

'He was not my case operative. I only trained him.'

'True, but you have to admit, you do have a history of reckless conviction, especially with personal matters.'

Shara sighs. 'I can't even believe we're still talking about *that*.'

'*I* am, even if you're not here to listen to it. It gets brought up in all the political circles whenever I try for funding.'

'It was seventeen years ago!'

'Voters might have short memories. Politicians do not.'

'Have I ever in my history abroad caused even a whisper of a scandal? Isn't that my sole purpose, to kill scandals before they start?'

'Among other things, yes,' says Vinya.

'You know me, Auntie. I am quite good at what I do.'

'I will not deny that you've been a blessing to my work, darling, no.' Then Vinya sighs, and thinks.

Shara keeps her face still and closed as she rapidly reviews the last five minutes. This conversation has not gone at all as she anticipated: she expected a harsh rebuke from her aunt, because it certainly seems to Shara that she has stumbled across some deeper, much more dangerous operation, one in which Pangyui was apparently involved. But so far Auntie Vinya has reacted as if Pangyui was just a simple historian on a diplomatic mission. *Which means she either doesn't know*, thinks Shara, *or she doesn't want me to know that she knows*.

So Shara does what almost always works in these situations: she waits. If you wait and watch, she's found, things so often reveal themselves, despite your adversary's best efforts. And though Vinya may be her aunt, there never was a relationship between a commander and their operative that wasn't somewhat adversarial.

'Well, then,' says Vinya. 'I suppose you ought to brief me. What's the situation there?'

Interesting, thinks Shara. 'Poor. Mutinous. It would be an understatement to say CD Troonyi did not maintain the embassy to the best of his abilities.'

'Troonyi . . . my God, I'd forgotten they'd stuck him there. Are there any young girls about?'

Shara thinks of the tea girl. 'One.'

'Was she pregnant?'

'Not that I could see.'

'Well. Thank the seas for small gifts.'

'What about Mulaghesh, the Polis Governor? She's been very . . . hands off with Bulikov. Still a keeper to the policies, in essence.'

'Yes.'

'And the policies still have *full* support?'

Vinya recites the boilerplate immediately. 'Saypur has always felt that its efforts should not be focused on ruins and dead myths, and countries that have no resources of interest, but on the South Sea and trading ports, and the future. So long as the citizens of the Continent don't stir anything up, we prefer not to intervene. Mulaghesh likes strict policies, so I expect she'll keep to this strictly.'

'Can I rely on her?'

'Probably. She's old military, fought in the rebellions. The brass is in her bones. You always do quite well with her sort. Now – what about the professor?'

'I'm collecting information on it as we speak,' says Shara – glib, trite, serviceable.

'And once you know who killed him, and why, what will you do?' asks Vinya.

'Take stock of the situation and see what threat it poses to Saypur.'

'So vengeance doesn't cross your mind?'

'One has no room for vengeance,' says Shara, 'when the eyes of the world are watching. We must be judicious and bloodless. I am to be, as always, a simple tool in the hands of my nation.'

'Enough of the rhetoric,' says Vinya. 'I've no idea who it actually works on any more.' She looks away to think. 'I'll tell you what, Shara. I will be generous with you. I'll give you a deadline on this – one week.'

Shara stares at her, incensed. 'One week!'

'Yes. One week to show me there's something more to the murder. The entire populace of Bulikov wished the poor man dead, darling! It could have been a *janitor*, for all you know. I will give you one week to show me there is some larger reason justifying your presence there, and then, if not, I'm pulling you out and I'll have someone else oversee the proceedings. Don't worry, I'm sure it won't be very interesting. It'll probably be all very procedural, darling. We've become very good at handling outrages, even if it's one as extreme as this. It's something of a speciality of ours.'

'One week—'

'Oh, is this the girl who just told me she was the highest ranking agent nearby? You made it sound like it'd only take a puff from your lips, and the house of cards would tumble.' Vinya waggles her fingers, imitating the snowfall spin of falling cards. 'If you are so well-prepared, my darling, surely it'll take mere *hours*.'

Shara adjusts her glasses, frustrated. 'Fine.'

'Good. Keep me informed. And I would appreciate it if you would keep your man from murdering anyone for at least a few days.'

'I can't promise that.'

'I know. But I thought I'd ask.'

'And if I defuse this situation in one week,' says Shara, 'if I do actually work the impossible this time, is there any chance that—'

'That what?'

'That I could be transferred.'

'Transferred?'

'Yes. Back to Ghaladesh.' Then, when Vinya stares blankly at her, 'We talked about this last time.'

'Ah. Ah, yes,' says Vinya. 'That's right, we did, didn't we?'

You know that, Shara thinks. *And we talked about it the time before that, and the time before that, and the time before that.*

'I must confess,' says Vinya, 'you are the only operative I know of who genuinely wants a desk job back at the home office. I thought you would love the Continent, it's all you ever studied in training.'

'I have been abroad,' says Shara softly, 'for sixteen years.'

'Shara . . .' Vinya smiles uncomfortably. 'You know you are my foremost Continental operative. No one knows more about the Divine than you . . . and what's more, almost no one in Ghaladesh knows that traces of the Divine still exist on the Continent, to some degree.'

How many times, Shara thinks, *have I heard this speech?*

'It's the policy of the Ministry to never disclose the continued existence of the Divine, however slight. Saypuris prefer to believe all that is history – dead, and gone. They cannot know that some miracles still work on the Continent . . . and they *certainly* cannot know that some Divine creatures still exist, though you and your man are very good at cleaning those up.'

Shara is silent as she reflects that her aunt has no idea what such a thing means.

'So long as the Divinities themselves remain gone,' says Vinya, 'and we are *so* happy that that is the continued situation, we have no reason to tell people what they don't wish to know.'

Shara opts to ask the obvious question. 'So, because I have seen so much that we cannot admit exists,' she says, 'I cannot come home?'

'And because of who you are, if you were to come home, you would be questioned extensively. And since you know so much no one else should ever know . . .'

Shara closes her eyes.

'Give me time, my love,' says Vinya. 'I am doing what I can. The powers that be listen to me more than ever before. Soon they can't help but be persuaded.'

'The problem is,' Shara says quietly, 'we operatives fight to protect our home. But we must return home occasionally, to remember the home we fight for.'

Vinya scoffs. 'Don't be so soft hearted! You are a *Komayd*, my child. You are your parents' child, and *my* child – you are a patriot. Saypur runs in your blood.'

I have seen dozens of people die, Shara wishes to say, *and signed the death warrants of many. I am nothing like my parents. Not any more.*

'Anyway,' says Vinya, 'I suppose this occasion is momentous. For other reasons than what we've discussed, I mean.'

'Why?'

Vinya looks around the edges of the glass. 'Well, darling, your performance of this little miracle is probably the first time it's been performed in Bulikov since the War. Doesn't that make you feel special?'

'Not particularly.'

'Well, you must feel good that it worked.'

'Why wouldn't it work?'

'Oh, I didn't mean the *miracle*. Don't think you're so opaque, darling. I know you only used it so you could convince me face to face to let you stay. A simple telegram wouldn't do, would it?' She smiles, eyes glittering. 'Please stay safe, my love. History weighs a little heavier in Bulikov. If I were you, I'd step carefully – especially since you're a direct descendant of the man who brought the whole Continent crashing down.' Then she reaches out with two fingers, wipes the glass and is gone.

It is the duty of the Ministry of Foreign Affairs to regulate that which could not possibly be regulated.

However, just because something is impossible, this does not mean that the people of Saypur should not expect it to be done: after all, before the War, didn't impossible things happen on the Continent every hour of every day?

Is that not why Saypur and, indeed, the rest of the world, sleeps so poorly every night?

Prime Minister Anta Doonijesh,
letter to Minister Vinya Komayd, 1701

Unmentionables

Bulikov University is a sprawling many-chambered structure, a dense network of stone and atriums and passageways, hidden behind towering walls on the west side of Bulikov. The University's stonework is stained with rain and dark blooms of mould; its floors and pavements are worn smooth, as if trodden on for many years; and its fat, swollen chimneys, which resemble wasp's nests more than any functional architectural feature, are of a make not used in several centuries at least.

But, Shara notes as she enters, the University's plumbing is nothing short of immaculate. As with most buildings, only pieces of it can be seen: connections to water mains, sprinklers in the ceiling, along with the usual taps and sinks. But what she sees is fairly advanced.

She tries not to smile. Because Shara knows that, despite the University's ancient appearance, the structure itself is little more than twenty years old.

'Which wing are we in now?' she asks.

'The Linguistics wing,' says Nidayin. 'And they prefer to call them "chambers".'

Shara blinks slowly at such a prompt correction. Nidayin, she finds, is not an unusual embassy officer, in that he is snotty, dismissive and self-important. However, he is also the embassy's public affairs representative, which means he is the person who formally gets ambassadors and diplomats into important places – like the University.

'Very long chambers,' says Pitry, looking around. 'It's a hallway, really.'

'The term "chambers",' says Nidayin severely, 'has a very *symbolic* meaning.'

'Which is what?'

Nidayin, who evidently has not expected to be quizzed in such a manner, says, 'I am sure it has no bearing on the investigation. It doesn't matter.'

Their footsteps echo on the stone. The University is empty after the death of Dr Pangyui. Perhaps it is the way the blue light of the lamps (the *gas* lamps, Shara notes) plays on the stone walls, but she cannot help but feel this is a profoundly organic structure, as if they are not in an institute of higher learning but are instead within some insect's hive, or the belly of some titanic creature. *But that*, she thinks, *is probably exactly what the architects intended*.

She wonders what Efrem thought of this place. She has already seen his rooms at the embassy and, as expected, found them completely barren, shorn of any detail at all: Efrem was a man who lived for work, especially *this* kind of work, in this historic place. She has no doubt that stuffed in some drawer in his office in the University are hundreds of charcoal sketches of the University's cornices, gates and, almost certainly, dozens and dozens of doorknobs, for Efrem was always fascinated by what people did with their hands: *It is how people interact with the world*, he told her once. *The soul might be within the eyes, but the subconscious, the matter of their behaviour, that is in the hands. Watch a man's hands, and you watch his heart.* And perhaps he was right, for Efrem was always touching things when he encountered some new discovery: he stroked table tops, tapped on walls, kneaded up dirt, caressed ripe fruit. For Efrem Pangyui, there was never enough of the world to experience.

'Well, now I'm curious,' says Pitry.

'It doesn't matter,' says Nidayin again.

'You don't know,' says Pitry.

'I *do* know,' says Nidayin. 'I merely do not have the appropriate resources in front of me. I would not wish to give incorrect information.'

'What rot,' says Pitry.

Sigrud sighs softly – which, for him, constitutes an exasperated outburst.

Shara clears her throat. 'The University has six chambers,' she says, 'because the Continentals conceived of the world as a heart with six chambers, each chamber housing one of the original Divinities. The flow between each of the Divinities formed the flow of time, of fate, of all events: the very blood of the world. The University was conceived as a microcosm of this relationship. To come here was to learn everything about everything, or so they wished to suggest.'

'Really?' says Pitry.

'Yes,' says Shara. 'But this is not the original University. The original was lost during the War.'

'After the Blink, you mean,' says Nidayin. 'It vanished with most of Bulikov. Right?'

Shara ignores him. 'The University has been rebuilt based on sketches and art made before the War. Bulikov was very insistent it be recreated exactly as it was: they tore down a great deal of the surviving ancient architecture so the University could be rebuilt with genuine ancient stone. They wanted it to be authentic – or, at least,' she says, gently touching a gas lamp, 'as authentic as one could make it while still allowing certain modern conveniences.'

'How do you know all that?' asks Pitry.

Shara adjusts her glasses. 'What sort of classes do they teach here?'

'Erm, these days, mostly economics,' says Nidayin. 'Commerce. Basic job training, as well. Chiefly because the polis has made a concerted effort to become a financial player in the world. Part of the New Bulikov movement, which has had a bit of a backlash lately since some people are interpreting it as modernisation. Which it is, really. There're sporadic protests around the University campus, most of the time. Either about New Bulikov or, well . . .'

'About Dr Pangyui,' says Shara.

'Yes.'

'I suppose,' says Pitry as he absently examines the doors, 'that they can't teach history.'

'Not much, no,' says Nidayin. 'What history they teach is strictly regulated, due to the WR. The Regulations sort of cripple everything they do here, to an extent. And they have trouble teaching science and basic physics, since for so long things here didn't *function* by basic physics. And, in some places, they still don't.'

Of course, thinks Shara. *How do you teach people science when the local sunrise refutes science every morning?*

Sigrud stops. He sniffs twice, then looks towards one door on the right. Like most of the doors at the University, it is thick wood with a thick glass window in the centre. Otherwise, it is bereft of markings.

'Is that Dr Pangyui's office?' asks Shara.

'Yes,' says Nidayin. 'How did he—'

'And has anyone besides the police been inside?'

'I don't believe so.'

Still, Shara grimaces. The police, she knows, will be bad enough. 'Nidayin, Pitry – I would like it if you would check all the offices and rooms in this chamber of the University. We need to know which other University staff might have been nearby, as well as the nature of their relationship to Dr Pangyui.'

'Are you sure we should be taking up such an investigation?' asks Nidayin.

Shara gives him a look that is not quite cold, perhaps the cooler side of lukewarm.

'I mean, not to speak out of turn, but . . . you are only the *interim* CD,' he says.

'Yes,' says Shara, 'I am.' She produces a small, pink telegram slip and hands it to Nidayin. 'And I am following orders from the Polis Governor, as you will see.'

Nidayin opens up the telegram and reads:

C-AMB THIVANI PRELIM INVEST POLIS FORCES ASSIST
<STOP> GHS512

'Oh,' says Nidayin.

'Strictly the preliminary investigation,' says Shara. 'But we must take advantage of evidence while it is still fresh, or so I am told. Would I be wrong?'

'No,' says Nidayin. 'No, you would not.'

He and Pitry begin their rounds, checking the adjacent offices. Within twenty feet they begin bickering again. *That should keep them busy for a while,* she thinks.

She tucks the telegram inside her coat. She knows she'll probably need it again.

Naturally, Polis Governor Mulaghesh sent no such telegram, but it's useful to have friends in every Comm Department, no matter what you're up to.

'Now,' says Shara. 'Let's see what's left.'

The office of Dr Efrem Pangyui initially resembles a massive rat's nest: it is a knee-high sea of torn paper, with his desk resembling a barge lost on its yellowed waves. Shara turns on the gas lamps and surveys the damage. She sees countless tacks on the corkboard on the walls, with scraps of paper still tacked up. 'The police must have torn them all down,' she says quietly. 'My word.'

It is a small, dingy office, not at all befitting a man of Pangyui's stature. There is a window, but it is of stained glass so dark it might as well be brick.

'We shall have to bag this all up and take it back to the embassy, I suppose.' She pauses. 'Tell me: how many followed us on the way here?'

Sigrud holds up two fingers.

'Professionals?'

'Doubt it.'

'Did Nidayin or Pitry see them?'

Sigrud gives her a look – *what do you think?*

Shara smiles. 'I told you. Stir up the hornet's nest . . . but back to the matter at hand.' She looks around. 'What do you think?'

He sniffs and rubs his nose. 'Well, obviously someone was looking for something. But I think they did not find it.' Shara nods, pleased to see her own conclusions were correct. Sigrud's one grey eye dances along the tides of paper. 'If they were looking for one thing, and found it, they would have stopped. But I see no sign of stopping.'

'Good. I see the same.'

Which leaves the question: what were they looking for? The message in Pangyui's tie? She isn't yet sure but, more and more, Shara doubts if Pangyui was murdered simply for committing heresy in Bulikov.

Assume nothing, Shara reminds herself. *You do not know until you know.*

'All right,' says Shara. 'Where?'

Sigrud sniffs again, shuffles through the paper towards the desk, and uses his foot to clear the floor on the side of the desk opposite where the professor would normally work. A large, dark stain still lies on the stone floor. She has to get very near before she catches the coppery smell of old blood.

'So he wasn't at his desk,' says Shara.

'I doubt it, no.'

She wishes she knew where he was lying when they found him, what was next to him, what was on his person. There were notes in the police report, of course, but the police report did not mention Pangyui's shredded clothing at all, so it's not exactly trustworthy. She supposes she'll have to work with what she has.

'If you could fetch me a bag for this paper, please,' she says softly.

Sigrud nods and stalks off down the hallway.

Shara surveys the room. She walks forward gingerly, and stoops and picks up a scrap of paper:

> . . . *but the contention is that the Kaj's history as an unusually entitled Saypuri does not undermine his actions. His father was a collaborator with the Continent, yes, and we know nothing of his mother. We know the Kaj was a scholar and something of a scientist, performing experiments in his home, and though he did not lose any of his own in the massacre, he . . .*

She picks up another:

> . . . *one wonders what the chamber of Olvos was used for in the original University, for it is suggested she disapproved of the actions of the Continent and, indeed, the other Divinities. Considered a Divinity of hope, light and resilience, Olvos's withdrawal from the world in 775 at the onset of the Continental Golden Age was considered a great tragedy. Exactly why she withdrew was hotly debated: some texts surfaced claiming Olvos predicted nothing but woe for the path the other Divinities had chosen, yet many of these texts were quickly destroyed, probably by the other Divinities . . .*

And another:

> *. . . by all indications, the Kaj's time on Continental shores was spent very*
> *sparsely before he died of an infection in 1646. He slept, ate and lived alone, and*
> *only spoke to give orders. Sagresha, his lieutenant, records in her letters, 'It was*
> *as if he was so disappointed in the homelands of those who had conquered and*
> *ruled over his people for so long that it wounded him. Though he never said so,*
> *I could hear him thinking it – should not the land of the gods be fit for gods?'*
> *Though, of course, the Kaj could not know that he was almost directly respon-*
> *sible for the devastation of the Continent, for it was the Kaj's successful*
> *assassination of the Divinity Taalhavras that brought about the Blink . . .*

Shara recognises a lot of this as Efrem's older writings, already published. He must have brought his old volumes here, and the police shredded
them during their 'search'. *Perhaps they enjoyed destroying so much celebrated*
Saypuri writing, she thinks. *That is, if it was really the police who did this.*

Her eye catches a bulky form in the corner. Upon examination, it is a
dense, impressive safe – and what's more, its door is ajar. She inspects the
lock, which is terribly complicated: Shara is not a skilled lockpick, but
she's met a few in her time, and she knows they'd blanch at this. Yet the
lock shows no sign of damage, nor does the door or the rest of the safe, nor
is there any scrap or sign of what the safe once held.

As she sits back to think, she notices one corner of paper jutting up from
the wreckage that is starkly different: it is not a page from an academic
publication, but an official form with the Ministry of Foreign Affairs seal
in the upper left corner and, in the upper right, the seal of the Polis Govern-
or's Office.

She fishes it out. It's a request form filled out by Efrem. Exactly what it
is requesting is hard to tell: the request itself is reduced down to a code,
ACCWHS14-347. Efrem has signed the bottom but there's another signa-
ture needed, and underneath the blank are the words: TURYIN MULAGHESH,
POLIS GOVERNOR, BULIKOV.

'Found something?' says Sigrud's voice from the door.

'I'm not sure yet,' says Shara.

As they bag up all the material, Shara finds that this is not the only document of the Polis Governor's that found its way into Efrem's possession: among the scraps of paper are dozens and dozens of entry permission stubs, probably handed to him by a guard when he was approved to enter . . . somewhere.

Shara counts them when they're done: there is a total of nineteen permission stubs here in the office. And Shara knows Efrem probably didn't keep them intentionally: they'd probably be worthless once his visit was over. He must have just emptied his pockets once he came back to his office.

Shara glances back at the safe in the corner. *And perhaps he brought back more than ticket stubs.*

Nidayin and Pitry both stumble in, looking quite harassed. Nidayin holds a long, smudged piece of paper in his hands. 'Well,' he says, 'we've finished. We have a total of sixty-three names, and we've recorded their departments, tenure, relation to the professor and—'

'Good work,' says Shara. 'Sigrud, if you could please add that to our collection. I believe we've done what we need to here. We'll go back to the embassy now. And then, Pitry, you will probably need to fill up the car again. I believe a short excursion beyond Bulikov is in order.'

'Where are we going?' asks Pitry.

Shara fingers the permission stubs in her pocket. 'To be frank,' she says, 'I don't quite know.'

When they exit the University and begin to cross to the car, Shara slows down.

Sigrud walks behind her. There is a soft hiss as he exhales through his nose.

She glances down and to the side, at his hands.

He makes a tiny gesture with his index and middle finger, no more than a tap against his thigh. She looks to the right.

They look like ordinary people sitting at the café. But then, of course, they would: a man buried in a thick grey coat, with oily hair and two days' worth of beard, who is slowly peeling back the packaging on a cigar; the other, a woman of about fifty or fifty-five, with skinny, bitter features, purplish, worn hands, and grey hair pulled back in a severe bun. The woman refuses to look up from her sewing, yet Shara can see her hands are trembling.

No. Not professionals.

'We'll drop you round the corner,' says Shara. 'Then, follow them.'

Sigrud nods and climbs into the car.

To get out of Bulikov by road involves a parade of admittance papers, of checkpoints, of bottlenecks and choked traffic, red and white striped gates and crossing guards and page after page of lists. All of the attendants – dressed in black or purple uniforms with dozens of brass buttons – are Continental. *Have we so deeply regulated this city*, thinks Shara, *that its very citizens are willing to choke it?* Her papers, of course, act as a magic wand, eliciting frenzied handwaves, sometimes even a salute, and she and Pitry navigate the network of checkpoints within half an hour – something a citizen of Bulikov accomplishes only if they wake up very, very, very early.

A Polis Governor's 'quarters' are always a tricky subject on the Continent. Shara knows that the official stance of Saypur on Governor's quarters, both of the Regional and Polis variety, is that they are only temporary: it's practically part of her script, as a Saypuri official. The official stance goes on to state that the Governor's quarters are monitoring stations established by Saypur solely to keep the peace until the peace is self-sustainable. But, as everyone on the Continent asks every day, when exactly will that be?

Judging by the twenty-foot concrete walls, fixed cannonry, iron gates and soldiers' shouts echoing over the walls (which are less than two miles from the walls of Bulikov), the indication is that the peace will not be self-sustainable for some time. Polis Governor Mulaghesh's office, for example, is imposing, stately, mostly barren and definitely, definitely permanent. Floor-to-ceiling windows stand behind her desk, and through them Shara sees green, rolling hills encircled by the concrete wall. She can also watch soldiers drilling on the parade grounds, dozens of soft blue headcloths bobbing up and down as the commandant barks out orders.

'Governor Mulaghesh will be with you shortly,' says the attendant, a chisel-faced young man with a starved, mean look to him. 'She's currently taking a constitutional.'

'I'm sorry, she's what?' asks Shara.

He smiles in a manner he apparently believes to be polite. 'Exercise.'

'Oh, I see. Then I'm happy to wait.'

He smiles again, as if to say — *How charming to think you had another option*.

Shara looks around the office. It has all the soul and ornamentation of an axe: everything is clean grey surfaces, strictly designed to function and to function well. The walls and ceiling and floor look so alike that Shara feels they are all cleaned with the same broom.

A small door at the side of the room opens. A shortish woman of about forty-five marches in, wearing a standard-issue grey tank top, light blue breeches and boots. She is drenched in sweat running in beads down her shoulders, which are immensely large and immensely brown. She stops and examines Shara with a cold eye, then smiles in a manner just as cold, and marches over to the desk. She grabs hold of the corner, kicks her right heel up and grasps the ankle with her right hand, stretching out her quadriceps.

'Well, hi,' she says.

Shara smiles and stands. Turyin Mulaghesh is, much like her offices, cold, spare, brutal and efficient, a creature so born and bred for battle and order that she cannot tolerate another manner of living. She is one of the most muscular women Shara has ever seen, sporting wiry biceps and a sinewy neck and shoulders. Shara has heard stories of the feats Mulaghesh performed during the minor rebellions in the aftermath of the Summer of Black Rivers, and she finds herself believing all of them when she studies the immense scarring along Mulaghesh's left jawline, not to mention her ravaged knuckles. She is, needless to say, a very unusual sort of person to occupy what's fundamentally a bureaucratic position.

'Good afternoon, Governor Mulaghesh,' says Shara. 'I am—'

'I know who you are,' says Mulaghesh. She releases the stretch, opens a drawer and takes out a cigarillo. 'You're the new girl. The — what is it? – Chief Ambassador.'

'Yes. Ashara Thivani, formally Cultural—'

'Yes, yes. Cultural Ambassador. Came in last night, right?'

'That's correct.'

Mulaghesh dumps herself down in her chair and puts her feet up. 'Seems like only two weeks ago they swept Troonyi in here. I'm surprised I still have a job, I thought the man'd burn down all the city in my time here. Just, honestly, a fucking oaf.' She looks up at Shara. Her eyes are steel-grey. 'But maybe he got the fire started. I mean, after all, Pangyui died on his watch.' She points to Shara with the butt end of the cigarillo. 'That's why you're here, right?'

'That's one reason, yes.'

'And another reason, I'm sure,' says Mulaghesh as she lights the cigarillo, 'would be for the Ministry to determine whether my actions – or *inactions* – could have contributed to their Cultural Emissary's death. Because it also, in a way, happened on *my* watch. Right?'

'That is not my priority,' says Shara.

'I commend you,' she says. 'You have evidently got the diplomat thing down to an art.'

'It's the truth,' says Shara.

'I believe it's the truth for *you*. Just probably not for the Ministry.' Mulaghesh sighs, wrapping her head in a wreath of smoke. 'Listen, I'm glad you're here, because if *you* tell them what *I've* been saying for the past year, maybe they'll listen. Because ever since I first got wind of this cultural expedition bullshit, I knew, I just *knew*, that this was all going to end in tears. Bulikov's like an elephant, see? It's got a long memory. Ahanashtan, Taalhavshtan, those places, they've got their act together. They're modernising. Getting train tracks in, doctors . . . shit, letting women vote.' She snorts, hawks and spits into a waste-paper basket at her desk. 'This place,' she gestures out of the windows, towards the walls of Bulikov, 'this place still thinks it's in its Golden Ages. Or that it *should* be. Every once in a while it forgets, and we get some peace, but then someone stirs up the nest again, and I have another crisis on my hands. A crisis *I* can't really intervene in, because the policy is: "Hands off." Policy, as always, sounds solid as shit in Ghaladesh, a whole damn ocean away, but when you've got those walls only a day's walk from you, it's all just words.'

Shara opts to interrupt. 'Governor Mulaghesh, before we continue . . .'

'Yeah?'

'Who do *you* think killed Dr Pangyui?'

Mulaghesh looks slightly taken aback. 'Me? Hell. I don't know. It could have been anyone. The whole city wanted him dead. Besides, I haven't been given the go-ahead to investigate.'

'But surely you must have some ideas.'

'Yeah. I do.' She studies Shara for a long while. 'Why do you care? You're just a CA. You're just here for the parties. Right?'

Shara reaches into her robes and produces her Ministry of Foreign Affairs badge.

Mulaghesh sits forward and, to her credit, examines it without a reaction.

After a long while, she reads from the name at the bottom, 'Komayd.'

'Yes,' says Shara.

'Not, I take it, Thivani.'

'No,' says Shara.

'Komayd. As in *Vinya* Komayd?'

Shara stares back at her, unblinking.

Mulaghesh sits back. She looks at Shara for some time, then asks, 'How old are you?'

Shara tells her.

'So . . . That thing, sixteen years ago. The Nationalist Party. Was that . . .'

With a great deal of effort, Shara's face shows no emotion.

Mulaghesh nods. Unless Shara is mistaken, she thinks she can see a sly gleam in her eye. 'Huh. Why didn't you say so at the start?'

'I'm afraid you started talking before I could say anything.'

'I guess that's true,' Mulaghesh says. 'I get mouthy after a run.' She sticks her cigarillo back between her teeth. 'So. You *are* here to investigate the professor's murder.'

'I am here,' says Shara as she puts away her badge, 'to see if anything in Bulikov poses a threat to Saypur.'

'In Bulikov? Shit. It's only crawled out of total squalor in the past fifteen years or so. When I got here it was probably no different than when the Kaj captured it. People were still shitting in buckets. It's hard to imagine how it could pose a threat.'

'They thought the same before the Summer of Black Rivers, when we introduced the Regulations and Bulikov rebelled, and the city was in an even worse state then. The passion of Bulikov far outweighs its limitations, it seems.'

'Poetic,' says Mulaghesh. She runs a thumb along the scar on her jaw. 'But probably true.' She slouches back farther in her chair, a feat Shara hadn't realised was possible, and thinks.

Shara knows she is wondering if it's wise to extend a hand to this new, mysterious official: so often in the Ministry good deeds and charitable actions win only woe, when someone loses their footing and all those who supported them get punished.

'I need your help, Governor,' says Shara. 'I cannot depend on the embassy.'

Mulaghesh snorts. 'Who can?'

'Quite right. And I am willing to do what is necessary to win your support.'

'Oh, really?'

'Yes. I wish to put this all to bed as quickly as possible. And I'd need your help to do so.'

Mulaghesh chews the end of her cigar. 'I don't know if you can give me what I want.'

'You may be surprised.'

'Maybe. I don't mind being a servant, Ambassador Komayd. And that's what we are, civil servants. But I've served enough. I want to serve elsewhere. Some place a lot better than this backwards ruin.'

Shara thinks she already knows where she's going. 'Ahanashtan?'

Mulaghesh laughs. 'Ahanashtan? You think I want *more* responsibility? By the seas, no. What I want, Ambassador, is to get stationed in *Javrat*.'

'Javrat?' says Shara, surprised.

'Yes. Way out in the South Sea. I want to go somewhere with palm trees. Sun. With *beaches*. Somewhere with good wine, and men whose skin doesn't look like beef fat. I want to get far away from the Continent, Ambassador. I don't want anything to do with this any more.'

Shara is a bit taken aback by this. The port city of Ahanashtan is the largest polis on the Continent, and it is also the polis with the strongest connection to Saypur. Its Polis Governor is one of the most powerful figures in the world, and presumably every Saypuri official on the Continent would love to get the job. Requesting the tiny island of Javrat, however, would mean Mulaghesh wants essentially to step out of the political game *altogether*: and Shara has never really met any Saypuri whose ambition didn't keep them in the game in perpetuity.

'So do you think,' says Mulaghesh, 'that that's possible?'

'It's . . . possible, certainly,' says Shara. 'But I expect the Ministry will be a little confused.'

'I don't want a promotion,' says Mulaghesh. 'I've got, what, two decades left of my life? Less? I want to take my bones somewhere warm, Ambassador. And all this gamesmanship . . . I find it sickening nowadays.'

'I will most certainly see what I can do to get that arranged.'

Mulaghesh smiles a grin that would not look out of place on a shark. 'Excellent. Then let's get started.'

'I'll tell you that this New Bulikov movement in the city has stirred up a big bucket of shit,' says Mulaghesh. 'It's been brewing for a while. People see there's money to be made in modernisation – in cooperation with Saypur, in other words – and they mean to make it. The rich folk in Bulikov, they don't want to cooperate at all, and they make enough noise so that the poor ones listen.'

'What would this have to do with Dr Pangyui?'

'Well, the big argument in the anti-New Bulikov movements is that they're "straying from the path".' To this statement Mulaghesh applies air quotes, an eye roll, a sneer – the works. 'This is not as things *were*, thus this is not how things should *be*. The most extreme of them call themselves, rather boldly, the Restorationists. Self-appointed keepers of Bulikov's national heritage, cultural identity. You know the kind of arseholes I'm talking about. So when Pangyui showed up, dissecting the

Continent's history and culture, well, it gave them a pretty big target to talk about.'

'Ah,' says Shara.

'Yeah. The Restorationists were losing the debate, because, shit, no one's going to vote against prosperity. So if you're losing the debate, you change the conversation.'

'He was a good distraction, in other words.'

'Right. Point at this filthy Saypuri, showing up with the blessing of this foreign power they're supposed to get in bed with, and scream and howl and bitch and whine about this horrific sacrilege. I don't think they actually cared much about Pangyui and his "mission of cultural understanding" – well, maybe *some* did – they just used him as a political chip. And now they've all officially denied having had anything to do with the murder, and their official position is that this was just honest political debate. You know, basic good old-fashioned, disgusting, slanderous political debate. Nothing out of the ordinary.'

Shara finds absolutely none of this surprising. The political instinct might wear different clothes in different nations, but underneath the pomp and ceremony it's the same ugliness. 'But does this have any bearing on Dr Pangyui's murder?'

'Maybe. Maybe not. Could it have stirred some nut into beating the professor to death? Could have. Does that mean the political factions in Bulikov are responsible? Maybe. Can we do anything about that? Probably not.'

'But what if the powers in Bulikov,' says Shara, 'are directly complicit?'

Mulaghesh stops chewing her cigar. 'And what would you mean by that?'

'We've inspected the professor's offices. They were ransacked. I suspect this could not have happened without *someone* in the Bulikov police knowing. Much of his material has been shredded, destroyed. Someone was looking for something.'

'What?'

'I don't know.'

'Then why come to me about it?'

'Well, it may depend on exactly *what* he was researching.' Shara reaches into her coat and takes out the entry permission stub, puts it on Mulaghesh's desk and slides it over.

Mulaghesh's face drops the second she sees it. She takes the cigarillo out, sits frozen with it in one hand, then lays it on the table. 'Ah, shit.'

'What would this be, Governor?' asks Shara.

Mulaghesh grunts, frustrated.

'I found dozens of these in his office,' says Shara. 'There are no communications about this. Whatever this is.'

'That's because we can't risk anyone finding out where it is.' She fingers one of the stubs.

'What are these, Governor?'

'Visitor badges,' says Mulaghesh. 'You clip them to your shirtfront, so we can see you have access. They expire every week, because, well, the access is so restricted. I guess he must have taken the expired ones home – though he had strict orders to *destroy* them. This is what you get for giving this sort of work to civilians.'

'Access to . . . what?'

Mulaghesh puts the cigarillo out on the table top. 'I thought you'd know. I mean, everyone *sort of* knows about the Warehouses.'

When Shara hears this, her mouth falls open. 'The Warehouses? As in . . . the *Unmentionable* Warehouses?'

Mulaghesh nods reluctantly.

'They're *real*?'

She sighs again. 'Yeah. Yeah, they're real.' She scratches her head and, once again, says, 'Ah, shit.'

'They showed me the one near here in my first week as Governor,' says Mulaghesh. 'Years ago. Drove me out into the countryside. Wouldn't tell me where we were going. And then we came across this huge section of bunkers. Dozens of them. I asked what was in them. They shrugged. "Nothing special. Nothing extraordinary." Grain, tyres, wire, things like that. Except in one. One was different, but it looked just like all the others. Camouflage, you see. Hiding it in plain sight. Very clever people, we

Saypuris. They didn't open the doors, though. They just said, "Here it is. It's real. And the safest thing you can do is never talk about it or think about it again." Which I did. Until the professor came, of course.'

Shara gapes at her. 'And *this* is where Dr Pangyui was going?'

'He was here to study history,' says Mulaghesh with a shrug. 'Where is there more history than in the Unmentionables? That's, well . . . that's why they're so dangerous.'

Shara sits in stunned silence. The Unmentionable Warehouses have always been a somewhat ridiculous fairy tale to everyone in the Ministry. The only suggestion of their existence lies in a line in a tiny subsection of the Worldly Regulations:

> Any and all items, art, artefacts or devices treasured by the peoples of the Continent shall not be removed from the territory of the Continent, but they shall be protected and restricted should the nature of these items, art, artefacts or devices directly violate these Regulations.

And as Shara and any other student of the history before the Great War knows, the Continent was practically *swimming* in such things. Before the Kaj invaded the Continent, the daily life of people on the Continent was propelled, maintained and supported by countless miraculous items: teapots that were never empty, locks that responded only to a drop of a certain person's blood, blankets that provided warmth and protection regardless of the temperature. Dozens upon dozens were cited in the texts recovered by Saypur after the Great War. And some miraculous items, of course, were not so benign.

Which begged the question: where are such items now? If the Divinities had created so many, and if the WR did not allow Saypur (in what many felt was an unusual and unwisely diplomatic decision) to remove them from the Continent altogether or destroy them, then where could they be?

And some felt the only answer could be: well, they're all still there. Somewhere on the Continent, but hidden. Stored somewhere safely, in warehouses so secret they were unmentionable.

But this had to be impossible. In the Ministry, where everyone was tangled up in everyone else's work, how could they hide storage structures of such size, of such importance? Shara herself had never seen anything in her career indicating they existed, and Shara saw quite a lot.

'How is that . . . how could that *be*?' asks Shara. 'How could something like that be *real*?'

'I think,' says Mulaghesh, 'because they're so old. They predate all intelligence networks in operation today. Hell, they're older than the Continental Governances for sure, way before we started communicating so closely with the Continent. The Ministry lets you know if you need to know, and you never did.'

'But *here*? In *Bulikov*?'

'Not *in* Bulikov, no. Nearby. After the Kaj died, his lieutenants took all the miraculous things he found and locked them up. They locked up so many that no one could ever move them without anyone on the Continent finding out where they were. So they had to keep them here, and build around them.'

'How many?'

'Thousands. I think.'

'You *think*?'

'Well, *I* never wanted to go inside. Who knows what's in there? It's all filed, organised, locked away, sure, but . . . I never wanted to know. Things like that are supposed to be *dead*. I wanted them to stay that way. Part of the reason I've never done much in my career as Governor of Bulikov, Ambassador, is that it's not Saypur's policy. But the other reason is that I was never meant to attract *attention*. There are a lot of things near Bulikov that need to be left alone.'

Shara, with a great deal of effort, manages to return to the issue at hand. 'But Pangyui didn't?'

'He was here to study the past in a way no one ever had before,' says Mulaghesh. 'I'm willing to bet that the Warehouse is probably the real reason he came. We've been sitting on top of a stockpile of history and I guess someone at the Ministry got impatient. They wanted to open the box.'

Shara feels more than a little betrayed to hear this news. Efrem never mentioned anything like this. *No wonder he was such an apt student in tradecraft*, she thinks. *He had already been hiding many secrets of his own.*

It feels quite impossible that Vinya would have no knowledge of any of this. *Do I really want*, Shara wonders, *to keep turning over these stones?*

She remembers how Efrem lay on the trolley in the embassy vault, his skull wearing the crude mask of his small, delicate face.

Something cold blooms in Shara's belly. *Efrem, did Auntie Vinya get you killed?*

'Do you know which artefacts he was studying?' asks Shara.

'He said he wished to study only the books in there, and a few inactive items.'

'Inactive?'

'Yeah. Most of them aren't miraculous any more. They're just . . . things. A box, a pen, a painting. But some . . . some are still alive. Before you ask, no, I don't know which ones. I don't know much about those things, and I don't *want* to know. All that was established back in the Kaj's age. And nobody's really been in the Warehouse, until Pangyui.

'He understood the dangers. He was remarkably well informed about all of it. I guess he'd read and studied enough of the old stories so that he already knew all about them before he walked through the door. He was careful. The ones he took out, he stored and watched safely.'

'He took some *out*?'

Mulaghesh shrugs. 'Some. From what he described, a lot of the Warehouse is just junk, really. There are piles and piles and piles of books down there, too. That was what the professor was primarily looking for, he said. He made some careful selections, and he studied them beyond the . . . circumstances of the Warehouse. Which, I guess, was pretty oppressive.'

The safe, thinks Shara. 'And do you think his murder had anything to do with the Warehouse?'

'You might think so,' says Mulaghesh. 'But I doubt it. Like I said, no one knows much about the Warehouse. The bunkers it's part of are monitored very closely. There haven't been any disturbances. To me, there are a lot more public reasons to have killed him.'

'But a danger as significant as the Warehouse . . .'

'If I was in charge, I'd have moved it piece by piece to the border,' says Mulaghesh. 'But I'm not. I guess the Ministry was too worried about exposing something like that. Listen, I can't do much in Bulikov, but I can watch. And no one's been tampering with the Warehouse. I'm sure of that. You asked for my advice, and my advice would be to look at the Restorationists.'

Shara considers it reluctantly. 'And I suppose,' she says, 'that it would not be possible to allow me access to this Wa—'

'No,' says Mulaghesh sharply. 'It would not.'

'I know I do not have approval, but if such a thing were to go unnoti—'

'Don't even finish that. It's treason to suggest it.'

Shara glares at her. 'I am nearly as well informed as Pangyui in such historical matters.'

'Good for you,' says Mulaghesh. 'But you weren't sent here for this. You don't have clearance. The way to keep these things secret is to keep people from talking about them. And that includes you, Ambassador Komayd.'

Shara readjusts her glasses. She defiantly files all this in the back of her mind for later perusal. 'I see,' she says finally. 'So. The Restorationists.'

Mulaghesh nods approvingly. 'Right.'

'Do you have any sources on them?'

'Not a single one,' says Mulaghesh. 'Or, at least, not a trustworthy one. I don't want to wade into that mess and have them start trumpeting that I'm watching them.'

'I suppose the New Bulikov supporters could be a help.'

'To an extent. There's one City Father who's a big proponent, which is unusual. But he probably doesn't want to mix too closely with Saypuris like us. *Collusion*, you see. There are some formal opportunities, though. He throws a monthly reception for his party, calling on the supporters of the arts. Sort of a fund-raising thing – it's an election year. He usually invites me and the Chief Diplomat, as a formality. So if you wanted a chance to talk to him, that'd be it.'

'What more can you tell me about him?'

'He's old money. Family's really established. They broke into the brick trade years back, and bricks are useful when you're rebuilding a whole damn city. They're political, too. A member of the Votrov family has been a City Father for, shit, sixty years or so?'

Shara, who has been nodding along with this, freezes.

She replays what she has just heard, then replays it again, and again.

Oh, she thinks, *I badly hope she did not say what I think she said.*

'I'm sorry,' says Shara. 'But *which* family is it?'

'Votrov. Why? What's so shocking about that?'

Shara sits slowly back in her chair. 'And his name . . . his first name.'

'Yeah?'

'Would it happen to be Vohannes?'

Mulaghesh cocks an eyebrow. 'You know him?'

Shara does not answer.

The words come crashing back down on her as if it'd only been yesterday.

If you were to come with me to my home, I'd make you a princess, he'd said to her when she saw him last.

And she'd answered, *What I think you truly want, my dear child, is a prince. But you can't have such a thing at home, can you? They'd kill you for that.*

And the cocksure grin had melted off his face, his blue eyes crackling with brittleness like ice dunked in warm water, and she'd known then that she'd hurt him – really, genuinely hurt him – found some place deep inside him no one knew about, and burned it into ash.

Shara shuts her eyes and pinches the bridge of her nose. 'Oh, dear.'

Columns pierce the grey sky again and again, stabbing it, slashing it. It bleeds soft rain that makes the faces of the crumbling buildings glisten and sweat. Though the War that littered this city with such scars is long over, the shrapnel is still fresh, the flesh and bones of the buildings still broken and exposed. Desiccated children clamber across the ruins of a temple, its collapsed walls dancing with the twinkles of campfires, its cavities and caves echoing with cries. The wretches make apish gestures to passers-by and harangue them for coin, for food, for a smile, for a warm place to sleep; yet there is a glitter of metal in their sleeves, tiny blades hidden among the filthy cloth, waiting to repay any kind gesture with quick violence. The new generation of Bulikov.

Those few that see Sigrud pass say nothing: they make no plea, no threat. They watch silently until he is gone.

A crowd of women cross the street before him, humble, shoulders hunched and eyes averted, their figures buried under piles of dark wool. Their necks and shoulders and ankles are carefully obscured. The putter and squeak of cars. The stink of horseshit. Pipes protrude from buildings several storeys up, sending waste raining down on pavements. A city too old and too established for proper plumbing. Colonnades stacked with faceless statues stare down at him, eyeless, watchful. Squatting, thick-walled structures with twisting loggias ring with music and laughter, homes of the powerful, the wealthy, the hidden. On their balconies men in thick black coats dotted with medals and insignias glower at Sigrud, wondering: what is this doing here? How could a mountain savage be allowed into this neighbourhood? Next to these bulbous mansions might be a puzzle-piece of a building facade, half a wall with windows empty, a wooden staircase clinging to the frames. And beyond these are winding rivers of stairs, some rounded and aged, some sharp and fresh, some wide, some terribly narrow.

Sigrud walks them all, following his marks. The man and woman flee straight from the University, and do not lead him on an especially merry chase: they are not professionals, and are quite blind to the art of the street. They bicker loudly, then softly, then loudly again. Though Sigrud keeps his distance, he hears some of it.

The man says: *This was expected. You were told of this.*

The woman answers, first softly, then more loudly as she gets angry: *These people showing up at my place of work! Where I spend my days, where I eat breakfast! Where I mopped floors for decades!*

Then the man: *You knew there were dangers! You did! And you quaver now? Do you not have faith?*

And the woman is silent.

Sigrud rolls his eyes. The incompetence of it all is dispiriting. He's not even sure whether he wants to bother hiding himself any more. His burgundy coat is rolled up and stuffed under one armpit – since this, of course, is a conspicuous flag – but still, a six-and-a-half-foot man would normally never lend himself well to obfuscation. But Sigrud knows that crowds are much like individual people: they have their own psychology, their own habits, their own natures. They unthinkingly assume specific structures – channels and corridors of traffic, bending around blockades – and break apart these structures in a manner that almost seems choreographed when you watch it. It's simply a matter of placing yourself within these structures, like hovering in the still curve of a shoal of fish as it twists and darts across the ocean floor. Crowds, like people, never truly know themselves.

The couple stops at one teetering, oddly rounded apartment building. The woman, grey-faced, twitching, nods as the man whispers his final orders to her. Then she enters. From the cover of a stable, Sigrud makes a careful note of the address.

'Hey!' A stable boy emerges from a side door. 'Who're you? What are you—'

Sigrud turns and looks at the stable boy.

The boy falters. 'Uh. Well . . .'

Sigrud turns back. The woman's companion is starting off. Sigrud stalks out of the stable and follows.

This chase is a little different. The man plunges ahead into a part of Bulikov that was obviously much more ravaged by the Blink, the War, and whichever other catastrophes happened to get wedged within that rocky period of world history. The number of staircases practically triples, or quadruples – it's a little hard for Sigrud's eyes to count them. Spiral staircases rise up to halt completely in mid-air, some only ten feet off the ground, some twenty or thirty. There is something faintly osseous about them, resembling the rippled horns of some massive, exotic ruminant. Birds and cats have nested in the top steps of some. In one ridiculous instance, a huge basalt staircase slashes down through an entire hill, sinking a sheer forty feet into the earth in a veritable chasm that has apparently managed to undermine several small houses, whose remains totter unnervingly on the lip of the gap.

Sigrud's quarry, thankfully, never mounts or starts down any of these truncated steps, but trots through the alleys and the streets, which are often just as schizophrenic as the stairs. Sigrud casts a bemused eye on the buildings that have seemingly been blended into other buildings, like toys shoved together by a child. What appears to be a rather stodgy law firm has one quarter of a bath house sticking out of its side, like some kind of unseemly growth. In some places these invasive buildings have been messily excised: a chunk of a shoe shop has obviously just been tugged out from where it was previously lodged inside a bank.

The pace of the hunt quickens. Sigrud's quarry zags left. Sigrud follows. His quarry ducks through the crumbling remains of a large wall. Sigrud stalks through a different gap, but maintains visual contact. His quarry — whom Sigrud is almost positive remains ignorant of his surveillance — sprints up a wobbly staircase to mount the roof of an old church. Sigrud, with some strategic, gingerly placed steps, hops up after him, closing the gap.

Sigrud crests the top and peers out over the roof. He sees his quarry running towards the edge, but the man shows no sign of stopping. Not when he is thirty feet away from the edge, or twenty, or five, and then he . . .

Jumps.

The last thing Sigrud sees of the man is the flutter of his grey coat as he plummets to the street below, arms outstretched and fingers spread.

Sigrud frowns, climbs on to the roof, and walks to the edge.

The street is nearly forty feet below. Yet there is no body, nor any mark of one ever having been there. There is nothing the man could have jumped on to: all the walls near this spot are blank and sheer. It is as if he fell, and then simply . . .

Vanished.

Sigrud grunts. This is inconvenient.

He considers trying to scale the wall, and decides this would be unwarranted. So he climbs back down the stairs and out on to the street.

There is no one, nothing. This part of Bulikov appears powerfully deserted.

Sigrud touches each cobblestone. None of them are warm; all of them are solid.

He sighs.

Working with Shara Komayd has introduced Sigrud to many confounding events, and dozens of things wondrous and terrifying and strange.

However, he has never found any of them particularly awe-inspiring or moving: he chiefly finds them to be irritating.

He turns round to start back to the embassy. But as he does, he gets the queerest feeling.

Did the street just change? Just at the corner of his eye? Though it seems impossible, he's sure it did: for one second, he did not see the tumbledown building fronts and deserted homes, but rather immense, slender skyscrapers of gleaming white and gold.

It is virtually impossible to gauge the amount of damage caused by the Blink.

This is not just a measure of the Blink's destruction, which was huge: rather, the nature of the Blink's destruction is of a sort so bizarre and so complex that we − Saypuri, Continental, or anyone who lived through it or came after it − cannot understand what was lost.

The facts, however, are simple, though perhaps superficially so.

In 1639, after having successfully completed the first assassination of a Divinity and overthrowing the Continental outposts in Saypur, Avshakta si Komayd, freshly crowned as Kaj, assembled a small, ragged fleet of ships and sailed for the Continent − then called the Holy Lands, of course.

The Holy Lands were utterly unprepared for such an action: having lived under the protection of the Divinities for thousands of years, it was inconceivable that anyone, let alone a Saypuri, could invade the Holy Lands, or − much more inconceivable − actually kill a Divinity. The Holy Lands and the remaining three Divinities (as Olvos and Kolkan had departed long ago) had grown quite concerned about the long absence of the Divinity Voortya, unaware that Voortya and her forces had been slaughtered in the Night of the Red Sands in 1638. So when a fleet was spotted off the south shore of Ahanashtan, the Divinities reacted quickly, thinking it to be their missing friends.

Such was their downfall. The Kaj had anticipated a coastal battle, and had outfitted several ships with the same machinery he'd used to assassinate Voortya. And the Divinities' concern was so great that it was Taalhavras himself, the leader of the Divinities, who met the fleet in the port of Ahanashtan.

The recorded impressions of the Kaj's sailors vary widely on exactly what happened. *Some reported seeing 'a man-like figure, twelve feet high, with the head of an eagle, standing on the port'. Others reported 'an enormous statue, vaguely mannish, covered in scaffolding, yet it somehow managed to move'. And others reported seeing only a 'beam of blue light, stretching up to the heavens'.*

However Taalhavras presented himself, the Kaj directed his machinery at him and immediately struck him down, just as he had Voortya.

But since Taalhavras was the builder god, all of what he built vanished the moment he vanished; and, judging by the enormous devastation of the Blink, he had built much more than anyone knew. Taalhavras had, in fact, made significant alterations to the very fundaments of the Continent's reality. The nature of these alterations probably cannot be understood by mortal minds. However, once these alterations vanished – one imagines supports, struts, bolts and nuts and so on falling out of place – the very reality of the Holy Lands abruptly changed.

The Kaj's sailors did not witness the Blink: they recorded only experiencing a terrible storm that kept them from landing for two days and three nights. They assumed that it was a Divine defence, and they only persisted through the determination of the Kaj himself. They could not know the cosmic collapse occurring mere miles away.

Whole countries disappeared. Streets turned to chasms. Temples turned to ash. Stars vanished. The sky clouded over, marking the permanent change to the Continent's climate – what was once a dry, sandy, sunny place would soon be cloudy, wet and bitterly cold, much like the Dreyling lands to the north. Buildings of Divine nature imploded into a single stone, taking all their occupants with them to what one can only assume was a terrible fate. And Bulikov, being the holiest of cities, and a recipient of much of Taalhavras's attentions, contracted inwards by miles in one brutal moment, disrupting the very nature of the city, and losing hundreds of thousands of people to ends best left unimagined. The Seat of the World itself, the temple and meeting place of the Divinities, completely disappeared, leaving behind only its bell tower, which shrank to only a few storeys tall.

In short, a whole way of life – and the history and knowledge of it – died in the blink of an eye.

No one, not even the Continentals, truly knows what Continental life was like before the Blink. All we have are scraps of history, many of which are meaningless to our modern eyes, filled with references to lost mysteries and dead mythologies.

Upon History Lost, *Dr Efrem Pangyui, 1682*

Dead languages

The tiny graphite strokes blend together in the light of the lamps. Shara *tsks*, lights another lamp, sets it at her desk and tries to read again. *Damn this city*, she thinks. *How backward must they be that our own embassy can't get enough gas to light a room?*

She's transcribed the professor's code on a number of papers, trying to render truth from the twisted characters like squeezing water from a stone. A cup of noonyan tea cools beside the documents. (Shara has decided to ease up on the sirlang: if she keeps going at this rate, she'll exhaust the embassy's stores in a week.) She bends so close to the documents that the heat from the lamps is insufferable.

It is an address, she thinks. She can tell just by how the characters are arranged. She has broken a bit of the code already, but she suspects it is not really a code in any conventional sense: rather, the message has been translated into a mashup of foreign alphabets. What she believes to be the consonants all have the top half of Gheshati, a dead alphabet from Western Saypur. And though it took her hours to figure out, the bottom halves, she thinks, are all in Chotokan, an incredibly rare and borderline impenetrable language from the mountains east of the Dreyling Republics.

Now she just has to figure out the vowels.

And then the numbers.

Oh, the numbers . . .

Her admiration for the professor has dimmed, somewhat: *Pangyui, you cryptic old lizard*.

She tosses back tea and sits back in her chair. She tries to believe that this is taking her so long because the code itself is difficult. She does not want to entertain the notion that she might, in truth, be deeply distracted.

*He's here. He's here in the city, with me. Maybe blocks away. Why didn't I con-
sider this? How could I have been so stupid?*

It had started, like so many of Shara's lifelong pursuits, with a game.

The first days of any term at Fadhuri Academy in Ghaladesh were always
the most tense. The bright young stars of every county and island in Saypur found themselves crowded together into Fadhuri's hallowed halls, and
quickly discovered that, despite everything their upbringing told them,
they might not actually be special: every student here was a genius back at
home, so every student arrived wondering if they would prove to be exceptional among the truly exceptional.

As a way to relieve the tension, the school tradition was to hold a Batlan
tournament on the weekend before term really started. It became such a
popular event that parents encouraged their children to drown themselves
in strategies and plays before arriving, perhaps assuming that a high place
in the tournament would ensure better grades and a better future.

Shara Komayd, then sixteen, was no such student. Not only was she
unshakeably confident that she was the most brilliant child on the grounds,
but she had always held Batlan in some contempt, thinking it a showy
game where chance was far too much of a factor: the roll of the dice at each
turn determined each player's capabilities, and it *did* make the game more
spontaneous, but it removed a lot of the players' control. She had always
preferred Tovos Va, a somewhat similar game which was far more cerebral
and much slower paced, rewarding plans thought out several plays ahead.
However, she rarely got the chance to play it: Tovos Va was a Continental
game, and was unheard of in Saypur.

But the lessons she'd learned in Tovos Va *did* translate to Batlan, to an
extent – though to mitigate the factor of chance, you had to plan very,
very far ahead. If you did so early enough, and played with enough foresight, decimating any normal Batlan player was child's play.

On that first weekend before term, Shara tore through the Batlan rank-
ings like a shark. She did not win: she *annihilated* the other players. Since
she essentially won the games in the first dozen plays, and had to play out
the next three dozen before taking the board, she found herself increasingly contemptuous of the other players, flailing in her traps as they

thought they were playing one game when in truth they were playing another. And she let her contempt show: she sighed, rolled her eyes, sat with her chin in her hand and groaned as her opponents made one blind, stupid move after the other.

The other students began to watch her with naked hate. When they discovered she was sixteen, two years younger than any normal Fadhuri freshman, the hate curdled to rage.

Shara became so sure that she'd utterly sweep the tournament that she barely paid attention to the standings. When she finally glanced at them, she saw another player was accomplishing nearly the same feat she was, eating through the players from the other side of the hall: VOTROV.

She leaned back in her chair and scanned the room to get a look at him. It did not take long for her to find him.

He was, to her surprise, not a Saypuri at all, but a Continental: a tall, thin, pale young man with blond-red hair, a strong jaw and bright blue eyes.

'I've made my play,' said Shara's opponent.

'Shh,' said Shara, who wished to watch this boy more.

'What?' her opponent said, incensed.

'Oh, fine,' said Shara, and she made two plays that would probably destroy him in the next round. Then she returned to looking at the Continental.

It was not uncommon for rich Continentals to send their children to Saypur for education. Saypur, after all, was now the wealthiest nation in the world, and the Continent was still quite dangerous. The boy certainly had an aristocratic look about him: he slouched in his chair with an air of bored pleasure, and he talked to his opponents constantly, merrily exchanging jibes with them as though at a coffee house.

The boy looked up and saw Shara watching. He grinned, and winked.

Disconcerted, Shara returned to her game.

Finally, after two hours of play, and after laying waste to half the students at Fadhuri, Shara found herself sitting down opposite the Continental. They were the only two players left; the rest of the school and faculty stood around them, watching.

Shara stared mistrustfully at the Continental boy, who sat with a cocksure grin, stretched his back, popped his knuckles and said, 'I'm quite looking forward to my first actual game, aren't you?' He started laying out his Batlan pieces.

'I don't know what you mean,' said Shara as she did the same.

'Mmm. Maybe,' he said. 'Tell me. Have you ever heard of Tovos Va?'

Something inside of Shara squeaked. She hesitated very slightly before laying out the next piece.

'It's very popular where I'm from,' said the boy brightly. 'Why, back in Bulikov, we had a yearly tournament. Now, which ones did I win? There were three tournaments I won in a row, I just can't quite remember which ones . . .'

Shara finished laying out her pieces. 'I suggest, sir,' she said, 'that you play, rather than talk.'

He looked at her arrangements, and laughed. 'So nice to see my suspicions were right! That looks a little like Mischeni's Feint,' he said. 'Or it *would* be, if this was Tovos Va. Good thing this is Batlan, eh?' He finished laying out his own pieces.

Shara glanced at them. 'And *that*,' she said, 'is Strovsky's Curl.'

He grinned triumphantly.

'Or, you would like me to think it is,' said Shara, 'though I suspect in three plays it will be a Vanguard Block and, after that, a basic flank.'

The boy blinked as if he'd been slapped. His grin vanished.

'But, good thing this is *Batlan*, eh?' said Shara savagely. She leaned in. 'You look so much prettier,' she said, 'with your face wiped clean of smugness.'

The students around them *oooooh*ed.

The boy stared at her. He laughed once, in disbelief. Then, 'Roll the dice.'

'Gladly,' said Shara.

She dropped the ivories, and the game began.

It was to be a four-hour slugfest: a game of endless beginnings, of defensive positions, of recombinations and rearrangements. It was, one teacher said, the most conservative game of Batlan he had ever seen played: but, of course, they were not really playing Batlan at all, but a different game altogether, a mix of Batlan and Tovos Va they were inventing as they fought.

He talked to her constantly, a ceaseless burble of chatter. For three hours Shara resisted, ignoring his jibes, but then the Continental boy asked, 'Tell me, is your life so devoid of entertainment that you have enough time to study obscure, foreign games?' He made a play that appeared aggressive, but Shara knew was a feint. 'Have you no friends? No family?'

'You assume your game is difficult to learn,' said Shara, nettled. 'To me, your game and your culture are childish frippery.' She ignored his feint, and pressed towards a front in a manner that would look suicidal to anyone who didn't know what was going on.

He laughed. 'It talks! The little battleaxe talks!'

'I am sure that to someone of your position, anyone who doesn't tolerate each of your whims with blind submission must seem positively uppity.'

'Perhaps so. Perhaps I've travelled solely to find backchat somewhere. But I wonder — what could have beaten you so badly that it's formed and honed such a sharp edge, my little battleaxe?' He swooped back around, redoubled his defences. (Some student nearby grumbled, 'When are they actually going to start *playing*?')

'You are mistaken, sir,' said Shara. 'You are merely sensitive. In fact, I suspect that to sit upon an uncushioned chair would surely score your princely buttocks.'

While the students laughed, Shara began to quietly construct a trap.

The Continental boy did not appear insulted: rather, there was an odd gleam in his eye. 'Oh, my dear,' he said. 'If you really wished to check, I'd not stop you.' He made a play.

'What does *that* mean?' asked Shara. She made another play, appearing to withdraw inwards, while in truth layering her trap.

'Don't claim to be so innocent,' he said. 'You brought the subject up, my dear. I am simply yielding to you.' He made another play, blindly.

'You don't *seem* to be yielding,' said Shara. She withdrew farther, adding bait, thinking: *Why is he suddenly playing so poorly?*

'Appearances,' said the boy, 'can be deceiving.' He rolled the dice, thrust out again.

'True,' said Shara. 'So. Do you want to end it now?'

'To end what now?'

'The game. We can just walk away now, if you like.'

'What, as a draw?'

'No,' said Shara. 'I just won. It'll take a few plays for it to happen, but . . . well, I did.'

The other students glanced at one another, perplexed.

The Continental boy sat forward, looked at her pieces, and reviewed the last few plays: evidently, he'd simply not been paying attention. Shara realised he hadn't looked at the board at all in the last plays, but only at her.

The boy's mouth fell open. 'Oh,' he said. 'Oh. I see.'

'Yes,' said Shara.

'Hm. Well. No, no. Let's do the honourable thing and play it out, shall we?'

It was a formality, one extended by a few lucky rolls of the dice, but soon Shara was picking his pieces off the board. Yet to her irritation, the boy didn't seem shamed, or abashed: he just kept smiling at her.

She made what she knew to be the second-to-last play. 'I must ask – how does it feel to be beaten by a Saypuri girl?'

'You,' he said as he laid his game's neck below her blade, 'are not a girl.'

She faltered as she made her play – what could he mean by that?

Shara picked off his final piece. The students around them erupted in a cheer, but she barely heard them. *Another of his mind games.* 'Before you ask, I'll play you again any time.'

'Well, honestly,' he said cheerfully, 'I'd much prefer a fuck.'

She stared at him, astonished.

He winked, stood up and walked away to be joined by his friends. She watched him go, and gazed around at the cheering students.

Had anyone else heard that? Had he actually *meant* that? Could he *really*?

'Who was that?' she asked aloud.

'Do you really not know?' said a student.

'No.'

'Really? You really didn't know you were playing Vohannes Votrov, the richest prick on the whole of the damnable Continent?'

Shara stared at the empty board, and wondered if the boy had been playing yet another, different game all along: neither Batlan, nor Tovos Va, but a game with which she was totally unfamiliar.

The numbers are going to shave years off Shara's life.

She has translated much of the professor's code. It now reads:

____ H_GH ST___T, SA_NT M___V__VA BANK, B_X ____, GH_V_NY TA___KAN _____

A security box, in a bank. A bank that bears the name of some saint. Ordinarily this would narrow her choices down quite a bit, but High Street is a very long street in Bulikov, and nearly every bank is named after a saint of some sort.

(Actually, Shara knows almost *everything* on the Continent is named after some saint or another. Saypuri historians gauge there were an estimated 70,000 saints before the Great War: apparently the Divinities considered granting sainthood an irritating formality to be signed off on without thought. When the WR were enacted, the idea of trying to remove sainted names from polis structures proved overwhelming, and in what was considered to be a very big concession, and with a very big shrug, Saypur simply gave up trying. Shara wishes they hadn't. It would make her job much easier now.)

And the numbers . . . Shara hasn't got to them yet, but she has glanced at them. Numerals and digits of any kind are always incredibly difficult in ancient languages: one particularly fervent cult of the Divinity Jukov refused to acknowledge the number 17, for example, though no historian has been able to figure out why.

She remembers a conversation she had with Dr Pangyui in their safe house in Ahanashtan:

'The amount of dead languages,' he said, 'are like the stars.'

'That many?' she asked.

'The Divinities were not stupid – they knew the best way to control what other nations thought was to control how they talked. And when those languages died, so did those ways of thinking, those ways of looking at the world. They are dead, and we cannot get them back.'

'Are you one of those academics who keeps trying to revive the Saypuri Mother Tongue?' Shara asked.

'No. Because Saypur was a big place, and had many Mother Tongues. Such vain, jingoistic missions do not interest me.'

'Then why waste your time looking at all?'

He lit his pipe. 'Oh, well, we all reconstruct our past because we wish to see how our present came to be our present, do we not?'

And yet Pangyui had lied to her. He had, in a way, used her, to further his own secret ends.

She returns to work, knowing she has many hours ahead, and also, perhaps, to try to keep herself from remembering more.

It was two months into term when she met him again. She was in the library, reading about the political exploits of Sagresha, lieutenant to the Kaj and celebrated war hero, when she noticed someone had sat down at the table by the window.

His head was bowed, his curly red-gold hair eclipsing his brow. He never seemed to sit in a chair right: he was angled sideways and almost on his back, with a tome in his lap about Thinadeshi, the engineer who had introduced the railways to the Continent.

Shara glared at him. She thought for a second, then stood up, gathered her books, sat down opposite him and simply watched.

He did not look up. He turned a page, and after a moment said, 'And what would you want?'

'Why did you say that to me?' she asked.

He looked up at her through his curtain of messy hair. Though Shara was no drinker, she could tell by his puffy lids that he had what the masters at Fadhuri called a 'morning head'.

'What?' he asked. 'From the tournament?'

She nodded.

'Oh, well.' He winced as if embarrassed, and returned to his book. 'Maybe to get a rise out of you. You seemed such a serious thing, after all. I hadn't seen you smile all day, despite your admirable record.'

'But what did you *mean*?'

This provoked a long, confused stare. 'Are you, erm, serious?'

'Yes.'

'What did you *think* I meant when I asked you for . . . a fuck?' he asked, slowly and uncertainly.

'No, not *that*.' Shara waved her hand. 'The part about me . . . not being a girl.'

'*That's* what you're mad about? *That*?'

Shara simply glared back.

'Well, I mean,' he said. 'Well, here. I have seen girls before. Many girls. You can be a girl at any age, you know. Girls at forty. Girls at fifty. There's a kind of flightiness to them, just like how a man at forty can have the impatience and belligerence of a five-year-old boy. But you can also be a *woman* at any age. And you, my dear, have probably been the spiritual equivalent of a fifty-three- or fifty-four-year-old woman since you were six years old. I can tell. You are *not* a girl.' He again returned to his book. 'You are very much a woman. Probably an *old* one.'

Shara considered this. Then she took out her own study materials and began to read opposite him, feeling confused, incensed and strangely flattered.

'That biography of Thinadeshi is shit, just so you know,' she said.

'Is it?'

'Yes. The writer has an agenda. And his references are suspect.'

'Ah. His references. Very important.'

'Yes.'

He flipped a page. 'Incidentally,' he asked, 'did you ever give much thought to the thing I said about fucking?'

'Shut up.'

He smiled.

They started meeting in the library nearly every day, and their relationship felt like a continuation of their Batlan game: a long, exhausting conflict in which little ground was ever ceded or gained. Shara was aware throughout that they were playing reversed roles, considering their nationalities: she was the staunch, mistrustful conservative, zealously advocating the proper way of living and building a disciplined, useful life, while he was the permissive libertine, arguing that if someone wished to do something, and if it hurt no one, and moreover if they had the *money* to pay for it, then why should anyone interfere?

But both of them agreed that their nations were in a bad, dangerous state.

'Saypur has grown fat and weak off commerce,' Shara said to him once. 'We believe we can *buy* our safety. The idea that we must fight for it, fight for it every day, never crosses our minds.'

Vohannes rolled his eyes. 'You paint your world in such drab cynicisms.'

'I am right,' she insisted. 'Saypur has got to where it is through military strength. Its civilian leadership is far too permissive.'

'What would you do? Have Saypuri children learn yet another oath, another pledge to Mother Saypur?' Vohannes laughed. 'My dear Shara, do you not see that what makes your country so great is that it allows its people to be human in a way the Continent never did?'

'You *admire* Saypur? As a Continental?'

'Of course I do! Not just because I wouldn't catch leprosy here, while I can't say the same of the Continent. But here, you allow people . . . to be people. Do you not know how rare a thing that is?'

'I thought you would wish for discipline and punishment,' says Shara. 'Faith and self-denial.'

'Only Kolkashtani Continentals think that,' Vohannes said. 'And it's a bastard way to live. Trust me.'

Shara shook her head. 'You're wrong. Fervour and strength are what keep the peace. And the world hasn't changed that much.'

'You think the world is such a cold and bitter place, my dear Shara,' said Vohannes. 'If your great-grandfather taught you anything, I'd have hoped it would be that one person can vastly improve the lives of many.'

'Saying something so admiring of the Kaj on the Continent would get you killed.'

'A *lot* of things on the Continent would get me killed.'

Both simply assumed that, as educated children of power, they would change the world, but neither could agree on the best way to change it: one day Shara would wish to write a grand, epic history of Saypur, of the world, and the next she would consider running for office, like her aunt; one day Vohannes would dream of funding a grand art project that would completely remake the Continental polises, and the next he would be shrewdly planning a radical business venture. Both of them hated the other's ideas, and gleefully expressed that hatred with unchecked vitriol.

In retrospect, they might have started sleeping together solely out of conversational exhaustion.

But it was more than that. Deep down, Shara knew she had never really had anyone else to talk to, to *really* talk to, until she met Vohannes, and she suspected he felt the same: they were both from famous, reputable families, they were both orphans, and they were both intensely isolated by their circumstances. Much like the game they'd played in the tournament, their relationship was one they invented day by day, and it was one only they could understand.

When she was not studying in her first and second year of college, Shara was engaged in what she would later feel to be a simply unfathomable amount of sex. And on the weekends, when the Academy maids would stay home and everyone could sleep in, she'd stay in his quarters, sleeping the day away in his arms, and she would wonder exactly what she was doing with this foreigner, this boy from a place she was supposed to hate with all her heart.

She did not think it was love. She did not think it was love when she felt a curious ache and anxiety if he was not there; she did not think it was love when she felt relief wash over her as she received a note from him; she did not think it was love when she sometimes wondered what their lives would be like after five, ten, fifteen years together. The idea of love never crossed her mind.

How stupid are the young, Shara would later think, *that they cannot see what is right in front of them*.

Shara sits back in her chair and studies her work:

3411 HIGH STREET, SAINT MORNVIEVA BANK, BOX 0813, GHIVENY TAORSKAN 63611

She wipes sweat from her brow, checks her watch. It is three in the morning. And, once she realises it, she finds it feels like it.

Now the real difficulty, thinks Shara. *How to get at whatever is in this box?*

There's a knock at her door.

'Come in,' she says.

The door swings open. Sigrud lumbers in, sits down before her desk and begins to fill his pipe.

'How did it go?'

He pulls an odd face: confusion, dismay, slight fascination.

'Bad?'

'Bad,' he says. 'Good, some. Also . . . odd.'

'What happened?'

He stuffs his pipe in his mouth with some hostility. 'Well, the woman of the two, she works at the University. She is a maid . . . Irina Torskeny. Unmarried. No family. Nothing besides her work. I checked her rotation – she cleaned the professor's office, quarters. All of it. She has been assigned to Dr Pangyui's offices since he got here.'

'Good,' says Shara. 'We'll look into her, then.'

'The other one . . . the man, though . . .' Sigrud recounts his confusing exploits in the ravaged neighbourhoods of Bulikov.

'So the man just . . . vanished?' asks Shara.

Sigrud nods.

'Was there a sound of any kind? Like a whip crack?'

Sigrud shakes his head.

'Hm,' says Shara. 'If it had been a whip crack, I would have thought it—'

'Parnesi's Cupboard.'

'Parnesi.'

'Whatever.'

Shara rubs her temple, thinking. Although Saint Parnesi has been dead for hundreds of years, his works continue to bother her: he'd been a priest of the Divinity Jukov who fell passionately in love with a Kolkashtani nun. As the Divinity Kolkan held very dour views on the appeal of sex, Parnesi found it difficult to visit his lover in her nunnery. Jukov, being a mercurial, clever Divinity, created a miracle that would allow Parnesi to hide in plain sight from enemies both mortal and Divine: a 'cupboard' or pocket of air, which he could step inside at any moment, which allowed him to infiltrate the nunnery easily.

But, of course, one could use the miracle for less jovial purposes. Just two years ago it took Shara the better part of three months to figure out the source of a documents leak in Ahanashtan. The culprits turned out to be three trade attachés who had, somehow, discovered the miracle, and if one of them had not been so liberal with his cologne – for Parnesi's Cupboard does nothing to mask scent – Sigrud might never have caught him. But caught him he did, and things had turned quite grisly . . . Though the man did quickly surrender the names of his associates.

'I feared the miracle had become popularised, after Ahanashtan,' says Shara. 'Something like that . . . it could be catastrophic. But if it's not Parnesi . . . and you're *sure* he vanished?'

'I can find people,' says Sigrud with implacable, indifferent confidence. 'I could not find this man.'

'Did you see him pull out a sheet of silver cloth? Jukov's Scalp supposedly did something similar . . . But no one's seen a piece of it in forty years. It would look like a silver sheet.'

'Your suggestions ignore a bigger problem,' says Sigrud. 'Even if this man was invisible, he would have fallen several storeys to his death.'

'Oh. Good point.'

'I saw nothing. I scoured the streets. I scoured the area. I asked questions. I found nothing. But . . .'

'But what?'

'There was a moment . . . when I did not feel like I was where I was.'

'What does *that* mean?'

'I do not quite know,' admits Sigrud. 'It was as if I was somewhere . . . older. I saw buildings that I did not think were really there . . .'

'What sort of buildings?'

Sigrud shrugs. 'There are not words for what I saw.'

Shara adjusts her glasses. This is troubling.

'Progress?' asks Sigrud, looking at the clutch of lamps and mounds of paper. 'I see you have drunk what looks like three pots of tea. So the news will be either very good or very bad.'

'Like you, the news is both. The message is a safety deposit box, in a bank. The only question is – how to get to it?'

'You are not sending me to rob a bank, are you?'

'Good *gracious*, no,' says Shara. 'I can only imagine the headlines . . .' *And*, she thinks, *the body count*.

'Are there no strings you can pull?'

'Strings?'

'You are a diplomat,' says Sigrud. 'The City Fathers, they are puppets, more or less, right? Can't you use them?'

'Unless the box is being watched. And it seems Pangyui was being watched very, very closely. He was dealing with things that I did not know he was dealing with. He did not tell me, it seems, the whole truth.' She looks up at Sigrud. 'I am not sure if I should tell *you*, in fact. But I will, if you ask.'

Sigrud shrugs. 'I do not really care, to be frank.'

Shara does not bother to hide her relief. One of the things she values most about her 'secretary' is how little he cares for the intricacy of obfuscation: Sigrud is a hammer in a world of nails, and he is satisfied knowing only that.

'Good,' says Shara. 'I would not wish to show we have an unnatural interest in Pangyui's researches. For them to know that we do not know what Pangyui knew would be . . . well, unwise. We will need to be more subtle in our arrangements. I am just not quite sure how, yet.'

'So what do we do now?'

At first Shara is not sure what to say. But then she slowly realises she has been thinking of a strategy all night: she was just not *aware* she was thinking of it.

Her heart sinks as she realises what the solution is: yet she is so sure it would work she knows she'd be a fool not to try it.

'Well,' says Shara, 'we do have one lead. Who do we have at the Ministry who's good with finance?'

'Finance?'

'Yes. Banking, specifically.'

Sigrud shrugs. 'I think I recall hearing Yonji is still there.'

She makes a note of it. 'He'll do. I'll have to contact him very soon to check . . . I *think* I am right. But I will need him to confirm the exact financial arrangements.'

'So we are still on our own? Just you – and I – against the whole of Bulikov?'

Shara finishes her note. 'Hm. No. I doubt if that will do. Start sending out feelers. I expect we will need to recruit at least a few bodies, or a few eyes. They cannot know this has any involvement with the Ministry. But you are usually quite good with contractors.'

'How much are we willing to pay them?'

Shara tells him.

'*That* is why I seem so good with recruits,' he says.

'Very good. Now the last thing . . . I must ask you – do you have any party clothes?'

Sigrud lazily gestures at his mud-spattered boots and smog-stained shirt. 'What about this,' he asks, 'isn't it appropriate for a party?'

In the predawn light, Shara waits for sleep, and remembers.

It was towards the middle part of their relationship, though neither she nor Vohannes knew it then. She had found him sitting beneath a tree, watching the rowing team practising in the Sharyoonith River, next to the Academy. The girls' team had just set their shell in the water, and were climbing in. When Shara joined him and sat in his lap, as she often did, she felt a soft lump pressing into her lower back.

'Should I be worried?' she asked.

'About what?' he said.

'What do you think?'

'I try not to think at all when outdoors, dear. It tends to ruin things so.'

'Should I be worried,' she said, 'that your favour might one day wander to another girl?'

Vohannes laughed, surprised. 'I didn't know you were so jealous, my battleaxe!'

'No one is jealous until they have reason to be.' She reached around, grabbed the lump. 'And *that* seems like a reason.'

He grunts, not displeased. 'I hadn't realised we were quite so formal.'

'Formal? This is an issue of *formality*?'

'It is to me. So, what is it to be, then? Are you saying you assume you are *mine*, and I *yours*, dear? Are you sure you wish to be *my* girl, for ever and ever, and belong only to *me*?'

Shara was silent. She looked away.

'What?' said Vohannes.

'Nothing.'

'What?' he said again, frustrated. 'What have I said now?'

'It's nothing!'

'It's obviously not nothing. The very air has just turned colder.'

'It *should* be nothing. It's . . . it's my thing. A . . . Saypuri thing.'

'Oh, just say it, Shara. Let me learn it, at least.'

'I suppose it doesn't mean anything to you, does it? Calling someone yours. Saying they belong to you. Me being *your* girl. But we don't say things like that here. And you might not understand . . . but then, your people have never been owned. And it sounds very different coming out of your mouth, Vo.'

Vohannes took in a sharp breath. 'Oh, gods, Shara, you know I didn't mean to—'

'I know you didn't. I know that to you, it was a perfectly innocent thing to say. But being owned, and making someone yours, they have different meanings here. We don't say them. People still remember what it was like, before.'

'Well,' said Vohannes, suddenly bitter, '*we* don't. We lost that. It was *taken* from us. By your damn great-grandfather, or whatever.'

'I hate it when you talk about tha—'

'Oh, I know you do. But at least *your* people have *your* memories, however unpleasant they are. You're allowed to read about *my* history here. Hells, this school's library has more information on us than we do! But if I tried to bring any of it home, I'd be fined or jailed – or worse – by *your* people.'

Shara, abashed, did not answer. Both of them turned to the river. A cygnet stabbed its dark bill down among the reeds; its long white neck came thrashing up with the pumping, panicked legs of a tiny white frog trapped in its mouth.

'I hate this,' said Vohannes.

'What?'

'I hate feeling we are different . . .' A long pause. 'And feeling, I suppose, that we do not really know each other.'

Shara watched as the rowing teams did sprints across the water, triceps and quadriceps rippling in the morning light. First the shells of the girls' team passed, followed by the boys, dressed in considerably less clothing, and showing quite a bit more muscle.

And was it her imagination, or did the lump in her back move just a little as the boys' team emerged from the shadow of a willow, and broke into sunlight?

He sighed. 'What a day.'

We are not ourselves. We are not allowed to be ourselves. To be ourselves is a crime, to be ourselves is a sin. To be ourselves is theft.

We are work, only work. We are the wood we tear from our country's trees, the ore we dig from our country's bones, the corn and wheat and grain we grow in her fields.

Yet we shall never taste it. We shall not live in houses made of the wood we cut. We shall not hammer and forge our metals into tools for ourselves. These things are not meant for us.

We are not meant for ourselves.

We are meant for the people across the water. We are meant for the children of the gods. We are as metal and stone and wood for their purposes.

We do not protest because we have no voice to protest with. To have a voice is a crime.

We cannot think to protest. To think these things is a crime. These words, these words you hear, they are stolen from myself.

We are not chosen. We are not the children of the gods. We are the soulless, we are ash-children, we are as mud and dirt.

But if this is so, why did the gods make us at all? And if we were meant only to labour, why give us minds, why give us desires? Why can we not be as cattle in the field, or chickens in their coops?

My fathers and mothers died in bondage. I will die in bondage. My children will die in bondage. If we are but a possession of the children of the gods, why do the gods allow us to grieve?

The gods are cruel not because they make us work. They are cruel because they allow us to hope.

Anonymous Saypuri testimonial, circa 1470

To do what he does best

The house of Votrov is one of the most modern homes in all of Bulikov, but you could never tell by looking at it: it is a massive, bulky, squat affair of dark grey stone and fragile buttresses. Tiny windows dot its bulging sides like pinpricks, some filled with the narrow flicker of candle flame. On the south side, away from the prevailing northern wind, it features massive, gaping balconies arranged in what appears to be a stack, each balcony slightly smaller than the one below it, ending at a tiny crow's nest at the top. To Shara, who grew up seeing the slender, simplistic wooden structures of Saypur, it is a primitive, savage thing, not resembling a domicile so much as a malformed, aquatic polyp. Yet in Bulikov it is quite new for, unlike so many homes of the old families, this house was built specifically to accommodate the cold, wintry climate. Which, one must remember, is a somewhat recent development.

To acknowledge things have changed, thinks Shara as her car approaches, *is akin to death for these people*.

Her stomach flutters. Could he really be inside? She never knew about his home before, and to see it now, to realise it is real and that he had a life beyond her, strangely disturbs her.

Be quiet, she says to the mutterings in her mind, yet somehow this only makes them louder.

A huge line of automobiles and carriages slowly shuffles forward to the Votrov manor entrance. Shara watches the rich and celebrated citizens of Bulikov emerge from their various methods of transport, one lapel flipped up to shield their faces from the frosty air before hurrying inside. After nearly half an hour, Pitry, tutting and wincing, pulls the car through the estate gates and up to the door.

The valet receives her with a look as cool as the night wind. She hands him her official invitation. He takes it, offers a curt nod, then gestures with one white-gloved hand to the door, which he is pointedly not holding open.

With a chorus of squeaks from the car's shock absorbers, Sigrud emerges and mounts the bottom step; the valet twitches almost imperceptibly, bows low to Shara and opens the door.

She steps over the threshold. *How many parties have I been to in my life*, thinks Shara, *with warlords and generals and proud murderers. And yet this one I dread more than any of those.*

In stark contrast to the exterior, the interior is stunningly lavish: hundreds of gas flames line the entry hall, each filtering through tinted chimneys to provide a flickering, golden hue; a staggeringly complicated chandelier of crystal slabs appears to drip down from the rounded ceiling, giving the impression of a massive, glowing stalactite; at the centre of the room, two huge hearths are filled with roaring fires, and between them a set of curling stairs twists upward to ascend the vaults of the home.

A voice not dissimilar to Auntie Vinya's says, *You could have lived here with him if not for your pride.*

He did not love me, she says back, *and I did not love him.*

Shara is not stupid enough to convince herself these are truths; but neither, she knows, are they wholly lies.

'The reason it's so big,' says a voice, 'is because he owns all the damn builders, of course.'

Mulaghesh stands to attention before a pillar. Just looking at her posture makes Shara's back hurt. Mulaghesh is dressed in her uniform, which is pressed, polished, spotless. Her hair is tied back in a brutal bun, and her knee-high black boots boast a mirror shine. Her left breast is covered in medals; her right handles the considerable overflow. Overall, she does not look well dressed but, rather, carefully assembled. Shara is almost tempted to search the seams of her coat for rivets.

'The original home vanished in the Blink,' says Mulaghesh. 'Or so I'm told.'

'Hello, Governor. You look quite . . . impressive.'

Mulaghesh nods, but does not take her eyes off the socialites milling before the fires. 'I don't like for these people to forget what I am,' she says. 'Despite all diplomatic pretences, we *are* a military presence in their city.'

Beside the hearth on the right is a plinth with five short statues standing on it.

'And those would be the reason for the occasion?' asks Shara.

'They would be,' says Mulaghesh.

She and Shara wander towards them.

'It's an art auction, benefiting the New Bulikov party and a number of other vaguely worthy causes. Votrov's become well known as an art fan. Pretty controversial stuff, too.'

Shara can see why: while none of the stone figures are nude to the extent that they'd show anything one would actually wish to see, they come *very* close, with the fold of a robe or the neck of a guitar just in the right place to shield things from view. There are three female statues, two male, but none are particularly physically lovely: they are bulky creatures, with wide hips and shoulders and fat thighs.

Shara squints as she reads the plate at the bottom of the plinth. ' "Peasants in repose",' she says.

'Yes,' says Mulaghesh. 'Two things Bulikov doesn't like to think about: nudity and the poor. *Especially* the nudity, though.'

'I am familiar with this city's stance on sexuality.'

'Not so much a stance as a glower, though,' says Mulaghesh. She picks up a horn-flute of ale from a passing footman and quaffs it. 'I can't even talk about it with them.'

'Yes, I wouldn't expect you could. Their disgust for our more . . . liberal marital arrangements is well known,' says Shara.

Mulaghesh snorts. 'It didn't seem liberal when *I* was married.'

As nearly all Saypuris were treated as chattels under the Continental Empire, many were forced into marriage or divorced on the whims of whichever Continental company or individual owned them. After the Kaj overthrew the Continent, Saypur's laws on marriage and personal freedom were greatly influenced by these traumas: in Saypur, two consenting spouses enter into a six-year contract, which at its end they can either renew or allow to expire. Many Saypuris have two, three, or even more spouses in their lifetimes; and while homosexual marriage is not formally recognised in Saypur, neither does Saypur's vehement observance of personal freedom allow the state to forbid it.

Shara observes the scandalous protuberance underneath one statue's robe. 'So one could categorise this work as counter-cultural.'

'Or as pissing in the eyes of the powerful, yeah.'

'A crass way of putting it,' says a voice. A tall, slender young woman dressed in a menagerie of furs walks to stand just behind them. She is terribly young, not much older than twenty, with tawny hair and high, sharp cheekbones. She manages to look both very Continental and yet also very urbane, two characteristics that often conflict. 'I would, instead, say that it is embracing the new.'

Mulaghesh raises her horn-flute in a sardonic toast. 'That I shall drink to. May its feet find earth and may it run fast and far.'

'But you do not sound like you think it likely, Governor.'

Mulaghesh grunts into her ale.

The young woman does not appear surprised, yet she says, 'I always find it disheartening that you are so doubtful of our efforts, Governor. I would hope that, as a representative of your nation, you'd lend us support.'

'I am not in a position to lend anything, especially support. Nor am I in a position to officially say much. But I am compelled to listen to your City Fathers quite frequently, Miss Ivanya. And I am not sure your ideas, ambitious as they are, grow in fertile ground.'

'Things are changing,' says the young woman.

'That is so,' says Mulaghesh. She stares balefully into the fire. 'But not as much as you imagine.'

The young woman sighs and turns to Shara. 'I hope the Governor has not saddled you with too much gloom. I would prefer it if your first social event in Bulikov had a *lighter* mood to it. You are our new Cultural Ambassador, are you not?'

'I am,' says Shara. She bows politely. 'Shara Thivani, Cultural Ambassador, Second Class.'

'I am Ivanya Restroyka, assistant curator to the studio that donated the pieces. It is a genuine pleasure to have you here with us, but I must warn you that not everyone here will greet you so warmly – fusty old attitudes are sometimes so hard to shrug off. Yet I hope that at the end of the night, you will count me a friend.'

'That is extremely kind of you to say,' says Shara. 'Thank you.'

'Come, allow me to introduce you to everyone,' says Ivanya. 'After all, I am sure that the Governor will not wish to sully herself with such social responsibilities.'

Mulaghesh picks up another ale. 'It's your funeral, Ambassador,' she says. 'But watch that one. She has a taste for trouble.'

'I merely have *good* taste,' says Ivanya, smiling beatifically.

It immediately becomes clear, that despite her youth, Miss Ivanya Restroyka is a seasoned socialite: she carves through the groups of the glamorous and the powerful like a shark through a shoal of fish. Within an hour Shara has bowed before or shook the hand of nearly every luminary at the reception.

'I wished to be an artist,' Ivanya confides to Shara. 'But it simply didn't turn out that way. I didn't have the . . . I'm not sure. The *imagination*, I suppose, or the ambition, or both. You have to be a bit outside things to make something new, but I was always very much *inside* things.'

A small hubbub breaks out before one of the hearths. 'What could that be?' says Ivanya, but Shara can already see: Sigrud stands with one foot up on the hearth, reaching into the fire to pull out a small, flaming coal. Even from here she can hear it sizzle as it touches his fingertips, but his face registers no pain as he lifts it to his pipe, sucks twice, exhales a plume of smoke, then tosses it back. Then he skulks away to a shadowed corner where he crosses his arms, leans up against a wall and watches.

'Who is *that* creature?' asks Ivanya.

Shara coughs. 'That is my assistant. Sigrud.'

'You have a *Dreyling* as your assistant?'

'Yes.'

'But aren't they *savages*?'

'We are all products of our circumstances.'

Ivanya laughs. 'Oh, Ambassador . . . You are *so* much more provocative than I could ever have hoped. This will be a grand friendship. Ah! What perfect timing!'

She breaks off from Shara and trots away to a tall, bearded gentleman slowly descending the stairs, picking his way down with a white cane. His right hip bothers him: every other step, his right hand snaps down to steady it, but he maintains a regal posture, dressed in a trim, somewhat conservative white dinner jacket, and sporting an ornate gold sash. 'And *there's* my darling. It took so *long* for you to come down! I thought it was women who took for ever to get dressed, not men.'

'I am going to put in some sort of pulley-lift in this damn house,' he says. 'These stairs will kill me, I'm sure of it.'

She drapes herself around his shoulders. 'You sound like an old man.'

'I feel like an old man.'

'But do you kiss like one?' Ivanya pulls him in, though he resists a little before indulging her. Someone in the crowd gives a soft *Whoop!* 'No,' she concludes. 'Not yet. Will I have to check every day, darling?'

'You will have to make an appointment, if so. I'm terribly busy, you see. Now. Who do we have sponging off me tonight?' he asks merrily.

He looks up at the crowd. The firelight washes over his face.

Shara's heart goes cold: she assumed the man was old, but he is not. In fact, he's hardly aged a day.

His hair is longer, and though it is streaked with grey at the temples it still has that odd reddish hue to it. His beard is bright copper-red, but it is short and closely cropped, rather than the mountainous ball of fluff popular among wealthy Continentals. Shara can still see the strong jaw, the ever-present smirk, and though his eyes have lost a bit of their wild gleam, they are still the same bright, penetrating blue she remembers so well.

The dilettantes and socialites gently descend on him.

'Oh, goodness,' he says. 'Such a crush. I hope you've brought your wallets . . .' He laughs as he greets them. Though he could only know a handful of them, he treats them as his oldest friends.

Shara watches, fascinated, horrified, terrified. *How little he has changed, really*, she thinks.

And she is surprised to find that she hates him for this. It is so terribly, unbearably rude for him to pass through all these years and come out the same person on the other side.

'Have you seen the pieces?' Ivanya asks him. 'You must see them when you can, darling, they're so delightfully *abominable*. I adore them. I can't *wait* to hear what the papers will say.'

'Probably many impolite things,' he says.

'Oh, of course, naturally. Huffing and puffing. As one should hope. Rivegny from the foundry is here – you've wanted him to attend for some time, haven't you? Well, he's *finally* showed up. I thought he'd be a rough sort of fellow, being a fellow captain of industry, but he's quite svelte, I think. You must talk to him. I will get you an envelope for the cheque. Oh, and we have the new Cultural Ambassador here, and do you know she has a North-man as her *assistant*? As in a *secretary*? And he's *here*, darling, he reached into the fire with his *hands* and it was just *absurd*! I can't stop laughing, I mean, the night is going *so* well.'

He looks up again, glances around the room, amused. And, at first, he looks past her. Shara reels from this slight as one would a sound blow.

But then a light goes on in his eyes, and he slowly drags his gaze back to her.

Within a matter of seconds, his face does many things: first she sees confusion, then recognition, then disbelief and anger. But after this medley of expressions, his delicate features settle on an expression she finds quite familiar: a smirk of the most cocksure, arrogant sort.

'New ambassador?' he says.

Shara adjusts her glasses. 'Oh, dear.'

Sigrud stares into the fire, massaging the palm of his gloved hand with one thumb. He recalls a saying from his homeland: *Envy the fire, for it is either going or not. Fires do not feel happy, sad, angry, depressed. They burn, or they do not burn.*

It took Sigrud several years to understand this saying, but it took many more for him to learn to be like the fire: merely alive, and no more.

He watches Shara and the man with the cane circle one another in the crowd. See how they stand, faces almost averted, but never quite completely: always they can watch one another, peering over someone's shoulder or glancing to the side to catch the other's feigned ignorance.

They watch without watching. It is, he thinks, a clumsy dance.

The man with the cane keeps checking his watch: perhaps, Sigrud thinks, to avoid appearing too eager. After he's made a good show of pumping the crowd, he grabs a footman and whispers into his ear. The footman orbits the crowd a handful of times before closing in on Shara, to whom he delivers a small white card. Shara, smiling, tucks it away, and after severing herself from the talkative young girl in the furs, she slinks upstairs.

Sigrud turns back to the fire. Lovers, certainly. Their movements sing of past caresses. He is amused: though small and quiet, Shara Komayd is as much a weapon as he is. But he realises this surprise is silly. All creatures on this Earth have a little love in their lives, however short.

He remembers the whaling ship *Svordyaaling*. The deck slick with blood and fat as the crew peeled away the skin of a dead whale as one peels an apple. The reeking, bleeding thing clutched to the side of the ship, trailed by churning clouds of gulls. On the days after a kill, after the chase, after the foreman hacked at the beast's lungs with a halberd until its blowhole sprayed blood, after they dragged it back to the ship across the ocean . . . On those days down below decks Sigrud would pull a locket from his jacket, and he would hold it in his hands, and open it and peer at it by candlelight . . .

Sigrud looks at his gloved, aching hand. He cannot recall what the locket looks like, nor can he recall the portrait inside. He thinks he remembers at least the feel of the locket in his hand. But perhaps he is imagining things.

'You seem occupied,' says a voice. A middle-aged woman, obviously wealthy and established, sits next to him by the fire. 'Perhaps a drink?' She holds out a goblet of wine.

Sigrud shrugs, takes it, downs it in one gulp. She watches, excited, curious.

'What a remarkable guest you are,' says the woman. 'I doubt if Votrov has ever had someone like you under his roof.'

Sigrud puffs at his pipe and watches the fire.

'So what would you be here for?' she asks.

He takes another long puff of his pipe. He considers it. 'Trouble,' he says.

Someone has made a ribald joke; a cross-section of the crowd bursts into laughter, and some of the more delicate members turn away, offended.

The clink of glassware, the mutter of laughter. Cheers ring out in some distant cavity of this warped house. *How hollow and horrible the wild noise of a party sounds*, thinks Shara, *when filtered through yards of stone*.

The spiral staircase keeps going up. She wonders if she will find him waiting at the top; if he is, she feels it would be wise to tip backwards, and tumble down these steps, rather than try to speak to him.

She gets control of herself, and climbs the stairs to what is ostensibly the library, but it is far too large to be one room. One wall boasts a massive family portrait. Not once in their two-year relationship did Vohannes ever mention his parents – which now strikes her as odd – yet they look much like she imagined: proud, regal, stern. Father Votrov is dressed in an almost militaristic uniform, with lots of medals and ribbons; Mama Votrov wears a plush, pink ballroom gown. *The sort of people who intermittently review their children*, she thinks, *rather than raise them*. But what surprises her more is that standing next to what looks like an eleven-year-old Vohannes is a second boy, slightly older, with darker eyes and paler skin. The two look so alike they could only be brothers, but Vohannes never mentioned him.

The wind rises, the candle flames dance. She licks her fingers, tests the air, and finds the source of the draft in a nearby window. She walks to it.

The lights of Bulikov stretch out below her like a sea of blue-white stars. The moon is weak tonight, but she can see strange, alien forms out among the rooftops: a half-collapsed temple, the ruined skeleton of an estate, the curlicue twist of tottering stairs.

She looks down. Three tin-hatted guards patrol the walls of the house of Votrov, with bolt-shots in their hands. This is interesting: she didn't see any guards when they arrived.

The click of a door handle. She turns and watches as someone fumbles the two side doors open, and the tip of a white cane pokes through.

Now is your last chance to run! says a voice in her mind. She is ashamed that she doesn't wholly dismiss it outright.

He enters, limping. His white furs are honey-golden in the light of the lamps. He half looks at her – he avoids eye contact – and walks to a drinks trolley, pours himself something. Then he begins to hobble over.

'This room,' he says, 'is far too large. Do you not agree?'

'That would depend on what it's being used for.' She is not sure what to do with her hands, her body: how many dignitaries she has met before, how many nobles, yet now such awkwardness comes plummeting down on her? 'I'm sorry to take you away from your party.'

'Oh, that. I've seen it before. Know how it ends.' He grins at her. It is still a blinding smile. 'I am not, as they say, on tenterhooks about the whole thing. Enjoying the view?'

'It's quite . . . splendid.'

'That's one word for it.' He joins her at the window. 'My father would talk endlessly about the view around here. About what *used* to be there, I mean. He'd point and say, "There, at that corner, that was where we had the Talon of Kivrey! And there, across the park, that was Ahanas' Well, and the line of people would stretch down the street!" I was impressed, enamoured, until I figured out the timeline and realised dear Papa had not been alive to see any of this. That was all long before his time. He hadn't really known, he'd just been guessing. And now, I don't really care to know what he meant, or what all those old things were.'

Shara nods stiffly.

Vohannes glances sideways at her. 'Well, go on.'

'Go on? Go on with what?'

'Go on and tell me. I know you're bursting at the seams to.'

'Well . . .' She coughs. 'If you really want to know . . . The Talon of Kivrey was a tall metal monument with a small door in the front; visitors would walk in through the door and find something waiting for them, something that would change their lives. Sometimes it would change their lives for the good – a bundle of medicine to bring home to a sick relative – or sometimes it would change their lives for the worse – a bag of coins and the address of a prostitute, who would later bring them to ruin.'

'Interesting.'

'It was probably a testament to the Divinity Jukov's strange sense of humour: a long, ongoing joke on everyone, in other words.'

'I see. And the well?'

'Oh, just healing waters. The Divinity Ahanas had them all over the Continent.'

He shakes his head, smiling. 'Still an insufferable know-all.'

She gives him a taut, bitter grin. 'And you're still so smugly, blithely ignorant.'

'Is it ignorance if you don't care to know it?'

'Yes. That is the *definition* of ignorance, actually.'

He looks her up and down. 'You know, you don't look *anything* like I expected you to.'

Shara is too affronted for words.

'I thought you'd be all in jackboots and military grey, Shara,' he says. 'Like Mulaghesh down there, but louder.'

'Was I such a terror in those days?'

'You were a bright, blessed little fascist,' says Vo. 'Or at least a savage little patriot, as many children of Saypur are. And I'd have expected you to come in here as the conquering hero, rather than slip in through the back door, like a little mouse.'

'Oh, *shut up*, Vo.'

He laughs. 'How remarkable it is that we so quickly fall into our old patterns after so many years apart! Tell me – should I arrest you for violating the WR? I noticed you mentioned a few forbidden names. '

'I think there's a clause in there,' says Shara, 'specifying that any ground the Ambassador walks on is considered Saypuri soil. Do you know, your asinine little speech was probably the longest I've ever heard you talk about your family?'

'Is it?'

'You never talked about them at all while we were at school.' Shara nods towards the painting on the wall. 'You definitely never told me you've got a brother.'

Vohannes' grin grows fixed. '*Had* a brother,' he says. 'And I probably didn't tell you because he wasn't a very good one. He taught me Tovos Va – so I suppose we should thank him for having brought us together.'

Shara tries to scan his comment for irony, and comes up inconclusive.

'He died before I ever went to school. He didn't die with my parents, not during the Plague Years, but . . . after.'

'I'm sorry.'

'Really? I wasn't, not much. Like I said, he was not a very good brother.'

'Your family did leave you a magnificent home. You never talked about that, either.'

'That's because it didn't exist yet.' He raps the stone floor with his cane. 'I tore the old Votrov manor down the second I came back from school, and had this one built. All my various legal guardians – the old trolls followed me around like ducklings after mama, honestly – all of them were horrified, just *horrified*. But it wasn't even the *real* Votrov manor! Not the centuries-old one everyone talked about, at least. No one knows where the hells that is any more, just like the rest of Bulikov. We all just pretended the house had always been *the* house, and nothing had ever happened. No Blink, no Great War, nothing. I regret including all these stairs, though.' He winces and touches his hip.

'That's how you injured yourself?'

He allows a pained nod.

'I'm sorry,' she says. 'Is it bad?'

'When it's wet out, yes. But be honest with me.' He spreads his arms and turns his head so light catches the side of his face. 'Beyond that, how cruel has time's blade been to me? Am I still the beauty you fell head over heels for at first sight? I am, admit it.'

Shara resists the urge to push him out of the window. 'You are a horrific ass, Vo. *That* hasn't changed.'

'I'll take that as a yes. I won't let you pull your polite little mouse role with me, Shara. The edges on the girl I knew could *never* be sanded down.'

'Perhaps you didn't know me as well as you thought,' says Shara. 'Do you wonder if your parents would approve of the house, as well as your little party?'

He grins broadly at her. 'I expect they'd approve of them just as much as they'd approve of me having a discussion with a Saypuri intelligence officer.'

Someone downstairs crows laughter. There is the tinkle of broken glass, and a sympathetic *Awww!* from the crowd.

Shara thinks, *And so we come to it.*

'I am happy to see you're not surprised,' says Vohannes. 'You didn't seem to be hiding it, anyway. There is no way that Ashara Komayd, top of her class at Fadhuri, niece of the Minister of Foreign Affairs, great-granddaughter of the damnable Kaj, could rise only to the lowly position of Cultural Ambassador.'

She smiles mirthlessly at his flattery.

'And though "Ashara" is a name as common as water,' he says, '"Komayd", well . . . you'd have to get rid of that fast. Hence the "Thivani".'

'I could have married,' says Shara, 'and taken my husband's name.'

'You are not married,' says Vohannes dismissively. He tosses the rest of his drink out of the window. 'I *know* married women. There are signals and signs, none of which you possess. Aren't you worried someone would recognise you?'

'Who?' says Shara. 'No one from Fadhuri is on the Continent besides you and me. All the politicos my family ran with are back in Ghaladesh. There's just Continentals and the military over here, and none of them know my face.'

'And if someone went hunting for Ashara Komayd?'

'Then they'd discover records indicating she retired from the public eye to teach at a small school in Tohmay, in the south of Saypur – a school that I think closed down about four years ago.'

'Clever. So. The only possible reason someone of your level – whatever it is – would come to be in Bulikov now, well, it'd have to be Pangyui, wouldn't it? But I've no idea why you've come to *me*. I avoided the man like the plague. Too many political consequences.'

Shara says, 'The Restorationists.'

Vohannes nods slowly. 'Ah. I see. How very political of you. Who better to tell you about them than one of the people they hate most in the world?' Vohannes considers it. 'Let us discuss this somewhere else,' he says. 'Somewhere with less of an echo.'

Morotka, the Votrov valet, stamps his feet in the cold. It is remarkably stupid that he's out here. The party started, what, one hour ago? Less? Yet as house valet, it's Morotka's duty to hold the door for all guests, call the cars up, and get the guests settled. And so many of these foolish people enjoy dropping in, being seen, making an appearance, whatever you'd like to call it, so they leave quite quickly. Mr Votrov is canny enough to know that these people, regretfully, are usually more important than most, and require unusual gladhanding. But could they not make their stay just long enough to allow Morotka a swig of plum wine, a pinch of snuff and a few seconds with his feet by the fire? No, no, of course not, so he stamps his feet in the cold and wonders if kitchen duty would suit him better. He doesn't mind carrots and potatoes. He could live with that.

There is a clunking to the west, like a can rolling along the street. Curious, he peers out. He sees one guard on the west manor wall – but shouldn't there be two? Mr Votrov prefers that his guests do not see the ugly necessities his rather radical positions require. But usually, once the reception begins, it's security as normal.

Morotka grunts. *Perhaps the fool is wise enough*, he thinks, *to shirk outdoor duty when he can*. Yet then he squints. Is there something on the wall? Something moving, very slowly, towards the remaining guard?

Headlights flare at the end of the drive. A car coughs to life and trundles towards the house.

'Oh, no,' says Morotka. He steps out and waves his arm. 'No, no, no. What are you doing?'

The car continues towards him. As it wheels around the drive, Morotka shouts, 'You come when you're called, all right? I haven't flagged you yet. I don't care what your master says, you come when you're called.'

As the car pulls up before him, Morotka sees movement on the manor wall out of the corner of his eye: a dark figure peeps up, points something at the remaining guard. There is a *click*, and the guard goes stiff, tumbles backwards, his tin hat bouncing off the wall to clatter and clunk to the street below.

There is the glimmer of a bolt-point in the window of the car. A voice says, 'But we *have* been called.'

Then a harsh *click*, and the car seems to fall away.

Sigrud stares into the fire, lost in his memories.

The blood in the water, the halberd in his hands. The monstrous shadow in the sea, thrashing, moaning, spouting gore. How he thought those days hellish, but he'd not known hell yet.

The leather of his gloved hand squeaks as he clenches his fist.

'Are you all right?' asks his companion. The woman examines him. 'Would you need another glass of wine?' She gestures to a footman.

Yet then Sigrud hears it, terribly faintly, but *there*: a very soft 'click', out at the front of the house. And he knows that sound very well.

At last. A distraction.

'Here,' says the woman. She turns back round with another goblet. 'Here you g—'

But she can only stare at the empty seat beside her.

'The enemy of old Bulikov,' says Vohannes, 'is not Saypur, and it is not me, or the New Bulikov movement. It's *time*.' They sit on a bed in one of the guest rooms. It is, like most of this floor, decorated in deep, warm reds and gold gilt. The estate grounds end just outside the window, and the walls gently curve around the house below. 'There's a tremendous age gap in Bulikov, you see: after the Great War and the Blink, it took so long for life to return to normal. So there's a dying portion of the population that still remembers the old ways, and devoutly clings to them, and there's a growing new portion of the population that never knew anything about them, and doesn't care. They just know they're poor, and they don't have to be.'

'The New Bulikov movement,' says Shara.

Vohannes waves a hand at her. 'That's just a name. What we're seeing is much bigger than politics. It's a generational shift, and I am definitely not its creator. I'm just riding the wave.'

'And the Restorationists hate you for it.'

'Like I said, they're fighting history. And everyone loses that fight.'

'Have they threatened you in any way, Vo?'

'Don't be ridiculous.'

'Then why the guards out the front?'

He pulls a face. 'Hmph. I prefer to be discreet about that. But trust you to see. They have never threatened me *directly*, no. But there's lots of political talk that teeters towards the violent side. The biggest offender being Ernst Wiclov, who is, more or less, the biggest player in the Restoration game. Another City Father. Rather dogmatic fellow. Throws a lot of money around. I suppose you could say he's my political opponent. I never engage him – I don't really need to – but he depicts me less as a political opponent, and more like a demon shat straight out of hell.'

'He sounds like a very wise man.'

'Don't try to be cute. You're terribly bad at it.'

'And this Wiclov,' says Shara, 'would he——?'

'Would he have been one of the biggest agitators behind the protests against Pangyui?' Vohannes smiles savagely, a surprisingly ugly expression. 'Oh, yes. I've no doubt he's neck deep in all this, and I'd not weep to see you set your dogs on him. The man is a reeking bag of goat shit with a beard.'

'There are two other City Fathers aligned with the New Bulikov movement,' she says, 'but neither attracts nearly as much hate as you.'

'Ah, well,' says Vohannes, 'I've become a bit of an iconic figure. I have always had a taste for fashion and architecture, you know that . . . And part of it is that it's fun to stir them up. I indulge in a bit of decadence right in the open, and offend their fusty old values of modesty and repression, and they let loose a string of hateful screeds that win me however many new voters.' A dainty puff of his cigarette. 'It's win-win, from my perspective. They also mistrust my background, though. Considering my education, they believe me half Saypuri.' Then a guilty look. 'But I do have a few projects of my own that may cause friction.'

'Such as?'

'Well, Saypur is the largest buyer of weapons in the world, of course. But all those soldiers are stuck using bolt-shots rather than rifles, just mechanised bows and arrows. The issue, as you may know, is one of *salt-petre*: Saypur and her supporting nations have almost none of it, and you can't make gunpowder without it. The Continent, however, has saltpetre aplenty——'

'So you want to make munitions for *Saypur*?' she asks, astonished. What she does not say is, *How have I not heard about this?*

He shrugs. 'My family made bricks. Mining isn't that different.'

'But, Vo, that's . . . Are you an *idiot*?'

'An idiot?'

'Yes! That's far, far more dangerous than any political shenanigans you've got planned! Collaborating with Saypur in basic trade is controversial enough, but making weapons? I'm surprised no one in Bulikov has murdered you yet!'

'Yes, well, it's not been publicly announced yet. The nation of Saypur moves slowly on deals like this, it seems. Nothing's been agreed. Though if you could possibly lend me any support on this, well . . . it could improve my situation, and Saypur's, *and* Bulikov's, quite considerably.'

'So you genuinely wish to become a war profiteer?'

'What I *wish*,' says Vohannes forcefully, 'is to bring industry and prosperity to Bulikov. Saypur's industry is war. It's the largest industry in the world. Bulikov is terribly poor, but this could bring it back, Shara.'

Shara laughs in disbelief. 'My, my, I've dealt with many petty bandit kings and warlords before, but never would I have thought to count Vohannes Votrov among them.'

Vohannes pulls himself up into a regal pose. 'I am doing what I must to help my people.'

'Oh, goodness, Vo,' she sighs. 'Please dispense with your rhetoric. I've heard enough speeches.'

'It's not rhetoric. And it's not a speech, Shara! I have tried to involve Saypur and her trading partners before, but Saypur does not lend us its favour – it wants to keep things the way they are, with Saypur completely in control of everything. It does not want to see wealth in Bulikov any more than it wants us chanting the names of the Divinities. If I must nakedly prostitute myself to bring aid to my city, to my country, I will gladly do so.'

He hasn't changed at all, really, she thinks, torn between amusement and shock. *He's still the noble idealist, in his own perverse way* . . .

'Vo, listen,' says Shara. 'I have worked with people who did the same thing you're doing now. If I have seen one of them, I've seen a hundred. And most of them now feed worms, or fish, or birds, or the very deep roots of trees.'

'So. You worry for my safety.'

'Yes! Of course I do! This is not a game I wish to see you in!'

'*Your* game, you mean,' he says.

'Yes! I'm mostly confused why you aren't happy where you are!'

'And where am I?'

'Well, it seems to me you've got vast wealth, a promising political future and an adoring mistress!'

'Fiancée, actually,' he says, with a touch of indifference.

Something inside Shara splits open. Ice floods into her belly.

'Ah,' she says.

I shouldn't care this much, she thinks. *I am a* professional, *damn it all. What a stupid, stupid thing to feel.*

'Yes. Wasn't wearing her ring today. Got a rock on it like a whisky tumbler.' He holds up a massive imaginary stone. 'She says it's conventional. Gaudy. Which it is, but. We haven't set a date yet, neither of us is the planning type.' He looks down at his hands. 'Sorry. Probably not a fun thing to . . . ah,' he coughs, 'to talk about.'

'I always knew you'd go on to do great things, Vo,' she says. 'But to be honest, I would *never* have pegged you as the marrying type. I mean . . .'

The silence stretches on.

Finally, he nods. 'Yes,' he says delicately. 'But. Certain practices, while acceptable abroad, are not quite so tolerated here. Once a Kolkashtani, always a Kolkashtani.' He sighs and begins to rub his hip. 'I need your help, Shara. Bulikov is a ruin of a city, yes, but it could be great. Saypur holds all the purse strings in the world – and I only need them loosened a fraction. Ask me something, ask me for anything, and I'll do it.'

Never has the reality of my job, she thinks, *seemed so unreal and so preposterous.*

But before she can answer, the screams start echoing up from the floors below.

'What is *that*?' says Vohannes.

But Shara is already at the window. She is just able to make out the form of two bodies resting in the shadows below the manor walls.

'Hm,' says Shara.

They kick the doors in and burst into the room in unison. It's perfect, really, a beautiful, deadly choreography, grey cloth rippling as they descend on the decadent partygoers. Cheyschek's mask is slipping a little – the left corner of his eye is now blind – but besides this he feels glorious, resplendent, chosen.

See these traitors and sinners quail and shriek. See them run. Look upon me, and fear me.

One of his compatriots kicks over the bar. Bottles shatter, fumes of alcohol flood the hall. Cheyschek and his brothers in arms scream at the people to get down, down, get down on the ground. Cheyschek points the bolt-shot at the one man who looks like he has some spine and howls in the man's face and throws him to the floor.

To be a tool of the Divine, thinks Cheyschek, *is thrilling and righteous.*

A woman shrieks again. Cheyschek screams at her to shut up.

It is over fast, and easy. Which is expected, from this soft, cultured sort. The Polis Governor, as expected, is here, though they have strict orders not to touch her. *But why, why?* he thinks. *Why forgive the one person who's approved so many unjust punishments?*

When the hostages are cowed, Cheyschek's leader (none of them know each other's name – they *need* no names, for they are all *one*) paces among the partygoers, grabbing them by the hair to pull up their heads and view their faces.

After some seconds, he says, 'Not here.'

'Are you sure?' Cheyschek asks.

'I *know* who I am looking for.' He looks among the crowd of hostages, picks one elderly woman, and lowers his bolt-shot until the bolt point hovers just in front of her left eye. 'Where?'

She begins to weep.

'*Where?*'

'I don't know what you mean!'

'Someone special is missing from here, yes?' he asks sardonically. 'And where could that person be?'

The old woman, ashamed, points at the stairs.

'You wouldn't be lying to me?' he says.

'No!' she cries. 'Votrov and the woman, they went upstairs!'

'The woman?' He pauses. 'So he's not alone? You're sure?'

'Yes. And . . .' She looks around.

'What? What is it?'

'The one in the red coat . . . I don't see him any more.'

'Who?' When she does not answer, he grabs a fistful of her hair and shakes her head. 'Who do you *mean*?' he bellows.

She begins sobbing now, pushed beyond answering.

Their leader lets her go. He points at three of them, says, 'Stay here. Watch them. Kill anyone who moves.' Then he points to Cheyschek and the other four. 'The rest of you, upstairs with me.'

They mount the stairs silently, rushing up like wolves through mountain forests. Cheyschek is trembling with joy, excitement, rage. Such a righteous thing, to bring pain shrieking down on them out of the cold night, traitors and sinners and the filthy ignorant. He had expected to find them, perhaps, in the throes of some pornographic rite, their blood polluted by foreign alcohol, the air stinking with incense as they shamed themselves willingly. Cheyschek has heard, for example, of places near Qivos where – with the full allowance of Saypur, of course – women walk the streets in dresses cut so short that you can see their . . . their . . .

He colours just to think of it.

To imagine such a thing is sinful. It must be excised from the mind and the spirit to remain clean.

Their leader raises a gloved hand when they hit the second floor. They stop. He swings his masked face around, peering through the tiny black eyeholes. Then he signals to them, pointing, and Cheyschek and two others fan out to search the floor while their leader and the others go upstairs.

Cheyschek sweeps the hallways, checks the rooms, but finds nothing. For such a large house, Votrov keeps it terribly empty. *Another damning indication of the man's excesses*, thinks Cheyschek. *He even misuses his country's stone!*

He comes to a corner, knocks twice on the wall. He listens and hears a second *knock-knock*, then a third, from farther in the house. He nods, satisfied that his compatriots are close, and keeps patrolling.

He looks out of the windows. Nothing. Looks in the rooms. Nothing but empty beds. *Perhaps Votrov keeps his lovers here, one in each room*, Cheyschek thinks, feeling scandalised and unclean.

Focus. Check in again. He knocks once more. He hears one *knock-knock* from somewhere else in the house, and then . . .

Nothing.

He pauses. Listens. Knocks again. Once more, there's a second echoing knock, but no third.

Perhaps he is too far away to hear me. But Cheyschek knows his instructions, and he begins to backtrack, following the halls back to the stairs.

Once he reaches the stairs, he knocks twice on the walls again, and listens.

This time, nothing – no second *or* third knock.

He fights the growing panic in his chest, and knocks again.

Nothing. He stares around, wondering what could be going on, and it is then that he sees.

There is someone sitting in the darkened second-floor foyer, sprawled back in a white overstuffed chair.

Cheyschek raises his bolt-shot. The person does not move. They do not seem to have noticed him. Cheyschek retreats to the wall, paces along the edge of the shadows with the sight of the bolt-shot on the person at all times.

Yet when he nears, he sees they are dressed in grey cloth, and there is a grey mask in their lap.

Cheyschek lowers the bolt-shot.

It is one of his comrades. Yet the man's mask is removed, and they were ordered to *never* remove their masks.

Cheyschek takes two more steps forward, and stops. There is a stripe of red and purple flesh running across the man's exposed neck, and he stares up at the ceiling with what can only be the eyes of the dead.

Cheyschek feels sick. He looks around for help, wishing to knock, to call for someone, but there is someone or some*thing* in the halls with them, and he does not want to give away his location.

This can't be happening. They were all supposed to be socialites, artists.

Then he freezes. He listens carefully.

Is there a gagging sound coming from the northern hallway?

He readies his bolt-shot. His pulse pounds in his ears. He stalks forward, rounds the corner, and sees . . .

One of his compatriots is standing in a doorway along the side of the hall, almost out of sight. His compatriot trembles slightly, jerking his shoulders with his hands at his sides, and there is something on his mask, something large and white-pink and rippled that extends outwards, into the doorway, where Cheyschek cannot see.

As Cheyschek nears, he sees that the something on his compatriot's face is actually some*things*: a pair of huge hands grasps the sides of the man's head, yet the thumbs have been shoved deep into the man's eye sockets, all the way up to the second knuckle.

His compatriot gags, gurgles. Blood spurts around the thumbs, painting the wrists, the walls, the floor.

Cheyschek sees now.

There is a giant man standing in the shadows of the doorway, and he is murdering Cheyschek's compatriot with his bare hands.

The giant looks up, his one eye burning with a pale blue fire.

Cheyschek screams, and blindly fires the bolt-shot. The giant man recoils, drops Cheyschek's compatriot and falls backwards. Then the giant lies in the hallway, completely still.

Cheyschek, weeping freely, runs to his compatriot and rips his mask off. When he sees what is below, his screams turn to howls.

He holds his dead compatriot in his arms. *See what befalls the honoured sons of my country*, he wishes to say. *See what happens to the righteous in such sullied times.* But he does not have the control for the words.

'At least I killed him,' he says to his dead friend, sobbing. 'Please let that be enough. Please. At least I killed the man who did this to yo—'

There is an irritated grunt. Cheyschek, startled, stops and looks around.

With a curious determination, the big man slowly sits up and looks down at his hands in his lap.

He opens his left hand. Inside it, glimmering in the light of the gas lamps, is Cheyschek's bolt — which has apparently been snatched out of mid-air before it could ever find its mark.

The big man looks at the bolt with bemusement, as one would the strange toy of a child. Then he looks up at Cheyschek, and his one eye is filled with a cold, grey-blue calm, like the heart of an iceberg.

Cheyschek fumbles to reload the bolt-shot. There is a flurry of movement. Cheyschek feels fingers around his throat, blood battering the backs of his eyes, the floor lifting away, and the last thing he sees is a glass window flying at him, breaking around him, before he is embraced by the cold night and, almost directly afterwards, the street below.

Shara is ready when the two men burst into the room: she is sitting perfectly still on the bed, hands raised. Vohannes is not so composed: he does not follow the advice she has just given him, but leaps to his feet, cane thrust forward like a rapier, damning them for this and that.

'Hands in the air!' shouts one of the men.

'Clearly I have done that,' says Shara.

'Get down on the ground!' bellows the other. They are dressed, she notes, in grey robes that have been tied tight around the joints and neck – it has the look of ceremonial wear – with strange, flat grey masks upon their faces.

'We will all sit down,' says Shara.

Vohannes isn't nearly so placid. 'I will fuck the mouths of all your ancestors before I listen to one word you vandals have to say!'

'Vo,' says Shara calmly.

'Get down! Down!' the second attacker shouts. 'Do it! Now!'

'Grab him!' says the first.

'Listen,' says Shara.

'Get fucked!' shouts Vohannes. He stabs at one of the men with his cane. The man grunts. 'Stop that!'

'Get *down*, damn you!' shouts the other attacker.

But Vohannes is already moving for another strike. One of the masked men grabs his cane: there is a brief struggle, Vohannes lets go of his cane, and both of them stumble back.

The attacker's bolt-shot *clicks*, and Shara ducks slightly to the left as the bolt soars out, parting the air just where her neck was, before burying itself deep in the headboard of the bed.

The three men, startled, stare at her and the quivering bolt behind her.

Shara clears her throat. 'Listen,' she says to the two attackers. 'Listen to me now. You have made a terrible mistake.'

'Shut up and get down on the ground!' shouts one of them.

'You need to lay down your weapons,' says Shara, voice as smooth as fresh milk. 'And surrender quietly.'

'Filthy shally,' growls one of them. 'Shut up, and get *down*.'

'Why, you—' Vohannes struggles to stand.

'Stop, Vo,' she says.

'*Why*?'

'We aren't in danger.'

'Shut *up*!' shouts one of the attackers.

'They almost shot you in the face!' says Vohannes.

'Well, we are in *some* danger,' she admits. 'But we just . . . we just need to wait.'

The two attackers, she notes, are growing increasingly uncertain, so when Vohannes says, 'For what?' they look a little relieved that he asked.

'For Sigrud.'

'What? What are you talking about?'

'We just have to wait,' says Shara, 'for him to do what he does best.' She says to the attackers, 'I will help my friend up now. I am unarmed. Please do not hurt me.' She reaches down and helps Vohannes up to sit on the bed.

'Who is . . . Sigrud?' asks Vohannes.

There is a horrific scream from nearby, and a burst of breaking glass. Then silence.

'That is Sigrud,' says Shara.

The two masked men look at each other. Though she cannot see their faces, she can tell they are disturbed.

'You need to put down your weapons,' says Shara. 'And wait here with us. If you do, you might survive. Be reasonable about this.'

One of the masked men, apparently the leader, says, 'It's a mind game. A filthy shally mind game. Don't listen to her. It's the butler making noises, or something. Go check it out. And if you see anyone, kill them, and do so with a clean conscience.' The second masked man, still shaken, nods and begins to walk out of the door. The leader grabs his shoulder, says, 'Only a mind game. We will be rewarded,' before patting him on the back and sending him on his way.

'You just sent him to his death,' says Shara.

'Shut up,' snaps the leader. He's breathing hard now.

'The rest of your men are dead, or dying. You need to surrender.'

'That's what you all say, isn't it? Surrender, surrender, always surrender. We're *done* surrendering. We can't *give* you any more.'

'I ask nothing of you,' says Shara.

'If you ask me to lay down my weapon, to lay down my freedom, then you ask everything of me.'

'This is not war. This is a time of peace.'

'Your peace. Peace for things like *him*,' he says with disgust, gesturing to Vohannes.

'Hey . . .' says Vohannes.

'You embrace sinners, cowards, blasphemers,' says the leader. 'People who have turned their backs on their history, on everything that we are. This is how you wage your war on us.'

'We,' says Shara forcefully. 'Are not. At war.'

The leader leans in and whispers, 'The *minute* a shally steps within the Divine City, I am at war with them.'

Shara is silent. The leader stands up, listens. There is nothing to hear.

'Your friend is dead,' says Shara.

'Shut up,' says the leader. He reaches over his shoulder and pulls out a short, thin sword. 'Stand up. I'll get you out of here myself.'

Shara, supporting Vohannes's limping weight, walks out of the guest room and down the hall while the leader stalks behind them.

After a few seconds, she stops.

'Keep going,' barks the leader.

'Can you not see ahead of you?' asks Shara.

He steps around them, and sees there is something lying in the hallway.

'No,' he whispers, and walks to it.

It is a crumpled, masked body lying in a copious pool of blood. Though it is hard to see through the soaking grey cloth, his neck appears to be slashed wide open. The leader kneels and gently reaches up behind the mask to touch the man's brow. He whispers something. After a moment, he stands back up, and the hand holding the sword is trembling.

'Keep moving,' he says hoarsely, and Shara can tell he is weeping.

They walk on. At first, the house seems terribly silent. But before they reach the stairs they hear the sounds of a struggle – wood snapping, the tinkle of breaking china and a rough shout – before seeing an open door to a large room on their left, with many shadows dancing on the threshold.

'The ballroom,' mutters Vohannes.

The leader walks forward quickly, sword held out in front, then he braces himself and wheels into the room.

Shara, dragging Vohannes, follows and looks in, though she already knows what she will see.

The ballroom is quite spacious and ornate, or at least it was. One masked attacker is kneeling on the floor, clutching his wrist and shrieking: his hand has been completely amputated, and blood spurts out to fan across the red floral floor. Another masked attacker sits in the corner, quite dead, with the handle of a short, black-bladed knife buried in his neck. In the centre of the room the dining table has been kicked over, and behind this barricade stands Sigrud, covered in sweat and blood, with one frantic and miserable masked attacker in a headlock under his left arm. With his right hand Sigrud holds the remains of the ballroom chandelier – which has apparently been ripped out of the ceiling – and he is using it to fend off another attacker, who attempts to engage him with a sword. But though it is hard to tell through all the glimmering crystals flying through the air, the attacker appears to be steadily losing, stumbling back with every blow, in between which Sigrud, using the fist holding the chandelier, manages to pummel the face of the unhappy man in his headlock.

The leader of the attackers stands agog at this sight for a moment, before holding his sword high, screaming at the top of his lungs, and rushing in, bounding over the table.

Sigrud gives him an irritated glance – *What now?* – and lifts up the head-locked man just in time for the man's back to receive the point of the leader's sword.

Both masked men gag in shock. Sigrud swings the chandelier around so that it hooks the blade of the free attacker, shoves the man to the floor, and releases the chandelier.

The leader lets go of the hilt of his sword, pulls out a short knife and, with an anguished scream, dives at Sigrud.

Sigrud releases the headlock on the dead (or dying) man, grabs the leader's wrist before the knife can strike home, headbutts the leader soundly, and then – to the vocal horror of Vohannes – opens his mouth wide, lunges forward and tears out most of the man's throat with his teeth.

The gush of blood is positively tidal. Shara feels a little disgusted at herself for thinking only, *This will definitely make the papers*.

Sigrud, now totally anointed with crimson, drops the leader, grabs the sword sticking out of the dead man's back and, without a thought, hurls it like a javelin at the shrieking attacker with the severed wrist. The point of the blade catches the man just under the joint of his jawbone. He collapses immediately. The sword wobbles, and though it is buried deep enough in the man's skull that it does not fall out, the wobbling is accompanied by an unpleasant cracking noise.

Sigrud turns to the groaning man trapped under the remains of the chandelier.

'No,' says Shara.

He turns to look at her. His one eye is alight with a cold rage.

'We need one alive.'

'They shot me,' he says, and holds up a bleeding palm. 'With an arrow.'

'We need *one* alive, Sigrud.'

'They *shot* me,' he says again, incensed, 'with an *arrow*.'

'There must be more downstairs,' says Shara. 'The hostages, Sigrud. Think. Take care of them – carefully.'

Sigrud makes a face like a child who has just been given onerous chores. He walks to the man with the knife in his neck, pulls it out, and stalks out of the room.

Vohannes stares around his ruined ballroom. '*This*?' he says. '*This* is what your man does best?'

Shara approaches the masked man struggling to lift the chandelier and begins to disarm him. 'We all have our talents.'

Sigrud spots no masked attackers guarding the hostages when he runs down the stairs. 'Oh, thank goodness you came, we—' says one woman, before fully seeing him. Then she begins shrieking.

Mulaghesh is not half so phased. She clears her throat, from beside a pillar in the foyer. The Polis Governor is hunched over a robed figure, and appears to be calmly garrotting him with a festively coloured ribbon. Mulaghesh looks at Sigrud, her left eye blooming dark from what must have been a terrific blow, and says, 'Two more. Out the door.'

When Sigrud makes it outside, the car is already trundling away but is not gaining much speed yet. His boots thud as he sprints across the cobblestones. He hears one of the men inside cry, 'Go! Go! Hurry!'

The answer comes, 'I am! I'm trying!'

The car shifts into a higher gear, but just before it can pull away, Sigrud leaps forward and grabs on to the back door.

'Shit!' shrieks one of the men. 'Oh, gods!'

Sigrud's hands are so slick with blood that he almost loses his hold. He wedges a foot on the running board, then reaches up with his right hand and stabs his black knife into the roof of the car.

'Shoot him, damn you!' cries a voice.

A bolt-shot appears in the window. Sigrud leans to the side. The bolt slices through the glass of the window, missing him by inches, but does not shatter the window. Sigrud punches through the window with his left hand, grabs the man who fired at him by the collar, and repeatedly slams him against the door and roof of the car.

The driver, now totally panicked, begins swerving through the street. Sigrud can see coffee house patrons, restaurant attendees and horse and cart drivers stare in amazement as they fly by. A small child points and laughs, delighted. Sigrud focuses on battering the man into submission.

Sigrud can feel it when the man goes unconscious, and he begins to haul the man out of the broken window with one arm, intending to hurl him from the car. But then the car makes a hard turn.

He looks up. The corner of a building flies at them. Sigrud immediately sees that the driver intends to scrape the car along the building's side, scraping off Sigrud as well.

Sigrud considers climbing on to the roof of the car, judges that he doesn't have enough time, pulls his knife free, and dives away.

It is a painful landing, but not as painful as what happens to the unconscious man dangling out of the broken window of the car: there is a wet *smack*, and something goes tumbling across the stony streets. Sigrud can hear the driver begin to scream in horror, and what's left of the passenger slips out of the window to roll into the gutter.

The car makes a wide turn and roars down an alley. Sigrud, now quite irritated, gets to his feet and sprints after it.

He turns down the alley. The car has come to a stop several yards ahead. He runs to the car, and flings open the driver's side door to see . . .

Nothing. The car is empty.

He looks around. The alley ends in the blank side of a building, yet before that there is nothing: no windows, no ladders, no sluice gates or manhole covers or doors.

Sigrud grunts, sticks his knife back in its sheath and slowly walks along the alley, feeling the walls. None of them give. It's like the driver has simply disappeared.

He sighs and scratches his cheek. 'Not again.'

I am the stone beneath the tree.
I am the mountain under the sun.
I am the river below the earth.
I dwell in the caves in the hills.
I dwell in the caves in your heart.
I have seen what lies there. I know what lives in your minds.
I know right. I know justice.
I am Kolkan, and you will listen.

The Kolkashavska, *Book Two*

A memory engraved

The officers' mess hall of the Bulikov Police Department is a unique vantage point for the unfolding panic. There are windows that allow the mess hall attendees to see into the front offices, where a full-scale riot is building — composed of politicians, reporters, outraged citizens and family members of the hostages — and one can also see back into the halls of the interview rooms, where the Bulikov policemen are still confused as to who exactly is a suspect, who should be sent to the hospital, and what on Earth to do with Sigrud.

'This is a new experience for me,' says Shara.

'Really?' says Mulaghesh. 'I would have thought you'd been arrested at least a couple of times.'

'No, no. *I* never get arrested. One of the perks of being a handler.'

'It must be nice. You seem very calm, for someone who's just been through an assassination attempt. How do you feel?'

Shara shrugs. The truth is she feels ridiculous, sitting here sipping tea with Mulaghesh while chaos surges around them. Their status immediately set them apart from the other rescued hostages, mostly due to Mulaghesh, whom all the police officers seem acquainted with. Mulaghesh holds a pack of ice to her eye and occasionally mutters curses about being 'too shitting slow' or, alternately, 'too shitting old'. She's already sent her orders to the local outpost, and a small squad of Saypuri veterans should be here shortly to watch over the both of them. Though Shara has not said so, she privately dreads this: one's own security often makes it hard to penetrate that of one's opponents. And Sigrud often provides enough security, anyway. Sigrud, however, is currently cooling off in a holding cell. The captured attacker is totally untouched, stuck in a tiny cell normally reserved for the most violent offenders.

An officer refreshes their teapot, which Shara promptly drains. 'That's your fourth pot,' notes Mulaghesh.

'So?'

'So, do you normally drink tea like that?'

'Only when I'm at work.'

'You seem like the type who is always at work.'

Shara shrugs mid-sip.

'If you continue at that pace, Ambassador, I would advise you to familiarise yourself with a urologist.'

'How's your eye?'

'Humiliating. But I've had worse.'

'It can't be too humiliating. He did wind up the loser of your scrap, beyond a doubt.'

'There was once a day,' sighs Mulaghesh, 'when I could dispatch such little cretins without bothering to breathe. No more, I suppose. What I would give' – she winces, prodding her eye – 'for the vigour of youth. Though I doubt I could *ever* match what your man did in that house, even in my prime. Where did you find him?'

'Somewhere quite bad,' says Shara simply.

Then she slowly retreats back inside herself. The susurrus of faraway shouting fades, and internally she begins to compose a list.

In Shara's estimation, lists form one half of the heart of intelligence, the second half being patience. Most espionage work, after all, is a matter of collecting data and categorising it: who belongs to which group, and why; where are they now, and how are we so sure, and do we have someone else in the region; and now that we have catalogued those groups, what level of threat should they be categorised under; and so on, and so on, and so on.

So whenever Shara is really puzzled by something, she takes her thoughts and sorts them, threshing them out like chaff from wheat, tunnelling down and through her mind as she tries to wring truth from everything she knows, a frequently endless list of annotations, qualifications, categorisations and exceptions:

1. Fact: I have been attacked less than one week after Efrem Pangyui.
   - You don't know for sure it was you they were attacking.
     - Then who?
     - Vo wants to make munitions for Saypur. So that's ample reason to kill him there.
     - Then why not simply kill Vo when they had the chance? They could have shot him the moment they walked into the room.
     - His deal is not official, and also not publicly known yet.
     - Doesn't mean anything – there could always be leaks.
   - Efrem was beaten to death with a blunt instrument in his office. These men were far more professional.
     - You think? Whoever attacked Efrem has not been captured, a mark of professionalism if ever there was one.
     - Professionalism and the incompetence of the local authorities are very different things.
   - Efrem may have been attacked in connection with the Warehouse.
     - Neither Vo nor I have any such connection.
     - I know it exists.
     - Unlikely that that's enough to get me killed, though.
   - All three of us are heretical to common Continental sensibilities by nature.
     - Not an efficient qualifier. What *isn't* heretical to common Continental sensibilities?

2. Fact: Efrem Pangyui was conducting research at the Unmentionable Warehouse.
   - Does Vinya know? How could she not?
     - Efrem working for the Continent? A traitor?
     - Don't be an idiot.
   - Why not tell me? What's buried in there that I shouldn't know about?
     - Probably a lot, of course.
   - Would Continentals have killed him to get access to the Warehouse?
     - Mulaghesh has asserted no one has entered the Warehouse besides Efrem.

- If Vinya knows about Efrem's operation, why is she letting me stay?
  - Maybe she thinks you're just too dense to figure this all out.
- Is she protecting me? From what?
  - Don't be ridiculous, you just got attacked, of course she's not protecting you.
- Does she want to get me killed?
  - She's your aunt.
  - She's Minister first, aunt second.
- Okay, then why would the *Minister* want me dead?
  - If Vinya wanted me dead, I'd be dead, end of story.
- Did Vinya want to get Efrem killed?
  - Seems quite likely Efrem was a Ministry operative. Why would you kill your own operative?

3. Fact: I have not slept in twenty-three hours.
   - I need more damn tea.

Shara sighs. 'No sign of your Captain Nesrhev yet?'

'No,' says Mulaghesh. 'Still not in. But it is four in the morning, and he doesn't live nearby.'

'You know where he lives? How would you know that?'

'Don't pretend to be such an innocent daisy, Ambassador,' says Mulaghesh. 'It doesn't suit you.'

Secretly, Shara smiles: *Vigour of youth, indeed.*

'Anyway. Even though Nesrhev and I have . . . *some* history together, I'm not sure it's enough to make him amenable to the idea of a foreign ambassador taking over an investigation as huge as this.'

'I'm not taking over,' says Shara. 'They'll have their investigation, and I'll have mine. I just want to talk to the captured man first.'

How much simpler this would be in Qivos, she thinks. *We could have just snatched him off the street and claimed he'd never been there in the first place.* She briefly reflects on how civilised countries increasingly pose an inconvenience to her, and for a moment she envies Vohannes for maintaining his idealism – however ineffective it may be.

An idea strikes Shara, and she grabs an old newspaper from another table. She flips through the pages until she finds an article with the headline: CITY FATHER WICLOV OPPOSES IMMIGRANT QUARTERS. Below this is a picture of a man with a round face, pinched in a stern expression, and a mountain of a beard. To Shara, he looks like the sort of man who must constantly debate whether he should yell or merely talk very loudly.

'Why are you reading about Wiclov?' asks Mulaghesh.

'You know him?'

'Everyone knows him. Man's a shit.'

'It was suggested to me,' says Shara, 'that he might have some connection to Pangyui's murder.'

'Did Votrov tell you that?'

Shara nods.

'I would watch yourself, Ambassador,' says Mulaghesh. 'Votrov might be giving you real targets, or he might just be giving you his personal shit list.'

Shara continues staring at the picture, but Mulaghesh has voiced one of her deepest concerns. *I'm flying blind,* she thinks. *Usually I have six months or six weeks to prepare an operation, not six hours.*

She drinks more tea, and chooses not to admit to Mulaghesh that she only ingests caffeine at this rate when her work is going very, very badly.

Captain Nesrhev – who is quite handsome, and at least ten years Mulaghesh's junior – finally arrives at four thirty in the morning. At first he is not amenable to much of anything, as is common among people awoken at such an hour; but Shara is skilled at the shell game of badges and paperwork, and after using the term 'international incident' a few times, he reluctantly consents to 'one hour, starting now'.

'That will do,' says Shara, who fully intends to ignore the time limit. 'What's happened to Votrov?'

'After he gave his statement, his little girlfriend bundled him up and took him home right away,' says Nesrhev. 'That man, you could lead him around by the dick, if you got a good grasp on it.'

Shara does not bother to pretend to laugh.

★

The captured man, as it turns out, is hardly more than a boy: Shara gauges him as around nineteen when she walks in. He sits up behind the big wooden table in the cell, glowering at her and rubbing his wrist, and says, 'Oh, it's you. What do *you* want?'

'Mostly to give you medical attention.' She holds the door open for the doctor, who is quite fatigued by now.

The doctor grows appalled as he examines the captured boy. 'Did this child fall through a pane of glass?'

'He was struck repeatedly with a chandelier.'

The doctor grumbles and shakes his head — *These people find such stupid ways to harm themselves*. 'Most of this is superficial, it looks like. The wrist is sprained pretty badly.'

'And what would you prescribe?'

'The same thing I'd prescribe for his myriad cuts and bruises,' says the doctor. 'Aspirin, bandages, rest.'

'I can give him two of those,' says Shara. She gestures to the doctor to proceed.

When he is finished, the doctor bows and excuses himself. Shara sits across from the boy and puts her satchel down beside her. It is quite cold in the room: the walls here are made of thick stone, and whoever designed the building opted not to place any heating in here.

'How are you feeling?' says Shara.

The boy does not answer, content to sulk.

'I suppose I could simply be direct,' says Shara, 'and ask you why you attacked me.'

His eyes flick up, hold her gaze for a moment, then flick away.

'*Was* that what you were sent there to do? Your colleagues did have ample opportunity.'

He blinks.

'What's your name?'

'We don't have names,' says the boy.

'You don't?'

'No.'

'Why not?'

He considers answering, but is reluctant.

'Why not?'

'Because we are the silenced,' says the boy.

'What does that mean?'

'We do not have a past. We do not have a history. We do not have a country.' His words have the beat of highly rehearsed lines. 'These things are denied to us. But we do not need them. We do not need these things, to know who we are.'

'And what are you?'

'We are the past come to life. We are what cannot be forgotten or ignored. A memory engraved.'

'You are Restorationists, then,' says Shara.

The boy is silent.

'Are you?'

He looks away.

'Your weapons, your dress, your car,' says Shara. 'All very expensive. Money like that getting moved around, people notice. We are looking now. Who will we find? Wiclov? Ernst Wiclov?'

No reaction.

'He's a well-funded supporter of the Restoration, isn't he? His political posters tend to feature a lot of weapon-oriented imagery, I understand. Will we find him at the back end of this, child?'

The boy stares into the table.

'You do not seem to me,' says Shara, 'a hardened, violent criminal. Then why act like one? Don't you have a home to go to? This is all just unpleasant politics. I can make it stop. I can get you out.'

'I will not talk,' says the boy. 'I cannot talk. I am silenced, by you and your people.'

'I'm afraid you are quite wrong there.'

'I am *not* wrong, woman,' says the boy. He glares at her, and as he looks away his eyes trail over her exposed neck and collarbone.

Ah. Old-fashioned, is he? 'I do hope I'm not breaking any rules,' says Shara. 'Will you receive some kind of punishment for being alone in a room with an unwed woman?'

'You are not a woman,' says the boy. 'You have to be human first. Shallies don't count.'

Shara smiles pleasantly. 'If that's true, then why are you so nervous?'

The boy does not answer.

In her own estimation, Shara does not consider herself excessively attractive, but she is always willing to try anything. 'I find it quite hot in here,' she says. 'Don't you? My hands sweat when I get hot.' She pulls off her gloves, finger by finger, delicately folds them and places them on the table. 'Do your hands sweat?' She reaches out to his injured hand.

He pulls away as if she's made of fire. 'Do not *touch* me, woman! And do not try to ply me with your . . . your secret femininity!'

It takes a lot of effort for Shara not to laugh. She has not heard that term spoken aloud outside her history classes, and she's *never* heard it spoken with such sincerity. 'For someone who refuses to talk, you're talking quite a bit now. But, I admit, you're still talking less than your friend.' She pulls a file out of her satchel and consults it.

'Who?' says the boy suspiciously.

'The other one we captured,' says Shara. 'He wouldn't give us his name, either. Even though he was close to death. But he talked about many other things.' Of course, none of this is true – Sigrud very much killed all of the other attackers, except for the one who vanished – but she smiles at the boy, radiating cheer, and asks, 'How does the disappearing trick work?'

The boy flinches.

'I know that's how you get across the city,' says Shara. 'Cars. People. They find some street or alley, head down it, and then *poof*. They're gone. It's quite miraculous.'

There is a gleam of sweat next to the boy's ears.

'He was rambling,' says Shara. 'Weak from blood loss, you see. I wasn't quite sure what was true and what wasn't, but I'm tempted to think almost all of it is. Which would be quite remarkable, really.'

'That . . . that can't be true,' says the boy. 'None of us would ever talk. Even when dying. Throw us in Slondheim, and we still wouldn't talk.'

'I could make that happen, actually,' says Shara. 'I've been to that prison. It's worse than you can imagine.'

'We would *never* talk.'

'Yes, but if you don't possess full control of your faculties, it's perfectly understandable. What else will he tell us? If you tell us now, and tell it to us honestly, we'll be lenient on you. We will make sure you get home. We can put all of this behind us. But if you don't . . .'

'No,' says the boy. '*No*. We could never . . . we *will* be rewarded.'

'With what?'

The boy takes a breath, disturbed, and begins to chant.

'What's that?' says Shara. She leans in to listen.

The boy is chanting, 'On the mountain, by the stone, we will be rewarded, holiest of holies. On the mountain, by the stone, we will be rewarded, holiest of holies.'

'Rewarded with jail, death, ' says Shara. 'So many of you have died already. I saw it. I know you did, too. Are they rewarded? Did they get what they wished?'

'On the mountain, by the stone, we will be rewarded, holiest of holies,' says the boy, chanting more loudly. 'On the mountain, by the stone, we will be rewarded, holiest of holies.'

'Are their families rewarded? Their friends? Or do they not even have these?'

But the boy simply keeps chanting, over and over again. Shara sighs, thinks and excuses herself from the room.

'I have need of you, soldier,' says Shara.

Sigrud opens his eye a crack. He is slumped in the corner of his cell. His hand is wrapped in bandages and he has been scrubbed somewhat clean of blood. Shara can tell he is awake, though: his pipe is still smoking.

'They will be releasing you in just a short while,' she says. 'I've managed to get all that arranged despite the . . . casualties. Hostages corroborate that you acted like a hero.'

Sigrud shrugs, indifferent, contemptuous.

'Right. Now. I asked you to send feelers out and look at hiring a few contractors. Did you have any luck?'

He nods.

'Good. We'll need some thuggish assistance, if you please. When you're released, I want you to snatch up that maid from the University. The one who worked alongside Pangyui, the one who was tailing us the other day.

We should have done it immediately, but we were occupied. Grab her, and get her to the embassy. I want to question her myself. I want your contractors to stay back and watch her apartment, and see if anyone comes or goes. I will need this done by' – she consults her watch – 'six o'clock this morning. And you must be discreet. Assume both you and she are being watched. Understand?'

Sigrud sighs. Then he pulls a face, as if mulling over his options and realising he really had nothing better to do today. 'Six a.m.'

'Good.'

'The survivor,' he asks. 'Is he talking?'

'No. And I can tell he's not the talking type.'

'Then what?'

Shara adjusts her glasses. 'I've stalled for more time, but not nearly enough to crack him via the normal means.'

'Then what?'

'Well.' She stares off into the corner of his cell in thought. 'I think I'm going to have to dose him.'

Sigrud grows much more awake. He looks at her, disbelieving. Then he smiles. 'Well, then. At least you will have entertainment.'

Shara stands at the cell door, watching the captured boy through the viewing slot. She checks her watch – forty minutes. The boy shakes his head as if shaking off a chill, then takes his cup of water and sips it. *Seven sips so far*, thinks Shara. *If only he were utterly parched.*

The boy slowly droops forward more and more, as if deflating. She checks her watch again: it's not going unusually slowly, but she wouldn't mind if it were faster.

'This couldn't possibly be all that riveting,' says Mulaghesh, joining her.

'It isn't,' says Shara.

'Mm. I'd heard our survivor wasn't talking.'

'No. He's a fanatic – unfortunate, but expected. I don't think he's the sort who's afraid of death. He's more worried about what happens after.'

The boy in the cell raises his head to stare into the wall. His face is awed, horrified, fascinated. He starts to tremble a little.

'What's wrong with him?' says Mulaghesh. 'Is he mad?'

'No, no. Well, maybe, considering what he did. But that's not what *this* is.'

'Then what is it?'

'It's an unorthodox method I picked up in Qivos. It's useful when you're crunched for time, though I'd prefer it if we had even more for this – four, five hours at least. But it's cheap. And it's easy. You just need a dark room, some sound effects . . . and a philosopher's stone.'

'A *what*?'

'Don't pretend to be such an innocent lily, Governor,' says Shara. 'It doesn't suit you.'

'You *drugged* him?'

'Yes. It's a powerful hallucinogenic, and it's actually common here, though it's not used for recreational purposes, really. Which is understandable, as it has some history on the Continent.'

Mulaghesh is still too aghast for words.

'There are dozens of stories of people using it to communicate more closely with the Divine,' Shara continues absently. 'Breaking down barriers, merging with the infinite, that kind of thing. It even amplified the performance of certain miracles: acolytes of the Divine used to ingest it before performing astounding, miraculous feats. Powerful substance – but still just a drug.'

'You just walk around with that kind of thing?'

'I had Pitry run and get it from the embassy. What I usually like to do is make them feel like they're at home, suffering a fever, with their family members nearby, or at least people claiming to be their family members, and most of the time they get so agitated they wind up telling us everything. I'm not sure if that'll be the case here, however, as the jail cell may induce a delirium of a much more . . .'

The boy gasps, looks at his arm, then up at the ceiling. Then he grabs the sides of his head, and sobs a little.

'. . . nightmarish sort.'

'Isn't this torture?'

'No,' says Shara quietly. 'I've seen torture. This is nowhere close. And besides, *this* gets somewhat accurate answers. Torture usually gets you whatever you want to hear. And people are usually much more forgiving of this method. Mostly because they're never quite sure any of it really happened.'

'I am so happy I chose to remain a soldier,' says Mulaghesh, 'and never went into your line of work. This puts a bad taste in my mouth.'

'The taste would be much worse if we did *not* get the information, which often saves lives.'

'And this means we shed our morals at the door?'

'Nations have no morals,' says Shara, quoting her aunt from memory. 'Only interests.'

'Probably true. But I'm still surprised you'd do something like this.'

'Why?'

'Well, I wasn't in Ghaladesh during the National Party Scandal. But no one needed to be, to hear all about it. *Everyone* talked about it. The man everyone assumed would be Prime Minister going down in utter flames. Not to mention the party treasurer attempting suicide – nothing more ignoble than a failed noble exit. But most of all, I remember hearing about this girl who caused it all, who rocked the boat so much.'

Shara swallows. Down the hall, a conversation between three policemen grows into outraged bickering.

'Not really her fault, they said,' Mulaghesh continues. 'Just passionate, and very young. Twenty at most, they said. She didn't know that there were just some corruptions you don't try and drive out, some rocks you don't turn over.'

A furious secretary stomps out of her office and shushes the three policemen, who cast ugly looks at one another before separating.

'She let her heart guide her,' says Mulaghesh, 'rather than her head. And mistakes were made.'

Shara stares into the room at the twitching boy, who now seems torn between laughing and crying.

'I always imagined,' says Mulaghesh, 'that that girl just happened to be a good sort in a rotten line of work. That's all.'

The boy leans back and rests his head against the stone wall, staring forward with blank, glassy eyes. Shara shuts the viewing slot in the door.

Enough.

'If you will excuse me,' says Shara, and she opens the door, slips in and shuts it behind her.

Never has she been so happy to walk into a jail cell.

The boy tries to focus on her, and asks, 'Who's there?'

Shara shushes him. 'Don't worry. It's me. You're fine.'

'Who? Who is it?' He licks his lips. He's drenched with sweat by now.

'You need to relax, please. You're in recovery now.'

'I am?'

'Yes. You had a bad fall. Don't you remember?'

He squints as he thinks about it. 'Maybe. I think I . . . I fell during that party . . .'

'Yes. We had to put you in a cool, dark place, for you to relax. You were very agitated, but you're going to be fine.'

'You're sure? You're sure I'll be fine?'

'We're sure. You're at the hospital. We just have to keep you here for a little bit longer, to make sure.'

'No! No, I need to go! I have to . . . to . . .' He fumbles with his seat, trying to stand.

'What do you have to do?'

'I have to make it back to everyone . . .'

'To who? To your friends?'

He swallows and nods. He's almost panting now. Shara imagines he is seeing blinding bursts of colour, rippling shadows, cold fires.

'Where would you need to go?' she asks.

He struggles with this question. 'N-no . . . I have to . . . to go.'

'You can't, I'm afraid,' she says soothingly. 'We have to take care of you. But we can send word to your friends. Where are they?'

'Where?' he says, confused.

'Yes. Where are your friends?'

'They're . . . they're in another place. It's a place from another place. I *think*.'

'All right. And where is this place?'

He rubs his eyes. When he looks back at her, she sees he has burst several blood vessels in them.

'Where?' she says again.

'It's not . . . not *like* that. It's an . . . older place. Where things ought to be.'

'Ought to be?'

'*How* things ought to be.'

'But how do you get to this place to see your friends?'

'It's hard.' He stares at the light in the ceiling. He looks away, like the sight of it pains him. Then he says, 'The world is . . . threadbarren. Threadbare.'

'All right?'

'It's incomplete. The city is. It has spots where a thing was, but there's nothing there now. It got taken away. Connective' – he furrows his brow – '*tissue*. But you can still get to them. To the places. If you belong. The gold is . . . smudged but it still shines. The pearl has cracked. Yet it is still the city. Still what I feel' – he taps his heart – 'here.'

'Is this how people disappear?'

He starts laughing. 'Disappear? What a . . . what a ridiculous idea.' The idea tickles him so much he almost falls out of his seat.

She tries another tactic. 'Why did you come to the party tonight?'

'Tonight?'

'Yes.'

'Oh.' He holds his head. 'Are you sure it was tonight? It seems so long ago.'

'It wasn't. It was just a few hours ago.'

'But I felt years pass through my fingers,' he whispers. 'Like the wind.' He reflects on it. 'We came for . . . metal.'

'For *metal*?'

'Yes. We were trying to buy some, but it was too slow. And we got worried. We didn't like him. We *hate* him. But we had to have him.'

'Votrov?'

'Yes. Him.'

Shara nods. 'And did the woman have anything to do with it?'

'Who?'

'The . . .' She thinks. 'The shally.'

'Oh. Oh, *her*.' He starts laughing again. 'Do you know, we had no idea she'd be there at all?'

'I see,' says Shara quietly. 'What do you need the metal for?'

'We can't fly through the air on boats of wood,' says the boy. 'That's what they said.' His eyes trace the passage of something invisible through the air. 'Oh, my goodness . . . how beautiful.'

Shara wonders if she perhaps overdosed him. 'Did you and your friends kill Dr Pangyui?'

'Who?'

'The shally professor.'

'Shallies don't have professors. They haven't the minds for it.'

'The little foreign professor who was . . . committing blasphemy.'

'All foreigners are blasphemous. Being alive is blasphemous, for them. There is only us. We are the children of the gods. All others are people of ash and clay. For them to live and not pay us fealty is the greatest of blasphemies.' He frowns and leans forward like his stomach hurts. 'Oh. Oh, dear.'

'There was a man here, studying at the University,' says Shara slowly and clearly. 'You didn't want him here. The city didn't, I mean. There was much outcry about it.'

The boy rubs his eyes. 'My head. There's . . . there's something in my head.'

'He died, just a few days ago. Do you remember?'

He whimpers. 'There's someone *in* there.' He raps the side of his head with his knuckles, hard enough to make a noise. 'Please . . . please help me get him *out* . . .'

'Someone attacked him at the University. They beat him to death.'

'Please. *Please!*'

'Tell me what you know about the professor.'

'He's inside my head!' shrieks the boy. 'He's inside my head! He's been jailed for so long! Let me see light, oh, let me see light!'

'Damn it,' says Shara. She walks to the cell door and places her hand on the viewing slot. 'You want light?'

'Yes!' screams the boy. 'By all the mercy of the gods, yes!'

'Fine.' Shara opens the slot. A trickle of light pokes through. 'There,' she says. She turns back to him. 'Now will you tell me—'

The boy has gone.

Not just the boy: half the room has gone. It is as if half the room has been cut off by a standing wall of black water, only now in the centre of it there is a little hole of yellow light, yellow like the sky before a storm.

'Oh,' says Shara.

The hole of yellow light widens. Shara feels like someone is reaching into her head with thick, massive hands, and opening a tiny door.

Shara just has time for one thought — *I thought* I *dosed* him — before she begins to see many things.

There is a tree, old and twisted.

It stands at the top of a lonely hill. Its branches form a dark dome against the yellow sky.

There is a rock below the tree. It is dark and polished, polished so deeply it looks like it is perpetually wet.

There is a face carved into the centre of the stone. Shara can just barely see it.

Then comes a voice, booming like thunder.

WHO ARE YOU?

They all vanish — the hill, tree and stone — and things shift.

The sun, bright and terrible and blazing. It is not the huge ball of light she is so accustomed to: it is as if the sky is a sheet of thin yellow paper, and someone is standing behind it holding an oily, flaming torch.

This land is lit by an ancient fire. Yet who started it?

Below the sun is a lone, strange mountain. It rises from the earth in a straight, rigid shaft. Its top is smooth and rounded — not unlike the stone she just saw — and its sides are straight and rippled. There is something fiercely, disturbingly organic about the mountain, though it might simply be how its smooth form looks in the shuddering light of the sun.

Then the voice again.

HOW DID YOU GET IN HERE?

Again, the scene vanishes.

A hillside swells before her, lit with firelight. It is night. Shadows leap about her: faces, hands, all feral, all twisted. Above her is the moon, huge and swollen like a spider's egg. The moon appears to balance on the top of the hill, and she thinks she can make out a figure with a tricorne hat dancing before it, thrusting something up to the sky – a jug? – as if asking the moon itself to partake.

Starlings pour across the night sky in a dark, cheeping flood.

I CANNOT SEE YOU. COME CLOSER TO ME.

The darkness vanishes. She feels herself being pulled away.

A road on a plain. Again, the yellow sky lit by a sun with the light of a dying torch. Besides this, there is nothing but the dusty road and the plain.

She is pulled along the road, as if she is flying mere inches above the earth.

Hills swell in the distance, lumpen and yellow and barren. She is ripped towards them as if pulled by a string, and she flies up their smooth sides until she sees a crack between two of the hills, a small aperture, a stab wound, a cave.

There is something in the cave, pulling her in.

She enters. The light dies around her.

They are hollow, these hills.

No, not hills – statues.

Yet whose likeness do they mimic?

There is someone at the back of the cave. She cannot see them. She thinks she can make out a tall form, draped in grey cloth, like that of a thick robe.

She sees no face, but she feels eyes all over her.

THERE YOU ARE.

She sees no hands, but she feels like she is in someone's grasp.

HOW DID YOU GET IN? NO, IT DOES NOT MATTER. LET ME OUT.

She sees no movement, but she feels like the walls close in around her.

LET ME OUT. YOU MUST LET ME OUT.

A flutter of grey cloth. It grows nearer, but she still cannot see.

THEY HAD NO RIGHT. THEY HAD NO RIGHT, TO DO THIS TO ME.

Shara struggles. She reaches out, tries to push away – *No! No!*
YOU MUST LET ME OUT.
In the darkness comes a bright flame.

It takes Shara a moment to realise she is standing in the jail cell. There is
a blazing fire in the centre of the cell, and the firelight on the stone
walls gives the cell a primeval look, not unlike the visions she has just seen.
But when she hears Mulaghesh's voice shouting, *'Get out of there! Shara!*
What are you just standing there for? Get the hells out of there!' she realises where
she is.

There is another voice. Someone is screaming, she realises.

Then the fire in the jail cell stands to its feet, looks at her, and
reaches out.

She sees a face through the flames, blistering and cracking.

It is the boy, yet he burns as if doused in petrol.

He opens his mouth to scream again. Shara watches as flames flood into
his mouth, down his throat. She can see his tongue bubbling.

The door behind her flies open. Mulaghesh grabs her and jerks her into
the hallway.

The cell door slams shut, its edges and cracks illumined with bright firelight. There is a pounding from the other side, and screaming. Policemen
come running, but they are unsure what to do.

'Oh,' says Mulaghesh. 'Oh, by the seas. What on *fucking Earth*. Someone get some blankets! We need to put that man *out*! Come on, everyone,
move!'

The pounding on the door weakens, softens. A smell pervades the
air, bubbling lipids like a chandler's shop. By the time the officers finally
manage to bring blankets and a doctor, there is a dark smoke seeping
through the top crack of the door.

They prepare themselves and rip the door open. Its opposite side is black,
charred. Beyond is a wall of smoke, streaming plumes like black water.

'No,' says Mulaghesh. 'No. Far too late. Far too late.'

A dark, crinkled shape surfaces among the sea of black. Shara moves to
look, but Mulaghesh pushes her away.

                                       *

Wild havoc. Hallways of people screaming and shouting, fighting to get out. Shara wishes to ask, *What's all the commotion about?* but she feels too stunned and slow to ask.

She sees Saypuri soldiers fighting through the crowd to get to her; feels Mulaghesh shove her into their arms; feels herself being ripped out of the stampeding throng.

She feels these things, but they do not register. *I suppose this is what shock feels like*, she thinks, rather curious.

She is stuffed into a car along with Mulaghesh and two soldiers. Pitry looks back at them from the driver's seat, alarmed. Mulaghesh tells him, 'The embassy. *Now.*' When they pull away, an armoured car bearing the Polis Governor's insignia on its side coughs into life and follows closely.

'Look *up*,' Mulaghesh tells the soldiers. 'On the rooftops. And keep an eye on the alleys.'

'What are you telling them to look for?' Shara asks softly.

'Are you in*sane*? For any more assassins! That's, what, *twice* in six hours? By the seas, I don't even know how he did it. He must have had a device on him, some flask with oil, or something. I don't know how the police missed it, unless one of them snuck it to him while he was imprisoned. Which I wouldn't put past them.'

Shara thinks, *She believes he attacked me.*

But he didn't. I know exactly what that was.

But I've only ever read about it.

'I was turned away,' says Shara. 'What did you see?'

'No, you weren't,' says Mulaghesh. 'You were looking right at him. I thought it was some kind of mind game you were playing with him. You went to the door, opened the slot so I could see in. Then you said something about light and turned round and you both just . . . *stared* at one another.'

'For how long?'

'Hell, I don't know. Then he just burst into flames. I didn't see him activate anything, push any button, light any match. He didn't even seem to *move*. Whatever he used, I want to know what it was. They might use more of them.'

'And . . . and did you hear a voice in the room?'

'A what?'

'A voice? While we stared at one another?'

Mulaghesh takes her eyes off the street to look Shara over. 'You're in shock. You need to lie back, and rest. Let me take over today. This is what I do, this is what I know. Okay?'

He spoke to me from the heart of the world.

*No – he **was** the heart of the world.*

'You don't need,' says Shara softly, 'to order your men about so.'

'Shara, just *lie back—*'

'No,' says Shara. 'Listen. That was not a planned, coordinated attack. And it was most certainly *not* an assassination attempt.'

'Then what was it?'

Shara debates not telling her. *Some secrets*, she tells herself, *can't be borne alone*.

She sits up and says to Pitry, 'Pardon, Pitry, but could you pull over briefly? And when you do, could you roll up the partition back here?'

'What?' says Mulaghesh. 'Why?'

'Because I'm afraid your soldiers will have to join Pitry in the front seat,' she says. 'This conversation will have to be private, you see.'

The broken buildings are like savage landscapes as they speed by, grey glaciers creeping down a mountain. A pale face appears at a window and a young girl heaves out a prodigious amount of what can only be human waste. The passers-by stop only briefly: not an unusual occurrence for them.

'I have read more about the history of the Continent than nearly anyone else alive in the world,' Shara says. 'Before me, the only person who knew more was Efrem Pangyui. He has now passed, of course. Which means it is only me.'

'What's your point?' asks Mulaghesh.

'I have read of instances of spontaneous combustion on the Continent. It has not happened in decades, but once, long ago, it happened occasionally. The cause of these episodes of spontaneous combustion was widely known here, back then: they were the result of Divine possession.'

'Of what?' asks Mulaghesh.

'Divine possession. A Divine being could project his or her intelligence into a mortal agent to commune with them directly – almost using them as a puppet, essentially. This was quite common among some of the lesser Divine beings – sprites, spirits, familiars and so on.'

'All of which the Kaj killed in the Great Purge,' says Mulaghesh. 'Right?'

'Presumably. But the *primary* Divinities could not possess a mortal agent to the same degree. Their very beings were too large, too powerful, too intense. The mortal body could not bear it. However, some particularly devoted followers of Voortya valued this experience very highly, despite the damage done. They would beseech her to "enter their selves" and "speak behind their eyes", as the story goes. But when Voortya would comply, after a matter of seconds, their mortal bodies would burst into flames. Sort of like spiritual friction, I suppose.'

Mulaghesh is silent for a long, long time. 'And . . . you're saying you think this is what happened.'

'I'm positive of it.'

'How so?'

'Because' – she takes a breath – 'whatever possessed that boy spoke to me. To you, outside the cell, it looked like we were simply standing still. But to me, something . . . took me somewhere. I was there for some time. It pulled me in. It wanted to see me. And it wanted me to let it out of . . . wherever it was.'

'It spoke to you?'

'Yes.'

Mulaghesh swallows. 'Are you quite sure of this?'

'Yes.'

'This wasn't a side effect of the drug you used on that boy? Maybe you absorbed it through your skin?'

'I'm sure the drug contributed, but not in the way you mean. Like I said, a philosopher's stone was often used to commune with the Divinities. Records indicate it acted like lubrication, in a way. I believe I might have unintentionally opened that boy up for . . . whatever it was, to possess him.'

'Whatever it was,' echoes Mulaghesh.

'Yes.'

'But it's . . . it's not a "whatever it was". Because you sound like you know what it was.'

'Yes.'

'Because if what you're saying is correct, then the only thing that made people combust was—'

'Yes. A primary Divinity.'

'And if you're saying that was what you saw, what took control of that boy, then that would mean—'

'Yes,' says Shara. 'It would mean at least one of the gods has survived.'

Winning the War — if such a lopsided conflict could even be discussed in such terms — is most certainly the single greatest shift in Saypur's history. And the Kaj is almost single-handedly responsible for the victory. However, both the Kaj and the War often overshadow the handful of years directly after the downfall of the Continent — which were just as crucial for Saypur as the death of the Divinities. But this period is almost completely forgotten.

This is probably because the events following the War are so unpleasant to remember.

After the Kaj had killed the last Divinity, it became evident that the Divinities had been protecting the Continent — and Saypur, to a certain extent — not only from outside attackers, but also from a number of viruses and diseases. Whether this was done intentionally by the Divinities, or if it was simply a coincidental bonus from residing within their sphere of influence, no one is quite sure. But for the twenty years after the death of Jukov, the last Divinity, horrific plague and rampant outbreaks became as seasonally predictable as rain and snow.

The estimated worldwide loss during the official Plague Years is innumerable. The Continent, being so dependent on the Divinities, was especially vulnerable: immediately after the Blink, nearly one third of all its population died of various ailments. Saypuri soldiers — who were just as vulnerable, being on the Continent — wrote letters home describing streets stuffed with rotting corpses, rivers of the dead piled twice as high as any man, endless trains of litters bearing bodies to pyres outside each polis. Every polis suffered an explosion of insects, rats, cats, wolves — almost any pest one can imagine. Everywhere one went on the Continent, one was met with the overpowering scent of rotting flesh.

Saypur, however, being a colony that only peripherally benefited from miraculous intervention, had better knowledge of non-miraculous sanitation. They quarantined the infected, and when soldiers arrived home, they promptly quarantined them as well – a decision that caused much outrage in Saypur at the time. Overall, though the Plague Years were far from easy, Saypur lost fewer than 10,000 lives to the sudden, massive influx of disease.

It is this self-sufficiency that also came to Saypur's aid in terms of technology. For the 876 years of its subservience, Saypur was forced to provide resources to the Continent chiefly by their own means – without Divine support. (Exactly why the Divinities needed Saypur to produce resources at all, rather than simply doing so with any number of miracles, is a favourite, and often rather infamous, question among Saypuri historians.) Having been forced to generate such technological innovation under threat, and now suddenly finding itself sitting upon a wealth of resources that could be called its own, Saypur underwent a phenomenal technological transformation overnight. Vallaicha Thinadeshi herself, who is generally acknowledged to be the greatest of the iconic engineers of this period, said that for two decades 'you could toss a stone out of any window in Ghaladesh, and strike four geniuses on the way down'. (It is perhaps noteworthy that the Kaj himself was an amateur scientist, performing many experiments on his estate.)

In contrast, the Continent – plague-ridden, starving – sank into its own helplessness. In the absence of any single ruling force, the polises succumbed to internal conflict. Bandit kings sprang up like mushrooms. During their withdrawal, some Saypuri soldiers recorded rumours of cannibalism, torture, slavery and mass rape. The people that were once the blessed luminaries of the world had, almost overnight, descended into monstrous, barbaric savagery.

It must have seemed to the newly founded Saypuri Parliament an easy if not satisfying decision: Saypur, for so long the subservient nation, would intervene in the Continent's affairs, and bring order. They would reinvade, this time under a banner of peace, and reconstruct.

But I am not sure they truly understood the memory of the Continent, which – despite the Blink, despite the Plague Years, despite the bandit kings – remains to this day quite long, and bitter.

They remember what they were, and they know what they have lost.

While Saypur has much to be proud of, we should consider that this decision may not have been as humanely motivated as we might wish — and pride, as the Continent learned, is often rewarded with hardship.

The Sudden Hegemony, *Dr Efrem Pangyui*

Dangerously honest

Hazy morning light trickles across the rooftops. The white expanse of the city walls appears to miraculously grow transparent, or maybe Shara's mind only imagines the diamond flecks of stars glittering above the dawning sun. *It's not really the sun*, she thinks. *I'm not seeing the sky. It's just the picture of the sun and the sky, produced by the walls. Or, at least, I think it is.*

The Bulikov pigeons can tell no difference: they emerge from their roosts, fluff their feathers, and descend to the city streets in wheeling clouds.

Shara is not afraid. She tells herself this repeatedly, in the calm, cool voice of a doctor.

I have never regarded knowledge as a burden, thinks Shara, *but how heavy this weighs on me.*

But inside her a small, quiet voice reminds her that this isn't completely surprising. Shara spent enough time buried in the restricted information at the Ministry to understand that the history taught in Saypuri schools is just one variation on a story, one with many, many holes. *But just because the nightmare you expected comes true*, she tells herself, *it doesn't make it any less terrifying.*

More and more, she worries about what could be in the Warehouse. And, more and more, she worries that someone other than Efrem could have gained access to it. That *should* be impossible; but having just had what *should* be a dead Divinity directly address her, she knows the impossible cannot really be ruled out.

She picks up the morning paper on her desk and reads, for the hundredth time:

ASSASSINATION ATTEMPT

The aristocratic quarter of Bulikov remains in a state of anxiety after an arts fund-raiser at the House of Votrov became a scene of violence and terror last night.

The fund-raiser, part of the 'Faces of New Bulikov' display, was attacked in the late evening by a group of armed, masked men whose intentions are as yet unknown. However, two attendees are thought to have been their targets: City Father Vohannes Votrov himself and Ashara Thivani, the new Cultural Ambassador of the Saypuri Embassy of Bulikov, and interim Chief Diplomat.

Four staff members of the House of Votrov were killed in the attack, but security forces at the reception protected all attendees and quickly eliminated the attackers. The Bulikov Police Department is currently investigating the identities of the men involved, and though the Saypuri Embassy has shown a keen interest in the case, their official involvement has yet to be determined.

Vohannes Votrov expressed grief for his slain staff members and regret that the attack happened, but said he was not surprised: 'With the current discourse we're seeing in the city, I am not shocked at all that some citizens felt violence was the only answer. They are told day in and day out that [New Bulikov's] vision for the city is one of destruction and death, that we are liars and deceivers. I have no doubt that such men felt they were acting out of a moral principle – and this I regret perhaps most of all.'

City Father Ernst Wiclov, a frequent opponent of Votrov and New Bulikov, was quick to condemn these accusations. 'The very idea that someone would capitalise on such a tragedy for political gain is abhorrent,' he said in an interview mere hours after the attack. 'This is a time for mourning and reflection, not self-righteous posturing.'

Mr Vohannes was not available for response.

There's a knock at the door, and Mulaghesh sticks her head in. 'I didn't want to open up shop for anyone, but I thought I'd make an exception for this – your boy is here.'

'My what?'

Mulaghesh pushes the door open the rest of the way to reveal Vohannes standing in the hallway, looking quite awkward despite his elegant grey suit and thick white fur coat.

'Ah,' says Shara. 'Come in.'

Vohannes limps in. 'I must say, I am happy to see you in one piece. Two attempts on your life in one day! I thought you were important, Shara, but not . . .' – he rubs his hip – 'not *that* important. And I also thought you'd be a lot better at your job, if everyone's trying to kill you.'

Shara rolls her eyes. 'I see your charm has not been dulled by all the excitement. Please sit down, Vo. I have some rather bad news for you.'

As he does, Shara finds she only hates herself a little for finding this all a fortunate coincidence: she needs Vohannes to be frightened in order to do what she wants him to.

'Bad news?' asks Vo. 'Beyond all the damage and . . . and *stains* done to my home?'

'We are happy to compensate you for that,' says Shara. 'Those damages were done, after all, by a Ministry employee.'

'That man works for the Ministry? For you? But he's a *Dreyling*, isn't he? Haven't they all become savages and pirates since their little kingdom collapsed?'

'Maybe so,' says Shara, 'but he saved your life.'

Vohannes pauses while taking out a cigarette. 'Well, I don't think . . . wait, *what? My* life?'

'Yes,' says Shara. 'Because those men were not there for me. They were there for you, Vo.'

He stares at her. The cigarette hovers an inch from Vohannes's open mouth.

'That would be the bad news I just mentioned,' she says gently.

'He . . . he what?'

'They were there, I think, to kidnap you, actually – not to kill you,' Shara continues. 'This does not necessarily make it better, though: they were not there to make a grand political gesture, and kill a public figure. They were there to accomplish real, definite goals, about which I know very little. This means they have something larger in mind, something that requires a lot of preparation. You were just a stepping stone in accomplishing that, whatever it is.'

Vohannes stares at her, and finally says, 'But . . . but I heard you were attacked at the police station.'

'A coincidence. They had no idea I'd be at your party. Bulikov, it seems, is a morass of plots and schemes. I can say, though, that you are quite lucky to be sitting in front of me,' she says mildly. 'I am probably the only person on the Continent right now who can help you.'

'Help me what?'

'Help you stay alive. Did you see how those men were dressed?'

His face grows slightly bitter. 'Kolkashtani robes.'

'Yes. Those haven't been seen on the Continent for decades. They were devotees of the Divinity Kolkan. This is not a matter of politics, I think, Vo – I think it is a matter of *faith*. These men are willing to die for what they believe. And they need something from you. And if they're willing to die, they're definitely willing to try again.'

'Try again to get . . . what?'

'The attacker I questioned was not in a state where he could provide much detail, but he said they specifically needed your *metal*. Do you know what that means?'

Vohannes stares into space for nearly a minute before he's capable of processing her question. 'My *metal*?'

'Yes. I don't believe he meant anything precious – gold, silver, or anything like that. But as you said, you're playing into the resources game . . . so I wondered.'

'Well, I told you my biggest project is saltpetre – which isn't a metal, you know.'

'I am familiar with the nature of metals,' she says. 'We *did* go to school together, you know.'

'Right, right. The only other thing I could think of' – Vohannes scratches an eyebrow, smoothes it down – 'would probably be the steelworks. But that's incredibly new.'

'Steel?'

'Yes. No one else on the Continent can produce steel – mostly because no one can afford the process.'

'But you can?'

'Yes, to a limited degree. It takes a specialised kind of furnace, which is expensive to build and maintain. It's a bit of a test project, and one I'm not very much interested in because it's so damn expensive. And because Bulikov isn't building anything big or grand enough to *require* steel.'

'But you *are* producing steel?'

'Yes. But I've no idea why some reactionary Restorationist would want it.'

'He suggested it was for ships that would sail through the air.'

'He said it was for *what*?'

Shara shrugs. 'It's what he said.'

'So this man is insane. Barking mad, surely. I admit, it's a bit of a relief to hear it.'

'He was in an induced state, let's say. But we can't question him any more, I'm afraid. The man has died.'

'How?'

Shara is silent. She briefly remembers the sight of the boy's face, flames filling his mouth as he tried to scream. 'I can't say at the moment,' she says. 'But it was unpleasant. All of this is unpleasant to me, Vo. And I don't like that you're at the middle of it. You're a lightning rod, it seems.' She gently touches the paper before her. 'And I do not want you to make it worse.'

Vohannes studies her. 'Oh . . . Oh, Shara. I hope you are not about to suggest what I think you are to suggest.'

'I will go ahead and assume you've had visitors from all your supporters and allies,' says Shara, 'and I will assume they have all told you, in varying terms, how you have just been handed some very valuable political capital. Being attacked, and surviving that attack, puts a powerful weapon in your hand. I will also assume that both you, and they, think it politically expedient to get on as many newspaper pages as possible.'

'I was attacked,' he says. 'Am I not allowed to decry my attackers?'

'Not when I am trying to catch them, no,' says Shara. 'I want you to stay out of the papers, Vo, and I do not want you to inflame the situation any more than it is.'

A short laugh. 'Really.'

'Really. This job is proving difficult. But you can make it easier.'

'*Your* job is difficult? Oh, so you just step into my city and all of a sudden it's *your* arena? *You're* the person dictating how everything should happen in Bulikov? Gods, were I a less enlightened person, Shara, I'd say such behaviour was typical of a—'

Shara cocks an eyebrow.

Vohannes coughs. 'Listen, Shara. I have spent my life building my career. I have thrown away fortunes doing it. And I have battered and battered on the invisible walls surrounding this Continent, trying to bring in aid, wealth, support, education, and now, just when it looks like I might be getting somewhere, just when it looks like I might unify the support of Bulikov, you want me to *stop*? When the City Father elections are next *month*?'

'This is bigger than votes.'

'It's not about *votes*. It's about the city, the Continent!'

'So is what I'm doing.'

'People depend on me!'

'People depend on me, too,' says Shara. 'They just don't know it.'

'Oh, you can justify almost anything by saying *that*.'

'I am not your enemy,' she says. 'I am your ally. I have been honest with you, Vo – dangerously honest. Now you must trust me. I want you to withdraw from the public eye, just for a little bit. If your movement is as successful as you claimed, stepping away can't be that damaging.'

This appeal to his vanity appears to appease him somewhat. 'How long?'

'Hopefully not long at all. The sooner I can get this done, the sooner you can return to your work, without your guards.'

'I . . . wait, what guards?'

Shara stirs her tea. 'Bodyguards. The Saypuri detail I'm going to assign to you.'

Vohannes stares at her and laughs. 'You . . . you can't put me under guard. That's ridiculous!'

'I can. You'll still be perfectly free to do as you like, to an extent. They'll just be watching over you.'

'Do you know how terrible this will look? Me going about town with a bunch of armed Saypuris in tow?'

'I thought we just discussed that you shouldn't be going about town at all,' says Shara. 'You will be a moderately private citizen, for a period of time, and a *safe* one, if I have my way. But you can shorten that period of time, if you do something for me.'

'Oh, my goodness' – Vohannes rubs his eyes – 'something you need doing? Is this how the Ministry always manages to get what it wants?'

'Sixteen people are dead, Vo. Including some of your household staff. I'm taking this seriously. And so should you.'

'I *am* taking this seriously. You're the one telling me to do nothing!'

'Not nothing. There's something being stored in a safety deposit box at a bank. I'm not sure what it is, but I know I need it.'

'And you want me to get it?'

She nods.

'How do you expect me to do that? Am I to don all black and infiltrate this place in the middle of the night? I would have thought you'd have people for this.'

'I expected you'd come up with an easier way than that. Primarily because you own the bank.'

Vohannes blinks. 'I . . . I do?'

'Yes.' Shara hands him a copy of Pangyui's decoded message.

He examines it. 'Are you *sure* I own it? Its name doesn't ring a bell.'

'It must be so nice,' says Shara, 'to be so wealthy that one is uncertain of which institutions one does and does not own. But yes. I have confirmed that you personally own this bank. If you could find some means, or excuse, to retrieve the contents of that box, and deliver it to me, then it may help us figure this all out. Which means I would no longer have to keep you under guard, and you could return to business as normal.'

Vohannes grumbles something about a violation of his rights, then folds up the address and angrily stuffs it in his pocket. He stands up and says, 'If you are my ally, I expect you to act like it.'

'And what does that mean?'

'You said yourself, we want the same thing: a peaceful, prosperous Bulikov, don't we?'

Shara instantly regrets saying this – for she knows the Ministry of Foreign Affairs desires no such thing.

'Work with me,' he says. 'Help me.'

'Is this about how you want to start making munitions?'

'I am talking about increased Saypuri engagement with Bulikov,' he says. '*Real* engagement. *Real* aid. Not this subterfuge. Right now, we are given but a trickle of water, when we need a flood to wash all this stagnancy away. Flex your muscles, Shara. Give me genuine political support.'

'We can't possibly voice support for a local politician. Maybe one day, but not right now. The circumstances—'

'The circumstances will never be right,' says Vohannes, 'because this will always be hard.'

'Vo . . .'

'Shara, my city and my country are desperately, desperately poor, and I genuinely think they are on a path that can only end in violence. I am offering you an opportunity to try and help us, and put us on a different path.'

'I cannot accept it,' says Shara. 'Not now, Vo. I'm sorry. Maybe one day soon.'

'No. You don't believe that. You're not an agent of change, Shara. You don't make the world better – you work to keep things how they are. The Restorationists look to the past, Saypur wishes to maintain the present, but no one considers the future.'

'I am sorry,' she says. 'But I cannot help you.'

'No, you aren't sorry. You are a representative of your country. And countries do not feel sorrow.' He turns and limps away.

Shara stands in front of the window again. Dawn is now in full riot across the roofs of Bulikov, giving a golden streak to all the wandering columns of chimney smoke. She takes a long sip of tea. *An import*, she thinks. *Maybe made in Ghaladesh*. She wonders, briefly, if she is not addicted to the tea's caffeine so much as the taste and scent of home, so far away.

She opens the window – wincing at the blast of cold air – closes the shutters outside, then closes the window.

She licks her finger, hesitates, and begins to write on the glass.

Why do I always do this, she thinks, *when I'm at my most vulnerable?*

Slowly, the shadows shift. The air gains a curious new current. Somewhere in the room, in some invisible manner, a door opens to somewhere else. And there in the glass, she sees . . .

An empty office.

Shara sits down to wait.

Twenty minutes later, Vinya Komayd arrives, holding many papers and clad in what she personally refers to as her 'battle armour': a bright red, highly expensive dress that is both attractive and tremendously imposing. It has always possessed the odd property of making Vinya the undeniable centre of the room. When Vinya spotted the dress in a store, she purchased five of them, then arranged it so the entire line was permanently removed from the shelves. *I could never trust such a dress to anyone else*, she remarked when she told Shara. *It's much too dangerous.*

'Important meeting?' asks Shara.

Auntie Vinya looks up, and frowns. 'No,' she says, slightly irritated. 'But important people were there. Why are you calling on the emergency line? If you've found something, send it through the normal channels.'

'I can't send this through the normal channels.'

'Do you distrust our normal channels?'

Shara doesn't bother to answer.

'I take that as a professional slight,' says Vinya. 'Since I oversee most of them. And I don't like the idea of your head owning the *only* copy of critical information. If you want to rise up, darling, you'll have to learn to share.'

'We have sixteen dead,' says Shara. 'Continentals. They were killed in an attack on a Bulikovian political figure – a City Father. Who survived.'

Vinya pauses. She looks at the piece of paper in her hand – work that obviously needs to get done, and soon – and sighs and lays it aside. She walks over to sit before the pane of glass, and asks, 'How?'

'They opted to attack during a social occasion. At which I was present.'

Vinya rolls her eyes. 'Ah. You and . . . what's his name?'

'Sigrud.'

'Yes. *How* many dead?'

'Sixteen.'

'So he's clocking up his normal rate, then. By all the damned seas, Shara, I've no idea why you keep such a man *on*! We have trouble with the Drey-lings every day. They're *pirates*, my dear!'

'They weren't always. Not while their king was still alive.'

'Ah, yes, their dead king they do so love to sing about. Him and their little lost prince, who'll one day sail back to them. I expect they also sing all day while burning half the northern Continental coastline! I mean, you must admit, my dear, these people are *savages!*'

'I think he's proved his worth, last night and many other nights.'

'Intelligence work is meant to avoid bloodshed, not generate it by the quart!'

'And yet intelligence work is as susceptible to its environs as anything else,' says Shara. 'We operate within a set of variables that we often cannot influence.'

'I *hate* it when you quote me,' says Vinya. 'All right. So what? So some bumpkins took a shot at an alderman, or whatever he is. That's not news, that's just your average weekday. Why would you contact me?'

'Because I am convinced,' says Shara, 'that there is some connection to Pangyui.'

Vinya freezes. She looks away, then slowly looks back. '*What?*'

'I suspect,' says Shara, 'that Pangyui's death was probably part of a reactionary movement here, meant to rebuke Saypur's influence and return the Continent – or at least Bulikov – to its former glory.'

Vinya sits in silence. Then, 'And *how* would you have determined that?'

'Because there were numerous agents of this reactionary movement who were watching him,' says Shara. 'Specifically – though I cannot confirm it yet – I think his death is probably related to their discovery of exactly *what* he was doing here. Which was *not* a mission of cultural understanding, as they were told.'

Vinya sighs and massages the sides of her neck. 'So. You found out about his little . . . historical expedition.'

'So you *do* know about the Warehouse?'

'Of *course* I know about the Warehouse!' Vinya snaps. 'It's why he went there, of course! If you know so much, you might as well know everything.'

'You signed off on this?'

Vinya rolls her eyes.

'Oh. So you *planned* this.'

'Of *course* I planned this, darling. But it *was* Efrem's idea. It was just one I had a very specific interest in.'

'And what was this idea?'

'Oh, well, I'm sure that you being the Divine expert that you are, you probably know all about it. Or you would, if Efrem had been allowed to publish it. His idea was not, as one says in the parlance of our era, *approved*. And it is still a highly dangerous idea.'

'And what idea was this?'

'We don't talk much about the Divine over here – we like such things to stay dead, naturally – but when we do, we, like the Continent itself, assume that it was a top down relationship: the Divinities stood at the top of the chain, and they told the Continentals and, well, the world what to do, and everything obeyed. *Reality* obeyed.'

'So?'

'So,' she says slowly, 'over the course of his career, Efrem quietly became less convinced this was the case. He believed there was a lot more subtle give and take going on in the relationship than anyone imagined. The Divinities projected their own worlds, their own *realities*, which our historians have more or less surmised from all the conflicting creation stories, and afterlife stories, and static and whatnot.' She waves her hand, eager to cycle through all the minutiae.

'Of course,' says Shara – for this is a topic that is well known to her.

One of the Continent's biggest problems with having six Divinities were the many, many conflicting mythologies: for example, how could the world be a burning, golden coal pulled from the fires of Olvos's own heart while *also* being a stone hacked by Kolkan from a mountain behind the setting sun? And how could one's soul, after death, flit away to join Jukov's flock of brown starlings, while *also* flowing down the river of death to wash ashore in Ahanas' garden, where it would grow into an orchid? All Divinities were very clear about such things, but none of them agreed with one another.

It took Saypuri historians a long while to understand how all this had worked for the Continent. They made no progress until someone pointed out that the discordant mythologies appeared to be mostly *geographical*: people near a Divinity recorded history in strict agreement with that Divinity's mythology. Once historians started mapping out the recorded histories, they found the borders were shockingly distinct: you could see almost *exactly* where one Divinity's influence stopped and another's began. And, the historians were forced to assume, if you were within that sphere or penumbra of influence, you essentially existed in a different reality where everything that specific Divinity claimed was true *was* indisputably true.

So, were you within Voortya's territory, then the world was made from the bones of an army she slew in a field of ice in the sky.

Yet if you travelled to be near Ahanas, then the world was a seed she'd rescued from the river mud, and watered with her tears.

And still if you travelled to be near Taalhavras, then the world was a machine he had built from the celestial fundament, designed and crafted over thousands of years. And so on and so forth.

What the Divinities felt was true *was* true in these places. And when the Kaj killed them, all those things stopped being true.

The final piece of evidence supporting this theory was the 'reality static' that appeared directly after the Kaj successfully killed four of the six original Divinities: the world apparently 'remembered' that parts of it once existed in different realities, and had trouble reassembling itself. Saypuri soldiers recorded seeing rivers that flowed into the sky, silver that would turn to lead if you carried it through a certain place, trees that would bloom and die several times over in one day, and fertile lands that turned into cracked wastelands if you stood in one exact spot, then instantly restore themselves once you'd left it. Eventually, however, the world more or less sorted itself out, and instances of reality static all but vanished from the Continent – leaving the world not quite ruined, but not quite whole, either.

Vinya continues. 'Efrem believed that the mortal agents and followers of these Divinities had played some part in *shaping* these realities. He was never sure how, though, because he never had access to the correct historical resources. *Dangerous* historical resources.'

'Which were all in the Warehouse.'

'Exactly. He actually wrote and submitted a paper about this theory, which promptly got sent to me as this sort of thing is very much looked down upon. I think they expected I'd imprison him, or exile him, or something.'

'But instead you gave him exactly what he wanted. Why?'

'Well, think about it, Shara,' says Vinya. 'Saypur is now the strongest nation in the world. Our might is undeniable. Nothing in the world even feigns to threaten us. Except, we know that the Divinities once existed. And though they were killed, we do not understand what they were, or how they did what they did, where they came from, or even *how* the Kaj killed them.'

'You're thinking of them as weapons.'

Vinya shrugs. 'Maybe so. Imagine it – imagine a weapon that could decimate a country with a gesture. If a Divinity wished a land to be bathed in fire, it would be bathed in fire. They would be, in a way, a weapon that would end modern warfare as we know it. No more armies. No more navies. No more soldiers of any kind – just casualties. After all, look at the Continent – they became so dependent on the Divinities that not only did they not know how to fight, they didn't even know how to dispose of their own *waste*.'

Shara feels a cold horror growing in her belly. 'And you wished . . . to *produce* one of these for Saypur?'

Vinya laughs. 'Oh, my *goodness*, no. No, no, no. I am *quite* happy where I am. I would be insane to invite in something that would wield – how shall I put this? – a greater authority than my own. What I would wish would be to prevent anyone *else* from getting one. *That* . . . that is something that has kept me and many a Saypuri up at night. If Efrem could answer exactly where the gods came from, and how they worked, then we could actively prevent them from recurring. And if he just happened to find some information about the Kaj's weaponry – about which we to this day know absolutely *nothing* – that would help me sleep a little better, too.'

'Knowing how to kill a god would help you sleep better?'

A flippant shrug. 'Such are the burdens of power,' says Vinya. 'Efrem was a little less eager to explore this avenue – I think it bored him, to be frank – but anything would be better than what we know now.'

'And we would know . . . well, we would know why we were denied, too,' says Shara.

Vinya pauses, and slowly nods. 'Yes. We would finally know.'

Neither of them says any more on the topic, but they do not need to: while no Saypuri can go a day without thinking of how their ancestors lived in abysmal slavery, neither can they go an hour without wondering – Why? Why were *they* denied a god? Why was the Continent blessed with protectors, with power, with tools and privileges that were never extended to Saypur? How could such a tremendous inequality be allowed? And while Saypuris may seem to the world to be a small, curious people of education and wealth, anyone who spends any time in Saypur soon comes to understand that in their hearts lives a cold rage which lends them a cruelty one would never expect. *They call us godless*, Saypuris occasionally say to one another, *as if we had a* choice.

'So we dressed it up as an act of diplomacy,' says Vinya. 'An effort to heal the gulf between our nation and theirs. We only wanted to peruse the books in the Warehouse. That's all. I . . . I honestly never thought Efrem was in any danger. We assumed Bulikov would continue being Bulikov – all squalor and filth – and he could simply go about his business.'

Shara pauses, wondering how to broach the most obvious question. 'And . . . I'm curious,' she says slowly. '*Why* did you not tell me about this when I first came to Bulikov?'

Vinya sniffs, and sits up. But for one second her dark eyes skitter and dance as she considers how to answer.

Shara leans forward slightly, and watches her aunt carefully.

'This was a highly, highly restricted project,' pronounces Vinya. Still her eyes search the bottom of the pane before wandering up to find Shara's face. 'If you had caught someone, good on you. If not, we would have pursued the matter through different channels.' Vinya smiles haughtily.

Lying, screams Shara's mind. *She's lying! Lying, lying, lying, lying!*

In that instant, Shara decides not to tell her aunt what she witnessed in the jail cell. It goes against every line of reasoning she can imagine – Vinya wishes to know how to destroy any new Divinity, so of *course* she'd want to know Shara has actually encountered such a being – but Shara feels something is very, very, very wrong. She knows she should discount her own paranoia, of course. *Paranoia about one's case officers and commanders*, as she's told her own sources, *is a perfectly natural feeling*. But her aunt has not been her normal shrewd self recently, and now every instinct Shara has is shouting that Vinya is lying. And after nearly seventeen years of interviews and interrogations, she's learned to trust her instincts.

With no small amount of disbelief, she begins to wonder if her aunt has somehow been compromised. Could someone possibly gather enough material to own and control the heir apparent to the Prime Minister's seat? *A corrupt politician*, thinks Shara sardonically, *what a wildly unconventional idea*. After all, one can't mount the last few steps on the ladder without a lot of nasty compromises. And, moreover, if one prised open any of Auntie Vinya's closet doors, surely a whole parade of skeletons would come tumbling out.

But Shara is surprised at how terribly guilty and ashamed she feels to make such a decision. This is, after all, the woman who raised her, who took care of her and oversaw her education after her parents died in the Plague. But just as Vinya is Minister first, aunt second, Shara has always been an operative first and foremost.

So Shara returns to her old maxim: *When in doubt, be patient, and watch.*

Vinya asks, 'Now. What is this movement you talked about?'

Shara summarises the New Bulikov movement in a handful of sentences.

'*Oh*,' says Vinya. 'Oh, I remember this. This is the thing with the man who wants to make us guns.'

'Yes. Votrov.'

'Yes, yes. Some ministers are really keen on it, but I've tried to stall it as much as I can. I do not want us to be dependent on a place like Bulikov for *anything*. Especially *gunpowder*. So Votrov is the man who got attacked last night?'

'Yes.' Shara measures exactly what to share now, and decides not to reveal that the Restorationists were after his steel.

'*Votrov* . . . that name is strangely familiar, for some reason.'

'We went to school together.'

Vinya holds up a finger. 'Ah. *Ah*. I remember now. That's *him*? The boy from *Fadhuri*? He's the one wanting to make us guns? I remember being terrified he'd get you pregnant.'

'Auntie Vinya . . .'

'He didn't, did he?'

'Auntie Vinya!'

'Fine, fine.'

'I don't think he will give up on the munitions proposal,' says Shara. 'Just as a note. He seems very insistent on trying to bring industry to the Continent.'

'He can be as insistent as he likes,' says Vinya. 'That's not happening on my watch. It's better for the Continent to remain the way it is. Things are tenuously stable right now.'

'Not here,' says Shara. 'Obviously.'

Vinya waves a hand. 'The Continent is the Continent. It's always been that way, ever since the War. And I hope you're not getting soft on me, Shara. You know every country in the world wants to bleed Saypur dry. And every single time they'll claim children are starving in the streets, bloodshed of the innocent, and so on and so forth. We hear it dozens of times every day. The wise look after their own, and leave the rest to Fate – especially if it's the Continent. But enough about this. So. You want me to extend your work there, I assume. What do you have that's so solid?'

'We'll be pulling in one of the Restorationists' sources for questioning shortly. Off the grid.'

'Who's this agent you wish to grab?'

'A maid.'

Vinya laughs. 'A *what*?'

'The University maid! Which, I remind you, is where Pangyui worked. Cases and operations, as you *know*, frequently run on some of the most menial of workers.'

'Hm,' says Vinya. 'Fair point. Speaking of which, have you found anything else on Pangyui's murder?'

Here it is, thinks Shara. She attempts to step back into a cold veil, and keep her face still. 'No, not yet. But we are following our leads.'

'No? Nothing?'

'Not so far. But we're working on it.'

'That's interesting.' Vinya's tongue, red as a pomegranate, explores an incisor. She smiles. 'Because I know you ran a check on a bank just two days ago. You haven't mentioned that.'

Shara's blood turns to ice. *She's watching my background checks requests?*

She scrambles for an excuse. 'I did,' she says. 'I was checking on Votrov.'

'Were you?' says Vinya. 'Votrov owns several banks in Bulikov. Many much larger than the one you asked for a check on. And *that* one he owns through a rather dense tangle of channels. So I'm curious – why that bank, in particular?'

'For the reasons you just outlined. It seemed likely that if he had anything to hide, it'd be there.'

Vinya nods slowly. 'But looking for something like *that* would require a full finance check. Which you did not initiate.'

'I became distracted,' says Shara. 'So many bodies, you see.'

Both Vinya and Shara's faces hang in the window panes, staring at one another, perfectly stoic.

'It would have nothing to do, then,' says Vinya quietly, 'with how that particular bank is the closest bank to Bulikov University with safety deposit boxes, would it?'

She knows.

'Safety deposit boxes?' asks Shara. Her words drip with innocence.

'Yes. That is, after all, your most preferred method of dead drops. You tend to like the finance people. They are so process-oriented, not unlike yourself.'

'I haven't had enough time here to do anything necessitating a dead drop, Auntie.'

'No.' Vinya's eyes appear to drift backwards into her head, and Shara gets the strange and horrible feeling of being looked through. Suddenly she understands how Vinya has commanded so many committees and oversight hearings with complete confidence. 'But you would have probably taught this method to Efrem.'

I hope I am not sweating right now. 'Where are you going with this, Auntie Vinya?'

'Shara, my dear,' says Vinya slowly, 'you're not *hiding* anything from me, are you?'

Shara attempts a tiny smile. '*I* am not the one who is hiding things.'

'I am your superior. It's my job to restrict what people know. And I will tell you what this all tastes like, to me. It tastes like you have stumbled across a dead drop of Pangyui's, and you have yet to access it. But you do not wish to report it until you review its contents. However, my dear, I *must* remind you' – her words are so frosty, Shara feels like she's been slapped – 'Pangyui was *my* agent. *My* operation. I don't run many ops these days, but when I do, I make sure they stay mine. And the product of that operation, whatever it may be, goes to *me* first. *Me*, Shara. It does not get digested by another operative who just *happens* to be there, an agent *not* assigned to that operation. Not unless that operative wishes to be very abruptly pulled out of that intelligence theatre. Do I make myself clear?'

Shara blinks slowly.

'Do you understand, Shara?' Vinya asks again.

Though Shara is perfectly passive, in her head she is engaged in rigorous debate. As she sees it, she has four options. She can:

1. Tell her aunt that she's had contact with a Divinity, and thus needs access to everything Pangyui has produced. (However, this would require telling a possibly compromised official about the most dangerous intelligence breakthrough in modern history.)
2. Withhold both the Pangyui dead drop and the Divine contact from her aunt and pursue her own investigation of both. (However, this would risk being pulled from Bulikov altogether, though all her aunt seems to care about now is the Pangyui dead drop.)
3. Give up the content of Pangyui's safety deposit box to her aunt, and continue investigating the Divine contact and Pangyui's death on her own.
4. Tell Vinya she isn't going to read the material, see what the maid has to say, and then decide from there.

Right, thinks Shara. *Number four it is*.

'If I find anything produced by Efrem,' says Shara, 'rest assured that I will deliver it to you first, Auntie Vinya.'

'*Without* your review?'

'Without my review, of course. I am only interested in Efrem's operation to the extent that it could have caused his death.'

Vinya nods, and smiles widely. 'What a satisfying briefing this has been!

So much intrigue, so much history, so much culture. I believe I may send you some messengers shortly. Because I suspect that Efrem's work *did* generate some product, and I expect you will find it soon.'

Translation: I *know* it already has generated product, and I'm sending someone to get it now before you can do anything with it.

'Thank you, Auntie,' says Shara. 'I appreciate all the support you can lend.'

'Oh, absolutely, dear,' says Vinya. 'An intelligence agency is only as strong as its operatives in the field. We *must* support our overseas operatives: wherever boot soles strike the ground is where the work gets done.' She smiles again, says, 'Take care, dear, and keep me posted,' and wipes the glass with her fingertips.

As her aunt's face dissolves, Shara wonders what speech she pilfered those lines from, and mutters, 'Ta-ta.'

People tell me what a great woman I am for helping the Kaj kill the gods. They tell me this with their eyes filled with tears. They paw at my clothing, wishing to touch me. They treat me as if I am a god myself.

But I say to them, 'I did not lift a sword to the gods. I did not strike them down. I loosed not a single shaft against them. That was him, and only him. He was the only one who knew how his weapon really worked. And when he died, he took his secrets to the grave.'

As he should have. Such a thing should never be known by people.

In truth, we almost did no fighting at all on the Continent. The gods were dead, or dying. The land was dead, or dying. We saw many horrors that I cannot describe, nor would I wish to. Most of the fighting done was in our souls.

The only people we made war against on the Continent was a tribe the Continentals called the 'Blessed'. They were, I was given to understand, descendants of unions between humanity and the Divine, creatures of perverse intercourse with either the gods or the creatures of the gods. These beings rallied some of the people of the Continent, most of them sick or starving, and fought us.

The fighting was bitter, and I hated the Blessed so. They were almost impossibly hard to kill. Yet their skin was not iron, nor were they strong of arm: they were simply lucky, impossibly lucky. Their lives were charmed, for they were

the children of gods, though it seems the more they muddied their blood with that
of other mortals, the less charmed they became.

There were not charmed enough, though. We cast them down with the
others. We slaughtered their tiny armies and shed their blood in the streets. We
piled their bodies in the town squares and we set them alight. And they burned
just the same as other men and other women. And other children.

The people in the towns came outside to watch the fires. And as they watched,
I could see their hearts and hopes die within them.

I wondered if we, soldiers of Saypur, were still men, still women, on the
inside.

Such is the way of victory.

> *Memoirs of Jinday Sagresha, First Lieutenant to the Kaj*

Shara checks the clock for the sixth time, and confirms that, yes, it is still
3.30 p.m. She sighs.

This day has been spectacularly ill-timed. Sigrud was bailed out just as
the working day started, which meant that when he arrived to pick up the
University maid, she'd already gone to work – and though there are many
powers Shara can exercise in her duties for the Ministry, walking into a
woman's workplace, picking her up, and then walking out with her is
something she can't quite pull off.

She guesses it is still about an hour and a half until the maid returns to
her apartment. Shara mutters to Pitry that she's going for a walk around
the corner, and he protests, but one glance from her silences him. Still, she
wears a coat with a hood, so she's not immediately identifiable as Saypuri.

The staggered streets and alleys unscroll before her: damp grey walls,
gleaming stones and khaki ice slurry. Her nose grows raw and brittle, her
toes numb. She thought the walk would clear her head, but all the suspicions and paranoia cling to her like fog.

Then she glances up, sees the man standing in the street ahead of her,
and stops.

He wears only a pale yellow robe: he has no shoes, no hat – in fact, he is
completely bald – and no gloves. Even his arms are bare, and, like his face,
they are deeply tanned by the sun.

She stares at him. *No . . . It can't be. That's illegal, isn't it?*

The icy wind rises.

The robed man takes no notice: he sees her watching, and smiles placidly. 'Looking for something?' His voice is deep and cheery. 'Or would you be here for warmth?' He points up.

A sign above him reads: DROVSKANI STREET WARMING SHELTER.

'I'm . . . not sure,' says Shara.

'Oh. Would you perhaps be here to make a donation?'

She considers it, and finds he intrigues her. 'Possibly.'

'Excellent!' he cries. 'This way, then, and I will show you all the good work we do here. So thoughtful and kind to give to us, on such a bitter day.'

Shara follows him. 'Yes . . .'

'People rarely wish to even go out of doors, let alone give.'

'Yes. Pardon me. Might I ask you something?'

'You may ask me' – he shoves open the door – 'anything you wish.'

'Are you . . . Olvoshtani?'

He stops and looks at her with the expression of a man both confused and slightly offended. 'No,' he says. 'That would be illegal, to follow a Divinity. Wouldn't it?'

Shara is not sure what to say. The robed man smiles his glittering grin again, and they continue into the shelter.

Ragged urchins and trembling men and women crowd around a wide, long fireplace, bedecked with many bubbling cauldrons. The room is filled with coughs and groans and, among the children, miserable whimpers.

'But your robes,' says Shara. 'Your bearing . . .'

'What have they,' he asks, 'to do with the Divine?'

'They're *historically* that of an Olvoshtani.'

'And *historically* when one wished to praise the Divine, one looked up to the sky, arms outstretched.' He hauls an empty cauldron out of the kitchens and pours soup into it, with a *rap, rap, rap* as he taps his spoon against the side of the pot. 'But if a man were to do this today, in the street, would he be arrested?'

Shara looks back into the kitchens. She sees many other shelter attendants there wearing pale yellow robes, cheerily working away, all hairless, all quite exposed to the frozen air. 'So if you are not Olvoshtani,' says Shara, 'what are you?'

'We're a warming shelter, of course.'

'Well, all right, but what are *you*?'

'A person, I suppose. A person who wishes to help others.'

She tries another tack. 'Why do you not warm yourself against the cold?'

'Cold?'

'It is freezing outside. I can see men hacking holes in the ice to fish from here.'

'That is the water's affair,' he says. 'The temperature of the wind, that is the wind's affair. The temperature of my feet, my hands, that is *my* affair.'

'Because,' says Shara, remembering the old texts, 'you have captured a secret flame in your heart.'

The man stops, and appears to struggle between trying to close off his face and looking positively delighted with what she has said.

'*Are* you Olvoshtani?' says Shara.

'How can I be Olvoshtani,' says the robed man, 'if there is no Olvos?'

Then it comes to her. 'Oh,' says Shara. 'Oh, I remember this. You are . . . Dispersed.'

The robed man makes a face – *If you wish to say so.*

When the Divinity Olvos abandoned the Continent, her people did not – not completely, anyway. Jukoshtan and Voortyavashtan were the first cities to record sightings of people resembling Olvoshtani priests, wearing yellow or red robes and sporting no other adornments – not shoes or gloves, or even hair – only too happy to expose themselves to the elements. These people appeared nomadic, travelling through villages and cities, walking the Earth with apparently no other agenda than to help people when they most desperately needed it. Yet they did not claim to be Olvoshtani, or priests, or part of any higher order: though some called them the 'Abandoned' or the 'Dispersed,' they did not declare themselves to be anything at all. 'We are here,' they were known to say. 'What more is there to be?'

'I am afraid you are mistaken,' says the robed man. 'We do not claim that name.'

'No, you wouldn't,' says Shara. 'You reject names, don't you?'

'There is nothing to reject. Names are other people's affairs. They are things to help people identify the things that they themselves are not.'

'So what are you doing, here in Bulikov? For what reason are you here?'

He gestures to the throngs of miserable people huddling by the fire. Some are families, with young children; a father pulls off his infant's tiny boots to bare her blueish feet to the warmth. 'This,' says the robed man, now without a trace of joy, 'seems reason enough.'

'So you live to offer hope, as the old texts say. To be a light in dark places.'

'Old texts say many things. *You* say *these* things as though they are special – as if it is unusual for one person to see another in pain, and wish to help. As if,' he says quietly, 'to do the extraordinary – or what you think is extraordinary – a person must be *told* to do so, by the Divine.'

'Well, don't you?'

'Do you? You have not donated yet, but if you did, would it be because you were told to?' He picks up a lump of black bread.

'No.'

'Do you – a Saypuri, obviously – need a Divinity to live your life?'

'That's different. We're from different countries.'

'I never saw a country before,' says the robed man. 'All I saw was the earth under my feet.'

'You do these things,' says Shara, insistent, 'because Olvos told you to.'

'I have never met Olvos,' he says. He spears the black bread with a thick wire, and holds it over the coals. 'Have you?'

'You would not be here, without Olvos,' says Shara. 'Olvos started your order. Without her, this shelter would not exist.'

'If this Olvos whom, if I recall, I am not legally allowed to acknowledge ever existed . . .'

Shara, irritated, impatient, waves her hand.

'. . . was ever here, then the greatest thing she ever gave us was the knowledge that we did not *need* her to do good things. That good can be done at any time, anywhere, to anyone, by anyone. We live our lives thinking up so many rules – ' he twists off some of the bread and, as the crust splits, a tiny bloom of steam rises up – 'when often things can be so simple.'

He offers the piece of steaming bread to her, and smiles. 'A bite? You look cold.'

Before she can answer, Pitry comes running down the street, calling for her. Shara flips him a ten-drekel piece – he snatches it out of the air with shocking speed, smiling – and she hurries out.

He still follows his god, in his own way, she thinks. Which begs the question: who else in Bulikov is doing the same thing, but with far less benevolent intentions?

The old woman sits in the embassy hallway, eyes beetroot-red from weeping. Her upper lip glistens with snot in the lamplight. Her knuckles are purple from ages of soaking in soap and water.

'That's her?' Shara asks quietly.

'That's her,' says Sigrud. 'I am sure.'

Shara watches her closely. So, this is one of the two expert agents who were watching them at the University just yesterday: Irina Torskeny, University maid from Pangyui's offices, who perhaps moonlights as a Restorationist. Could this sad old creature somehow be complicit in Efrem's death?

Shara frowns, sighs. *I really cannot afford a second botched interrogation*, she thinks. 'Put a table and two chairs in the corner of the reception hall, by the window,' she tells Pitry. 'Brew some coffee. Good stuff – vitlov, if you have it.'

'We do, but it's expensive,' says Pitry.

'I don't care. Do it. Get our best porcelain, too. Quick as you can.'

Pitry scampers away.

'She thinks you are about to kill her,' says Sigrud softly.

'Why would she think a thing like that?' asks Shara.

He shrugs.

'She didn't put up a fight?'

'She came,' says Sigrud, 'as if she'd been expecting it all day.'

Shara watches the old woman a moment longer: Irina tries to wipe away her tears, but her hands tremble so much she resorts to using her forearm. *How much more I would prefer it*, Shara thinks, *if she were just some simple thug*.

When the reception hall is arranged, Pitry leads the old woman over to where Shara waits, seated before a small, modest table bearing two teacups, saucers, biscuits, sugar, cream and a steaming pot of coffee. Despite the cavernous space, this corner now has the atmosphere of someone's tidy front room.

'Sit,' says Shara.

Irina Torskeny, still sniffling, does so.

'Would you like some coffee?' Shara asks.

'Coffee?'

'Yes,' says Shara. She pours a cup for herself.

'Why would you give me coffee?'

'Why wouldn't we? You are our guest.'

Irina considers it, and nods. Shara pours her a cup. Irina sniffs the steam uncurling from the tiny cup. 'Vitlov?'

'I'm eager to hear your opinion of it,' Shara says. 'So often the people we serve feel obliged to compliment everything we do. It's polite, but not quite honest – do you see?'

Irina sips it. She smacks her lips. 'It is good. Very good. *Surprisingly* good.'

Shara smiles. 'Excellent.' Then her smile grows slightly sad. 'Tell me – why were you crying?'

'What?'

'Why did you cry just now?'

'Why?' Irina thinks, and finally says, 'Why would I *not* cry? There are only reasons to cry. This is all I have now.'

'Have you done something wrong?'

She laughs bitterly. 'Don't you know?'

Shara does not answer; she only watches.

'Looking back, I have done nothing *but* wrong things,' says Irina. 'Everything, all of it . . . it has been a huge mistake. This is what they need of you, isn't it? This is what idealists and visionaries ask of you – to make their mistakes for them.'

'Who have you made mistakes for?'

Again, the laugh. 'Oh, they are too clever to allow an old thing such as me to know too much. They knew I was – how should I say? – a risk. A necessary one, but a risk. Oh, my mother, my grandmother . . . I think of how they would feel to look at me now, and I—' She almost begins crying again.

Before she can, Shara asks, 'Why were you necessary?'

'Why? I was the only one who worked with him, wasn't I?'

'The professor?'

She nods. 'I was the only person who had access to his affairs behind the University walls. And they came to me, and they said, "Are you not a proud child of Bulikov? Does not the past burn in your heart like a smouldering cinder?" And I said yes, of course. They were not surprised, or gracious – I expect people say yes to them a lot.'

Shara nods sympathetically, though internally she is rapidly recalibrating her approach. She has dealt with sources such as this woman only a few times before: people so angry, so worn down, so anxious that the information comes spilling out of them in a dangerous flood. Questioning her will be like riding a rabid horse.

She tries a calmer tone. 'What is your name?'

Irina dries her eyes. 'Do you not know it?'

Shara gives her a sad look that could mean anything.

'My name is Irina Torskeny,' says the old woman softly. 'I am a University maid. I have worked soap and water into those walls, into those floors, for twenty-four years of my life. I was here when it was built – *re*built. And now I feel I will die and those stones shall forget me.'

'And you worked with Dr Pangyui?'

'*Worked*? Pah. You say it as if I was his colleague, his peer. As if he consulted me, saying, "Here, Irina, take a look at this." I was his *maid*. I picked up his teacups. Swept his floor, polished his brass, dusted his bookshelves . . . all those bookshelves.' Her righteous bitterness recedes. 'Will you kill me?'

'Why would we do something like that?'

'For his death. For allowing your countryman to die.'

' "Allow"? It doesn't sound like you killed him.'

'No. No, I did not do the deed. But I think I . . . I think I made it happen.'

'How, Irina? Please tell me.'

She takes a breath, coughs. 'He had only been at the University a few days before they contacted me. They came to my apartment. I had gone to meetings, you see. Rallies for people who did not wish to deal with sh— . . . Saypuris any more.'

Shara nods. She understands, and Irina sees she understands.

'Do you hate me for this?' asks Irina.

'I might have, once,' says Shara, in a moment of such honesty that she surprises herself.

'But you don't now?'

'I don't have the time or the energy to hate,' says Shara. 'I only wish to understand. People are what they are.' She smiles weakly and shrugs – *What can one do?*

Irina nods. 'I think that is a wise way to look at things. I was not so wise. I went to these meetings. I was angry. We all were. And these men found me there.'

'Who?'

'They never told me their names. I asked, but they said it was not safe. They said they were in danger, always in danger. From who, they did not say.'

'How many were there?'

'Three.'

'What did they look like?'

Irina describes them, and Shara takes notes. But her descriptions for the first two – short, dark-eyed, dark-haired, excessively bearded – could describe almost any man in Bulikov. But the last one is different.

'He was tall,' Irina says. 'And pale. And terribly starved. It was like he ate only broth, the poor thing. He could have been quite handsome, if he took care of himself. He spoke the least. He only watched me, really. Nothing I said seemed to surprise him. They knew I worked at the University – how, I don't know. But they asked me to serve them, to serve Bulikov. Just like the old days. And I did.' Irina coughs again. 'I was to spy on him, the professor. I was to pilfer his pages, open his drawers, look among his folders.'

'For what?'

Irina colours, but does not answer.

'What were you looking for, Irina?'

'*I* was not going to look for anything.'

'Then how were you to know if you'd found something?'

Irina turns an even brighter red. 'I would just . . . I would just have to *guess*.'

'Why?'

'Because, the words' – she is on the verge of tears again – 'I look at them on the page, and they don't make sense to me.'

'What do you mean?'

'I was never taught such a thing, you see? We had no school here, in Bulikov, when I grew up. And when they brought schooling to us, I was too old, and I could never figure it out. I could only pretend. I would hold a book, and pretend to look at it, and . . .' She purses her mouth, giving Shara the strong impression of a humiliated child. 'I *tried*.' She reaches into her pocket, and pulls out a crumpled up piece of what looks like anti-Saypuri propaganda. 'I tried to learn. I *wanted* to learn to be righteous. I wanted to know. But I could only ever pretend.'

Shara is not surprised; much of the Continent is still illiterate. 'So what did you do, when they asked you to spy on him?'

'I told them I would. I did not want to let them down. And I . . . I hated him. I hated the professor, always so giddy to be reading our histories, when we, when I . . .' She trails off. Then, 'What I chose to bring to them was a list.'

'A list of what?'

'I do not know. The professor worked from this list *all* the time, so I knew it had to be important. But to me, it was just a list, with lots of information. Many squares, going all across the page, up and down, side to side, with letters and numbers in them. I did this over a period of weeks. I could not take it *out* – he would know if I did, and he only had pieces of this list at a time – so I would sneak out one page, maybe two, or three or four, and take it to the broom cupboard and copy it, sketching it. The first time was hard, but after that I could do it in minutes. Even if I didn't know how to read, I knew how to copy,' she says with a slight sniff of vanity. 'Then I would bring them the copies.'

'How many copies of pages did you bring them?'

'Dozens. Maybe more than a hundred, over the course of many weeks. I was quite good at it,' she says, pleased with herself. 'And they were *so* pleased when I first brought it to them. They were overjoyed. They *wept*. I felt . . . I felt . . .' She trails off, unable to finish the thought.

'Why did you stop?'

'They asked me to. Not at first – but after the first time, when I brought them copies, they were less and less pleased. "Oh, this is good, but it is not what we were looking for, not what we need at all." As if it was all my fault! But then, one day, the tall pale one, he saw something on the list, and he did not *smile*, exactly, but his eyes, they crinkled, and he nodded. And the men laughed and said, "Good! Good, good, very good." As if they'd found what they needed. And they never asked me to get anything else again.'

Shara feels an immense dread welling up in her throat. 'What day was this?'

'Day? I am not sure.'

'Month, then.'

'It was still warm. It must have been late autumn. The Month of Tuva, I think.'

'Is there *anything* else you can tell me about this list?'

'I do not know anything more than what I said.'

'You copied it. You copied hundreds of pages of it.'

Irina thinks. 'Well. There were page numbers.'

'*Besides* those.'

'Besides those, there was . . . there was a stamp in the corner. No, not a stamp – a sign of some kind, in the corner of every page. Like a . . . a bird on top of a wall.'

Shara is quiet. Then, 'Did it have a crest on its head? And did it have its wings outstretched?' She holds out her arms to show her.

'Yes. I had never seen a bird quite like it.'

That's because it lives only in Saypur, thinks Shara, who knows this insignia well. *There could be only one list bearing the stamp of the Polis Governor's Office that would excite the Restorationists so much.*

'What does it all mean?' asks Irina.

'I'm not sure yet,' says Shara.

'I thought I hated the professor,' says Irina. 'But when I was told he was dead, I realised I never really did. I *wanted* to hate him. But I hated things far larger than him. I hated feeling so . . . humiliated.' She looks at Shara, her eyes wet with fresh tears. 'What will you do with me? Will you kill me?'

'No, Irina. I am not in the business of hurting innocents.'

'But I am *not* innocent. I got him *killed*.'

'You cannot know that. As you said, you hated things far larger than you – and I think things far larger than you or me, or even the professor, are in play here.'

Irina looks hopeful, relieved. 'Do you think so?'

Shara tries not to let her face hint at her dread. 'I know so.'

Then both women look up as shouts echo up from the street outside: '*Let me through! Let me through!*'

'What is that?' says Irina.

Shara leans over and pulls a curtain aside with a finger. There is a small crowd that has gathered before the embassy gates: Shara can see the glimmer of a golden sash, suggesting a City Father; numerous official-looking men in off-white robes; and before them, on the inner side of the gates, is Mulaghesh, arms crossed, feet fixed in a martial pose, emanating contempt like a fire makes smoke.

Shara smiles at Irina. 'Excuse me.'

Shara can hear the bellowing before she even exits the front doors. 'This is a political and ethical travesty, do you hear me!' shouts a man. 'A crime that verges on a declaration of *war*! Grabbing a woman from her home? An old maid, who's spent her life serving one of Bulikov's most beloved and revered institutions? Governor, I *insist* you step aside and release her immediately! If you do not, I will do everything in my power to guarantee this becomes an international incident! Am I clear?'

Mulaghesh mutters something back, but it is too quiet to hear.

'Attack? *Attack*?' the man's voice answers. 'The only attack we should be concerned with is the attack on the rights and privileges of the citizens of Bulikov! And allow me to remind you, Governor, the only blood shed today was Continental! You Saypuris might claim fear and alarm, but I note it was not *your* children who died.'

Shara crosses the courtyard. She can see Sigrud lurking in the shadows, leaning up against the embassy wall. The City Father outside grips the bars of the gate as prisoners do their cell doors. He is tall, for a Continental, and his face is brown and bright red: Shara imagines a potato that has been glazed and fired in a kiln. Half of his face, however, is concealed behind a thick, woollen beard that almost climbs up to his eyes.

Shara recognises him. *The photo in the paper*, she thinks, *does not do the real Ernst Wiclov justice.*

Behind him stand at least twelve bearded men in the plain, off-white robes of Bulikovian advocates. Each of them observes Mulaghesh with small, unimpressed eyes, and in their right hands they carry leather brief-cases like most men would swords.

Now we must deal with lawyers, too, thinks Shara. *If I were to die now, I'd count myself lucky.*

'As this embassy is technically Saypuri soil—' says Mulaghesh.

Wiclov laughs. 'Oh, I am *sure* you would be delighted to see all the world called Saypuri soil!'

'As this embassy is part of Saypur,' says Mulaghesh, through gritted teeth, 'we have no obligation to inform you of who is, or who is not, on our property.'

'But you do not have to! For my own friends and colleagues personally observed the woman being brought here!'

Shara glances at Sigrud, whose brow is furrowed in concern: normally he can spot nearly any tail, so if anyone escaped his watch, then they must be talented indeed.

Wiclov continues. 'I tell you, Governor Mulaghesh' – he intentionally butchers the pronunciation of her name – 'if a child of Bulikov is harmed or threatened by your familiars in any way, then the streets will ring with calls to tear down your embassy, and your quarters, and to cast you out as we should have done years ago!'

'You can cut the rhetoric, Wiclov,' says Mulaghesh. 'There's no crowd. There's just you, me and an empty courtyard.'

'But there *will* be a crowd if you do not release that woman! I guarantee that there will be *riots* if that poor woman is not released!'

'Released? Anyone who's here is here voluntarily.'

'Voluntarily! After being visited by *that*?' Wiclov points a finger at

Sigrud, who scratches his nose, bored. 'This is intimidation! Threats! How is that any different than capturing her?'

Shara clears her throat and says, 'You are mistaken, sir. Mrs Torskeny has been having coffee upstairs with me. I can personally testify to that.'

He shifts his scornful gaze to her. 'And who are you? Oh, are you the replacement for that vile oaf Troonyi? Are you to interject yourself into frivolous parties, to dribble gin upon the floor and bray with laughter at worthless frippery? If so, then I no more accept your authority in this matter than I would a drunken simpleton!'

Shara blinks slowly. It has been a while since she's been spoken to like that. She asks, 'You would be Ernst Wiclov, I take it?'

He nods savagely. 'I know my name must be on one of your lists somewhere. "Enemy of Saypur", I am sure. I am *proud* to wear the target you lay upon my chest!'

'Quite the opposite, sir,' says Shara. 'I only read about you in the paper last night.'

Mulaghesh covers her mouth to prevent a laugh.

Wiclov colours. 'Insolence is one of the rare things your kind actually excels in,' he says. 'Little miss, neither you nor your Governor can lie your way out of this. There are no diplomatic tricks to play. The facts are plain: you are holding a citizen of Bulikov hostage, almost certainly as an act of petty revenge for the scuffle last night!'

'Scuffle?' says Mulaghesh. 'Sixteen people are dead. *Violently* dead. I was there, I saw the bodies. Did you?'

'I do not need any further confirmation,' he says, 'of your people's barbarism.'

'First a scuffle, now barbarism,' says Mulaghesh.

'The matter is moot,' says Wiclov. 'Do you have a woman named Irina Torskeny on your property? If you persist in lying, and claiming that you do *not*, then I and my colleagues shall make the case at the highest level that your actions are in violation of multiple international treaties! Your names and your careers shall be *dragged* through the streets! I shall personally see to it that you are banned from our lands, never to return again! Does *that* make sense to you?'

Shara grimaces. She is not, of course, intimidated by such ridiculous bluster: but Wiclov appears quite talented at attracting undue attention, and that is not something she needs right now. Ever since her visions in the jail cell, Shara has felt like she is sitting on a drum of volatile explosives, and people keep trying to kick the drum over.

'Ah!' shouts Wiclov suddenly. 'There she is! There she is!'

Everyone turns round. Shara's heart drops when she sees Irina Torskeny peeping out from the embassy front doors.

'Do you see!' shouts Wiclov. 'Do you see her? She *is* being held captive! I told you so! That's her, is it not?'

Shara marches over to Irina, who is staring at Wiclov with wide, awed eyes. 'Irina, you should not be downstairs,' says Shara. 'It isn't safe.'

'I heard my name,' she says softly. 'Is that a *City Father*? Is it City Father *Wiclov*?'

'Do you know him, or any of these men?' asks Shara quietly.

Irina shakes her head. 'Are they asking for *me*?'

'Irina!' shouts Wiclov. 'Do not listen to her! Come over to me, Irina! Do not listen!'

'I believe someone was watching your apartment,' says Shara. 'They were tracking you, keeping tabs on you, even after you did work for them.'

'Irina! Walk to us! Ignore her!'

'I would advise you not to go with them, Irina. I do not know why they are here for you, but I can't think it's honest.'

Irina stares across the courtyard.

Wiclov rattles the bars on the gates. Mulaghesh snaps at him to stop it, but Wiclov shouts, 'They mean you harm, Irina! They mean to do you and Bulikov ill! Do not listen to that silly woman!'

'Irina, I would *not* advise it,' says Shara. 'The men behind these actions are terribly dangerous. You know that.'

'But a City Father would never—'

'I can hear you!' says Wiclov – an obvious lie. 'I can hear you talking to her, telling her to give up her rights as a child of Bulikov! Do not listen to her, Irina Torskeny!'

'Irina,' says Shara. '*Think.*'

But Wiclov continues, 'She is not of your race, of your people! And she is not sacred, like you and I, and all your brothers and sisters. Saying such a thing violates their laws, but you know in your heart it is true!'

Irina looks up at Shara, and Shara can tell she's made up her mind. 'I'm . . . I'm sorry,' she whispers, and she crosses the courtyard.

Wiclov rattles the bars again, bellowing for Mulaghesh to open the gates. Mulaghesh looks to Shara. Shara tries to think of something, anything, but nothing comes. Mulaghesh nods stiffly, face bitter, and machinery begins clanking and wheels start spinning, and slowly the gates draw back.

> *To stretch your years across the waves,*
> *To bend your soul across the cliffs,*
> *To wash your hands in blood and salt,*
> *To close your eyes to the chorus of wood.*
>
> *We are a blade in the wind,*
> *An ember among the snow,*
> *A shadow under the waves,*
> *And we remember.*
>
> *We remember the sea-days, the river of gold,*
> *Days of happy conquest, treasure unending.*
> *They called us barbarians,*
> *But we knew we lived in peace.*
>
> *For violence we know all too well,*
> *Violence, our unwelcome friend.*
> *How long we lived in its shadow*
> *Until the kings pulled us from its depths.*
>
> *From the window a dart of steel,*
> *From the torch a guttering flame*
> *To creep up rafters, crawl across thatch,*
> *A cry in the dark, unanswered.*
>
> *We lost him, we lost his family,*
> *Our family, for we have lost our king.*

We could not even mourn his passing.
They spirited Harkvald's body away,
Fed it to the waves, to the creatures of the sea,
Fed it to the harvest from which we fed our children.

Red days these are now, dark days,
Days of piracy and lawlessness,
Days of warfare never-ending,
Days of empty shores and full graves.

We remember him. We remember his family,
We remember his lost son.
We remember the Dauvkind.

And we know, one day,
He will return
And save us from ourselves.

                    Anonymous Dreyling song, 1700

What history tells us

Shara stands in the courtyard, watching the small crowd depart. Mulaghesh and Sigrud slowly cross over to her. 'Well,' says Mulaghesh, 'that didn't go well.'

Shara agrees — in fact, the past thirty-six hours have not gone well at all. In her opinion, they have been nothing short of disastrous.

She reviews the situation: the Restorationists know about the Unmentionable Warehouse. Worse, it sounds very likely that they've learned of something *in* the Warehouse that would be quite terribly useful. *The question is*, thinks Shara, *have they somehow managed to get inside the Warehouse yet? And if they have, have they started using whatever it is they've found? Is that why I contacted that Divinity?*

And stranger still: *Why kill Pangyui after they've got their hands on what they wanted from him? Especially if it brings 'bad people' to Bulikov.*

Shara rubs her eyes. A tiny growl of frustration squeaks out of her throat.

Pitry coughs from the doorway. 'Are . . . are you okay?'

'No,' says Shara softly. 'No, I am not.'

'Is there anything I can get you?'

Shara's index and thumb find the webbing of her opposite hand, and she pinches, hard. The dull pain fails to break through the ice currently solidifying in her mind.

Only one thing to do, then.

'I need,' she says, 'a knife.'

'What?' says Pitry.

'A knife. A very sharp one.'

'Uhh,' he says, alarmed.

'And an iron skillet.'

Mulaghesh cocks her head. 'What?'

'And two fresh onions, parsley, salt, pepper, paprika – and about three pounds of goat, I think.'

Sigrud groans and covers his face.

Shara ignores him, and walks back into the embassy. 'Come on,' she says, and waves to them.

'What?' says Mulaghesh. 'What the hells?'

Sigrud grumbles for a moment, but reluctantly explains. 'She always cooks, when she is really angry.'

Shara stops, and points at Sigrud without looking. 'Are you still in touch with your contractors?'

'Of course,' says Sigrud.

'Have them follow her. And report back to us hourly.'

'Do you not wish for me to do it?'

'I need you with me,' says Shara. She marches down the embassy halls. 'We're going to sort some things out.'

'What kind of things?' asks Mulaghesh.

'Dead things,' says Shara. 'Or things that should *be* dead.'

What a pleasant thing it would be to be a knife, always eager to take the path of least resistance, always drawn to the weak points, falling through tendons and skin and rind like a blade of grass swept downstream. The knife slips and slides, skids and curls, leaving piles of tiny scrolls of orange peel, lemon peel, melon rind, like a mound of curling ticker tape. It saws slowly against flesh, parting vein and muscle, tendon and gristle, breaking the goat cutlet down until it no longer resembles any part of any living creature.

All you need is one good knife, and one good skillet, thinks Shara. *With these simple tools one can create anything*.

Shara lights a match, hunts for the gas jet. Blue flames bloom along the oven, caressing the skillet. She douses the skillet with oil, then grabs an onion.

'There were six of them, originally,' says Shara quietly. Her face flickers with the light of the gas flames. 'Or at least six that made themselves known. Olvos, the light-bearer. Kolkan, the judge. Voortya, the warrior. Ahanas, the seed-sower. Jukov, the trickster, the starling shepherd. And Taalhavras, the builder.'

Mulaghesh clenches her right fist; her knuckles emit a chorus of cracks. 'I know all this. Everyone knows this.'

'You know *part* of it,' says Shara. She stands before the ovens in the spacious embassy kitchens, which once catered to numerous social events before Troonyi oversaw the embassy's decline. Mulaghesh and Sigrud sit at the servants' table producing a small cloud of smoke, Mulaghesh with her cigarillo, Sigrud with his pipe; Pitry runs back and forth from the pantry, bringing more vegetables, spices, salted meats. 'There's a lot of it that is not taught. The Worldly Regulations might demand silence from the Continent on this subject, but there are just as many strictures about it in Saypur. Historians are permitted to publish some discoveries; others are filed away to be forgotten. Especially when it comes to the Ancients, the Most Heavenly, the Divine. All six of them sprang to life on the Continent – how long ago, no one is quite sure – all six of them built their domains here, and all six of them fought like cats and dogs for what we estimate to be over five hundred years.'

'I didn't know they fought,' says Mulaghesh. 'I thought they were allies.'

Shara's knife makes a seam on the onion's skin; she plucks at it, peels it back, then tosses the glossy outer layer away. 'They were, eventually. But at first they fought like mad, for territory, followers, anything. But sometime in the early 700s they chose to stop fighting, and unite. Shortly after that, they chose to expand. *Rapidly* expand. This would be the beginning of the Continental Golden Age, and the beginning of Saypur's slavery to the Continent. Of which we know much, of course, though we would prefer otherwise.' She pulls out a cutting board, tests its flex, and slaps it on the counter. 'But imagine the Continent like a pie – for it is roughly circular – with six pieces cut. And there, at the centre, the spoke of the wheel.'

'Bulikov,' says Sigrud. The word is a wad of smoke from his lips.

'Yes,' says Shara. She splits the onion, slaps one half down on the cutting board, and grips it hard enough that its tiny veins bleed white. The knife makes a staccato clattering; there is a wave of white blocks, and the onion appears to disintegrate. 'The Seat of the World. No one's city, and everyone's city, established when they chose to unite. After all, each Divinity had their own city. Kolkashtan for Kolkan, Taalhavshtan for Taalhavras, Ahanashtan for Ahanas, Jukoshtan for Jukov, and Voortyavashtan for Voortya. So Bulikov was meant to belong to everyone.'

'But you only listed five,' says Pitry from behind a small mountain of celery.

'That's true. Olvos did have a city, once. But she abandoned the Continent just after the Divinities opted to unite. And when she left, her followers deserted her city. They left it to be claimed, one historian recorded, by ash and dust. No one even knows where it was.'

'Why did she leave?' asks Mulaghesh.

'No one quite knows. Maybe she just wasn't a sociable Divinity. Maybe she disagreed with something. Maybe she did not wish to take part in the Great Expansion, when the Continent would conquer almost all the known world. Whatever the reason, she has faded from history: the last time anyone saw or spoke to Olvos was in 775.'

'Wait, wait,' says Mulaghesh. 'So everyone's known for all these years that one of the Divinities still exists? I thought the Kaj killed *all* of them!'

'Yes, but which ones have you been *told* he killed, specifically? In specific instances?' Shara counts off on her fingers. 'Voortya he killed in Saypur, in the Night of the Red Sands. Taalhavras and Ahanas he killed when his army first landed on the Continent's shore. And Jukov he killed in Bulikov just after capturing it. When, exactly, have you been told the definitive account of the assassination of Olvos? Or Kolkan, for that matter.'

'But . . . but everyone agrees history grew murky after the Kaj invaded,' says Mulaghesh. 'No one's entirely sure *what* happened. He could have killed Olvos or . . . or Kolkan then, right?'

'Partly true. We only know what the scraps of history tell us. We know the Kaj used his weapon – whatever it was – on the Divinities, and they vanished. But that does not necessarily mean they are gone from the present altogether. Some miracles still work. The Divine have not completely left the Continent, despite our efforts and wishes. History is even inaccurate about how the Kaj killed the ones we *know* he killed. Jukov, for example, he killed *three years* after capturing Bulikov — something that is never mentioned in conventional texts.'

'I didn't know that,' says Pitry. 'I thought Jukov was executed in the Great Purge. That's what they taught us in school.'

'That is because Jukov's evasion is not a popular subject,' says Shara. 'It makes the Kaj look weak. Jukov didn't attack or confront the Kaj's forces — he only hid from them. Yet the Kaj moved on, or perhaps he knew that sometimes you must defeat your enemy's spirit before you can defeat their body. Which was why he started the Purge.'

Shara crushes garlic with her knife, dices it and tosses it in with the onions. 'The Great Purge was not the righteous act that's often depicted in Saypuri history books. The Kaj did not use his weaponry to bloodlessly eliminate all the Divine creatures of the Continent at once. Nor did he drive them back into heaven, or into the seas.'

'Then what?' says Pitry.

'They were dragged from their homes, into the streets,' says Shara. She turns the knife over in her hands. The handle is slick and oily. 'They were corralled and driven like animals, and slaughtered in much the same way. Unlike their creators, Divine creatures may be killed via conventional means.'

Sigrud grins nastily, relishing some vicious, treasured memory.

'Bulikov, for example, is host to several mass graves,' continues Shara. 'Who knows what sort of bones we would find if we dug them up? The delicate wings of a *gityr*, Ahanas' winged ponies? The finger bones of a *hovtarik*, the twenty-fingered harpist from the courts of Taalhavras? The marred bones of a *mhovost*, the knuckle-men, Jukov's pet horror? Presuming, of course, that the Kaj and his army did not destroy them beyond recognition — which, quite frankly, I think is probably the case. Perhaps they felt justified. Had not every Saypuri lived their lives under the boot heel of these creatures? Were they not dangerous monsters? But one soldier wrote of screams of pain coming from the fires, and of how some of these creatures had the appearance and demeanour of children, and begged for mercy. Of which they received none.'

Mulaghesh is silent; her cigarillo's smoke has dwindled to a slow bleed. Sigrud runs his finger along the blade of his black knife. Pitry, lost in thought, tries to scoop the spilled flour back into its canister, with poor results.

Shara checks the rice, which has been soaking in chicken broth, and the sauce, which is dark and creamy. This she sniffs, and adds a touch of garlic. 'When the Purge came to an end, Jukov finally emerged. He had been hiding, it is said, in a pane of glass in a window – exactly what this means, I can't say. Again, I only know what history tells us. Jukov sent word to the Kaj directly, asking him to meet. Alone. To the surprise of his lieutenants, the Kaj agreed. But perhaps the Kaj had some foresight, for when he met the last Divinity, it is recorded he saw that Jukov was no threat: the Divinity was weeping uncontrollably, distraught over the death and mayhem that had been wreaked upon the Continent.'

'He should have come to Saypur, then,' says Mulaghesh bitterly. 'Then he would have been prepared for such misery.'

'Probably true. The two of them met in an abandoned temple. A ruin, really, though the reports of the Kaj's lieutenants are unclear as to exactly where this temple is, or was. They were there for most of one night. What the two of them said there, no one knows. When he did not return, the Kaj's lieutenants feared the worst. But then the Kaj emerged, having personally slain Jukov – yet the Kaj was weeping. Over what, he would not say.' Shara wipes off the knife. 'The Kaj became moody and silent after this last, final victory, and took to wine. He died of an infection less than four months later – one of the first deaths of the Plague Years, most likely.'

Sigrud snuffs and rubs his nose. He appears only mildly interested in such stories.

Mulaghesh, however, eats up every word. 'So Jukov *was* the last god killed.'

Shara salts the goat meat, then tosses it in with the simmering vegetables. 'Yes. The Plague Years came just after, the last bit of Divine protection falling away, so we know for sure that he is gone from this world.'

Mulaghesh thinks. 'It feels damn odd,' she says, 'to list Divinities as you would suspects for a robbery. As if we could go out and line them up against a wall and have the victim come in and point the criminal out. So, the only *confirmed* dead gods – or at least, the ones that other people *saw* die – are Voortya, Taalhavras, Ahanas and Jukov?'

'That would be a fair summary,' says Shara.

'Which leaves Olvos and Kolkan.'

'Yes.'

'You haven't said anything about Kolkan.'

'True. We know quite a bit about his existence. His end, though . . . no one knows that. We don't even think anyone on the *Continent* ever knew.'

'Did he also leave, like Olvos?' asks Pitry.

Shara wipes her hands clean on a rag. 'No. He did not. Or at least, we do not think so.'

'Then what happened to him?'

Shara checks the time. Twenty minutes until it's all ready.

'That,' she says, sitting down, 'is a very different story.'

'Kolkan, it is said, was a Divinity of judgement and order. He was the Man of Stone, He of the High Places, the Far Shepherd. He's depicted in many different aspects, but his most dominant appearance is as a man seated on a mountain, with both hands extended forwards, palms up. Waiting to weigh, balance and judge, you see. He was by far and away the most active Divinity out of the six. Jukov played tricks with his mortal followers, turning them into animals – wolves, sometimes, but most frequently brown starlings – and sometimes even going so far as to impregnate them, regardless of gender, if you can believe it.'

Pitry's mouth falls open, but Shara continues.

'Taalhavras and Ahanas, being builders and growers, had larger affairs, and were only broadly concerned with mortal life. Olvos, as you know, was content to leave. And Voortya *was* quite active in her own right, personally leading war parties and raids. But none of them compare to Kolkan, who was fascinated by – if not fixated on – the affairs of mortal creatures.'

Shara gently turns the goat meat over. Fat snaps and sizzles. She withdraws her hand before a gobbet of oil can leap on to her knuckle.

'Kolkan wanted nothing more than for his followers to lead a good and ordered life. After the city of Kolkashtan was established, he told his followers to come to him with any questions, any concerns, and he would be there to answer them, to judge them and to help them. And they responded quite enthusiastically. There are records of lines of people five, ten, fifteen miles long. Of people fainting, starving, growing sick and infirm as they waited. The historical accounts are vague, but it's estimated Kolkan listened to however many millions of people, judging day and night, sitting in one place, for over one hundred and sixty years.'

'By the seas,' mutters Mulaghesh.

'Yes,' says Shara. 'Historians have agreed that it probably had some effect on Kolkan. Eventually he realised that this process was not efficient. So, he ended his period of judgement, emerged from his temple and began creating edicts, based on what he had learned during his time judging.'

Sigrud pulls a cured ham from the pantry. He sits, carves off a perfect scroll with his black knife, begins chewing it, then absently saws at the rest of the hard flesh.

'Over the space of two years, Kolkan produced twelve hundred edicts. By our modern standards, they were wildly invasive, often arbitrary rules: do not stack this type of stone upon this type; a woman's hair should not be braided in this manner; these times of day are the appropriate times to speak, and these for silence; these meats can be cured, these cannot. And so on, and so on, and so on. You would think normal people would resist, and try and free themselves. But the Kolkashtanis did not. They welcomed these rules, all twelve hundred of them. For, after all, if their Divinity said they deserved them, then did they not deserve them?'

'You can't be serious,' says Pitry.

'I am quite serious. They genuinely tried to follow his edicts, no matter how bizarre. But, naturally, no one is perfect, and very few completely followed the edicts. But the *edicts* couldn't be wrong — people enjoyed being told what to do — so, at some point, Kolkan decided the issue was that there wasn't a big enough impetus to *follow* the edicts.'

Shara lifts the top off the pot of rice. A rolling bloom of steam rises up, fogging her glasses. She steps back, sets the lid down, and polishes her glasses.

'This was how the Writs of Punishment began. A living, ongoing, constantly edited document about how people should be . . . *encouraged* to follow the edicts. Over time, one sees an increasing tendency to – how shall I put this? – mar the flesh.'

'Mar?' says Mulaghesh.

'Whipping. Branding. Hobbling. Blinding. And amputation for the worst offenders – striking off the right hand of a thief, and so on. Never death. Kolkan had decreed that life was *sacred*. Even he would not violate this proclamation. One of the most prominent punishments was called the Finger of Kolkan: a small round stone that would, when touched to flesh, grow heavier and heavier and hotter and hotter. Punishers would tie down the victims, place the Finger on their leg, or stomach, or chest, or—'

There is a squeak from Sigrud's leather glove. His right hand is a trembling fist, his jaw is clenched around his pipe, the black knife is buried deep in the pork leg.

Shara coughs. 'You get the idea,' she says. 'These punishments were carried out with almost no objection. The people did not fight. They welcomed these punishments with the sober obsequiousness of the condemned.

'Over time, Kolkan's punishments and rules became more and more severe, and odder and odder. He became fixated on flesh and desire, on sexuality and lust. He wished to wholly censor these subjects. His first method of repression may be ironically familiar to any Saypuri. For he banned any public acknowledgement of the female sex or anatomy.'

'What!' says Mulaghesh. 'That's not . . . that's not like the Worldly Regulations at all! We're trying to suppress something *dangerous*!'

'And to Kolkan, there was nothing more dangerous than sexuality. Saypuri historians are not sure why he opted to suppress the *female* sex. It's a highly debated point among certain specialists. But Kolkan demanded that his clerics and saints force women to completely shroud their figures in public, and to make illegal any mention of the female anatomy, sexuality or form – any of it – in public. This was referred to as the "Excision of Impurities". It led to a darkly amusing conundrum: how do you make a law outlawing saying a thing if you are not allowed to say that thing, even in the law? The lawmakers settled on the vague term "secret femininity", which can mean anything, really. So the law allowed for either mercy, or great cruelty, depending on the arbiter.'

The chill of the jail cell, the clutch of the shadows. The young boy, whispering: *Do not tempt me with your secret femininity!*

'Things grew worse and worse. He began to insist that *all* his followers "veil their flesh" and deny themselves *all* mortal pleasures: the taste of food, drink, the feeling of naked human skin, even comfortable sleep, for all of Kolkan's followers were forced to sleep on beds of stone. Physical pleasure of any kind was not to be encouraged. And his punishments grew grotesque. Castration. Clitoridectomy. Terribly extreme amputations. And so on.

'Yet now the other Divinities began to take notice. While Divinities did have many interactions among themselves – even relationships – they were mostly happy to stay out of one another's Divine business. But Kolkan's new fixations began to spill over. For example, he insisted Bulikov adopt his personal views on sexuality – homosexuality and promiscuity, for example, which were allowed under the more permissive Divinities, became illegal in Bulikov. Jukov was a particularly passionate opponent of this, but Kolkan's perspective took root, and has never left Bulikov, despite what happened later. Eventually, Jukov convinced the other Divinities to act.'

'Act how?' asks Mulaghesh. 'You can't tell me no one knows about a second *war*.'

'No,' says Shara. 'There was no war. Because in 1442, Kolkan simply disappeared. With no explanation whatsoever.'

A pause.

'He just . . . disappeared?' asks Pitry.

'Yes.'

'Like with the Kaj's weapons?' asks Mulaghesh.

'Not quite,' says Shara. 'None of Kolkan's works disappeared. Kolkashtan remained intact. But there were a few alterations: overnight, all those who were mutilated by Kolkan's methods were suddenly whole, and healed. Except for the ones who had passed on, of course. This is strange in its own right, but the victims could *also* no longer recall ever being punished – it was as if those memories had been painted over in their minds.'

'Then how' – Sigrud rolls his eyes up as he formulates his question – 'do you even *know* they were punished?'

Shara nods. 'A fair point. It took a while, but Saypuri historians have pinpointed 1442 as a year of great historical confusion. They've tracked it regionally – all historical records, journals and testimonies in Kolkashtan and Bulikov went suddenly and completely blank for the specific years of Kolkan's punishments. We only know what we know from texts recovered far from Kolkashtan and Bulikov – these, somehow, escaped what seems to have been a historical purge.'

'And you assume it was the other four Divinities,' says Mulaghesh.

'I assume so – especially because the other Divinities did not remark upon Kolkan's sudden absence at all. We have recovered no indications of a proclamation, or explanation. They didn't even mention him. It was as if he'd simply never existed. Reality was edited – no, *overwritten*.'

'And this,' says Mulaghesh, 'do you think it was *this* that you saw? A vanished Divinity, but not a dead one?'

Shara thinks. She finally says, 'No.'

'Why not?'

'Our attackers were dressed and definitely spoke like traditional Kolkashtanis. But I have read accounts of communing with Divinities. And what I encountered in that jail cell was nothing so coherent. It was like a cacophony of voices, of images – many people in one. I do not know what to call it. Even Kolkan would have made much more sense than the thing I spoke to, I think.'

They are silent. Sigrud belches softly. 'What happened' – another belch – 'to the people?'

'The people?'

He waves a hand. 'Of Kolkan.'

'Oh. Do you know, they more or less kept doing the same things? They wore Kolkashtani robes, followed Kolkashtani precepts, even enforced the Writs of Punishment, to an extent. They had faint memories of Kolkan, and they retained his edicts – those that were not erased – and they continued doing what they'd always done. It was never as terrible and punitive as it had been under Kolkan himself, but the same perspective, the same beliefs, these persist in Kolkashtan and Bulikov even today, as you know.'

'So the reason Votrov's art show was so scandalous,' says Mulaghesh slowly, 'is because of what some mad god believed *three hundred years ago*?'

'More or less.'

She checks the time, then the goat: much of the fat has rendered out. She scoops the diced meat out and allows it to drain.

'I suppose these things are like momentum,' she says. 'Once you get started, it's hard to stop.'

Fat strikes the stove top, and sizzles like lava rushing into the sea.

Sigrud, Mulaghesh and Pitry eat like starving refugees. There is curried goat, soft white rice, fried vegetable pastries, pork-wrapped melon. Within minutes all of Shara's artful displays are reduced to ravaged scraps.

'This is' – Mulaghesh hiccups – 'amazing. This is the best curry I've had in years. As good as at home. Where did you learn to cook?'

'From another operative.' She sips her tea, but does not eat. 'You get stuck in one place a lot, during an operation. You learn to make do with what you have.'

Shara sits back, looks up. Smoke-stains trail across the stone ceiling. There is an oily sheen to them: grease deposits, no doubt, from dozens of bubbling meals.

'You are absolutely positive, beyond a shadow of a doubt, that there has been no disturbance at the Warehouse?'

'None,' says Mulaghesh around a mouthful. 'I sent a runner there just now to check. But I am confident that they don't have the resources to mount an attack on the Warehouse.'

'Why?'

'The attack on Votrov took a lot of manpower. It wasn't a distraction. If anything, it smacks of desperation to me. I don't think they could mount two such operations at once.'

'But we will increase security at the Warehouse.'

'Most definitely.'

'Inside, and outside.'

'Well, no.' Mulaghesh coughs and wipes her mouth. 'We don't have any security inside the Warehouse.'

'None?'

'No. No one goes into the Warehouse.'

'Not even patrols?'

'Even if I wanted to do patrols, I doubt if I'd be able to order anyone in there. That place is full of ghosts, Shara. What's there, we don't want to disturb.'

'But you do have a list of what's *in* the Warehouse?'

'Oh, yes. Definitely.'

'And I don't suppose,' she says slowly, 'that you have more than one copy? Since Efrem was taking out parts of the list to study, I assume you'd want a backup in case something happened to it.'

'We have two copies, yes. What are you thinking?'

'I am thinking,' says Shara slowly, 'that Irina Torskeny told me she copied around a hundred pages from the list before the Restorationists found either what they were looking for, or something that would be useful to them.'

'So?'

'So. We know it was the *last* few pages they were interested in. Once they found what they were looking for, or what would help them, they stopped. This occurred in the Month of Tuva, according to Irina. So we simply need to pull the segments of the list that he checked out during that period—'

'And we'll know what it is the Restorationists found! Of course! Damn, that's brilliant!'

'No, it's narrowing it down from a needle in a haystack to a needle in a slightly smaller haystack,' says Shara. 'From what Irina told me of this list, there are dozens of entries on each page. So we would be reducing the quantity from thousands of entries to check to . . . oh, maybe only a few hundred.'

Mulaghesh's face falls. 'A few hundred?'

'It's a starting point, at least,' says Shara. 'And speaking of Irina . . .' She turns to look at Sigrud.

'We are watching,' says Sigrud.

'You're certain of the men you hired?'

'I know what we are paying them,' he says. 'For a job this simple, it will be no trouble. She's been returned to her house, I am told. They have left her there, alone. And we are watching.'

'You must make sure not to miss her. She's one of our last solid leads. And we must keep a close eye on Wiclov.'

'We' – Sigrud pulls his knife free of the ham shank – 'are watching.'

Shara taps the side of her teacup. *Sit on your leads*, the saying goes, *until they crack under your weight.*

'If you only drink tea when you work,' says Mulaghesh, 'I advise you switch to coffee. I see a lot of work in our future, and coffee packs more punch.'

'Coffee refreshes the body,' says Shara. 'Tea refreshes the soul.'

'And is your soul so bruised?'

Shara opts not to respond.

'Aren't you going to eat?' says Pitry. 'Have some before we eat it all.'

'We could never eat all this,' says Mulaghesh.

'Mm. No,' says Shara, through the fog of thought.

'Why? Aren't you hungry?'

'That's not the issue. I tend to find,' says Shara as she refills her tea, 'that the taste reminds me a little too much of home. If I want a taste of Ghaladesh, I prefer it to be tea.'

The coffin sits inside the shipping crate perfectly, hardly an inch of space on any side. *I wonder*, Shara thinks, *if there's a market for crates for coffins. Do so many people die overseas?*

'Do you want us to nail it shut now?' asks the foreman. He and his three employees do not bother to try and hide their impatience.

'Not just yet,' says Shara quietly. She touches the surface of the coffin: lacquered pine, something most Saypuris would never be buried in. 'Could you give me a moment, please?'

He hesitates. 'Well, the train to Ahanashtan is set to leave within an hour. If it goes out late, then . . .'

'Then they dock your pay. Yes. I will gladly pay the difference, if I make you late. A moment. Please?'

The foreman shrugs, gestures to his men, and Shara is alone in the alley behind the embassy.

There ought to be more ceremony than this, but there almost never is. Her operative in Javrat; the dockworker they turned in Kolkashtan; the peddler from Jukoshtan, going door to door selling cameras, taking pictures of the residents, ostensibly as part of his pitch . . . none of them she ever truly laid to rest. They wander in her mind still, just as they often did in life.

If I could go home with you, she tells the coffin, *just to see you rest, I would*.

She remembers when he first came to her in Ahanashtan, how delighted she'd been to see he was exactly the bright-eyed, nattily dressed little man she'd always imagined him to be.

After a day of training, he was impressed with how well read she was. 'What university did you study at? I am so sorry, I'm unfamiliar with your publications.' And when she told him that she was not published, that she would *never* be published, that her line of work was *far* outside the world of academia, he paused, thinking, and asked, 'I am sorry, I must ask. You are . . . ehm . . . Ashara *Komayd*, yes? Everyone seems a little reticent to say so. But that is the case, yes?'

Shara smiled a little, and reluctantly nodded.

'Ghonjesh and Ashadra – they were your parents?'

She stiffened, but nodded again.

He reflected on this a moment. 'I knew them, you know. Very distantly. Back in the reformist days. Did you know that?'

In what sounded like a very small voice, Shara said, 'Yes.'

'They were much more active than I was. I stayed behind my desk and wrote my letters and my articles, but they actually *went* to the slums, to the Plague areas, setting up medical tents and hospitals. I suppose they knew the danger – the Plague was so infectious – but they did it anyway. I sometimes think I was a coward, in light of what they did. A cloistered academic to the core.'

'I don't think so,' Shara said.

'No?'

'I think you . . . you changed history. You changed history when we *needed* it changed.'

He grew a little stern at this. '*Change*? No, I did not *change* anything, Miss Komayd. I told what I thought was the truth. Historians, I think, should be keepers of truth. We must tell things as they are – honestly, and without subversion. That is the greatest good one can do. And as a Ministry servant, you must ask yourself – what truth do you wish to keep?'

And after that, Shara felt he held back a little, as if he'd sniffed her out, sensed she was a creature with different values than his, maintaining an agenda and a story he knew he'd one day refute. And Shara had wished to say, *No, no, please don't spurn me – I am a historian, just as you are. I seek the truth, just as you do.*

But she could not say this, for she knew in her heart that this would be a lie.

> *I have never met a person who possessed a privilege who did not also exercise that privilege to the fullest extent that they possibly could. Say what you like of a belief, of a party, of a finance system, of a power – all I see is privilege and its consequences.*
>
> *States are not, in my opinion, composed of structures supporting privilege. Rather, they are composed of structures denying it – in other words, deciding who is not invited to the table.*
>
> *Regrettably, people often allow prejudice, grudges and superstitions to dictate the denial of these privileges – when really it's much more efficient for it all to be a rather cold-blooded affair.*
>
> Minister of Foreign Affairs Vinya Komayd,
> Letter to the Prime Minister, 1688

Another wintry morning. As Shara opens the embassy front door, the courtyard guard, up to his nose in furs, turns and says, 'He's at the front gate. We didn't let him in, because——'

'I understand,' says Shara.

She crosses the embassy courtyard, reflecting that it feels so different in the day, clean and cold and glittering, than it did the evening before, when Wiclov bayed through the bars like a guard dog. The trees bow with what looks like layers of black glass; the embassy's numerous corrosions and cracks are filled with pearly white, as if given fresh repair overnight. The mug of coffee in her hand leaves a river of steam behind like a ship leaving bubbles in its wake.

The gates rattle open. The boy stands in the embassy drive, holding a silver plate aloft. He is dressed in what she recognises as manservant's clothing, but it seems he has walked some way: his upper lip is frosted with icy snot. If he were not shivering so fiercely, the expression he makes at her could almost be a smile.

'Ambassador Thivani?'

'Who are you?' she asks.

'I . . . have a m-message for you.' He holds the silver plate out to her. In its centre is a small white card.

Shara fumbles at it with her cold hands, and squints to read:

HIS EMINENCE VOHANNES VOTROV
CITY FATHER OF THE 14TH, 15TH AND 16TH WARDS
OF THE POLIS OF BULIKOV
INVITES YOU TO A SPLENDID EVENING
TO BE HELD AT 7.30 P.M. TONIGHT
AT THE GHOSHTOK-SOLDA DINNER CLUB
SHOULD BE A LOT OF FUN

Shara crushes the card. 'Thank you,' she says, and tosses it away. *Of all the luck*, she thinks. *The one thing to break is the one thing I told Vinya I wouldn't look at.*

'Pardon, miss,' says the boy. 'I hate to interrupt, but . . . c-can I go?'

Shara glowers at him for a moment, then shoves the cup of coffee into his hand. 'Here. This'll do you more good than it will me.'

The boy trudges away. Shara turns and trudges back to the embassy front door.

A child begins crying in the street beyond the embassy. A snowball fight has taken a bad turn. One salvo contained an excessive quotient of ice, and children throng the pavements, with pointed fingers and persistent cries of: *Not fair, not fair!*

Upon the opening of the door, the interior of the Ghoshtok-Solda Dinner Club appears to be a solid wall of smoke. Shara is perplexed by this sight, but the attendants do not seem to notice: they gesture as if this dense block of fog is a perfectly welcoming sight. The outside wind comes sweeping through, turning the smoke to swirling clouds and slashing it into thin wisps, and Shara can just barely see the wink of candlelight, the sheen of greasy forks, the faces of men laughing.

Then the overwhelming reek of tobacco hits her, and she is almost blown backwards.

As she enters her eyes begin to adjust. The smoke is not quite so thick as she initially imagined, yet the ceiling remains all but invisible: chandeliers and lamps seem to be suspended from the heavens. The desk attendant looks at her – surprised, slightly outraged – and requests a name, as if he could not expect a Saypuri to provide anything more.

'Votrov,' says Shara.

The man nods stiffly – *I should have known* – and extends a sweeping arm.

Shara is led through a labyrinth of booths and private rooms and bars, each stuffed with men in suits and robes, all gleaming grey teeth and gleaming bald heads and gleaming black boots. Cigar ashes dance in the smog like red-orange fireflies. It's as if the whole place is smeared over with oil and smoke, and she can feel the smoke snuffling bemusedly at the hem of her skirt, wondering – *What is this? What alien creature has infiltrated this place? What could this be?*

Some tables go silent as she passes. Bald heads poke out of booths and watch her. *I am, of course, a double offence*, she thinks as she maintains her composure. *A woman, and a Saypuri.*

A twitch of velvet curtain, and a grand backroom is revealed. At the head of a table the size of a river barge sits Vohannes, half hidden behind a tent of newspaper and slouched in a cushioned chair with his light brown (but muddy) boots propped up on the table. Behind him, in very comfortable-looking chairs, sit his Saypuri bodyguards. One looks up, and waves and shrugs apologetically – *This wasn't our idea.* Vohannes's tent of newspaper deflates slightly; Shara spots a bright blue eye peeking over the top, then the tent collapses.

Vohannes springs up as quickly as his hip allows, and bows. 'Miss Thivani!'

He would make an excellent dance hall emcee. 'It's been less than two days,' she says. 'There's hardly need for such ceremony.'

'Oh, but there's plenty of need for ceremony! Especially when one is meeting . . . how does the saying go? The enemy of my enemy is my—'

'What are you talking about, Vo? Do you have what I asked you to get?'

'Oh, I have it. And what a *joy* it was to get. But first . . .' Vohannes claps twice. His gloves – white, velvet – bear smudges from the newsprint. 'Oh, sir, if you could, please fetch us two bottles of white plum wine, and a tray of snails.'

The attendant bows like a spring toy. 'Certainly.'

'*Snails?*' says Shara.

'Are you fine gentlemen' – Vohannes turns to the Saypuri guards – 'in need of any refreshments?'

One opens his mouth to respond, glances at Shara, rethinks his answer, then silently shakes his head.

'As you wish. Please.' Vohannes gestures to the chair next to him with a flourish. 'Sit. So glad you could make it. You must be terribly busy.'

'You have picked an interesting venue for our meeting. I believe a leper would have received a more cordial welcome.'

'Well, I figured that if I meet you at your place of work, you might as well meet me at mine. For though this place may look like a lecherous din of old fogies, Miss *Thivani*, I guarantee you, here is where Bulikovian commerce lives and dies. If one could see all the flow of finance, envisioning it as a golden river hanging above our heads, here, right here, among all this smoke and all the crass jokes, all the boiled beef and bald heads, would be where it forms its densest, most impenetrable, most inextricable knot. I invite you to look and reflect upon the rickety, shit-spattered ship that carries Bulikov's commerce forward into the seas of prosperity.'

'I get the strangest sense,' says Shara, 'that you do not *enjoy* working here.'

'I have no choice,' says Vohannes. 'It is what it is. And though it may *look* like one building, it's actually several. Any house in Bulikov is a house divided, and this house is cut to ribbons, my battleaxe. Each booth could be colour-coded for its party allegiances. You could draw lines on the floor – if the warped floorboards would allow it – highlighting barriers some club members would never dare to cross. But recently, this club – like Bulikov – is beginning to align itself around two main groups. *My* group and, well . . .'

He slaps his paper in her lap. A smallish article has been circled: WICLOV TAKES STAND AGAINST EMBASSY.

'You've been accumulating some ink, my dear,' says Vohannes.

Shara eyes the article. 'Yes,' she says. 'I have been notified of this. What do you care about it?'

'Well, I have been ruminating on ways I could help you.'

'Oh, dear.'

'And I can help you quite a lot with Wiclov.'

A waiter materialises out of the smog with a bottle of white plum wine. He proffers the bottle to Vohannes; Vohannes glances at the label, nods and lazily extends a hand, which is promptly filled with a brimming crystal glass. The waiter looks doubtfully between them, as if to say – *And do you really want me to serve her, as well?* Vohannes nods angrily, and the waiter, exasperated, gives Shara a perfunctory version of the same ceremony.

'Cheeky shit,' says Vohannes as the waiter leaves. 'Do you get a lot of that sort of thing?'

'What are you proposing, Vo?'

'What I am *proposing*, is that I can get you somewhere on Wiclov. And I would do this out of the godly goodness of my own heart . . . provided you also bury that fat bastard.'

Shara sips her wine, but does nothing more. She sees there is a suitcase sitting beside Vohannes, as white and velvet and ridiculous as his gloves. *By the seas. Have I honestly enlisted a clown as an operative?* But, she notes, there's a second suitcase on his opposite side. *Were the contents of the safety deposit box that extensive?*

'How would you get us somewhere on Wiclov?'

'Well, that's the tricky bit. I'm not the sort for sneaky, underhanded political machinations, despite what is happening . . . ah . . . right now. My style is much more' – he twirls a slender finger, thinking – 'grand idealist. I win support specifically because I *don't* dirty myself.'

'But now you are willing to do so.'

'If that fly-ridden turd of a human being is genuinely, *really* connected
to the people who attacked us, who killed Pangyui, it would not grieve my
heart excessively to see him removed from the political theatre, no. But
while I can't plant the dagger in his back, perhaps I could pass the dagger
along to someone more talented in its use.'

The waiter looms back out of the reeking mist with a large, flat stone
covered in small holes. The stone swims with butter, and the holes appear
to be stuffed with tiny beige buttons.

'What are you saying, Vo?' she asks again.

Vohannes sniffs and picks up a fork the size of a needle. 'I have a friend
in Wiclov's trading house. That's how he made his money, you
know – Wiclov is one of the few old-guard icons to actually dabble in
trade. Made his living with potatoes. Seems appropriate for him, somehow. Something that grows in the mud, away from the sun.' He spears a
snail, pops it in his mouth, grunts, and says around it, '*Haat*. Mm.' He
manoeuvres the little ball of flesh on to his teeth, breathes and swallows.
'Very hot. Anyway. I have convinced this contact within Wiclov's trading
house to pass along all investments and purchases Wiclov has made in the
past year.' He smiles triumphantly and taps the second suitcase beside his
chair. 'I am sure there is something very rotten going on under his robes,
let's say. Probably nothing smutty, unfortunately – once a Kolkashtani,
always a Kolkashtani, and Wiclov is about as Kolkashtani as they get – but
something. And I would love you to find out.'

Shara cuts to the chase. 'Is he funding the Restorationists?'

'I've taken a glance at the pages, and I admit that I haven't seen *that*,
unfortunately. Though there is some oddness that stands out.'

'Like what?'

'Like the loomworks.'

'Like . . . wait, the *what*?'

'Loomworks,' says Vohannes again. 'Wiclov has bought, outright *bought*,
three loomworks around the city. You know, the big weaving factories
they used to make rugs?'

'I understand the general idea.'

'Yes. He's *bought* them. Not cheap, either – and he hasn't changed the
names.'

'So you think he doesn't want anyone to know,' says Shara.

'Yes. But there must be *something* else in all his history. I just can't see it. But then, I don't have a massive intelligence agency behind me.'

She considers it. 'Did he buy these loomworks after the Month of Tuva?'

'Ah . . . well, I can't recall off the top of my head with complete accuracy, but I *suppose* so.'

Interesting, she thinks. 'How good is your source?'

'Quite good.'

'Yes, but *how* good?'

Vohannes hesitates. 'I know him very personally,' he says slowly. 'That should be enough for you.'

Shara almost questions him further, but then she understands. She coughs uncomfortably, and says, 'I see.'

She watches him take another sip of wine. He is sweating, and pale; suddenly he seems wrinkled and breakable, as delicate as finely made linen.

'Listen, Vo. I . . . I am going to do something I don't often do for willing sources.'

'What's that?'

'I am going to give you the chance to reconsider.'

'You what?'

'I am going to give you the opportunity to rethink what you're doing here,' says Shara. 'Because if you offer me those papers again, I *will* use them. It would be unprofessional of me not to. And when someone asks where I got them from – and they *will* ask – then I will have to tell them. I can't predict what will happen, but once this is all played out, there is a chance that, in the future, in some very public, very accessible forum in Saypur, someone will testify that Vohannes Votrov, City Father of Bulikov, provided valuable material to the government of Saypur with the full understanding that another City Father would be damned by it. And a thing like that . . . it has repercussions.'

Vohannes watches a candle flame slowly waltz on its taper.

'I've seen it before,' says Shara. 'I've lost sources this way before. I *use* people, Vo. That's what I do now. It is not pretty. It has many consequences. And . . . and if you offer me this material again, I *will* take it, because I have to. But I want you to really think about what could happen to you if you hand over that suitcase.'

Vohannes fixes his bright blue eyes on her. *They must still be*, she imagines, *the same blue as when he was an infant*.

'Come work for me,' he says suddenly.

'*What?*'

'You seem unhappy where you are.' He stabs a snail and blows on it. Droplets of butter rain on the tablecloth. 'Come work for me. It'd be a change of pace. We're not the old guard. None of my companies are. We're doing big new things. And also I can pay you perfectly despicable amounts of money.'

Shara stares at him, disbelieving, and laughs. 'You're not serious.'

'I am gravely serious. Serious as death itself.'

'I am . . . I am *not* going to work for you, Vo.'

'Then, hell, take over.' He glugs wine, eats another snail. 'It's all just a headache for me. Run my businesses. Direct my money. I'll just sit around, getting elected and, I don't know, sitting on parade floats or some such.'

Shara puts her face in her hands, laughing.

'What are you laughing about?' He gallantly tries to keep sounding serious, but his smile betrays him. 'What? I'm serious here. Come be with me.' The smile fades. 'Come live with me.'

Shara stops laughing. She winces, groans. 'Oh, Vo. *Why?*'

'Why what?'

'Why did you have to say *that*?'

'I meant . . . oh, come now, I meant live in *Bulikov*.'

'It didn't sound like it. And . . . and that's exactly what you asked me when you graduated.'

Vohannes, sheepish, looks at the Saypuri guards. 'Could you, ah, gentlemen please excuse us for a moment?'

The guards shrug, and take up stations outside the backroom door.

'That . . . Shara, that *obviously* is not what I meant,' says Vohannes. He laughs desperately.

'Is this why you invited me here? For fine dining and propositions?'

'This is *not* fine dining. I can only taste tobacco, for the gods' sakes.'

Silence. Then a throaty laugh from the next room contorts into laboured coughing.

'Bringing me back won't make us happy,' says Shara.

Vohannes, stung, sits back in his chair and stares into his glass.

'I'm not who I was,' she says, 'and you aren't who you were.'

'Why must everything be so *awkward*?' he says, now sulky.

'You're *engaged*.'

'Oh, yes, engaged.' He raises his hands, drops them – *And what does that mean?* 'We're a very merry couple. We carouse a lot. Make the papers.'

'But you don't love her?'

'Some people need love in their lives. Others, not so much. It's like buying a house: "Do you want a central fireplace? Do you want windows in your bedroom? Do you want love?" It's not part of my necessary package.'

'I don't think that's true of you.'

'Well, it's not like I have a *choice*,' he snarls. 'Have you *seen* those men when you walked in? Can you *imagine* what they would . . . ?' Again, he fights for composure. 'I'm dirtier than you know, Shara.'

'You don't know dirty.'

'You don't know *me*.' He stares at her. His cheeks tremble. One tear quivers at the inner corner of his right eye. 'I can give you Wiclov. He deserves it. Take him. Take him and burn him.'

'I'm sad to see you so happy to persecute Kolkashtanis.'

He laughs blackly. 'Don't they *deserve* it? I mean, my own damn *family*. You want to talk about persecution, why don't you talk to the people who did so with zeal for hundreds of years, even without their damn' – he glances around, lowers his voice – 'god?'

'Aren't they still your people, the very ones you want to help? Do you really want to reform Bulikov, Vo, or burn it to the ground?'

Vohannes is so struck by this he cannot speak for a moment.

'Your family was Kolkashtani?' asks Shara quietly.

He nods.

'You never told me.'

His skin grows pale and papery again. His brow wrinkles as he considers it. 'No,' he says. 'No, I didn't. I didn't feel like I needed to – most of Bulikov was Kolkashtani back then. Still is. *Lots* of the Continent still is. They got used, I suppose, to living without a Divinity. After the Kaj and the War, the transition was just so much easier for Kolkashtanis than anyone else.'

He pours off the rest of one bottle of wine, one of his rings making a chipper *tink, tink, tink* as he taps out the last drops.

'My father was a *rich* Kolkashtani, so that was even worse. To most Kolkashtanis, you show up to the world with plenty to be ashamed of – born in shame – but to the rich ones, you show up *poor*, too. Just one more thing, y'see. Strict man. If we did anything wrong, we had to go and cut a switch' – he extends his index – 'the size of our finger for him to beat us with. If we picked one too small, then *he* got to choose for us. And though he was a stingy man in life, he was never so stingy with his switches.' A glug of wine. 'My brother loved him. They loved each other, I suppose I should say. Maybe it was just because Volka was older – father always had a grudge against children for having the insolence not to act like reasonable adults. And when my father died, my brother never forgave . . . well, everything. The world. Saypur, especially – since we Continentals assumed the Plague was a Saypuri invention.

'Volka joined up with a group of pilgrims when he was fifteen, and went on a trek to the icy North to try and find some damn temple. Left me with a bunch of nannies and servants when I was nine years old. And he never came back. I got news years later that the whole bunch of them had died. Froze to death. Expecting a miracle' – Vohannes lifts his wine glass to his lips – 'that never came. Maybe I want to ruin Wiclov, sure. Perhaps he's an obstacle to the future of the Continent, for I don't see him ever wishing to see a bright new future, but rather the dead, dull, dusty past. Either way, I wouldn't shed a tear to see him go.'

Shara shuts her eyes. *How easily*, she thinks, *my corruption spreads*. 'If you offer me it again, I'll have to take it.'

'Do it, Shara. If this is what you do for a living, I'd love to see you do it to him.'

Shara opens her eyes. 'Fine. I will. I presume the contents of the safety deposit box are in the other suitcase?'

'You presume correctly.' He picks it up, slams it down on the table, and starts to open it.

'No, no,' says Shara. 'Don't.'

'What? Why?'

'I . . . made an unfortunate promise.' *And Auntie Vinya remembers what promises are made to her . . . and which ones are broken.* She wonders if she is willing to disobey her aunt, and crack the suitcase open. To do so, she feels, could bring hell shrieking down on her, especially after Vinya's threat. *A last resort, then,* she thinks, wondering if this is how fools rationalise their poor choices. 'If you can just give me the suitcase, the Ministry would be more than happy to reimburse you.'

'You want me to just *give* you the suitcase?' Vohannes is agog at the idea. 'But this luggage is worth a fortune!'

'How much?'

'*I* don't know . . . *I* didn't buy them. I have people for that.' He grumbles and inspects the suitcases. 'It *ought* to be worth a fortune.'

'Send us an invoice, and we'll compensate you accordingly.' She slides one suitcase off the table. It is only mildly heavy. *Paper?* she thinks feverishly. *Books? Some artefact?* Then she takes the other suitcase from Vo. She stands, a suitcase in each hand, and feels quite absurd, as if she is about to depart for a relaxing vacation at the beach.

'Why is it,' says Vohannes as he walks her to the door, 'that whenever we finish our business, it feels like neither of us has got what we wanted?'

'Perhaps we conduct the wrong sort of business.'

Escaping the air of the club is like swimming up from the depths of the sea. *I shall have to throw these clothes away,* she thinks. *The very fabric has been poisoned.*

'Oh,' says a voice. 'Is it . . . Miss Thivani?'

Shara looks up, and her heart plummets. Sitting in the back of a long, expensive white car is Ivanya Restroyka, face as pale as snow, lips painted bright, bloody red. She looks somehow more colourless than when Shara saw her last, at Vohannes' party. One curl of black hair escapes her fur hat to curl across her brow and behind her ear. Yet despite these carefully cultivated features, she stares at Shara with a look of unabashed shock.

'Oh,' says Shara. 'Hello, Miss Restroyka.'

Ivanya's dark eyes slide to the club door and dim with disappointment. 'So. You were the one he was meeting tonight.'

'Yes.' *Think quickly now.* 'He was making some business introductions for me.' Shara slowly walks to the car window. 'He has a lot of business he wishes to drum up with Saypur. It was very good of him to do it.' A good lie: serviceable, sound, maybe one-sixth true.

'At *this* club. The most old guard of any club in Bulikov.'

'Yes. I suppose, as they say, times are changing.'

Ivanya glances at the white suitcases and nods, obviously disbelieving. 'You knew him once, didn't you?'

Shara pauses. 'Not really, no.'

'Mm. Might I ask something of you, Miss Thivani?'

'Certainly.'

'Please . . . be careful with him.'

'I'm sorry?'

'For all his bravado, for all his bluster, he's so much more fragile than you think.'

'What do you—'

'Did he tell you he broke his hip falling down the stairs?' She shakes her head. 'He was at a club. But not a club quite like this. It was a club where men went to meet men, I suppose you could say, but . . . there the similarities end.'

Shara feels her heart beat faster. *I knew all this already. But why does it surprise me so?*

'The police raided the club the night he was there,' says Ivanya. 'Bulikov, as you probably know, has never really given up many of its Kolkashtani inclinations. Such *practices* are terribly illegal. And they were quite brutal with the people they caught. He almost died. Hips are quite difficult things to fix, you see.' She smiles sadly. 'But he never learns. That's why he got into politics, you see. He wanted to change things. It was, after all, Ernst Wiclov who ordered the raid.'

A flock of drunken men exit the club, laughing. Smoke clings to their collars in a lover's embrace.

'Why are you with him?' asks Shara.

'Because I love him,' says Ivanya. She sighs sadly. 'I love him, and I love what he is, and what he wants to do. And I wish to look out for him. I hope you want to do the same.'

Headlights splash over the long white car. Shara hears Pitry's voice calling her name from the embassy car. The door of the club opens, and Vohannes emerges, his white fur coat gleaming in the light of the lamp posts.

Ivanya smiles. 'Farewell, Miss Thivani. I wish you a good evening.'

Shara still remembers the day of that awful discovery: long ago, towards the end of the second term of her second year at Fadhuri, when she was walking up his building's stairs and Rooshni Sidthuri came rushing down them. She'd said hello, but Rooshni — mussed, sweating — said nothing back. And when she went into Vo's room, and saw him sitting shirtless in his desk chair, feet up on the windowsill and hands behind his head, for some reason warning bells went off in her mind — for he only ever seemed to do that after making love.

As they talked — innocuously enough — she sidled over to the bed. Felt the sheets.

How damp they'd been, and in one spot — right where the hips and waist would be, were you to lie upon it — just positively drenched.

How young Rooshni had hurried, as if the building was burning down.

She did not confront him then. But she began to watch. (*This is what I've always been*, she'd think, much later. *Someone who does not intervene in her own life, but only watches, and works behind the scenes*.) She watched how Vo seemed to spend so much time with young men, the way he embraced them. She watched the way he watched them, the way his posture grew more languid, relaxed around them.

Does he even know it? she wondered then. *Do I?*

And one day she could bear it no more, and she quietly walked into his apartment while he and – she cannot even remember the boy's name now, Roy something or other – moved so slowly and so gently against one another in the very bed where Vo had whispered how much he loved her in her ear not more than two days ago.

The look on their faces when she cleared her throat. The boy, hustling out of the door. Vo, screaming in rage at her, while she stood silently.

He'd wanted her to scream back at him. She could tell. But she would not give him that. This was not a fight. They had not both done wrong. She could not imagine a purer betrayal.

The worst of it was how much the boy had looked like her. Shara had never and would never possess a particularly feminine form: she had, she thought, a boy's body, all shoulders and no hips, and certainly no breasts. *Was I just a substitute?* she thought afterwards. *A way to fabricate forbidden love without ever doing anything forbidden?* And if so, she was still inadequate, unable to capture the essence of the real thing.

He begged her to say something, to respond to him, to fight back. But she had not. She walked out of his apartment and, more or less, out of his life for the remainder of their school careers.

(She is still somewhat proud of this: how tranquil she was, how cold, how maintained. And yet also ashamed: was she so shocked, so cowardly, so withdrawn that she could not even allow herself to *shout* at him?)

She threw herself into schoolwork, suddenly inflamed with a sense of patriotic discipline. He approached her after his graduation, months later, packed and ready for the train trip to the docks, and on to Bulikov. He begged her to come with him, begged her to help him be the man he so dearly wished to be. He tried to bribe her, spin a storybook lie, told her she could be a princess back in his home, if she wished. And Shara, all ice, all cold steel, had hurt him as best she could – *What I think you truly want, my dear child, is a prince. But you can't have such a thing at home, can you? They'd kill you for that* – before she shut the door in his face.

One day you'll know, her Auntie Vinya told her. *And understand. You'll figure yourself out. And things will be all right.*

One of the few times, Shara often reflects, that Auntie Vinya was quite terribly and completely wrong.

★

When I entered the hills near Jukoshtan I felt quite terribly afraid. The moon was yellow-brown, like a tea stain. The hills were stark and white, with short, twisted trees. And the ground was so uneven that it always forced you down, walking the floor of the valleys, lost in darkness. Or so it felt.

Sometimes I saw firelight flickering on the trunks of the twisted trees. There were cries in the dark: animals, or people pretending to be animals, or animals pretending to be people. Sometimes there were voices. 'Come with us!' they whispered. 'Come join our dance!'

'No,' I said. 'I am on an errand. I have a Burden. I must deliver my Burden to Jukov himself, and no one else.' And they laughed.

How I wished I was back in Taalhavshtan. How I wished I was home. I wished I had never taken this Burden from Saint Threvski. And yet, I was also curious – I do not know if it was the voices on the winds, or the sniggers from the trembling trees, or the light of the yellow moon, but Jukoshtan was a place of hidden things, of constant mystery, and I secretly wished to see more.

I turned a corner and came to a valley filled with small skin huts. A bonfire roared in their centre. People danced around the fire, shrieking and singing. I shrank up against a tree and watched, horrified, as people copulated frenziedly on the sandy ground.

I heard someone step behind me. I turned, and saw an old man was standing on the path behind me, dressed in regal robes. His hair was braided and tied up to stand upon his head, as many respectful Taalhavshtani gentlemen did then.

He apologised for startling me. I asked him his business, and he said he was a trader from Bulikov. I could tell he thought me the same, from my Burden.

'A savage bunch, are they not?' he asked.

I told him I could not understand how they lived this way.

'They believe themselves free,' he said. 'But in truth, they are enslaved to their desires.'

He told me his tent was nearby, and well-hidden, and he offered me shelter in this strange place. He seemed a kind old thing, and I accepted, and followed him through the bent trees.

As he walked he said, 'I sometimes wish I was younger. For I am old, and not only am I frail of flesh, but I am bound by the many things I have been taught over the years. Sometimes I wish I had the courage to be so young, so loud, so unfettered and so unburdened.'

I told him he should be proud of himself to have lived to such an age without indulging in corrupt impulses.

'I am surprised,' he said. 'A creature as young as you, and you are wholly uninterested in such forbidden wildness?'

I told him I was repulsed by it — a lie, I knew.

'Do you not wonder if slavery to one's desires could, just a little, make you free?'

I felt myself sweating. My Burden felt so heavy around my neck. I admitted that my thoughts sometimes strayed to forbidden places. And that tonight, they seemed to stray to such places more frequently.

He turned sharply below the dark canopy of trees. I could no longer see him, but I followed his voice.

'Jukoshtan, the city itself, is also a forbidden place, in a way,' said his voice from ahead. 'Did you know that?'

I passed the old man's robes, lying on the sandy ground — discarded, it seemed, as he walked.

A flock of brown starlings took flight from the trees ahead, soaring up into the night sky.

'It moves, shifts,' said his voice. 'It dances through the hills.'

I passed a wig, hanging from a tree — the old man's braided hair.

'It is never where one expects it to be,' said his voice.

I passed a flap of cloth hanging from a bush. Yet it was not cloth, but a mask — a mask of the old man's face.

His voice floated through the trees. 'Much like Jukov himself.'

I entered a clearing. In the centre of the clearing was a low, long tent of animal skins. On the branch of every tree in the clearing sat a small brown starling, and each watched me with dark, cold eyes.

I could see footprints leading up to the tent's entrance. I followed them, and stood before it.

'Come inside,' whispered a voice, excitedly, 'and lay down your Burden.'

I hesitated. Temptation spoke to me. And I listened.

As the starlings watched, I took off my robes, and stepped out of my sandals. I shivered, naked, as I felt the cool wind on my skin. Then I stepped inside.

This was how I came to know Jukov, Sky-Dancer, Face-Peddler, Lord of Song, Shepherd of Starlings. And before he ever touched me, I think I already loved him.

Memoirs of Saint Kivrey, priest and 78th wife-husband of Jukov, circa 982

Survivors

Mulaghesh runs.

She runs over the frozen hills, through muddy roads, around dank forests. She runs though her breath burns in her chest and her legs protest with each step.

At forty-eight, she knows she will soon be beyond the age when she can do this to herself. *So I had better enjoy it while I can*, she thinks. *If I really want to do this.* She likes running because it is the purest combat sport possible – the only thing you're fighting is yourself, with every step. And it's been so long since she really fought anyone (her still-dark eye aches a little with each footfall), so maybe this is the only kind of fighting she can do now.

It has been nearly a week since she last saw Shara Komayd, but Mulaghesh cannot stop thinking about what the 'ambassador' told her. *By the seas, I hope that girl's wrong*, she thinks. The thought saps her of her strength – the next hill feels so much harder than the last – yet she cannot stop thinking about it.

One of the gods is alive. Maybe they never really left at all.

Mulaghesh, like everyone in the military – everyone in Saypur – grew up wanting to be the Kaj. Yet now that she just might get her opportunity, the idea terrifies her. Every child of Saypur grew up with the Divinities pacing just past the border of their nightmares: huge, dark unmentionables swimming in the deeps of history. Shara talks about them as if they were politicians or generals, but to Mulaghesh and the rest of Saypur, they will always be the bogeyman's bogeyman, beings so dreaded that merely mentioning their names feels like an illicit and terrible act.

Give me a real war any day, she thinks. *Something with trenches and bolts.*

Something human. Something that bleeds. As a veteran of the Summer of Black Rivers, Mulaghesh must see the irony in wishing for those awful days of mud and thunder, and the struggle in the dark. A short, glorious war, as all Saypuris agree, but one Mulaghesh wishes she'll never see again.

Still. Better that than this.

How confident that young girl is. Has she read so much? Or is that what it's like to be a descendant of the Kaj?

Yet Mulaghesh remembers how, the day after, young Shara Komayd trembled under her blanket, trying to concentrate on holding a cup of tea . . .

By the seas, she thinks again, *I hope that girl's wrong.*

She trots back into her quarters to find a small stack of papers on her desk. There is a note on the seat of her chair from one of her lieutenants: 'Pulled the records, here are the pages checked out that month. Took a while. Might want to give the kids a day off . . . only a suggestion.'

She examines the papers: there are twenty pages from the list of items in the Unmentionable Warehouse.

Mulaghesh has never looked at this list – she never wanted to – but she casts an eye over a page now, reviewing notes written decades ago by the now-dead Saypuri soldiers who locked all these things away:

368. Shelf C5-158. Glass of Kivrey: Small marble bead that supposedly contains the sleeping body of Saint Kivrey, a Jukoshtani priest who changed gender every night as part of one of Jukov's miracles. Miraculous nature – undetermined.

369. Shelf C5-159. Small iron key: Name is unknown, but when used on any door the door sometimes opens on to an unidentified tropical forest. Pattern has yet to be determined. Still miraculous.

370. Shelf C5-160. Bust of Ahanas: Once cried tears that possessed some healing properties. Users of the tears also had a tendency to levitate. No longer miraculous.

371. Shelf C5-161. Nine stone cups: If left in a place where they receive sun, these cups would refill with goat's milk every dawn. No longer miraculous.

372. Shelf C5-162. Ear of Jukov: An engraved, stone door frame that contains no door. Iron wheels on the base. Speculated that it has a twin and, no matter where the other Ear is, if the doors are operated in the correct manner one can pass through one door and come out of the other. We speculate that the twin has been destroyed. No longer miraculous.

372. Shelf C5-163. Edicts of Kolkan, books 783 to 797: Fifteen tomes mostly dictating Kolkan's attitudes on dancing. Total weight: 378 pounds. Not miraculous, but content is definitely dangerous.

373. Shelf C5-164. Glass sphere: Contained a small pond and over-hanging tree Ahanas was fond of visiting when she felt troubled. No longer miraculous.

Twenty pages. Nearly two hundred items of a miraculous nature, many of them terribly dangerous.

'Oh, boy,' says Mulaghesh. She sits down, suddenly feeling quite terribly old.

Shara's bag clinks and clanks, rattles and thumps as she walks down the alley. It took her most of the day to assemble the bag — pieces of silver, pearl, bags of daisy petals, pieces of blown glass — and though she packed it quite well, there's so much in it that she sounds like a one-man band seeking a corner to play at. She's grateful when she comes to the alley, so she can stop.

She inspects the alley carefully. It is, like most alleys, a forgotten little strip of interstitial stone, but this one bends around the curved wall of the west building, which is not more than three blocks from the House of Votrov.

She looks at the ground, where a twisting trail of tyre marks on the stone takes on the look of sloppy brushwork. *They turned here, at the corner*, thinks Shara, *and went down the alley*. She paces a few steps down, over an exposed pipe, around a pile of refuse. The black rubber is fainter here, but some streaks can still be seen. *Over this bump, over the pipe*. She looks up, spots a demolished waste bin and a smattering of broken glass. *Tipped over the bins, and . . .*

The tyre marks disappear. Beyond this, the alley is clean and immaculate – or at least as clean and immaculate as any alley can be.

'He stopped,' she murmurs, 'got out, and . . .'

And what? How does a man simply disappear into thin air?

Shara does not bother, as Sigrud did on the night of Vohannes's party, to check the stones and walls of this place. She simply takes out a piece of yellow chalk and draws a line across the alley floor. *Somewhere at this line*, she thinks, *there is a door. But how to find it?*

She sets her bag down. Her first trick is an old and simple one: she takes out a jar, fills it with daisy petals – *Sacred to Ahanas*, thinks Shara, *for their wilful recurrence* – shakes the jar, and dumps out the petals. Then she takes a bit of graveyard mud, smears it across the glass bottom of a jar, wipes it clean and applies the mouth of the jar to her eye, like a telescope.

The alley looks exactly the same through the lens of the jar. However, she can see a bit of the walls of Bulikov in the distance – and these glow with a blue-green phosphorescence bright enough to light up the evening sky.

She takes the jar away. Of course, now the walls do not glow; they are a dull grey, as always. But, viewed through a lens that discerns works of the Divine, they naturally stand out.

Yet this means that, whatever door the attackers disappeared through, it was not made by the Divine, unlike the walls of Bulikov.

Which should be impossible, thinks Shara. *Anything capable of making someone disappear* should *be Divine in nature*.

She begins to pace the alley. For the past four nights, Shara has been visiting this place and the one other spot where Sigrud witnessed a disappearance; in these spots she performs select tests and experiments, mostly in vain. She has nothing else to do: Sigrud watches Mrs Torskeny in her apartment; Pitry, Nidayin and a select few other embassy staff members are combing through the year's worth of investments Wiclov has made. Shara wishes she were there, overseeing them, but her knowledge of the Divine makes her more suited to this task.

And, strangely, Wiclov has not been seen in Bulikov since spiriting away Mrs Torskeny. 'He is in his country estate near Jukoshtan,' his office informed them, 'on family business.'

So many disappearances, thinks Shara as she returns to her bag. *And so precious few answers.*

She tries a multitude of other tricks: she casts poppy seeds on the ground, but they fail to align in any one direction, indicating a Divine breach in the world. She writes a third of a hymn of Voortya on a parchment, and carries it down the alley: were it to pass through a holy domain of Voortya, the hymn would be instantly completed, in Voortya's savage handwriting. (This failure does not surprise her. None of Voortya's miracles, however slight, have worked since the Night of the Red Sands.)

Another trick.

How did you disappear?

Another.

How did you do it?

And another.

How?

She performs one final test, rolling a silver coin down the alley. If it encounters some Divine obstacle, placed here intentionally or not, it should stop and fall flat, as if magnetically drawn to the ground, but it does not, merely plinks ahead before spinning round and tottering to a stop.

She sighs, reaches back into her bag, and takes out her thermos of tea. She sips it. It is stale and musky, having been stored for too long in a place that is too damp.

She sighs again, clears some space on the ground and sits in the alley with her back against the wall, remembering the last day of her training, the last hour she spent on Saypur's soil, the last time she tasted really good tea.

'How did you do it?' asked Auntie Vinya. 'Tell me. How?'

Young Shara Komayd, exhausted, dehydrated and starving, gave her aunt a puzzled look as she stuffed food into her mouth. The rest of the mess hall at the training facility was empty, causing the sounds of her chewing to echo.

'You stuck to your story, no matter how they badgered and questioned you,' said Vinya. 'Every answer right. Every single one, for all six days. Do you know how often that's happened? Why, I think you might be only the second or third in the Ministry's history.' She peered at her nineteen-year-old niece over her half-moon glasses, obviously pleased. 'Most of them break down on the third day, you know, after no sleep. The music gets to them – the same bass line, over and over. It shakes something loose. And when they are asked a question, they finally give the wrong answer. But you sat through it as if you heard nothing at all.'

'Did you?' asked Shara around a mouthful of potato.

'Did I what?'

'Did you break?'

Vinya laughed. 'I *created* this process, dear. I've never had to sit through it. So tell me – how did you do it?'

Shara sloshed down tea. 'Do *what*, Auntie?'

'Why, keep going. You didn't break down after *six days* of psychological torture.'

Shara paused, the tines of her fork stuck in a chicken breast.

'You don't want to tell me?' asked Vinya.

'It's . . . embarrassing.'

'I'm your *aunt*, dearest.'

'You're also my commanding officer.'

'Oh . . .' She waved a hand. 'Not tonight. Tonight's our last night together for a long while.'

'A *long* while?'

'Well. Not *that* long, dear. So, how?'

'I thought . . .' Shara swallowed. 'I thought about my parents.'

Vinya's mouth flexes. 'Ah.'

'I thought about what they must have gone through, when they died. I've read the stories, I know that the Plague is an . . . a hard way to go.'

Vinya nodded sadly. 'Yes. It is. I saw.'

'And I thought about them, and about what all of Saypur must have gone through under the Continent. All the slavery, and the abuse and the misery. And suddenly it was so easy to sit through it. The music, no sleep, no water, no food, the questions, over and over. Nothing they could ever do to me would be like that. Nothing.'

Vinya smiled and took off her glasses. 'You are, I think, the most ferocious patriot I have ever seen. I am so *proud* of you, my dear. Especially
because, well, we were worried, for a bit.'

'About what?'

'Well, my dear, I always knew you had a fancy for history. That was always
your forte at Fadhuri. Especially studying *Continental* history. And then when
you came to us, and we gave you access to the *classified* material – where we
keep the things we don't even allow them to teach at Fadhuri – why, you
spent *hours* in there memorising all those mouldy old texts! This fascination,
in government, is considered a little . . . unhealthy.'

'But they explained so much!' said Shara. 'I had only been taught pieces
of things at Fadhuri. So much had been missing, but then there it all was,
right on the shelves!'

'What we should concern ourselves with,' said Vinya, 'is the *present*. But
what is more, Shara, I admit I was worried that you were tainted by that
boy you used to dally about with at school.'

Shara's face soured. 'Don't talk to me about him,' she snapped. 'He's
dead to me. He was worthless and deceitful, as is the rest of the damnable
Continent, I bet.'

'I know, I know,' said Vinya. 'You have gone through a lot. I knew
when you came out of school that you wanted to change the world, for it
to live up to all your dreams of how Saypur should be.' She smiles sadly.
'And I know that that is probably why you investigated Rajandra in the
first place.'

Shara looked at her, startled. 'Auntie . . . I-I don't want to ta—'

'Don't fear the past, darling. You must accept what you did. You suspected Rajandra Adesh of wrongdoing. You thought he was misusing
funds from the National Party. And you were right. He *was* misusing
party funds. He was wildly, *wildly* corrupt. That's true. And I think by
exposing him, you wished to impress me, impress us all. But you must
know that if corruption is powerful enough, it's not corruption at all – it's
law. Unspoken, unwritten, but law. Such was the case here. Do you
understand?'

Shara bowed her head.

'You have ruined the career of the man everyone thought would inherit the Prime Minister's seat. You have destroyed a ruling party's leadership. Your investigation pushed the party treasurer to attempt suicide. The poor bastard couldn't even competently pull off his own suicide – he tried to *hang* himself in his office, but wound up ripping the water pipes clear out of the ceiling,' Vinya tuts. 'You are a Komayd, dear, and that will protect us, to an extent. But this will have repercussions for *years*.'

'I'm so sorry, Auntie,' says Shara.

'I know. Listen, the world is full of corruption and inequality,' says Vinya. 'You were raised a patriot, to love Saypur and to believe that its virtues must be extended to all the world – but this is not your job. Your job in the Ministry is not to *stop* corruption and inequality: rather, these are tools in your bag to be used to aid Saypur in every way possible. Your job is to make sure the past never happens again, that we never see such poverty and powerlessness again. Corruption and inequality are useful things: if they benefit us, we must own them fully. Do you see?'

Shara thought of Vohannes then: *You paint your world in such drab cynicisms.*

'Do you see?' asked Vinya again.

'I see,' said Shara.

'I know you love Saypur,' said Vinya. 'I know you love this country like you loved your parents, and you wish to honour their memory, and the memory of every other Saypuri who died in the struggle. But you will serve Saypur in the shadows, and Saypur *will* ask you to betray its virtues in order to keep it safe.'

'And then . . .'

'Then what?'

'Then, when I'm done, I can come home?'

Vinya smiled. 'Of *course* you can. I'm sure your service will only last a handful of months! We'll see each other again very soon. Now eat up, and get some rest. Your ship leaves in the morning. Oh. It is so *good* to see my niece working for me!'

How she smiled when she said that.

In the morning, thinks Shara. *Nearly sixteen years ago.*

In those sixteen years, Shara has taken more cases and done more work than nearly any operative in the world, let alone on the Continent. But though Shara Komayd was once a vigorous patriot, her fervour has been leached out of her with each death and each betrayal, until her passion to feed Saypur has shrunk to a passion merely to protect Saypur, which has then shrunk further into the mere longing to see her home country once more before she dies: a prospect which she sometimes thinks very unlikely.

Repetition, conditioning, fervour and faith, she muses as she sips tea in the alleyway. *All come to so little. Perhaps this is what it's like to lose one's religion.*

And, what is more, she has begun to question whether she is really in exile. She wonders: as disastrous as it was, could the National Party scandal *still* be on everyone's minds? Is that *really* why she is being kept away? She wishes she had been smart enough to establish a few connections to Parliament while she was still in Saypur. (Though it's true, she remembers, that all her experiences with the Divine make her about as dangerous and illicit as the Unmentionable Warehouse itself. There are many reasons, she feels, why her homeland could reject her.)

'Ambassador Thivani?'

She looks over her shoulder. Pitry stands at the mouth of the alley with the car parked just beyond; she must have been so lost in her memories that she didn't even hear him arrive.

'Pitry? What are you doing here? Why aren't you working on Wiclov's finances?'

'Message from Sigrud,' he says. 'Mrs Torskeny's been moved. He says Wiclov and one other man have escorted her from her home. He's given me an address, not much more.'

There is a clanking flurry as Shara packs all her materials. She walks down the alley, grabs the silver coin, and jumps into the back seat of the car.

They've already driven a quarter of a mile before she notices the coin has lost some of its lustre. She holds it up to the windows to catch some light.

Her eyes open in surprise. Then she smiles.

'At last,' she says quietly, 'something to go on.'

The coin is no longer silver at all: it has been completely transmuted into lead.

★

Shara and Pitry enter a quarter of Bulikov decimated by the Blink: she watches, fascinated, as truncated buildings and tapering streets pass by. As they drive down one block, a laundry on one corner stretches, twists and contorts itself until it forms half of a bank on the next corner. One set of quaint homes feature unusually large and warped front doors that would not, one imagines, ever have been fashioned with humans in mind. *They must have simply appeared overnight*, thinks Shara.

'Any progress with Wiclov's history?' she asks.

'We think so,' says Pitry. 'You were right about the loomworks. He is the confirmed owner of three of them in eastern Bulikov. But we noticed that at the same time as Wiclov started buying the loomworks, he also started purchasing materials from a *Saypuri* company: Vidashi Incorporated.'

'Vidashi.' The name is only vaguely familiar to her. 'Wait . . . the ore refinery?'

'Yep,' says Pitry. He wheels the car around a winding curve. 'It seems Wiclov has been buying very small increments of steel from them. Every month, like clockwork. Very arbitrary amounts, too – between one thousand five hundred pounds and one thousand nine hundred pounds every time. We're not sure wh—'

Shara sits forward. 'It's the weight check,' she blurts out.

'What?'

'The weight check! The Ministry of Foreign Affairs carries out automatic background checks on purchasers of large quantities of materials! Oil, wood, stone, metal. We want to know who we're selling to, if they buy large enough amounts. And for steel, the weight check amount must be—'

'Two thousand pounds,' realises Pitry. 'So the Ministry has never checked on him.'

Which leads Shara to wonder: why try and kidnap Vohannes if you're already purchasing steel through legitimate means?

Unless I spooked them, she thinks. *I wanted to stir up the hornet's nest, didn't I? They must not have acquired enough steel for whatever it is that they're making. So when Pangyui was killed, and a Ministry operative arrived, they became nervous and desperate.*

She stares out of the window, her mind racing. What could they possibly be building? What use could someone have for so much steel?

She keeps thinking about it until she sees something peeking over the rooftops at her: a huge black tower, a ten-storey stripe of ebony against the grey night sky.

Her heart twitches.

Oh, no, thinks Shara. *They can't be taking her* there. *Not there.*

She has not been to see this place yet. It seems unreal to believe it still exists.

Of all the things the Kaj threw down, why did he leave *that* still standing?

Pitry parks in an alley. The darkness in an old doorway trembles; Sigrud emerges from the shadows and paces across the street.

'Please do not tell me they went in there,' says Shara as she climbs out.

'Into where?' asks Sigrud.

'The bell tower.'

Sigrud stops, bemused. 'Why do you ask?'

Shara sighs and readjusts her glasses. 'Show me,' she says.

The streets of Bulikov are almost impenetrably dark at night in quarters most affected by the Blink: no one has been able to lay gas lines, as the disturbances reach deep down into the earth. One construction company made a valiant attempt, only to discover a sheet of iron three feet thick, forty feet tall and (they estimated) a quarter of a mile long, simply suspended in the loam below the streets. No one could logically explain its existence: eventually, like so many aberrations, they assumed it was one of the unintended and inexplicable consequences of the Blink. Though the iron sheet *could* be dealt with, the company withdrew its bid, perhaps out of concern about what else might be buried below Bulikov.

At the centre of this damaged neighbourhood is a wide, empty park. Sapling firs grow in the damp soil: recent transplants, as all the natural vegetation in Bulikov died when the climate abruptly changed. Behind these is a long building with one huge tower at the north end: a belfry with a very curious, skeletal structure at the top, a metal globe-like frame that appears to have once held a carillon, but is now empty. The base of the structure is formed from rambling clay walls with a flat roof to which time has not been kind: the roof dips and curves like a field marred by a glacier.

'They went in there?' asks Shara.

'No,' says Sigrud. He points to a long, dismal-looking municipal structure at the edge of the park. 'Wiclov and one other man took her in *there*. Just adjacent to it. Why do you worry so?'

'Because *that*' – Shara nods at the bell tower – 'is the oldest structure in Bulikov, after the walls. It was at the centre of Bulikov, originally, though the lopsided effects of the Blink considerably changed that. The Centre of the Seat of the World. Normally just called the Seat of the World, though outsiders called Bulikov the same.'

'A temple?'

'Something like that. Supposedly it was like Saypur's parliament house for the Divinities. Though I always imagined it would look much grander – it is quite shabby, I must say, and I remember reading it had *amazing* stained glass – but I'm told the Blink did not leave it unscathed. Apparently the tower was originally much, much taller. Each Divinity had a bell housed there, and the ringing of each bell had different effects.'

'Such as?'

She shrugs. 'No one knows. Which is why I'm reluctant to be here. So it *was* Wiclov who came?'

'Wiclov and one attendant. They came and took Torskeny to that little building. Then, forty minutes ago, Wiclov and his attendant departed. No sign of Torskeny.'

'That's rather bold of them to operate in the open. Where did they go afterwards?'

Sigrud's face darkens.

'Let me guess,' says Shara. 'They took a series of turns through the streets, and then they suddenly—'

'Vanished,' says Sigrud. 'Yes. This is the third time. Yet I have remembered' – he taps the side of his head hard enough for it to make a noise – 'each place where these people have disappeared. The only pattern I see is that they are all within *this* quarter, and the one to the west.'

'The ones most damaged by the Blink,' says Shara. 'Which supports a theory I've just now half confirmed.' She runs a hand over the scarred brick wall behind them. 'They are exploiting some damage or effect of the Blink for their own ends.'

'How are you so sure?'

'A piece of silver,' says Shara, 'changed into lead not more than an hour ago as it passed through the alley where their car disappeared. This sort of thing was only ever witnessed immediately after the Blink.'

'How are you so sure it wasn't a miracle?'

'Because I used all the tricks I knew of to look for miracles,' says Shara, 'and found none. No Divine workings at all, leaving only the Blink as a possible cause. It is worth noting, though, that no one has ever been able to adequately study the Blink. The Continent protects its damages like a bitter old woman does grudges. I plan to do so, when we have time – for now, let's investigate what we have.'

When they near the municipal building, Shara hangs back to allow Sigrud to inspect. He stalks around it, then shakes his head and gestures to her to come. 'Nothing,' he says as she joins him. 'Door is unlocked. No one in the windows, from what I can see. But much of the building has no windows.'

'What is this place?'

'Something the city had built. Think it might have been intended for development – make the neighbourhood into something better. But then they gave up, maybe.'

I would have, too, thinks Shara.

Sigrud goes to the door and pulls out his black knife. He peers inside, then silently enters. Shara waits a beat, and follows.

The interior of the building is almost completely devoid of furniture and ornamentation. The rooms continue on through the building's length, connected by a series of small doors. The building's most remarkable attribute is that, unlike nearly every structure nearby, this one has gas: little blue jets flicker along the ceiling, allowing the barest illumination.

'They left the lights on,' mutters Shara.

Sigrud holds a finger to his lips. He cocks his head, listening, and makes a queer face, like he's hearing an upsetting noise.

'Someone's here?' asks Shara softly.

'Cannot quite say.'

Sigrud stalks forward into the building, peering into each room before Shara follows. Each room is like the one before it: small, bland, empty. Mrs Torskeny is nowhere to be found. The doorways, Shara notes, all line up, more or less: look through one door, and you look through all.

Except the door at the very end, which is shut, and its keyhole flickers with a faint yellow light.

I like this less and less, thinks Shara.

Again, Sigrud stops. 'I hear it again. It is . . . laughing,' he says finally.

'*Laughing*?'

'Yes. A child. Very . . . quiet.'

'From where?'

He points at the closed door.

'And you can hear nothing more?'

He shakes his head.

'Well,' says Shara. 'Let's proceed.'

As she expects, all the rooms leading up to the closed door are empty. And as they draw near, she hears it, too: laughter, faint and soft, as if behind that door a child is playing a merry game.

'I smell something,' says Sigrud. 'Salt . . . and dust.'

'How is that remarkable?'

'I smell them in remarkable quantities.' He points at the door again, then squats to peer through the keyhole. One squinting eye on his face is spotlit; his eyelid trembles as he strains to see.

'Do you see anything?'

'I see . . . a ring, on the floor. Made of white powder. Many candles. *Many*. And clothes.'

'Clothes?'

'A pile of clothes on the floor.' He adds, 'Women's clothes.'

Shara taps him on the shoulder, and she takes his place at the keyhole. The light pouring through the keyhole is staggering: candelabra line the walls in a circle, each holding five, ten, twenty candles. The very room is alive with fire: she can feel the heat on her cheek in a concentrated beam.

As her eye adjusts, she sees there is a wide circle of something white on the floor – *Salt? Dust?* – and at the edge of her vision she thinks she can see a pile of clothes, just on the opposite side of the white circle.

Her heart sinks when she sees the dark blue cloth that is almost the exact shade Mrs Torskeny was wearing when she last saw her.

Then something dances into view . . . something gauzy and white, moving in drifting sweeps – the hem of a long white dress? Shara jumps, startled, but does not take her eye away. She sees a head of hair at the top of the cloth, thick black locks that shine in the candlelight, before the white thing trots away.

'There's someone in there,' Shara says softly.

Again, the childish laugh. Yet something is wrong.

'A child,' she says. '*Maybe* . . .'

'Step back,' says Sigrud.

'But . . . I'm not sure . . .'

'Step back.'

Shara moves away. He tests the knob: it's unlocked. He squats down low, knife in hand, and eases the door open.

Immediately the laughter turns to shrieks of pain. Shara is positioned so she cannot see what's inside – yet Sigrud can, and he drops any suggestion of threat. He glances at her – concerned, confused – and walks in.

'Wait,' says Shara. '*Wait!*'

Shara bolts around the open door and inside.

Things move so fast that it's difficult for Shara to see. There is a blaze of light from the candelabra, which are so densely crowded that she has to dance around them, and a wide circle of white crystals on the floor – salt, probably. Sitting in the centre of the ring, dressed in a huge, shining white dress, is a little girl of about four, with dark black locks and bright red lips. She sits in the ring of salt, rubbing at her knee . . . or Shara *thinks* she rubs her knee, for almost all of the little girl is hidden below her white dress. Shara cannot even see her hands, only the kneading motion under the white cloth.

'It hurts!' cries the little girl. 'It *hurts!*'

The scent of dust is overwhelming. It seems to coat the back of Shara's throat.

Sigrud walks forward, uncertain. 'Should we . . . do something?' he asks.

The salt.

'Wait!' says Shara again. She reaches out to grab his sleeve and hold him back; Sigrud is so much larger than she is that he almost knocks her over.

The little girl spasms in pain. '*Help* me!'

'You don't want me to do anything?' asks Sigrud.

'No! Stop! And look.' Shara points down. Two feet away is the outer edge of the circle of salt.

'What is that?' asks Sigrud.

'The salt, it's like a—'

'*Please* help me!' begs the little girl. 'Please! *Please*, you *must*!'

Shara looks closer. The dress is far too big for such a small girl, and there is a lump under it, as if her body is swollen and malformed.

I know this, thinks Shara. 'Just stop, Sigrud. Let me try and . . .' She clears her throat. 'If you could, please,' she says to the little girl, 'show us your feet.'

Sigrud is bewildered. '*What?*'

'*Please!*' cries the little girl. 'Please, do something!'

'We will help you,' says Shara, 'if you show us your feet.'

The little girl groans. 'Why do you care? Why do you . . . it hurts so *bad*!'

'We will help you quite quickly,' says Shara. 'We are experienced in medicine. Just, please . . . show us your feet!'

The little girl starts rocking back and forth on the ground. 'I'm *dying*!' she howls. 'I'm *bleeding*! Please, *help* me!'

'Show them to us. Now!'

'I take it,' says Sigrud, 'that you do not think that's a little girl.'

The girl lets out a long, tortured shriek.

Shara grimly shakes her head. 'Look. Think. The salt on the ground, ringing her in. Torskeny's clothes, which look to have been dropped on the ground just where she crossed the salt.'

The little girl, still shrieking in pain, tries to crawl over to them. Yet her movements are so *odd*. The girl doesn't use her hands or arms at all (Shara thinks, *Does she even have any?*) but she appears to kick over to them, crawling on her knees. It's like she's a cloth puppet with a hard little head on top, yet her cheeks and her tears and her hair all look so real.

But she never shows her feet. Not once throughout this strange rolling motion.

The taste of dust thickens: Shara's throat is clay, her eyes sand.

There is something under the dress. Not a little girl's body – something much larger.

Oh, by the seas, thinks Shara. *It couldn't be.*

'Help me, *please*!' cries the girl. 'I'm in so much pain!'

'Step back, Sigrud. Don't let it get close to you.'

Sigrud does so.

'No!' shouts the girl. Wormlike, the girl crawls to the very edge of the salt ring, mere inches away from them. 'No! Please . . . please don't leave me!'

'You're not real,' Shara says to the little girl. 'You're bait.'

'Bait?' says Sigrud. 'For what?'

'For you and me.'

The little girl bursts into tears and huddles at the edge. '*Please*,' she says. 'Please just pick me *up*. I haven't been held in so *long*.'

'Drop the act,' says Shara angrily. 'I know what you are.'

The little girl shrieks; the sound is like razors on their ears.

'*Stop*!' shouts Shara. 'Stop your nonsense! We're no fools!'

The screams stop immediately. The abrupt cessation of sound is startling. The girl does not look up; she sits bent in half, frozen and lifelessly still.

'I don't know *how* you're still alive,' says Shara. 'I thought all of you died in the Great Purge.'

The thick locks quiver as the girl's head twitches to one side.

'You're a *mhovost*, aren't you? One of Jukov's pets.'

The little girl sits up, but there is something disturbingly mechanical about the motion, as if she's being pulled by strings. Her face, which was once contorted into a look of such heart-piercing agony, is now utterly blank, like that of a doll.

Something shifts under the dress. The little girl appears to drop into the cloth. There is a sudden rush of dust.

Cloth swirling around it, it stands up slowly.

Shara looks at it, and immediately begins to vomit.

It is man-like, in a way: it has a torso, arms and legs. Yet all are queerly long, distended and many-jointed, as if its body is nothing but knuckles, hard bulbs of bone shifting under smooth skin. Its limbs are wrapped in white cloth stained grey with dust, and its feet are like a blend between a human's and a goose's – huge and syndactyl and webbed – with three fat toes, each with tiny perfect toenails on them. Yet its head is by far the worst part: the back is roughly like the head of a balding man, sporting a ring of long, grey straggly hair around its skull; but instead of a face or jaw, the head stretches forward to form what looks like a wide, long, flat bill – like, again, that of a goose. Yet rather than the tough keratin normally seen in ducks or geese, the bill is made of knuckled human flesh, as if a man's fingers were fused together and both hands were brought together to form a joint at the heel of his palms.

The *mhovost* flaps its bill at Shara, making a wet *fap, fap, fap*. Somewhere in her mind she hears echoes of children laughing, screaming, crying. As its fleshy bill wags Shara can see it has no oesophagus, no teeth – just more bony, hairy flesh in the inner recesses of the bill.

She spews vomit on to the floor again, but is careful to avoid the salt on the floor.

Sigrud stares blankly at this abomination, pacing in front of him like a bantam cock, daring him to attack it. 'Is this,' he asks slowly, 'a thing I should be killing?'

'*No*,' gasps Shara. More vomit burbles out of her. The *mhovost* flaps its bill at her – again, the echoes of ghostly children. She thinks, *It's laughing at me*. 'Don't break the ring of salt! That's the only thing keeping us alive!'

'And the little girl?'

'She was never there. This creature is miraculous by nature, though darkly so.'

She spits bile on the floor. The *mhovost* gestures to her belligerently. The human nature of its movements is revolting: she imagines it saying, *Come on! Come on!*

'You killed Mrs Torskeny, didn't you?' asks Shara. 'They led her here and she broke the salt barrier.'

The *mhovost*, in a bizarrely effective pantomime, looks at the pile of clothes, and shrugs indifferently – *That old thing?* It waves dismissively – *It was nothing.* Then, again, it flaps its bill at them.

'I so wish' – Sigrud is turning his knife over and over in his hand – 'that it would stop doing that.'

'It wants you to break the circle. If it can get at you, it'll swallow you whole.'

Fap, fap, fap, fap.

Sigrud gives her a sceptical look.

'It's a creature of skin and bone,' says Shara. 'But not its *own* skin and bone. Somewhere inside it, I fear, are the recycled remains of Mrs Torskeny.'

The *mhovost* prods its belly with its many-jointed fingers, as if probing for her.

A joker. But it would be, of course, considering who made it.

'How are you alive?' asks Shara. 'Shouldn't you have perished when Jukov died?'

It stops. Stares at her, eyelessly. Then it walks backwards, forwards, backwards, forwards, as if it's testing the edges of the salt ring.

'What is it doing?' asks Sigrud.

'It's mad,' says Shara. 'One of the creatures made by Jukov in his darker moods – a knuckle-man, a voice under the cloth. It's meant to mock us, to goad us. The only way to identify them is to ask to see their feet, because that's the one thing they can never really hide. Though I've no idea how it's alive . . . *Is* Jukov dead?' she asks the creature.

Still pacing back and forth, the *mhovost* shakes its head. Then it stops, appears to think, and shrugs.

'How are you here?'

Again, a shrug.

'I knew they could last for *some* time,' says Shara, 'but I did not think that a Divinity's creatures could persist so long after their death.'

The *mhovost* extends a repulsively long, flat hand and tilts it back and forth – *Maybe. Maybe not.*

'The two men who were here,' says Shara. 'Did they trap you here?'

It resumes pacing back and forth. Shara presumes she's just angered it, so she must be right.

'How long have they kept you trapped in this building?'

The creature mimes a laugh (Shara again reflects on what an astonishing pantomime it is) and waves a hand at her – *What a silly question!*

'A long time, then.'

It shrugs.

'You don't look underfed. How many others have you killed?'

It shakes its head, waggles a finger – *No, no, no, no.* Then it lovingly, thoughtfully caresses its stomach – *What makes you think they're dead?*

Children laugh in the empty chambers of Shara's head. She resists the urge to retch again. 'How . . . how many have they pushed within this circle?'

It flaps its bill. Shrugs.

'A lot?'

Another shrug.

Shara whispers, 'How are you *alive*?'

The *mhovost* begins waltzing across the circle, twirling gracefully.

'I very much wish to kill this thing,' says Sigrud.

The *mhovost* spins around and waggles its bony behind at Sigrud.

'Much more than I do most things,' he adds. 'And we have killed Divine creatures before'

'Listen to me, abomination,' says Shara coldly. 'I am descended from the man who killed your race, who pulled your Divinities down to the Earth and laid them low, who ruined and ravaged this land within *weeks*. My forebear buried dozens, *hundreds* of your brothers and sisters in the mud, and there they *rot*, even to this day. I have no qualms about doing the same to you. Now, tell me – is your creator, the Divinity Jukov, truly gone from this world, never to return?'

The *mhovost* slowly stands. It appears to reflect on something – for a moment, it almost appears sad. Then it turns round, looks at Shara and shakes its head.

'Then where is he?'

A shrug, but not half so malicious and gleeful this time: this gesture is doleful, confused, a child wondering why it was abandoned.

'These two men who were here. One of them was fat and bald, yes?'

It starts pacing the edge of the ring, walking in a frantic circle.

A *yes*, Shara assumes. 'And the other one – what did he look like?'

The *mhovost* adds a decidedly swishy step to its pacing. It puts one hand on its hip, bends the other hand effeminately at the wrist; and as it pivots across the ring, it strokes the bottom of its bill as if luxuriating in its gorgeous features.

That, thinks Shara, *does not sound like the sort of person Wiclov would normally dally with.*

'How did Wiclov trap you here?' she asks.

The *mhovost* stops, looks at her and bends double in silent laughter. It waves at her as if appreciating a merry joke – *What a ridiculous idea!*

'So it *wasn't* Wiclov,' says Shara. 'Then who?'

It bends its wrist, affects a feminine posture, and shakes its head in a manner that could only be called *bitchy*.

'The *other* man trapped you here. Who is this other man?'

It performs an agile flip, assumes a handstand, and begins trotting around on its palms.

'Who was he?'

The light in the room flickers as the candelabra flames dance. And all the flames bend, Shara notices, at the exact same angle.

A breeze?

She examines the walls. In the far corner, deep in amber shadows, she thinks she spies a crack in the stone – perhaps a panel, or a door.

She looks down at the floor. The salt ring fills the room almost perfectly: it's impossible to reach the door without going through the *mhovost's* little enclosure. *Like a guard dog.*

'What's through that door?' asks Shara.

The *mhovost* looks up at her, does yet another flip, and lands on its feet. It cocks its head, canine-like, and theatrically scratches its bald head with one quadruple-jointed finger.

The Divinities, she remembers, *could only be killed with the Kaj's weaponry. But their creatures were more vulnerable, and all had their own weaknesses.*

Shara comes to a decision. 'How many have you devoured during your imprisonment here?'

Again, it doubles over in mock laughter. It dances over to where Sigrud stands and mimes inspecting him, pretending to squeeze his thighs, test his belly.

'I believe it was many,' says Shara. 'And I believe you enjoyed it.'

In one swoop, the *mhovost* slides over to her. It runs one finger along the sides of its mouth: a disturbingly sexual gesture.

Shara looks at a candelabrum beside her. 'These are very illegal, of course.' She picks up one candle, flips it over. Inscribed on the bottom, as she expected, is a symbol of a flame between two parallel lines – the insignia of Olvos, the flame in the woods. 'These candles never go out, and they give off such a bright white light.' She holds a hand to its flame. 'But the heat they give . . . *that* is quite real, and no illusion.'

The *mhovost* stops, and slowly withdraws its finger from its mouth.

'There's a reason all these candelabra are here, isn't there?' asks Shara. 'Because if, by any chance, you got out of your cage, a dusty, dry creature like you would have to tread *very* carefully to avoid catching alight.'

The *mhovost* drops its hand, and takes a step back.

'I bet Mrs Torskeny ran to you, didn't she?' says Shara softly. 'Seeing a little girl, in need.'

Shara remembers the old woman bent over her coffee. *I tried to learn. I wanted to learn to be righteous. I wanted to know. But I could only ever pretend.*

Angry, the *mhovost* flaps its bill at her: *fap, fap, fap, fa—*

With a flick, Shara tosses the candle at it.

The creature catches fire instantly: there is a *whump* sound, and an orange blaze erupts from its chest. Within seconds it is a dark man-figure flailing in a billowing cloud of orange and white.

Somewhere in the back of her head, Shara hears children screaming.

She remembers, again, the boy in the jail cell – *How I repeat myself.*

The flaming creature veers across the salt ring, seeming to bounce off invisible walls. Scraps of flickering cloth float away from it like glowing orange cherry blossoms. It grasps its head, its monstrous mouth open in a silent cry.

Its form fades; the flames die away; a gust of ash dances around the candelabra. Then it is gone, leaving only scorch marks on the floor.

> *And Olvos said:*
> *'Nothing is ever truly lost.*
> *The world is like the tide*
> *Returning, for an instant, to the place it occupied before,*
> *Or leaving that same place once more.*
>
> *'Celebrate, then, for what you lose shall be returned.*
> *Smile, then, for all good deeds you do shall be visited upon you.*
> *Weep, then, for all ills you do shall return to you,*
> *Or your children, or your children's children.*
>
> *'What is reaped is what is sown.*
> *What is sown is what is reaped.'*
>
> Book of the Red Lotus, Part IV, *13.51 – 13.59*

Recreations

Shara strides across the room. As her feet cross the salt, she braces herself for some terrible misfortune – perhaps the thing would resurrect itself, and fall upon her – but there is nothing.

She feels the crack in the wall, pries at it with her finger, but it does not budge. 'Come and look,' she says. 'Do you see a handle? Or a button? Or maybe a lever?'

Sigrud gently pushes her aside with the back of one hand. Then he takes a step back, and soundly kicks the door in the wall.

The *crack* sounds deafening in this silent place. Half of the door caves in. The remainder, suddenly powdery, shatters and falls to pieces like a mirror. White, acrid clouds come pluming up.

Shara touches the broken door, which leaves a chalky residue on her fingers. 'Ah,' she says. 'Plaster.' She cranes her head forward to look into the dark.

Earthen stairs, going straight down in a steep angle.

Sigrud picks up one of the sputtering candelabra. 'I think,' he says, 'we may need one of these.'

The stairs do not end: they stretch on and on, soft and moist, formed of dark, black clay and loam. Neither she nor Sigrud talks as they descend. They do not discuss the horror they have just encountered, nor does he ask her how she knew how to dispatch it in such an able fashion: five or six years ago, they might have, but not now. Both of them have been at this strange sort of work for so long that there are few surprises left: you encounter the miraculous, do as you need with it, and go back to work. *Though that*, Shara reflects, *was the worst in a long while*.

'What direction do you think we're going?' asks Shara.

'West.'

'Towards the belfry?'

Sigrud considers it, and nods.

'So, soon we will be underneath it.'

'More or less, yes.'

Shara remembers how the gas company gave up this quarter, choosing to leave what was buried below Bulikov alone.

'A question comes to me,' says Sigrud. 'How could someone make this without anyone noticing?'

Shara inspects the walls of the tunnel. 'It looks like it's been in use for a while. Much of it's been worn away. But it almost looks like, when this tunnel was first made, they made it by *burning* it.'

'What?'

She points to the charred marks, and the sandier places that appear molten, like glass.

'Someone *burned* a hole this deep?' asks Sigrud.

'That's how it appears,' says Shara. 'Like a blowtorch flame through a stack of metal.'

'Have you seen such a thing before?'

'Actually, no. Which I find quite troubling, frankly.'

The white candlelight prances on the earthen walls. A strange breeze caresses her cheek. Shara adjusts her glasses.

The stairs seem to melt away below her. The walls fall back, then become stone – no, a stone *mural*, carved in a marvellously intricate pattern. Though the fluttering light makes it hard to see, Shara is sure she spots the flimsy form of Ahanas and the pointing hand of Taalhavras among the patterns.

The walls keep falling back. Then they aren't there at all.

'Oh my word,' says Shara.

The candlelight beats back the dark. The shadows withdraw like a curtain to reveal a vast chamber. Shara catches glimpses, flashes, flickers of distant stone.

'Oh, my *word*.'

She looks out. The chamber is huge, and oddly uterine, from what she can see: both the ceiling and floor are huge and concave, and both come to a point in the exact centre, connecting to form something similar to a stalagmite. The chamber has six atria, joining in the centre like the petals and stigma of a fabulously complicated orchid bloom. And every single inch of the walls, ceiling and floors are engraved, with glyphs and sigils and pictograms of strange and bewildering events: a man pulls a thorned flower from a skull, and ties its stem around his tongue; three vivisected women bathe in a rocky stream, their eyes like glass beads, while a stag watches from the shore; a woman stitches up an incision in her armpit, with the blank face of a man bulging out of the slit, as if he is being stitched up inside her; four crows circle in the sky, and below them, a man draws water from the ground with a spear . . . On and on and on, images of great and terrible meaning that are incomprehensible to her.

'What' – Sigrud snorts, hawks, swallows it with a gulp – 'what is this place?'

Around the centre, where the 'stalagmite' forms, Shara sees soft earth has collected on the ground. *But*, she wonders, *where did it come from?* She paces forward, taking halting steps as she crosses the sloping floor.

The stalagmite, she sees, is actually a curling stairway, with five columns holding it up: it originally had six, but one, she sees, has been removed.

Six atria, she thinks, *six columns, and six Divinities*.

The stairway ends in a blocked gap in the ceiling, filled with loose stone and crumbling loam, as if whatever was above has caved in.

'Of course,' she says. 'Of *course!*'

'What?' asks Sigrud.

She examines one column: it is beautifully wrought, engraved to resemble the trunk of a pine tree, with a line of flame crawling up its bark. The next column is straight and rigid, and features a complicated repetitious design, like the visual expression of many mathematical formulae. The next column is carved to resemble a pillar of teeth or knives, thousands of blades melted together and pointing upwards, like the trunk of a palm tree. The next looks like a twisted loop of old vines, with many woody stems curled around one another; there is a slight bend in the column, artfully suggesting some flex. And the final of the five remaining columns is a twisting, chaotic tornado of blossoms, fur, leaves, sand, anything and everything.

Shara bunches her fists and trembles like a schoolgirl. 'This was it!' she cries. 'This had to be it! *Really* it! Down here, all along!'

'*It* being what?' says Sigrud, who remains unimpressed.

'Don't you see? Everyone says the bell tower of the Seat of the World shrank during the Blink! But that's not true! Because *that's* the base of the bell tower!' She points at the columns around the staircase. 'Those stairs are the way up!'

'So . . .'

'So the tower never *shrank*! The whole temple must have *sunk* into the mud! That shabby little clay shack up in the park was *never* the true Seat of the World! Which is what everyone, even everyone in *Bulikov*, still thinks. *This* is it! This is the Seat of the World! This is where the Divinities met!'

As Shara has devoted most of her adult life to history, she can't help but be overwhelmed with giddiness, as unpatriotic as it may be; but one unmoved part of her mind speaks up.

This can't all be coincidence. The most sacred structure in Bulikov just happened to sink so it remained hidden for nearly eighty years? And Ernst Wiclov *was the one to tunnel underground to reach it? You don't do something like that unless you know about it – and you wouldn't know about it unless someone told you.*

Shara plucks one candle out of Sigrud's candelabrum. 'Go and send word to Mulaghesh. *Now*. If word gets out to the general populace of Bulikov that this is still here, and we have to publicly seize this place, it'll be the Summer of Black Rivers all over again. And have her throw up a net for Wiclov. All checkpoints around and inside Bulikov will need to be on the lookout for him. We've got enough to at least bring him in for questioning.'

'What will you do?' asks Sigrud.

'Stay down here, and inspect.'

'Will that candle be enough for you?'

'This is actually for *you*.' She holds the lone candle out to him, and points to the candelabrum. '*I'll* be needing that, please.'

Sigrud cocks an eyebrow, shrugs, and hands her the candelabrum. He retreats up the earthen tunnel. The faint white light comes bouncing down the stairs, then dims, leaving Shara alone in the vast chamber.

The candles fizz and spit. Somewhere, the limp *plink* of dripping water. And a thousand stone eyes watch her silently.

It takes some time to recalibrate her train of thought: the chamber was *not* an underground cave, she reminds herself, but a temple meant to be above ground. This explains the huge, gaping holes in the walls of each bulging atrium: they were once giant windows, and though it's difficult to tell from where she stands on the staircase, all but one of them is now broken. *So this is what happened to the famous stained glass of the Seat of the World*, she thinks. *Broken and buried in the mud of Bulikov.*

She looks out at the six atria. Each atrium has a different style, presumably aligning with each Divinity, just like the columns holding up the staircase. Shara sees the sigils of Olvos, Taalhavras, Ahanas, Voortya, Jukov and then . . .

'Hm,' says Shara.

Despite its burial, it seems the Seat of the World is *not* in perfect condition: one atrium is utterly blank of any engravings at all, as if someone came in and sanded down the floor, ceiling and walls.

But Shara sees someone has very recently attempted to restore the floor of this blank chamber, laying out engraved stones of a much darker hue than the rest of the temple. The restoration isn't complete yet, leaving a jumbled and distorted mess of images, words and sigils on the floor, telling half-stories and partial myths, and leaving huge swathes of the chamber blank.

Over and over again, these dark new stones show the same image: a human-like figure seated in the centre of a room, listening to someone. The accompanying sigil is familiar to her: a scale, represented by two dashes supported by a square fork.

Kolkan's hands, she remembers, *waiting to weigh and judge.*

She looks behind her. The pillar corresponding with the blank atrium is missing.

Shara gets the powerfully absurd feeling that she is staring at edited history.

This was once as decorated as the other five sections, thinks Shara. *But I'm willing to bet it all went blank in 1442, right after Kolkan disappeared from the world.* She looks out at the jigsaw collection of new pictograms. *But now someone's come back to correct the record.*

She smirks. *Perhaps they're taking the term 'Restorationists' a bit too seriously.*

It's a futile task. By her estimation, there are thousands of square feet of floor, ceiling and wall needing to be completely restored. And whoever was attempting to do so obviously had no idea what originally decorated Kolkan's chamber. And where did these stones come from, anyway?

Shara hops down and begins inspecting the new pieces of stone on the floor. The stones themselves are fascinating – a dark, smooth ore of a like she's never seen before – and their pictograms are of deeds and events Shara has never heard of. Kolkan, depicted as a robed, hooded figure, splits open a naked human form, and a pure, bright light comes spilling out to rain upon the rounded hills.

It's from another temple, maybe. She traces one carving with her finger. *Someone actually took the stone from one of Kolkan's surviving temples and tried to rebuild it here, to restore Kolkan in the Seat of the World.*

Could Ernst Wiclov really do something like this?

She sees movement ahead, and slowly looks up. Something is twitching on the wall.

After a moment's inspection, she sees there is a large, empty frame of some kind standing upright just a few yards ahead of her; the quivering candle flames must have caused its shadow to dance on the stone wall behind it.

She looks around at the other chambers. None of them have a frame of any kind. Whoever tried to restore Kolkan's chamber – presumably the same person who made the earthen stairway down, and also thought to trap the *mhovost* as a revolting sort of watchdog – must have brought it here.

She walks over to it. It's a stone door frame, about nine feet tall. But then, she recalls, Continentals generally were much taller in the years before the Blink: they were less malnourished in those days. Like so many things originating during the Divine era, the frame features exquisite stonework that gives it the likeness of thick fur, dry wood, chalky stone and starlings. Yet none of this artistry has any relevance to Kolkan, at least as far as Shara's aware: Kolkan generally disdained ornamentation of any kind.

She touches the carved starlings in the door frame. 'And weren't you a favourite of Jukov?'

As she touches it, the door slides back. She looks down at its base. The door frame is mounted on four small wheels made of iron. Shara gives it another push – with a squeak, it slides back further. *Why on Earth would anyone want a mobile door frame?*

She looks at the window frame in the wall of Kolkan's atrium. Each atrium originally had its own window, with stained glass for each Divinity. Shara has read scores of letters describing the beauty of the Divine glass of the Seat of the World – blues and reds the eye could not properly interpret, but still *feel* – and while she is sorry to see it all broken, she's a bit puzzled to see that Kolkan's glass remains whole, but is perfectly blank and clear. She slowly waves the candelabrum back and forth, watching the reflection: it's a big, transparent but otherwise utterly ordinary window. *Perhaps it simply went blank*, she concludes, *when Kolkan vanished. But if so, why is it still whole, and all the others are broken?*

She lifts the candelabrum, and gazes around at the other chambers.

Once, when she was very young, Aunt Vinya took her to the National Library in Ghaladesh. Shara was already an avid reader by then, but she had never realised until that moment what books meant, the possibility they presented: you could protect them for ever, store them up like engineers store water, endless resources of time and knowledge snared in ink, tied down to paper, layered on shelves. Moments made physical, untouchable, perfect, like preserving a dead hornet in crystal, one drop of venom hanging from its stinger for ever.

She felt overwhelmed. It was – she briefly thinks of herself and Vo, reading together in the library – a lot like being in love for the first time.

And to find this here, under the earth, as if all the experiences and words and histories of the Continent could be washed away by the rain to leach through the soil and drip, drip, drip into a hollow in the loam, like the slow calcification of crystal.

In the dark, under Bulikov, Shara Komayd paces over ancient stones, and falls in love again.

*

The rumble of footsteps. Shara looks up from a pictogram of Olvos to see the staircase glowing bright with candlelight.

Mulaghesh enters, flanked by Sigrud and two soldiers with candelabra. She takes one glance at the vast temple and her shoulders droop – *Oh, what a mess this is.* She sighs, 'Ah, *shit.*'

'It's quite a discovery, isn't it?' calls Shara as she walks across the atrium.

'You could say that,' Mulaghesh says, 'yes.'

'You have men posted to guard the entrance?'

'I have five soldiers outside, yes.'

'This is' – Shara steps around a puddle of mud – 'enormous. *Enormous!* I'd imagine this is the most significant Divine discovery since the War, since the Blink! The greatest historical discovery in . . . well, *history.* To discover any piece of this place, any fragment of these pictograms, would be borderline revolutionary in Ghaladesh, but to have found *the entire building*, whole, and more or less unharmed, is, is . . .' Shara, breathless, inhales. 'It boggles the mind.'

Mulaghesh stares at the curving ceiling. She strokes the scars on her jaw with her knuckles. 'It sure does.'

'Here! Look here, at this section!' Shara stoops. 'These few yards of carvings offer more knowledge about Ahanas than anyone's found in *years.* We know almost nothing about her! Ahanashtan, as you probably know, is one of the places most deeply affected by the Blink – almost all the city seemed to *vanish*, you see. Almost everything that's there now was built by Saypur.'

'Uh huh.'

'But this mural proves *why* it vanished! It corroborates the theory that Ahanas actually *grew* the city, sowing miraculous seeds that grew into living buildings, homes, streets, lights. Peaches that glowed at night, like street lights; vines that funnelled in water and carried away waste. It's *fascinating.*'

Mulaghesh scratches the corner of her mouth. 'Yeah.'

'And when Ahanas died, *all* of that vanished. What's more, it provides a *second* explanation for the gap in knowledge: if what this says is true, Ahanashtanis thought all life and all parts of the body were sacred – they never used medicine, never cut their hair, never shaved, never trimmed their fingernails, never brushed their teeth, never . . . well . . . cleaned their nether selves.'

'Yeesh.'

'But that was because they didn't *have* to! Ahanas was able to meet every single one of their needs! They lived in complete harmony with this massive, organic city! But after the Blink, when disease started rampaging through the Continent, they must have refused every medicine, every ministration. So nearly every Ahanashtani on the Continent must have *died out*! Can you imagine! Can you imagine that?'

'Yeah,' says Mulaghesh. Then, amiably, 'So, you know we're going to have to cave in that tunnel, right?'

'And this section here,' says Shara, 'it . . . it . . .' She bows her head and lets out a slow breath. Then she looks up at Mulaghesh.

Mulaghesh smiles grimly, and nods. 'Yeah. You know. You know we can't possibly keep something like this secret. Not something this big. We'd post guards. Then someone would ask questions about those guards, what they're guarding, and they'd keep asking questions until they found out. Or we'd try and excavate it, study it, document it, and someone would see all the equipment, all the personnel, and they'd ask questions, and they'd keep asking questions until they found out. Trouble' – Mulaghesh files away a rough nail on the edge of one engraving – 'is unavoidable. And worse, *Wiclov* knows about it, so if we try and stay here and do *anything*, it's putting a knife in his hands: "Look at Saypur, keeping our most sacred temple secret in the Earth, getting their dirty foreign fingers all over it." Can you imagine that fallout? Can you imagine what would happen, Ambassador? Not just to your investigation, but to the Continent, to Saypur?'

Shara sighs. This is an argument she expected, but she'd hoped the solution wouldn't be quite so drastic. 'You really want to . . . to just cave it *in*? You think *that's* our best option?'

'I'd prefer to fill the damn tunnel up with cement, but the equipment would attract too many eyes. I've already asked our engineers about it – there are some wooden struts at the door that are definitely load-bearing. It wouldn't take more than thirty minutes.'

'There's *evidence*, though. Someone's been here, restoring the

Kolkashtani atrium. They even put a stone door frame in here, though I've no idea why. It *must* be whoever's working with Wiclov!'

'Are you certain of it to the extent that you would risk Continentals discovering this place?'

Shara rubs her eyes, then sits back and stares out at the Seat of the World. 'Looking at it, I just know,' she says, 'that I could spend a lifetime studying this.'

'If you were a historian,' says Mulaghesh. 'But you're not.'

Shara flinches, stung.

'You're a servant, Ambassador,' says Mulaghesh softly. 'We both have a duty. Neither of us will be doing it down here.'

In Shara's head, Efrem Pangyui is saying, *What truth do you wish to keep?*

The candelabra stutter.

A thousand shadows dance. Ancient faces glower, vanish.

'Do it,' says Shara.

The trudge back up the stairway feels interminable. Shara commits herself to memorising everything she saw, everything she read. *By all the seas*, she tells herself, *we won't lose this, too.*

'So there was nothing miraculous down there?' asks Mulaghesh.

'Not that I saw,' says Shara absently.

'That's a relief,' Mulaghesh says. She pulls an envelope from her coat pocket and holds it out to Shara. 'We've been reviewing the stolen pages of the list from the Warehouse. The idea of finding any more of this, out in the open, gives me nightmares. These twenty pages are what we think got the Restorationists so excited – or something in them, at least. But they probably got much, much more.'

If there is one thing that could break Shara's concentration, it's this. She snatches the envelope from Mulaghesh's hand, tears it open, and reads:

356. Shelf C4-145. Travertine's boots: Footwear that somehow makes the wearer's stride miles long – can cross the Continent in less than a day. VERY IMPORTANT to keep one foot on the ground: there were originally two pairs, but the testing wearer jumped, and floated into the atmosphere. Remaining pair still miraculous.

357. Shelf C4-146. Kolkan's carpet: Small rug that MOST DEFIN-ITELY possesses the ability to fly. VERY difficult to control. Records indicate Kolkan blessed each thread of the rug with the miracle of flight, so theoretically each thread could lift several tons into the air – though we have not yet attempted such, nor will we. Still miraculous.

358. Shelf C4-147. Toy wagon: Disappears on nights of a new moon, reappears on the full moon full of copper pennies bearing the face of Jukov. Once returned with a load of bones (not human). Still miraculous.

358. Shelf C4-148. Glass window: Originally was the holding place of numerous Ahanashtani prisoners, trapped inside the glass. When Ahanas perished, the panes bled for two months – prisoners were never found or recovered. No longer miraculous.

358. Shelf C4-149. Edicts of Kolkan, books 237 to 243: Seven tomes on how women's shoes should be prepared, worn, discarded, cleaned, etc.

'Oh,' says Shara softly. 'Oh, my *word*.'

Mulaghesh stops briefly to light a match on a stone protruding from the tunnel wall. 'Yeah.'

'*This* is what's in the Warehouse?'

'They just had to get hold of a part of the list with an unusually large amount of active, miraculous items. A lot of glass pieces, though—'

'The Divinities were fond of using glass as a safe place,' Shara murmurs.

'What do you mean?'

'They stored things in them, hid in them. All Divine priests knew many Release miracles. They'd be sent a simple glass bead, perform the appropri-ate miracle, break the glass, and then' – she waggles her fingers – 'mountains of gold, a mansion, a castle, a bride, or . . . whatever.' She trails off as she reads, struggling between fascination and horror as she flips through the rest of the entries. She's barely aware when they emerge from the tunnel, registering only the bright light from the candelabra in the *mhovost*'s room.

Mulaghesh nods to two young soldiers with axes and sledgehammers. 'Go on,' she says.

The soldiers enter the tunnel.

Shara reads the last pages.

Her hands clench: she nearly rips the paper in half.

'Wait!' she says. 'Wait, stop!'

'Wait?' asks Mulaghesh. 'For what?'

'Look,' says Shara. She points at one entry:

372. Shelf C5-162. Ear of Jukov: An engraved, stone door frame that contains no door. Iron wheels on the base. Speculated that it has a twin and, no matter where the other Ear is, if the doors are operated in the correct manner one can pass through one door and come out of the other. We speculate that the twin has been destroyed. No longer miraculous.

'Do you remember,' Shara asks, 'the stone door in the Kolkashtani atrium we just saw?'

'Yeah.' Mulaghesh's face does not change as she lifts her eyes from the page to Shara. 'You . . . you think—'

'Yes.'

Mulaghesh has to think for a moment. 'So if that's the other Ear down there . . .'

'And if its twin is still in the Warehouse . . .'

The two stare at each other for one second longer. Then they dash back down the stairway.

Sigrud and the other two soldiers watch, bewildered, before following.

'Taking everything into account, it still seems wisest,' Mulaghesh intones from the shadows, 'to just destroy the damn thing.'

Shara holds the candelabrum higher to inspect the door frame. 'Would you prefer that we leave *not* knowing if someone used the door to access the Warehouse?'

A click as Mulaghesh sucks on her cigarillo. 'They could have gone in there, touched something they shouldn't have, and died.'

'Then I, personally, would like to have a body.' She studies the sculpted door, looking for a word, a letter, a switch or a button. *Though they wouldn't need anything mechanical*, she reminds herself. *All mechanics of the miraculous operate in a much more abstract manner.*

Sigrud lies on the temple floor, staring up as if it's a sunny hillside with a blue sky above. 'Maybe,' he says, 'you must do something to the *other* door.'

'I would prefer that, yes,' says Shara. She mutters a few lines from the *Jukoshtava*: the door remains indifferent. 'Then this door would be more or less useless. Provided security is firm at the Warehouse.'

'And it *is*,' snaps Mulaghesh.

Shara tries praising the names of a few key Jukoshtani saints. The door is unmoved. *This must be what it's like*, she thinks, *to be a lecher trying out lines on a girl at a party.*

'I rather think,' she says finally, 'that I am going about this the wrong way.'

Mulaghesh suppresses a ferocious yawn. 'Whatever gave you that idea?'

Shara's eye strays across a distant pictogram in Jukov's atrium depicting an orgy of stupendous complexity. 'Jukov did not respect words, or shows of fealty. He was always much more about action, wildness, with nothing planned.' At the head of the orgy, a figure in a pointed hat holds aloft a jug of wine and a knife. 'Sacrifice through blood, sweat, tears, emotion.'

She remembers a famous passage from the *Jukoshtava*: '*Those who are unwilling to part with their blood and fear; who refuse wine and wildness; who come upon a choice, a chance, and tremble and fear – why should I allow them in my shadow?*'

Wine, thinks Shara, *and the flesh.*

'Sigrud,' she says. 'Give me your flask.'

Sigrud lifts his head, and frowns.

'I know you have one. I don't care about that. Just give it to me. And a knife.'

Sparks as Mulaghesh taps her cigarillo against the wall. 'I don't think I like where this is going.'

Sigrud clambers to his feet, rustles in his coat. There is the tinkling of metal — unpleasant instruments, surely — and he produces a flask of dark brown glass.

'What is it?' asks Shara.

'They said it was plum wine,' he says. 'But, from the fumes, I think the salesman, he might not have been so honest.'

'And have you tried it?'

'Yes. And I have not gone blind. So.' He holds out a small blade.

This will either work, thinks Shara, *or be very embarrassing*. Sigrud uncorks the flask — the fumes are enough to make her gag — and she tugs off her free hand's glove with her teeth. Then she steels herself and slashes the inside of her palm.

Mulaghesh is appalled. 'What in the—'

Shara puts her mouth to the wound and sucks at it. It is bleeding freely: the taste of salt and copper suffuses her mouth, almost chokes her. Then she rips her hand away, and hurriedly takes a pull from the flask.

It is not — most *certainly* not — any sort of alcohol she has ever tasted before. Vomit curdles in her stomach, washes up her oesophagus; she chokes it back down. She faces the door frame, gags once, and spews the mixture of alcohol and blood over it.

She is not in control of herself enough to even see if it worked: she hands the flask and knife back to Sigrud, drops to all fours, and begins to violently dry heave, but as she lost most of the contents of her stomach when she first saw the *mhovost*, there is nothing to expel.

She hears Mulaghesh say, 'Um. *Uhh* . . .'

There is a soft scrape as Sigrud's black knife escapes from its sheath.

'What?' croaks Shara. She wipes away tears. 'What is it? Did it work?'

She looks, and finds it is difficult to say.

The interior of the door frame is completely, impenetrably black, as if someone has inserted a sheet of black graphite in it while she wasn't looking. One of Mulaghesh's soldiers, curious, steps behind the doorway: none of them are able to see through to her. The soldier sticks her head out the other side, and asks, 'Nothing?'

'Nothing,' says Mulaghesh. 'Was it supposed to do' — she struggles for words — '*that*?'

'It's a reaction, at least,' says Shara. She grabs the candelabrum and approaches the door frame.

'Be careful!' says Mulaghesh. 'Something could . . . I don't know, come *out* of it.'

The blackness inside the doorway, Shara sees, is not as solid as she thought: as she nears it, the shadow recedes until she spots the hint of tall, square metal frames on either side of the doorway, and a rickety wooden floor.

Shelves, she realises. *I'm seeing rows and rows of shelves.*

'Oh, my seas and stars,' whispers Mulaghesh. 'What is that?'

And would this – Shara's heart is trembling – *be the view from shelf C5-162, where the other Ear of Jukov sits?*

Shara reaches down and picks up a clod of earth. She gauges the distance, and tosses it into the doorway.

The clod flies through the door frame, into the shadows, and lands with a *thunk* on the wooden floor.

'It passes through,' remarks Sigrud.

'That,' says Shara, 'would be a major security breach.'

And so, she muses, *Lord Jukov allows us in his shadow.*

This deeply concerns her, though she does not say so. Not only has she just found that one of Jukov's Divine creatures was still alive, but now one of his miraculous devices appears to still work. *Who actually witnessed Jukov's death*, she thinks, *besides the Kaj himself?*

She returns to the task at hand. 'Let's take a look, shall we?'

There is a passing shadow – the candle flames in her candelabrum shrink to near nothing – an unsettling breeze, then the creak of wood below her feet.

Shara is through.

She takes a breath, and immediately starts coughing.

The interior of the Unmentionable Warehouse is musty beyond belief, much more so than the Seat of the World: it is like entering the home of a hugely ancient, hoarding old couple. Shara hacks miserably at the bloody handkerchief around her hand. 'Is there no ventilation here?'

Mulaghesh has tied a bandana around her head before stepping through. 'Why the hells would there be?' she says, irritated.

Sigrud enters behind her. If the air bothers him, he doesn't show it.

Mulaghesh turns round to look at the second stone door frame, sitting comfortably in the lowest spot on shelf C5. Shara can see Mulaghesh's two soldiers watching them from the other side of the door, anxious.

'Could we really be here?' Mulaghesh asks aloud. 'Could we really have been transported miles outside of Bulikov, just like that?'

Shara holds up the candelabrum: the shelves tower above them nearly three or four storeys tall. Shara thinks she can make out a tin roof somewhere far overhead. The skeletal form of an ancient rolling ladder lurks a dozen feet away. 'I would say we are here,' she says, 'yes.'

The three of them stand in the Unmentionable Warehouse, and listen.

The dark air is filled with sighs and squeaks and low hums. The rattle of pennies, the scrape of wood. The air pressure in the room feels like it is constantly changing: either something in the Warehouse has confused Shara's skin, inner ear and sinuses, or there are countless forces applying themselves to her, then fading, like ocean currents.

How many miracles are down here with us, Shara wonders, *functioning away in the dark? How many of the words of the Divinities still echo in this place?*

Sigrud points down. 'Look.'

The wooden floor is covered in sediments of dust, yet this aisle has been marred by recent footprints.

'I presume,' says Mulaghesh, 'that that would be the passage of our mysterious opponent.'

Shara fights to concentrate: there are many paths of footprints, none of them completely clear. Their trespasser must have paced the aisles many times. 'We need to look for any sign of tampering,' she says. 'Then, after that, we need to look and see if anything's *missing*. I would expect that, if there's anything missing, it'd be something from these pages, since these are the records that interested the Restorationists. So' – she flips through the pages – 'we'll want to look at shelves C4, C5 and C6.'

'Or he could have just randomly stolen something,' says Mulaghesh.

'Yes. Or that.' *Thank you*, she thinks, *for highlighting the futility of our search*. 'We all have a light, don't we? Then let's spread out, and keep an eye on each other. We'll get out of here as fast as we can. And I don't think I need to say this, but do *not* touch *anything*. And if something asks for your attention, or for your interference . . . ignore it.'

'Would these *items* really have minds of their own?' asks Sigrud.

Shara's memory supplies her with a litany of miraculous items that were either alive, or claimed to be. 'Just don't touch anything,' she says. 'Stay clear of all the shelves.'

Shara takes shelf C4, Mulaghesh C5, Sigrud C6. As she walks down her aisle, Shara reflects on the age of this place. *These shelves are nearly eighty years old*, she thinks, listening to the creaking. *And they look it.* 'The Kaj never intended for this to be a permanent fix, did he?' she whispers as she looks down the aisle. 'We just kept ignoring it, hoping this was a problem that would go away.'

Each space on the shelves is marked by a tiny metal tag with a number. Beyond this, there is no explanation for the contents, which are beyond random.

One shelf is occupied by most of a huge, disassembled statue. Its face is blank, featureless, save for a wriggling, fractal-like design marching across the whole of its head. *Taalhavras*, thinks Shara, *or one of his incarnations*.

A wooden box covered in locks and chains wriggles; a scuttering noise comes from within, like many small, clawed creatures scrabbling at the wood. Shara quickly steps past this.

A golden sword shines with a queer light above her. Beside it sit twelve short, thick, unremarkable glass columns. Beside these, a large silver cup with many jewels. Then mountains and mountains of books and scrolls.

She walks on. Next she sees sixty panes of glass. A foot made of brass. A corpse wrapped in a blanket, tied with silver twine.

Shara cannot see the end of the aisle. *One thousand four hundred years*, she thinks, *of miraculous items*.

The historian in her says, *How fortuitous the Kaj thought to store them all.*

The operative in her says, *He should have destroyed every single one of them when he had the chance.*

'Ambassador?' calls Mulaghesh's voice.

'Yes?'

'Did you say something?'

'No.' Shara pauses. 'At least, I don't think I did.'

A long silence. Shara surveys a collection of silver thumbs.

'Is it possible for these things to talk in your head?' asks Mulaghesh.

'Anything is possible here,' says Shara. 'Ignore it.'

A bucket full of children's shoes.

A walking stick made of horsehair.

A cabinet spilling ancient parchments.

A cloth mask, made to look like the face of an old man.

A wooden carving of a man with seven erect members of varying length.

She tries to focus: her mind keeps searching through all the stories she's memorised, trying to place these items in the thousands of Continental legends. *Is that the knot that held a thunderstorm in its tangle, and when untied brought endless rain? Could that there be the harp of a* hovtarik, *from the court of Taalhavras, which made the tapestries come alive? And is that the red arrow made by Voortya, that pierced the belly of a tidal wave and turned it to a gentle current?*

'No,' says Sigrud's voice. 'No. That is not so.'

'Sigrud?' says Shara. 'Are you all right?'

A low hum from a few yards away.

'No!' says Sigrud. 'That is a lie!'

Shara walks quickly down the aisle until she sees Sigrud standing on the opposite side of a shelf, staring at a small, polished black orb sitting in a velvet-lined box.

'Sigrud?'

'No,' he says to the orb. 'I left that place. I am . . . I am not *there* any more.'

'Is he all right?' calls Mulaghesh.

'Sigrud, listen to me,' says Shara.

'They died because' – he searches for an explanation – 'because they tried to *hurt* me.'

'Sigrud . . .'

'No. No! No, I will not!'

In the velvet box, the glassy black orb rotates slightly to the left; Shara is reminded of a dog cocking its head – *Why not?*

'Because *I*,' Sigrud says forcefully. 'Am *not*. A *king*!'

'Sigrud!' shouts Shara.

He blinks, startled. The black orb sinks a little lower in the velvet, as if it's disappointed to lose its playmate.

Sigrud slowly turns to look at her. 'What . . . what has happened?'

'You're here,' she says. 'You're here in the Warehouse, with me.'

He rubs his temple, shaken.

'The things here are . . . they're very old,' she explains. 'I think they're bored. And they've been feeding off one another. Like fish trapped in a shrinking pond.'

'I have found nothing missing,' he grumbles. 'The shelves are quite full. *Over* full, even.'

'Me neither,' says Mulaghesh's voice from the next aisle. 'You don't want us to climb the ladders, do you?'

'Does it look like the ladders have been moved?' asks Shara. 'Look at the dust.'

A pause. 'No.'

'Then it would have been something on the first few shelves.'

Shara directs her own attention to the lowest shelves of her remaining aisles, and continues her search.

Four brass oil lamps. A blank, polished wooden board. Children's dolls. A spinning wheel whose wheel is slowly rotating, though there seems to be no flax, and certainly no spinner.

Then, in the final spot, just ahead . . .

Nothing.

Maybe nothing. Nothing that she can see, at least.

Shara thinks. *Something missing?*

She strides towards the empty space. Her eyes are so used to seeing random material in the corner of her vision that she does not pay much attention to what's below her. But as she nears the blank space on the shelf, she thinks, briefly, *Did I see something shining on the ground?*

A wire, maybe?

Something catches at her ankle. Pulls. Breaks — a tinny *ping*!

There is a tinkle of metal from the next aisle over; a tiny steel key goes skittering across the boards.

Immediately Sigrud roars, '*Down! Now!*'

A puff of black smoke across the aisle to her right.

Then a wild blossom of orange flames, and a concussive blast.

A wave of heat batters her right side. Shara is lifted off the ground. She crashes into the shelves next to her, sending ancient treasures flying: a leather bag tumbles through the air, vomiting an endless stream of golden coins; a streamer of pale ribbon strikes the ground and turns to leaves.

Dust and metal and old wood spin around her. She falls to the ground, paws at a shelf, but cannot stand.

A fire rages to her right. Smoke coils and curls across the ceiling, like a black cat finding sanctuary in a sunbeam.

On her left, the statue of Taalhavras crashes off the shelf. Sigrud awkwardly clambers through to kneel beside her.

'Are you all right?' he asks. He touches the side of her head. 'You have lost some hair.'

'What damned miracle,' she pants, 'was that?'

'No miracle,' he says. He looks back at the spreading fire. 'A mine. Incendiary, I think, or it did not ignite properly.'

'What the *hells* is going on over there?' shouts Mulaghesh's voice.

Somewhere in the darkness, many tiny voices chatter.

Flames rush across the dust on the floor, hop on to one shelf, burrow into the blanket-wrapped corpse.

'We need to leave,' says Sigrud. 'This place, so dry and old, will burn down in moments.'

Shara looks out at the growing flames. The top of the shelf on her right is almost completely ablaze. 'There was a blank space,' she murmurs, 'on that shelf ahead. Something has been stolen.' She tries to point; her finger drunkenly wanders to the ground.

'We need to leave,' says Sigrud again.

There are popping sounds out in the darkness. Something screeches in the fire.

'What in *shitting hell* is going *on* over there?' bellows Mulaghesh.

Shara looks at Sigrud. She nods.

He effortlessly hauls her up on to one of his shoulders. 'We are leaving!' he shouts to Mulaghesh.

Sigrud sprints down the aisle, turns right, and makes a beeline for the stone door frame.

A ruby-red glow filters through the forest of towering shelves.

Decades, thinks Shara. *Centuries. Aeons. More.*

Gone. All gone.

Sigrud sets Shara down when they're back in the Seat of the World.

She coughs, and weakly asks, 'How bad am I?'

He asks her to wiggle her fingers and toes. She does so. 'Good,' he says. 'Mostly. Lost a lot of an eyebrow. Some hair. And your face is red. But not burned, not seriously. You are lucky.' He looks up at the inferno raging on the other side of the stone door frame. 'I do not think whoever set that trap knew what they were doing. But when I heard it . . .' He shakes his head. 'Only one thing in the world sounds like that.'

Mulaghesh leans on one of her soldiers and, in between hacking coughs, attempts to light another cigarillo. 'So the sons of bitches *mined* the Warehouse? Just in case we followed?'

A broiling heat comes pouring through the stone door frame.

At every moment, thinks Shara, *they've been one step ahead of me.*

'Let's cave that damn tunnel in,' says Shara, 'and be done with this damned place.'

In the darkness of the Warehouse, legends and treasures wither and die in the flames. Thousands of books turn to curling ash. Paintings are eaten by flame from the inside out. Wax pools on the floor, running down from the many candles stacked across the shelves, and makes a twisted rainbow across the wooden slats. In some of the deeper shadows, invisible voices sob in grief.

Yet not all the items meet destruction.

A large clay jug sits on a shelf, bathing in heat. Upon its glazed surface are many delicate black brushstrokes: sigils of power, of containment, of tethering.

In the raging heat, the ink bubbles, cracks and fades. The wax seal around its cork runs and drips down its side.

Something within the bottle begins growling, slowly realising its prison is fading away.

The jug begins to tip back and forth. It plummets off its shelf to shatter on the ground.

The jug erupts in darkness. Its contents expand rapidly, sending shelves toppling like dominoes. The jug's prisoner keeps growing until its top nearly touches the ceiling of the Warehouse.

One yellow eye takes in the flames, the smoke, the burning shelves.

A high-pitched voice shrieks in victorious rage: *Free! Free at last! Free at last!*

I am gentle with you, my children, for I love you.

But love and gentleness do not breed purity: purity is earned through hardship and punishment and edification. So I have made these holy beings to help you find your way, and teach you the lessons I cannot bear to:

Ukma, sky-walker and wall-walker, watcher and whisperer. He will see the weaknesses in you that you cannot, and he will make you fight them until you rise above yourself.

Usina, traveller and wanderer, window-creeper and ash-woman. Beware the poor wretch you mistreat, for it may be Usina, and her vengeance is long and painful.

And for those who cannot be purified, who will not repent, who will not know the shame that lives in all our hearts, there is Urav, sea-beast and river-swimmer, he of many teeth and the one bright eye, dweller of dark places. For those sinners who are blind to light, they will spend eternity within his belly, burning under his scornful gaze, until they understand and know my righteousness, my forgiveness and my love.

The Kolkashavska, *Book Three*

You will know pain

Vod Drinsky sits on the banks of the Solda and tries to convince himself he is not as drunk as he feels. He has had most of a jug of plum wine, and he tells himself that if he *was* quite drunk then the wine would start to taste thick and sour, but so far the wine continues to taste quite terribly beautiful and sweet to his tongue. And he *needs* the wine to survive in the cold – why, look at how his breath frosts! Look at the huge ice floes in the Solda, the way the black water bubbles against the spots as thin and clear as glass! A cold night this is, so he thinks he should be forgiven his indulgence, yes?

He looks east, towards the walls of Bulikov, huge white cliffs glimmering in the moonlight. He glowers at them and says, 'I should!' A belch. 'I *should* be forgiven.'

As he watches, he realises there is a queer, flickering orange light on the hill behind him.

A fire. One of the warehouses in the complex up there is burning, it seems.

'Oh, dear.' He scratches his head. Should he call someone? That seems, at the moment, to be a difficult prospect, so he takes another swig of wine, and sighs and says again, 'Oh, dear.'

A dark shadow appears at the chain-link fence around the warehouse complex. Something low and huge.

A long, stridulous shriek. The dark shape surges against the chain-link fence; the woven wires stretch and snap like harp strings.

Something big comes rushing down the hillside. Vod assumes it is a bear: it *must* be a bear, because only a bear could be so big, so loud, panting and growling. Yet it sounds much, *much* larger than a bear.

It comes to the treeline, and leaps.

Vod's drunken eyes only see it for an instant. It is smoking – perhaps an escapee of the fire above. But through the smoke, he thinks he sees something thick and bulbous, something with many claws and tendrils gleaming in the moonlight.

It strikes the river ice with a huge *crack* and plummets through into the dark waters below. Vod sees something shifting under the ice: now the thing looks long and flowing, like a beautiful, mossy flower blossom. With a graceful pump, it propels itself against the river current and towards the white walls of Bulikov. As it turns over, he sees a soft yellow light burning on its surface, a gentle phosphorescence that deeply disturbs him.

The creature disappears downriver. He looks at the broken ice: it is at least two feet thick. Suggesting, then, that whatever leaped in was very, very heavy.

Vod lifts his jug, sniffs at it and peers into its mouth, unsure if he wishes to buy this brand again.

Fivrei and Sohvrena sit under the Solda Bridge in a tiny shanty, nursing a weak lamp. It is an unusual time to fish on the Solda, but the two men know a secret few do: directly under the bridge, where the Solda is widest and deepest, dozens of trout congregate, presumably, as Fivrei claims, seeking food and warmth. 'As far away from the wind as they can get,' he says each time he drops his black line into his tiny hole.

'And they,' grumbles Sohvrena, 'are wise.'

'Do you complain? How many did you catch last night?'

Sohvrena holds his mittened hands closer to the fire in the suspended brazier. 'Six,' he admits.

'And the night before that?'

'Eight. But I must weigh the amount of fish I catch against the toes I lose.'

'Pah,' says Fivrei. 'A real fisherman must be made of sterner stuff. This is man's work. It calls for a man.'

But a man's other work, thinks Sohvrena, lies in the soft, warm arms of a woman. Could he be unmanly for wishing he were there, rather than here?

A soft tapping fills the shanty.

'A catch?' asks Sohvrena.

Fivrei inspects his tip-up, which is suspended over the six-inch hole in the ice; the white flag on the black line quivers slightly. 'No,' he says. 'Perhaps they are playing with it.'

Then high-pitched squeaks join the tapping, like someone rubbing their hands against a pane of glass. Before Sohvrena can remark upon it, the flag on his own tip-up starts to dance. 'The same here,' he says. 'Not a catch, but it . . . moves.'

Fivrei tugs his black line. 'Maybe I am wrong . . . wait.' He tugs the line again. 'It is caught on something.'

Sohvrena watches the flag twitch on Fivrei's tip-up. 'Are you *sure* it's not a catch?' asks Sohvrena.

'It does not give. It's like it's caught on a rock. What *is* that intolerable squeaking?'

'Maybe the wind?' Sohvrena, curious, tugs at his own line. It also does not give. 'Mine is the same. *Both* of our lines are caught on something?' He shakes his head. 'Something is wrong. We had nothing on our lines a few minutes ago.'

'Maybe flotsam is being washed downstream, and our lines are caught.'

'Then why don't our lines just break?' Sohvrena inspects the ice below them. Perhaps he is seeing things, but he imagines a soft yellow glow filtering through the frost in one spot.

'What is that?' he says, pointing.

Fivrei does a double take, and stares at the yellow light. 'What *is* that?'

'That's what I just said.'

The two men look at it, then at each other.

The fire in the brazier has melted away some snow on the ice; they stand and begin to clear away more with their feet, until the ice becomes more transparent.

Fivrei gapes. 'What on . . . by the heavens, what is . . . ?'

Something is stuck to the opposite side of the ice, directly underneath them. Sohvrena is reminded of a starfish he once saw, brought back from the coast, but vastly huger, nearly thirty feet in diameter, and with many, many more arms, some of them wide, some of them thin and delicate. And in the centre, a bright, glowing eye and a many-toothed mouth that sucks against the ice, its black gums squeaking.

The taps and pops increase. Sohvrena looks up at the ends of the beast's arms, and sees many tiny claws scraping at the ice around them in a perfect circle.

'Oh, no,' says Sohvrena.

The light blinks twice. Sohvrena thinks, *An eye. It's an eye.*

With a great *crack*, the ice gives way below them, and a mouth ringed with a thousand teeth silently opens.

The Vohskoveney Tea Shop always does a roaring trade whenever the weather dips; Magya Vohskoveney herself understands that it is not necessarily the quality of the tea that draws in customers – since she herself holds the opinion that her tea brewers are untalented clods – but between the endless flow of steaming water, the bubbling cauldrons and the dozens of little gas lamps lit throughout her establishment, Magya's tea shop is always churning with a sweltering humidity that would seem suffocating in normal weather, yet is downright inviting in the brutal dark of winter.

The tea trade has rocketed on the Continent in the past decades: what was previously considered a distasteful Saypuri eccentricity has become much more appealing as the climate on the Continent grows colder and colder with each year. And there is the additional factor that Magya has discovered a mostly forgotten old bit of folk herbalism: teas brewed with a handful of poppy fruit tend to feel so much more *relaxing* than other types of tea. And after implementing this secret recipe, Magya's trade has quintupled.

Magya squints at the crowd from the kitchen door. Her customers cling to tables like refugees seeking shelter. Their hair curls and coils and glistens in the heat. The brass lamps cast prisms of ochre light on the soaking wooden walls. The west windows, which normally look out on to a scenic stretch of river, are so fogged over they look like toast with too much butter.

One man at the bar paws his cup limply, blinking owlishly; Magya stops a waiter, nods at the man, says, 'Too much,' and sends the boy on his way.

'A good trade, for the hour,' says one of her servers, stopping to mop his brow.

'Too good, in fact,' says Magya. 'Everything is full except the second-floor balcony.'

'How is that *too* good?'

'We shan't let greed overcome wisdom, my love.' Magya taps her chin, thinking. 'No special batches for the next week.'

Her server attempts to control his astonishment. '*None?*'

'None. I'd prefer not to arouse any suspicion.'

'But what will we say when people complain about the *quality* of the tea?'

'We will say,' Magya answers, 'that we have been forced to use a new type of barrel that's affected the flavour. I don't know, some Saypuri trade rule. They'll believe that. And we'll tell them we shall be rectifying the situation shortly.'

Her server is rudely hailed by a couple at the bar, a middle-aged man with an arm thrown around a very giddy and curvy young woman. *In my grandmother's day*, thinks Magya, *such a public display would get you flogged. How times have changed.* 'Go on,' she says. 'Give them something to fill their mouths, and shut them up.'

Her server departs. Magya's eye, always seeking trouble, finds something concerning on the upper balcony: one of the lights in her lamps has begun to flicker.

She grunts, climbs the steps, and sees she is wrong. The lamp is not flickering, but it is jumping on its chain, hopping up and swishing about like a fish on a line.

'What on Earth . . . ?' Magya looks up the chain at the beam it is attached to.

She watches, awed, as the beam actually *buckles* up, as if something on the roof is pulling at it. There are even cracks in the plaster of the roof, which spread like fractures in ice bearing too much weight.

Magya's first instinct is to look out of the window, but she remembers that the windows are opaque with condensation. Yet she sees she is mistaken again: something has partially wiped the condensation away from the outside of the west windows.

But what could do that, thinks Magya, *as we're on the river, thirty feet up?*

She goes to the window, wipes away the inside moisture, and peers through the blurry glass.

The first thing she sees is a single yellow light on the river shore below.

The second thing she sees is something large, black and glistening stuck to the wall of the shop, like a tree root covered in tar, yet it is uncoiling, adhering itself to more and more of the wall.

And the third thing she sees is right in front of her. What appears to be a long, slender black finger rises up on the other side of the window, and the dark claw at its end reaches forward and delicately taps the glass once.

'What—?' says Magya.

Then a burst of thunder, a rain of plaster dust and wooden shards, and the treasured humidity of the Vohskoveney Tea Shop goes ballooning up into the winter night sky in a roiling rush as its ceiling and upper wall are completely torn off.

Magya blinks as the wind assails her. Most of her patrons are too stunned to scream, but some manage to find their voices. The lower wall follows suit, crumbling out on to the frozen river, pulling the second-floor balcony – and Magya Vohskoveney – with it.

As Magya falls, she sees the same fate has befallen many of her customers. *We shall be dashed on the ice*, she thinks madly, *like a handful of eggs*. But in those unending seconds as she tumbles over and over, she sees the ice is not there: there is only the yellow light, the churning of many tentacles, and a quivering, many-toothed mouth juddering open.

'I said I want *every* soldier available working to help those fire teams!' bellows Mulaghesh downstairs. 'Make sure to stress that as *much* as you can in a telegram! And let the corporal know that if there is any reluctance on his part to put his soldiers to such work, then there will be *dire* consequences!'

Shara winces in her office. Mulaghesh has completely taken over the embassy offices downstairs, commandeering every telegraph machine, and posting troops at all entrances. Normally she would be doing this from her quarters, but the embassy was much closer. 'Contact General Noor at Fort

Sagresha,' Mulaghesh shouts. 'He needs to be notified of this, and tell him we need all the support he can offer. Interrupt me as soon as you hear, even if I specifically say *not* to interrupt me!'

Shara rubs her temples. 'By the seas,' she mutters, 'can the woman speak at any other volume?' Shara is content to let Mulaghesh handle this disaster, and since this is technically Mulaghesh's jurisdiction, Shara has plenty of reasons to stay out. But privately she wishes Mulaghesh and the rest of them would just leave.

Sigrud sits in the corner of her office and sharpens his black knife. The *scritch, scritch* seems to grow until Shara's head echoes with it.

'Must you do that now?' she asks.

Sigrud scrapes the knife more softly. 'You seem to be in a mood.'

'I was nearly blown up tonight.'

He shrugs and spits on the knife. 'Not the first time.'

'And we burned down thousands of years of priceless history!' she hisses, not daring to shout it.

'So?'

'So I have . . . I have *never* experienced such a failure in my professional career! And I do not enjoy failure. I am *unused* to it.'

The *scritch, scritch* slows as he thinks. 'It is true that we have never encountered a mistake such as this.'

'*A* mistake? Ever since we've set foot in Bulikov, we've done nothing but stumble!' She quaffs tea with the air of a sailor drinking whisky.

'I suppose it is good to get all of your mistakes out in one run.'

'Your optimism,' says Shara, 'is not appreciated. I almost regret coming here.'

'Almost?'

'Yes, almost. Because as . . . as *shit-bedecked* as this operation is, I still wouldn't trust it to anyone else in the Ministry. Think what would happen if Komalta was here, or Yusuf!'

'I didn't even know those two were still alive. I thought they'd have managed to get themselves killed by now.'

'Exactly!' She stands up, walks to the window and pushes it open. 'I need air. My head is filling up with *noise*!' She breathes for a moment, listens, then rubs her eyes in exasperation. 'Even the streets outside are screaming! Is there no quiet place in this whole damnable ci . . .' She trails off. 'Wait, what time is it?'

Sigrud joins her at the window. 'Late. Too late for much noise.' He tilts his head. 'And it *is* screaming. You were not exaggerating.'

Shara surveys the dark streets of Bulikov. 'What's going on?'

Another howl in the night. Someone comes sprinting down the street outside, shrieking incoherently.

'I've no idea,' says Sigrud.

Downstairs, Mulaghesh is angrily dictating a response to General Noor specifying that this was *not* a direct attack, because that would be an indictment of their security, but Noor should be responding as if it *was* a direct attack, as they need assistance *immediately*.

Shara opens the window all the way. She hears a rumble towards the river. A cloud of white dust rises above the rooftops. 'Did a *building* just collapse?' she asks.

More people are running through the streets. Candles are lit in windows; doors are flung open. A man cries *What's wrong?* over and over. Finally someone answers, *There's something in the water! Something in the water!*

Shara looks to Sigrud, but can only say, 'What?'

Then a shout from downstairs. 'Shara!' cries Mulaghesh's voice. 'There's some idiot here to bother you!'

Shara and Sigrud troop downstairs. Pitry stands in the entryway with a very nervous-looking Bulikov police officer.

'A message from the Bulikov Police Department,' says Pitry, 'for Ambassador Thivani from Captain Nesrhev.'

'Get rid of this guy,' says Mulaghesh. 'I'm drowning in enough shit as it is.'

Shara fruitlessly searches for her inner calm. 'What would be the issue?'

The officer swallows, sweats. 'Ah, w-we're evacuating all homes and buildings near the river. The embassy's a priority' – he says this as if to suggest, *And I just* had *to get this duty* – 'so we need all of you outside, immediately.'

Mulaghesh finishes another communication, then breaks away. 'Wait, what the hells are you talking about? We're not going anywhere.'

'Well, Captain Nesrhev—'

'Is a fine and good officer, but he can't tell us to do a damn thing. This is Saypuri soil.'

'We're quite aware of that, Governor, but it's . . . it's *emphatically* suggested that you and the Ambassador evacuate.'

'Why?' Shara asks.

The officer is sweating profusely. 'We're . . . well, we can't quite say just yet.'

'Would this have to do with what's happening outside?' asks Shara.

The officer reluctantly nods.

'And what *is* happening outside?'

The officer appears to debate telling them; then his shoulders slump as if he's about to make an embarrassing confession. 'There's something in the Solda River,' he says. 'Something big.'

'And?'

'And it's killing people. Snatching them off the banks.'

Mulaghesh massages the centre of her forehead. 'Oh, by the seas!'

'It's even come up on the shore and attacked the buildings,' says the officer. 'It's . . huge. We don't know what it is, but we're evacuating every quarter near the river. And that includes the embassy.'

'And this just started happening very recently?' asks Shara. 'Within the past few hours?'

The officer nods.

Shara and Sigrud share a silent moment of communication. Shara's eyes say, *From the Warehouse?* Sigrud gives a grim nod. *Absolutely.*

'Thank you for notifying us, officer,' says Shara. She extends a hand, and Sigrud tosses her her coat. 'We will be glad to leave the embassy. Where is Nesrhev now?'

'He's staked out on the Solda Bridge, watching for it,' says the officer. 'But why d—'

'Excellent.' Shara pulls her coat on. 'We'll be only too happy to join him.'

The Solda Bridge's short walls leave them almost totally exposed to the cold wind, so nearly all of them are crouched down as low as they can to escape it. Shara wishes she'd wrapped every extremity in furs, and her feet in a layer of rubber, and Mulaghesh has not stopped swearing since leaving the embassy, though her curses shiver a bit more now. Captain Nesrhev sits against the wall, receiving messages and runners from his officers, who are hidden among the streets and homes that line the river. Only Sigrud leaves his face exposed, kneeling and staring into the bitter wind across the wide, frozen expanse of the river.

Shara peeps over the wall. The Solda resembles a jigsaw puzzle, with huge holes in the ice in perfect circles and half-moons. On the west bank, two buildings have had their facades and walls completely ripped off: white limestone lies crumbled on the mud like cottage cheese. 'And that . . .' asks Shara. 'That was where it attacked?'

'Yes,' says Nesrhev. 'We didn't see it. We were alerted too late. It's a miracle' – he checks himself, but Shara waves him on – 'it's a *good thing* it hasn't attacked the bridge, whatever it is. Though we hope the bridge is too strong for it. It's the only way across the Solda for four miles.'

'How many killed?' asks Mulaghesh.

'Twenty-seven reported missing or dead, now,' says Nesrhev. 'Plucked from the banks of the river, or sucked through the ice, or ripped from their homes.'

'My word,' murmurs Shara. 'So what *is* it?'

Nesrhev hesitates. 'We are told,' he says slowly, 'that it is a sea monster, with many arms.'

There is a pause as Shara absorbs this; Nesrhev and the officers watch, waiting to see how this will be received. 'Like a dragon?' she finally asks.

Nesrhev is relieved to be taken seriously. 'No, like . . . like a sea beast. But enormous.'

Shara nods. *A many-armed creature of the sea*, she thinks. *That's a very short list of possibilities.*

'So do you know what in all the hells this could be?' asks Nesrhev.

Shara watches as part of the ruined buildings tumbles off and drops into the river with a *plook*. 'I have some ideas,' she says. 'But . . . well, I will just say that I suspect this thing is in violation of the WR.'

For the first time, the veteran Nesrhev looks shocked. 'You're saying this thing is *Divine*?'

'Perhaps. Not everything Divine was good or godly,' says Shara.

'So what are you going to do?' asks one of Nesrhev's lieutenants. 'Arrest it?'

Sigrud makes a *tch* sound.

Shara sits up. 'Do you see it?'

'I see' – he tilts his head, squints – '*something*.'

Everyone peeks over the wall of the Solda Bridge. Several hundred feet south, a faint yellow light slips under the dense ice towards the east bank.

'Mikhail and Ornost are there,' says Nesrhev, concerned. 'Just behind the wall on the bank.'

The yellow light pauses. Then a faint cracking and creaking echoes across the river. Shara watches in amazement as a wide circle appears in the ice, as if someone is carefully sawing at it from under the water.

'Viktor,' says Nesrhev to one of his officers, 'go over there and tell the two of them to get *away*, get away *now*.'

The officer sprints away.

The circle of ice slowly sinks and slides underneath the frozen river. *A dexterous creature, then*, thinks Shara. The yellow eye creeps to the centre of the hole. Nesrhev lets loose a florid string of curses. Something very small and thin pokes out of the hole in the ice and rotates through the air, as if smelling for something. Then many more thin appendages – tentacles? – appear at the edge of the hole in the ice.

The yellow eye sinks lower. *It readies*, Shara realises, *for a leap*.

It bursts out of the water, sending shards of ice flying; its eruption is so powerful that a fine mist washes over them, even from here.

Nesrhev and his officers begin screaming; Mulaghesh's hand flies to her mouth; Shara and Sigrud, well used to horrors such as this by now, silently watch and observe.

It is not quite a jellyfish, not quite a squid, and nor is it a prawn, exactly, but a thirty-foot combination of all three: a slightly translucent creature with a long, black-shelled back and – maybe – a head, with the face almost concealed in a squirming bundle of thrashing tentacles that are long enough to start probing the shore, rising up like the hundreds of spearpoints of a phalanx.

Two shapes spring up on the banks and run away, screaming. One figure looks to be too slow. A tentacle whips towards it, and the figure spins – 'By all the gods, *no*,' whispers Nesrhev – but another officer comes running up with a flaming torch, which he hurls at the approaching tentacles. The creature pauses at this interruption just long enough for the officers to slip out of reach, up the banks of the Solda.

The creature climbs farther up the bank and screeches at them with a strangely avian call. Its tentacles search the riverbank, pluck up stones and hurl them at the retreating officers. None of the stones strike the officers; most find a home in the roof and walls of a small and unfortunate house. Then the creature shrieks twice more before retreating back, below the ice, where it drifts downriver.

'My *gods*,' says Nesrhev. 'My *gods*. What *is* that thing?'

Shara nods, satisfied that her hunch was correct. 'I think I know.' She polishes her glasses on her scarf. *He who waits in dark places*, she thinks. *And pulls down the unworthy and devours them*. 'I believe, Captain Nesrhev, that we have just seen the fabled Urav.'

A brief silence.

'*Urav*?' asks an officer. 'Urav the *Punisher*?'

Nesrhev swats at him furiously, as if to say, *Do you* know *who you are speaking in front of?*

'Don't stare so, Captain,' says Shara. 'It's perfectly all right for you to admit that you know of it. Even if it *is* against the WR to acknowledge such a thing. These are extenuating circumstances.'

'I thought Urav was a fairy story,' one officer reluctantly says.

'Oh, no,' says Shara. 'Kolkan was fond of using familiars and Divine creatures to do his work. Urav was the worst, and the most dangerous – and possibly his favourite.' She watches the yellow eye twirl under the ice, perhaps observing the shore, looking for sinners. *And to Urav*, Shara remembers, *who isn't a sinner?* 'The creature of the depths, in whose belly the souls of the damned cower under his gaze.'

'Then what the hells is it doing in my city killing innocent people?' demands Nesrhev.

'I can't immediately say,' says Shara, which is a lie. She recalls something she read in Ghaladesh: after Kolkan's sudden disappearance, Urav, without the oversight of its creator, reportedly went mad. Jukov was forced to capture it, luring it into a jug of wine distilled from human sin, and trapping it there.

And if all that is true, thinks Shara, *then there's only one likely place where that jug could have been stored.*

She silently curses herself for tripping on that wire. *Who knows what else I've released back into the world?*

'What on Earth can we do against such a thing?' asks Mulaghesh.

'Well,' says Shara, 'Divine creatures *can* be killed by normal means. They have their own agency, to an extent, which makes them vulnerable. I mean, look at the Great Purge – that was done with knives and spears and axes.'

The officers shift uncomfortably to hear such forbidden subjects discussed aloud. Some look outraged, even scandalised; Shara is happy she did not mention she personally accomplished this same feat mere hours ago.

'I do not like the idea,' says Nesrhev, 'of putting my officers at risk, and having them shoot at this thing in the ice.'

'Bolts wouldn't penetrate the ice, anyway,' says Mulaghesh.

'We should wait for the ice to melt,' says Nesrhev, 'or maybe start bonfires on it to melt it, and then see what we can do.'

'And what would you do then?' asks Mulaghesh. 'Attack it in boats? With spears? Like a whale?'

Nesrhev hesitates; he looks around at his officers, who look none too pleased with the idea.

Sigrud makes another *tch*, as if weighing something in his mind. Then, 'I can kill it.'

Silence.

Everyone slowly turns to look at him.

Shara glances at him, concerned. *Are you sure you want to start this?* But Sigrud's expression is inscrutable.

'What?' says Mulaghesh. '*How?*'

'It is a . . .' He makes the constipated face that he always does when trying to translate a Dreyling word. 'A thing of the water,' he finishes. 'And I have killed many things of the water.'

'But . . . are you *serious?*' asks Nesrhev.

'I have killed,' says Sigrud, 'many things of the water. This would be different.' He watches, keen-eyed, as Urav considers carving another hole in the ice before abandoning it. 'But not *that* different.'

'What exactly would you have my men do?' asks Nesrhev.

'I do not really think' – Sigrud scratches his chin, considering – 'that I would need any of your men at all.'

'You are genuinely suggesting that you, by yourself, can kill a Divine horror like *that*?' asks Mulaghesh.

Sigrud contemplates it; then he nods. 'Yes. The circumstances are favourable. The river is not big.'

'The Solda,' says Nesrhev, 'is almost a mile wide!'

'But it is not the sea,' says Sigrud. 'Not the ocean. Which I am used to. And with the ice' – he shrugs – 'it is very possible.'

'It's killed almost thirty people tonight, sir,' says Nesrhev. 'It would be an easy thing for it to kill you.'

'Perhaps. But. If so . . .' Again, Sigrud shrugs. 'Then I would die.'

Nesrhev and the other officers stare at him in disbelief.

Shara clears her throat. 'Before we continue down this line of thinking,' she says, 'I'd first like to ask if Captain Nesrhev would approve.'

'Why the hells would you care about that?' asks Nesrhev. 'It's up to you if your man wants to get himself killed.'

'Well, despite all the Regulations, that thing under the ice *is* considered holy by most of the Continent,' says Shara. 'It is, after all, a creature of stories and myths valued by your culture. It's part of your heritage. If you wish us to kill it – to kill what is, in effect, a living legend – we would want to have your express permission to do so.'

Nesrhev's face sours. 'You,' he says, 'are trying to cover your arse.'

'Perhaps. But Urav is an integral part of some of *your* treasured myths. *We* are not Continentals. To some Continentals, if we are successful in killing Urav, it would be tantamount to destroying a historic work of art.'

'In this case, though,' says Mulaghesh, 'it's a work of art that's running around murdering innocent people.'

Shara nods. 'Quite.'

Nesrhev grimaces. As he wrestles with his position, three policemen come staggering up, panting: one of them is Viktor, the officer sent to warn Mikhail and Ornost; the other two are presumably those same two men. One of them is clutching his right arm, which is slick with blood.

'Mikhail's hurt,' says Viktor. 'It got his arm, and it . . . it took some fingers.'

Nesrhev pauses. He looks out at the soft light under the ice. Then, 'Both of you, get back to the station and to the infirmary.' He looks to Sigrud. 'What do you need?'

Sigrud looks back out at the river. 'I will need,' he says thoughtfully, 'two hundred feet of towing rope, three lengths of sailing rope a hundred feet in length, a lantern, two halberds, five strong fishing spears and several gallons of fat.'

'Of *what*?' says Mulaghesh.

'Of fat,' says Sigrud. 'Animal fat. Whale if you have it – beef or pork if you do not.'

Mulaghesh looks to Shara, who shrugs – *I have no idea, either.*

Sigrud strokes his beard. 'And I will need you to get a good fire going, for when I finish. Because to do this, I will likely have to be naked.'

'Flaxseed,' says Shara, and drops it into the cauldron of warm beef fat. 'Willowgrass. Twine of six knots. And cedar pitch.' She looks back at the wheelbarrow of ingredients brought to her from the embassy. Screams echo up the river – again. She ignores them. 'Salt and silver . . . that might be harder.' She slips a tiny silver dessert spoon into a bag of rock salt and shakes it up. 'But this, I hope, should do.' She dumps it into the cauldron as well.

Pitry watches her, torn between fascination and disbelief. 'You really think this will do something?'

'I hope so,' says Shara. She takes a fistful of arrowroot and drops it in. 'The Divine familiars each had aversions to very specific elements . . . We're not sure, as always, if this was *intended* by the Divinities – maybe as a way to give their mortal followers some method of defence against the Divinities' own creations, just in case – or if it was purely by accident, something each Divinity, maybe by nature, could never prepare for. Either way, the Divine creatures were strongly repelled by these elements: they caused asphyxiation, burning rashes, paralysis, even death.'

'Like an allergy?' asks Pitry.

Shara pauses, realising Pitry has just said something Saypuri historians have been struggling to articulate for years. 'Yes. Exactly that.'

'And Urav is allergic to . . . to *all* of this?'

'I have no idea. These are some elements that often repelled Divine creatures. I am hoping,' she says as she drops in some wormwood, 'that one or two of these will have some effect. A broad spectrum of elements, you could say.'

Sigrud and Nesrhev's officers are almost finished: they've successfully looped the thick towing rope around the bridge itself, and fastened it securely. Shara can see the seaman in Sigrud coming out now: he ties knots in seconds, heaves coils of the dense rope around his shoulders, scales the bridge like he has hooks on his toes. He dumps the three lengths of sailing rope over the bridge; they land with a *thud* on the ice. He lets the remaining length of towing rope drop to the ice as well, nearly a hundred or so feet. Urav, so far, has remained ignorant of their efforts, choosing to harry the docks a mile or so downriver, seeking anyone who's chosen to ignore the evacuation order.

Sigrud walks over to where the weaponry is wrapped in waxed canvas. He picks up one fishing spear, which has a barbed tip as thick as Shara's arm; at its back is an iron loop, meant for some incredibly thick line. *What sort of fish*, Shara thinks, *could that possibly be intended for?* Sigrud tests its flex, nods in satisfaction, and kneels and runs his finger along the halberd's blade. 'Good iron,' he says. 'Good workmanship.'

'And you don't doubt,' asks Shara, 'the wisdom of your course?'

'We have done such things before,' says Sigrud. 'What makes this so different?'

'This is not like the *mhovost*.'

'*That*,' says Sigrud contemptuously, 'was not even a challenge.'

'Well. It is not like the *dornova* in Ahanashtan, either,' says Shara. 'This is not some common imp or wretch for you to brutally execute!'

'Next you will say it is not like that dragon.'

'That was a *small* dragon,' says Shara. She holds her hands up about three feet apart. 'And besides, *I* was the one who finally killed that one.'

'After I did all the work,' says Sigrud with a sniff.

'As entertaining as our exploits may be,' says Shara, *'that'* – she points a finger at the river – 'is the closest thing to a walking, talking Divinity the world has seen in decades!'

He shrugs. 'As I told you,' he says, 'it is a thing of the water. Things of the water, they are all alike, deep down. No matter who made them or where they came from.'

'But are you so terribly sure of yourself that you're really willing to try this *alone*?'

'The more you are at sea,' Sigrud explains, 'the more you learn. And the more you learn, the more help and assistance is a troublesome bother. Dealing death, after all, is a solitary affair.' He takes off his coat, shirt and breeches, revealing some very ancient long underwear. He is covered in rippling muscle, huge in the shoulders and back and neck, yet rather than appearing bulky there is something lean and lupine about Sigrud: he is like an animal that burns far more energy fighting for its food than it gains in consuming it. 'And I have always been so much better at dealing it alone.'

He peels off the long underwear's shirt. Shara has seen him shirtless – and more – in their time together, but she is always shocked by the variety of horrific scars curling across his arms and back: she can see brands, whips, slashes, stabs. Yet she knows the greatest damage he has ever sustained lies hidden behind the glove on his right hand.

He begins stripping off the rest of the long underwear. 'I don't *think*,' says Shara, 'that it will be necessary for you to take off *all* of your clothi—'

'Bah,' says Sigrud, and drops his drawers, utterly unselfconscious.

Shara sighs. Nesrhev and his officers, all dour, stolid Bulikovians, stare at this frank display of nudity.

Mulaghesh grins like a shark. 'There are times,' she says, 'when I kind of like my job.'

Sigrud is now totally naked except for his boots, the sheath for his knife (which is now strapped around his right thigh), and the glove he wears on his right hand. He reaches into the cauldron of fat and scoops up a handful. He cocks an eyebrow at the arrowroot and the other substances floating in it – 'Insurance,' explains Shara – and he shrugs and begins to slather it on his shoulders, chest, arms and thighs.

'Uh, let me know if you need help with that,' mutters Mulaghesh. Shara shoots her a scolding glare; Mulaghesh grins again, unrepentant.

Sigrud saves his face and hair for last; with this final touch, he resembles something primeval, a filthy, savage creature humanity left behind long ago. 'I think,' he says, 'I am ready.' He looks to Nesrhev. 'Try to keep the thing towards the bridge, if it comes to it.'

'I don't know how much we can do,' says Nesrhev. 'But we'll try.'

'Do only that,' says Sigrud. 'I want it focused on me. On *me*, do you hear?'

Nesrhev nods.

'Good.' Sigrud looks up and down the length of the bridge, as if not quite convinced it will hold. Then he heaves up the armful of weaponry and starts down the bridge towards the shore.

Mulaghesh hands out a lantern, which he takes. 'Good luck, soldier,' she says.

Sigrud nods absently, as if being greeted by familiar passers-by on a contemplative walk.

He stops next to Shara. 'If I *do* die tonight,' he says. He hesitates, staring out at the icy expanse of the Solda. 'My family . . . will you . . . ?'

'I will always make sure your family is taken care of,' says Shara. 'You know that.'

'But will you tell them . . . about me? About who I was?'

'Only if it's safe to do so.'

He nods, says, 'Thank you,' and starts off down the bridge.

Shara says, 'Listen, Sigrud, if it comes to that, it is likely Urav will *not* kill you.'

He looks back. 'Eh?'

'It's likely the people taken tonight aren't even dead. They may be *worse* than dead, actually. According to the *Kolkashavska*, in Urav's belly, you are alive, but you are punished, filled with pain, shame, regret. Under its gaze, no one holds hope.'

'How does it gaze at you,' asks Sigrud, 'in its own belly?'

'It's miraculous by nature. Inside of Urav, I think, is a special kind of hell. And the only thing that saves anyone is the blessing of Kolkan.'

'Which you can give me?'

'Which no one has received since he vanished, nearly three hundred years ago.'

'So what are you saying?'

'I am saying that, if it looks like Urav *will* devour you' – she looks down at where he has strapped his knife – 'then it might be wise to take matters into your own hands.'

He nods slowly. Then, again, he says, 'Thank you.' And adds, 'It would probably be wise for you to get off the bridge, by the way.'

'Why?'

'One never knows,' says Sigrud, 'how a good fight will go.'

Sigrud's boots make hollow *thumps* as he walks across the ice. He can tell right away that the ice is slightly less than two feet thick. *A good ice*, he thinks, *for sleighs and horses*.

He walks on and on over the frozen river. The wind bites and snaps at his ears. His arms and legs are bejewelled from millions of ice flecks trapped in the fat on his body: soon he is a glimmering ice-man, trudging across a vast grey-blue field.

He recalls an occasion like this: riding over the ice, the sleigh scraping behind him; the thud of the horse's hooves; and glancing behind and seeing Hild and his daughters buried in a pile of furs in the sled, giggling and laughing.

I do not wish to think of these things.

Sigrud blinks and focuses on the ropes dangling from the bridge ahead. The lights of Bulikov seem very far away now, as if this massive metropolis is but a small, seaside town on a very distant shore.

How many times did he see such a sight in his sailing days? Dozens? Hundreds?

I do not wish to think of these things, he says to himself again. But the memories arise painfully, like a thorn working its way free from flesh.

The chuckle of water. The sunless days. The bonfires on the rime-crusted beaches.

He remembers the last time he sailed. A young man he was, returning home, eager to see his family. But when they docked on Dreyling shores, he and the crew found the villages in absolute upheaval.

The king. They have killed the king, and all his sons. They are burning the houses, they are burning the city. What are we to do?

How shocked he was to hear this. He did not understand then ... could not understand how all this could happen. And no matter how many times he asked − *All his sons? All? Are you sure?* − the answer was the same. *The Harkvald dynasty is no more. All the kings are dead, gone, and we are lost.*

The ice crackles underneath Sigrud's feet. *The world is a coward*, he thinks. *It does not change before your face; it waits until your back is turned.*

Sigrud walks on over the Solda. The fat on his limbs is calcified now; he is milky white, crackling, a chandler's golem. He keeps walking to where the towing rope dangles from the centre of the bridge. While he was on it, the Solda Bridge seemed quite narrow, less than forty feet wide. Underneath, it's a massive black bone arcing across the sky.

He tells himself it will hold. If he does this right, it will hold.

He hears lapping water. He looks to the right, under the shadow of the bridge, and sees a geometrically perfect circle in the ice. A dense layer of wooden flotsam bobs up and down, trapped in the hole. A shanty, probably − and its occupants, long gone.

Finally he arrives at the dangling rope. He loops the end of the thick towing rope, then uses the sailing rope to tie it fast, holding the loop. The knot is familiar: his hands move and loop and thread the rope without him even thinking about it.

As he ties the knot, he remembers.

He remembers how he raced to his home after hearing the news. He remembers finding it burned and blackened and deserted; the farmland scarred, salted.

He remembers unearthing the fragile white bones lost in the moist ashes of his ruined, burned-out bedroom.

He remembers digging the graves in the courtyard. The jumble of charred bones, random, incomplete, a tangled human jigsaw.

He could not recognise his wife and two daughters in them. But he separated the bones as best he could, buried them, and wept.

Enough. Stop.

Sigrud ties the remaining lengths of sailing rope to the loop, then ties their other ends to the fishing spears. Then he stabs the fishing spears down in the ice in a line, each fifty feet apart.

He sets the lantern down before the centre spear, and uses the point of the halberd's blade to carve four deep, long lines in the ice, each converging on one point, just before the lantern. When he finishes, it looks like a giant star in the ice. Then he sits on the point, bare buttocks on the ice, halberd across his knees, and waits.

A duck honks disconsolately.

A spatter of screams from the east bank. The blasting wind.

Though he wishes to focus, the memories are merciless.

He remembers when he heard that a new nation had been formed, called the 'Dreyling Republics', but both that name and the title of 'nation' were laughable: they were mere pirate states, sick with corruption and avarice.

Sigrud, grieving, raging, chose to fight, like many did. And, like many, he failed, and was thrown in Slondheim, the cliff prison, a fate worse than death, they said.

And they spoke the truth. He is not sure how many years he spent in solitary confinement. Five. Ten. Maybe more. Living off gruel, ranting in the dark. Part of this was his own doing, of course: whenever they let him out, he tried to kill anyone who came close to him, and he often succeeded. Eventually they decided he would get no more chances: Sigrud was to live in the dark until he died.

But then one day the slot in his cell door opened, and he saw a face unlike any he'd seen before: a woman's face, brown-skinned and long-nosed, with dark eyes and dark lips, and she had *glass* on her face, two little pieces of glass before each eye. Yet all his puzzlement vanished when the face said, 'Your wife and children are alive, and safe. I have located them. I will be back tomorrow, if you wish to speak to me.'

The slot slammed shut. Her footsteps faded away.

This was how Sigrud first met Shara Komayd.

How many years has he spent with her? Nearly ten? It does not matter, he finds. The new years have no more meaning to him.

Sigrud blinks his eyes; his lids stick from the fat. He thinks of the children he never knew, now grown, and the young woman who was once his wife. He wonders if she has a new husband, and his children a new father.

He looks down at his scarred, gleaming hands. He does not recognise them any more.

On the horizon, a soft yellow light blinks below the ice.

Sigrud rubs fat from the palms of his hands, tests the grip on his halberd.

This is as it should be, he thinks. *The cold, the dark, and the waiting death.*

He waits.

The yellow light swims closer, closer, its movements smooth and graceful. Sigrud hears something tapping the ice, like a blind man with his cane. *It listens*, he thinks, *to the reverberations, to see what lies on the top*.

The ice creaks below him. The yellow glow is now twenty feet away; the light itself is nearly a foot wide. *Like the eye of a giant squid*, he thinks, and remembers, long ago, how he ate one that had been stewed in fish stock. *And that one was quite a fighter.*

He cannot see through the ice, but he hears something popping fifteen, maybe less than fifteen feet away. He looks and sees a circle is being carved around him, and he also sees he estimated the thing's breadth well: the edges of the circle all cross the four lines he carved in the ice. It begins to look like he is sitting in the middle of a big white pie with eight slices.

He slowly stands. The ice complains under his feet, weakened by so many carvings. He plucks up the fishing spear and stands in the centre of the circle.

Something dark swirls underneath him. The yellow light is almost under his feet.

I wonder, thinks Sigrud, *if I will find out how you taste*.

He readies the spear in his right hand. He takes a breath. Then, well before the thing under the ice is done carving the circle, he raises the halberd in his left hand and swings the massive blade down.

The weakened ice breaks apart underneath him immediately, and he plummets through into the icy water.

Urav – as Shara called it – darts back, surprised by this intrusion. Sigrud is tiny before its huge, swarming bulk, a swallow flying against a black thundercloud.

He sees a mass of waving arms, a huge, black-veined bright eye, and below that a mouth six feet wide . . . but it is not yet open.

He whips the fishing spear forward. The barbed blade sinks deep into Urav's black flesh, mere inches beside its huge eye.

Urav's mouth snaps open, but in pain rather than attack. Its eye rolls to focus on Sigrud, but he swings the halberd forward and cracks the creature in the mouth. Glittering teeth go spinning through the water like fireworks.

Urav writhes in pain and rage. Its tentacles snap out, grip Sigrud's legs, but the thick layer of fat makes it impossible to find a grip . . . and what is more, the tentacles withdraw suddenly as if the fat itself burns them: Sigrud can see the black skin bubbling where they touched him.

If Shara finds out her gambit worked, he thinks, *there'll be no living with her.*

The water is churning about him. He feels another tentacle try and grip his ankle; this too slips off. Urav marshals all its attention to himself, the countless limbs swirling around, preparing to strike.

Out, out now, he thinks, and he reaches up with his left hand, finds the sailing rope – it holds fast – and lifts himself up and out of the water, on to the ice.

His body is partially in shock from the temperature change, but he forces himself to forget about it, and instead focuses on sprinting to the fishing spear on the right. He hears ice shattering behind him, glances back to see Urav struggling against the sailing line, cracking through the ice around it. But the line holds fast.

Enraged, the creature bursts up on to the ice, its thousands of arms dragging its bulbous head forward. One tentacle pops forward and grasps Sigrud's left arm; its claw digs a hole in the skin of his biceps. He trips forward, and feels himself being dragged back. He struggles against it; the tentacle maintains its grip, even though he can see it is sizzling where it touches him.

Urav growls in pain and fury, gnaws at the ice, chopping it into coarse snow. *No. No, I will not let you go.*

Sigrud hacks at the tentacle once, twice with the halberd. This proves enough to weaken its grip and, with a low *pop*, Sigrud squirts free. *Praise the seas*, thinks Sigrud as he runs, *for cows with rich diets*.

'Shoot!' shouts Nesrhev from up above. 'Pepper the damn thing!'

Bolts whiz through the air, plunk into the ice. Many bite into Urav's hide; it screeches wildly and thrashes against the sailing line, which thrums like a guitar string.

Sigrud reaches the second fishing spear, but Urav is now focused on the men on the bridge. Its tentacles rise like a swarm of cobras and strike at the bridge above. There is a chorus of shrieks; two bodies twirl through the air, falling from the far side of the bridge. *Please*, thinks Sigrud, *do not be Shara*.

One tentacle curls down, a struggling police officer clutched in its grip, and stuffs the man into Urav's gaping mouth. A huge crack as the ice begins to protest against the battle.

This, thinks Sigrud, *is not what I wanted*.

He runs forward, halberd clutched under one arm, and throws the second fishing spear. He very nearly misses as the creature thrashes against the rope, but the spear finds its way deep into Urav's back. Urav howls again, and whips round. The yellow eye glares at him. Sigrud catches the quickest glimpse of a tentacle speeding at him like a tree trunk rushing down a river; then the world explodes in stars and lights and he goes sliding across the ice.

He expects another attack: it doesn't come. Groaning, he lifts his head and sees that Urav has turned in the ropes, and is now entangled; the sailing rope from the first spear he threw, however, has snapped, so the tangle is not permanent.

Sigrud growls, shakes his head, tests his limbs: they work, more or less. The halberd is beside him, but it has snapped, making it more like a short axe. He picks it up and trots towards the third and final fishing spear.

Get it tangled up, he thinks, *let it wear itself out, then beat it to death. Hack at its lungs until it drowns, drowns in its own blood*.

Stones begin to plummet from the Solda Bridge.

Unless, he thinks, *it tears the bridge apart*.

He watches as Urav strikes the bridge over and over again. More small stones tumble into the water.

He wishes Nesrhev had never given the command to fire. He wishes Urav had stayed focused on him, only him.

This is why I hate being helped.

Urav's thrashing has shredded almost all the ice under the bridge; the chunk with Sigrud's final fishing spear in it bobs up and down like the floater of a fishing pole. With a sigh, Sigrud dives into the water – the cold is like a hammer to his head – swims to it, pulls the spear free, and climbs the rope until it pulls him to sturdier ice.

His limbs are numb, hands and feet reporting that they no longer exist. Urav twists against the rope, opens its mouth to shriek; Sigrud doesn't hesitate, and hurls the fishing spear into the roof of the creature's mouth.

It wails in pain, twists, fights against its many bonds, exposing its soft, black, jelly-like underside.

Now, thinks Sigrud.

He rushes forward with the halberd, dodges a tentacle, slides over on the ice, clambers to his feet.

He is past the fence of swirling tentacles. He begins mercilessly hacking at the creature's belly.

Urav howls, yammers, shrieks, struggles. Black blood rains down on Sigrud in a torrent. His body reports either icy cold or boiling heat. He keeps slashing, keeps hacking.

He remembers burying his children, or the bones he thought were his children.

He keeps hacking.

He remembers looking up in his jail cell, and seeing a needle of sunlight poking through, and trying to cradle that tiny pinhole of light in his hands.

He keeps hacking.

He remembers watching the shores of his homeland fade away from the deck of the Saypuri dreadnought.

He keeps hacking.

Eventually he realises he is screaming.

I curse the world not for what was stolen from me, but for revealing it was never stolen long after the world had made me a different man.

Urav groans, whines. The tentacles go slack. The beast seems to deflate, slowly falling back like an enormous black tree. The many ropes twang and whine with the weight, and Urav hangs in their net, defeated.

Sigrud is dimly aware of cheering up on the bridge. But he can still see the organs inside the creature pumping and churning. *Not dead, not dead yet*.

A bright golden eye surfaces from the sea of tentacles at his feet. It narrows, examining him.

Suddenly the limp tentacles are not limp: they fly up, grab the weakest leg of the bridge, and pull.

Sigrud is briefly aware of a dark shadow appearing on his right, and growing; then a huge stone pierces the ice mere yards away.

Sigrud says, '*Shi*—'

The ice below him tips up like a seesaw, and he is thrown forty feet at least. Then he knows nothing but the cold and the water.

He feels water beat on his nose and mouth. A stream worms its way into his sinuses, tickles his lungs, almost evoking a cough.

Do not drown.

Air burns inside him. He turns over, looks up; the sky is molten crystal, impenetrable.

Do not drown.

He can see Urav above him, fighting against the ropes. Above the creature is a solid black arch: the bridge.

Sigrud kicks his legs, aims for a widening crack in the ice above.

The solid black arch of the bridge grows a little less solid. Through the lens of the churning water and ice, it appears to vanish; then a stone ten feet across bursts into the dark water. Ropes of bubbles twist and twirl around it; Sigrud darts away, and is buffeted up by its force.

Do not drown, he thinks, *and do not be crushed*.

More stones crash down, causing enormous concussions that push him up, up.

The water surface is a membrane, keeping him trapped; he is not sure if he can break through. He claws at it with his hands, opens his mouth . . . and tastes wintry air.

Sigrud hauls himself out of the water and on to the ice. This far from the bridge the ice is thankfully solid. He looks back, and sees the bridge is not there at all: it is collapsing into the water, causing huge waves . . . and he cannot see Urav anywhere.

Sigrud, weak, shivering, kneels on the ice and looks for some sign of hope: a fire, a rope, a boat, anything. Yet all he can see is the orb of soft, yellow light slipping through the water towards him, shoving the chunks of ice aside as if they were tissue paper.

'Hm,' he says.

He looks at his hands and arms: the fat has been completely washed away during the fight, presumably taking away whatever protection Shara provided with it.

Then there is a swarm of tentacles around him, and a trembling, widening mouth – one that is missing many teeth – and then a soft push on his back, ushering him in.

Sigrud opens his eyes.

He sits on a vast, black plain. The sky above him is just as black; he only knows that the plain is there because on its horizon is a huge, burning yellow eye, which casts a faint yellow light across the black sands.

A voice says: YOU WILL KNOW PAIN.

Sigrud looks to his left and right; around him is a vast field of seated corpses, ashen and dry, as if all the moisture has been boiled out of them. One is dressed like a police officer; another holds a fishing trap. All the corpses are seated facing the burning eye, and each face, though desiccated and grey, bears a look of terrible suffering.

Then he sees that the chests of the corpses are moving, gently breathing.

Sigrud realises, *They are alive*.

The voice says: YOU WILL KNOW PAIN, FOR YOU ARE FALLEN.

Sigrud looks down. He is still naked, still wearing only his boots, his knife and the glove on his right hand.

He touches the knife, and remembers what Shara said – *It might be best to take matters into your* own *hands*.

The voice says: YOU WILL KNOW PAIN, FOR YOU ARE UNCLEAN.

Sigrud takes out the knife and considers laying the blade against his wrist, opening up the vein . . . but something causes him to hesitate.

The voice says: YOU WILL KNOW PAIN, AND THROUGH YOUR PAIN YOU WILL FIND RIGHTEOUSNESS.

He waits, the tip of his blade hovering over his wrist. The black plain mixes like paint, swirling until it forms the walls of his old prison cell in Slondheim, where the dark days leached the life out of him bit by bit. *Is this*, he wonders, *the miraculous hell of Urav?* It seems so, but he does not lower the knife, not yet.

Set in the door of his cell is a great yellow eye. The voice says: YOU *WILL* KNOW PAIN. YOU *WILL* KNOW SUFFERING. YOU *WILL* BE PURGED OF YOUR SIN.

Sigrud waits. He expects that maybe all the old wounds and fractures and injuries he received in this place will suddenly blare to life, aching with all the agony he experienced here . . . but it doesn't come.

The voice, now sounding slightly frustrated, says: YOU *WILL* KNOW PAIN.

Sigrud looks around, knife point hovering over his wrist. 'Okay,' he says slowly. 'When?'

The voice is silent.

'Is this not hell?' asks Sigrud. 'Should I not be suffering?'

The voice does not answer. Then the walls rapidly transmute into a variety of horrifying situations: he lies upon a bed of nails; he dangles over an active volcano; he is trapped at the bottom of the sea; he is returning to the Dreylands, and sees smoke on the horizon. Yet none of these scenarios cause him any physical or mental pain.

He looks around. 'What is going on?' he asks, genuinely confused.

The walls swirl again. He is back on the black plain, with all the wheezing, ashen corpses, and the bright yellow eye is glaring furiously at him. He wonders, momentarily, if he is immune simply because he is a Dreyling, but this seems unlikely.

Then he realises the palm of his right hand is gently throbbing. He looks at his right hand, hidden in its glove, and understands.

The voice says: PAIN IS YOUR FUTURE. PAIN IS YOUR PURITY.

Sigrud says, 'But you cannot teach me pain' – he begins to tug at the fingers of the glove – 'because I already know it.'

He pulls the glove off.

In the centre of his palm is a horrendous, bright red scar that would resemble a brand if it was not carved so deeply in his flesh: a circle with a crude scale in the middle.

Kolkan's hands, he remembers, *waiting to weigh and judge*.

He holds up his palm to the bright yellow eye. 'I have been touched by the finger of your god,' he says, 'and I lived. I knew his pain, and carried it with me. I carry it now. Every day. So you cannot hurt me, can you? You cannot teach me what I already know.'

The great eye stares.

Then, it blinks.

Sigrud lunges forward and stabs it with his knife.

From the riverbank, Shara and Mulaghesh stare at where Urav has retreated below the water.

'Go!' shouts Nesrhev. '*Go!*'

Both Shara and Mulaghesh are soaking wet, having hauled Nesrhev from the Solda sporting two broken arms, a broken leg and mild hypothermia.

'For the love of the gods, get me *out* of here,' he cries.

Shara ignores him, staring at the river, awaiting some unbelievable twist: perhaps Urav will resurface, spit Sigrud out, and send him skipping across the water like a stone.

But there is only the gentle bob of the ice on the dark water.

'We need to get away,' says Mulaghesh.

'Yes!' shouts Nesrhev. 'Yes, by the gods, that's what I've been *saying*.'

'What?' asks Shara softly.

'We need,' says Mulaghesh again, 'to get away from the river. That thing is angry now. I know you don't want to leave your friend, but we need to *go*.'

Police officers scream orders to one another from the banks, Nesrhev howls and moans on the riverbank. No one is sure how to get across the Solda. There is no coherent authority to any of it, but the policemen seem to have voted en masse to pour petrol on the river and set it alight.

'We *definitely* need to go now,' says Mulaghesh.

Shara devises a sling out of her cloak, and the two set Nesrhev in it and begin hauling him up the riverbank. The remaining officers are backing a wagon of barrels up to the river. They do not even try to unload and dump them, they just hack at the barrel sides with an axe until the barrels burst and drain into the river.

Shara riffles her mind for some solution, some arcane trick – a prayer of Kolkan, a word from the *Jukoshtava* – but nothing comes.

Fire crawls across the river in snaking coils. River ice hisses, turns smooth as marble, and beats a rapid retreat.

They've almost reached the river walk when the blanket of fire begins to dip violently. 'Look!' Shara says.

The fire begins to churn and hiss.

'Oh, please,' whines Nesrhev. 'Please don't stop.'

The writhing form of Urav bursts up through the Solda, shrieks horribly, and begins battering the surface with its many arms.

'The fire!' cries a voice. 'It works!'

Yet Shara is not so sure. Urav does not seem to be reacting *to* anything: rather, it appears to be having an attack of some kind. She is reminded of an old man she once saw have a stroke in a park, how his limbs trembled and flailed.

Urav, screaming and gurgling, carves through the ice, splashes through the lake of fire, beats its arms on the riverbank, cannons into the remnants of the Solda Bridge, before finally beaching itself on the river walk, its great, trembling mouth opening and closing, whining and keening like a frightened dog.

'What in hells is going on?' asks Mulaghesh.

Urav opens its mouth, screeches a long, sustained pitch . . . and a tiny black tooth pops out of its belly, just below its gaping maw.

No, not a tooth: a knife.

'No,' says Shara. 'No, it can't be.'

Urav shrieks again; the knife wriggles, and slowly begins sawing its way down the creature's belly. Hot blood splashes to the ground, sizzles on the icy river. A hand, fingers clenched together to form a blade, punches through the long slash.

'You have *got*,' says Mulaghesh, 'to be *joking*.'

In what can only be described as a horrific perversion of a vaginal birth, there is a spurt of viscera, a flood of putrid entrails, and then the fat- and blood-drenched form of Sigrud slips out of the gash in the dying monster to lie on the ground and stare up at the sky, before rolling over, getting on to his hands and knees, and vomiting prolifically.

Shara is dimly aware of distant cheering as she sprints down the river walk to where Sigrud lies. She is forced to slow down once she nears him: the stench is powerful enough to be nigh impenetrable, but she fights through it to kneel beside him.

'How?' she cries. Some tiny gland dangles from his ear; she delicately removes it. 'How did you *do* it? How could you have possibly survived?'

Sigrud rolls on to his back, gulping air. He coughs and hacks and reaches into his mouth to pull out some kind of long, stringy grey tissue. 'Lucky,' he gasps. He throws the tissue away; it strikes a puddle of entrails with a wet *flup*. 'Lucky and stupid.'

Something inside Urav's dead bulk shifts, and more viscera slips out in an oozing landslide. Shara pulls Sigrud to his feet before it can pool around them. She notices he is not wearing his glove on his right hand, something she has never seen him go without.

Sigrud looks back at Urav with disbelief. 'To think . . .' He applies a finger to his right nostril, and blows a small ocean of brackish blood from his left. 'To think that whole *place* was inside that creature.'

'What was it? Was it really hell in there, Sigrud?'

Sigrud kneels as another cough grips him. A gathering crescendo of cheers and whoops echoes across the Solda. Shara looks up to see not only scores of policemen gathering on the shores to celebrate, but also common citizens, men and women and children pouring out of their homes to clap and sing.

Oh dear, thinks Shara. *This was rather public, wasn't it?*

A series of flashes from her left: three photographers have set up their tripods, and are winding up their cameras to take another round of snapshots.

And behind them is someone she never expected to see.

Vohannes Votrov stands at the back of the crowd. He appears to have eschewed his normally ostentatious wardrobe in favour of a dark brown coat and black shirt, buttoned up to the neck. He looks gaunt and pale, and he watches Shara with an expression of placid disdain, as one would watch an insect beat against the pane of a window. It takes her a moment to notice that he does not have his cane.

The crowd surges around Vohannes and the photographers. Sigrud and Shara are swept up in the tidal wave of claps on the back and bellowed congratulations. When she manages to look back at the photographers, he is gone.

I fault no one for praising Saypur's history — history, after all, is a story, one that is sometimes wonderful. But one must remember it in full — as things really were — and avoid selective amnesia. For the Great War did not start with the invasion of the Continent, nor did it begin with the death of the Divinity Voortya.

Rather, it began with a child.

I do not know her name. I wish I did — she deserves to be named, considering what happened to her. But from court records, I know she lived with her parents on a farm in the Mahlideshi provinces in Saypur, and I know that she was a simple child, one touched by nature in a manner to stunt her intelligence. Like many children of a certain age, she had an attraction to fire, and perhaps her simple nature made this attraction even stronger.

One day in 1631, she found an overturned, abandoned wagon in the road. It had been bearing boxes and boxes of paper — and seeing all this paper, I think, and knowing no adult was nearby, was all too tempting for her.

She built a little fire in the road, burning pages with a match, one after the other.

Then the wagon's passengers returned. They were Continentals, wealthy Taalhavshtanis who owned many nearby rice paddies. And when they saw her burning the paper, they became enraged — for she was unknowingly burning copies of the Taalhavshta, *the sacred book of Taalhavras, and to them this was a grave transgression.*

They took her before the local Continental magistrate and pleaded for justice for this heretical indiscretion. The girls' parents begged for mercy, for she was simple, and did not know what she had done. The townspeople joined their call, and asked for a light punishment, if any.

The Continentals, however, told the judge that if any Saypuri was willing to put the sacred words to flame, then they should be put to the flame as well. And the judge – a Continental – listened.

They burned her alive in the town square of Mahlideshi with all the towns-people watching; court records tell us they hung her from a tree by a chain, and built a bonfire at her feet – and when she, weeping, climbed the chain to escape the fire, they cut off her hands and feet, and whether she bled to death or burned to death first, I cannot say.

I do not think the Continentals expected the people to react as they did – they were, after all, poor Saypuris, not individuals of any strength or might. But this gruesome sight caused the entire town of Mahlideshi to revolt, tear down the magistrate's office and stone its inhabitants to death, including the executioners of the girl.

For one week, they celebrated their freedom. And I would like to say that the Colonial Rebellion started then, that Saypur was so inspired by this brave stand that the Kaj rose up and took the Continent at this moment. But the next week the Continentals returned in force.

Mahlideshi is no longer on any map, save for a charred spot of land along the shore, and a lump of earth a sixth of a mile long – the last resting place of the victorious citizens of Mahlideshi.

Word spread of the carnage. A quiet, hateful outrage began to seep through the colonies.

We do not know much about the Kaj. We do not even know who his mother was. But we know he lived in the province of Tohmay, just beside Mahlideshi; and we know that it was just after this massacre that he began his experimenta-tions, one of which must have created the weaponry he would eventually use to overthrow the Continent.

An avalanche dislodges a tiny stone into the ocean; and, through the myster-ies of fate, this tiny stone creates a tsunami.

I wish I did not know some parts of the past; I wish they had never hap-pened. But the past is the past, and someone must remember, and speak of it.

Upon History Lost, Dr Efrem Pangyui, 1682

Salvation

'No breaks,' says the doctor. '*Probably* some fractures. *Definitely* bruising, to the point that I would expect some bone bruising as well. I would be able to tell, of course, if the patient would permit me to examine him more closely.'

Sigrud, leaning back in the bed with a pot of potato wine in his lap, allows a grunt. One half of his face is a brilliant red; the other is black and grey, like mouldy fruit. In the light of the weak embassy gas lamps, he looks positively ghoulish. So far he has only allowed the doctor to prod his stomach and witness that he can move his head, arms and legs; beyond this, Sigrud only answers the doctor's requests with sullen grunts.

'He reports no abdominal pain,' says the doctor. 'Which is, I must say, unbelievable. And I also see no signs of frostbite – *also* fairly unbelievable.'

'What is *frostbite*?' asks Sigrud. 'I have never heard of this frostbite.'

'Are you implying,' says the doctor, 'that Dreylings *never* get frostbite?'

'There is cold' – Sigrud takes a massive swig of wine – 'and less cold.'

The doctor, flustered, frustrated, says to Shara, 'I would say that if he survives the night, then he will survive entirely. I would also say that if he wants to survive *in general*, he should allow medical professionals to do their *job*, and not treat us as if we are molesters.'

Sigrud laughs nastily.

Shara smiles. 'Thank you, doctor. That will be all.'

The doctor, grumbling, bows, and Shara leads him outside. A crowd is milling in front of the embassy gates, having followed them here from the river. 'If you could,' says Shara, 'we would appreciate your discretion. If you could avoid discussing any details of what you saw here.'

'It would be against my profession,' says the doctor, 'and, what is more, this examination was conducted *so* poorly that I would prefer no one ever to know about it.' He claps a hat on his head and marches away.

Someone in the crowd shouts *There she is!* and the gates light up with photography flashes.

Shara grimaces and shuts the door. Photography is a relatively new innovation, less than ten years old, but she can already tell she will hate it. *Capturing images*, she thinks, *carries so many complications for my work*.

She re-enters and heads up the stairs; the embassy staff watch her go with black-rimmed eyes, exhausted, waiting for permission to turn in.

Mulaghesh descends in a harried stomp. 'Warehouse fire's out,' she says. She lifts a bottle to her lips and drinks. 'I'm locking down the embassy until we decide if this city will kill us or not for destroying their god's pet, or whatever that was. The City Fathers have elected to deal with the bridge themselves. I'm getting drunk and sleeping here. You can deal with it.'

'I shall,' says Shara lightly.

'And you had better make *sure* I wind up in Javrat when this is all over!'

'I shall.'

She leaves Mulaghesh behind, enters Sigrud's room and sits at the foot of his bed. Sigrud is running a forefinger around the mouth of the bottle, again and again.

'Are you *really* all right?' Shara asks.

'I think so,' says Sigrud. 'I have survived worse.'

'Really?'

Sigrud nods, lost in thought.

'*How* did you survive?'

He thinks, then lifts his right hand, which is wrapped in medical gauze. He unravels it to reveal the brilliant pink-red carving of a scale in his palm. 'With this.'

She looks at it. 'But that . . . that isn't the *blessing* of Kolkan.'

'Maybe not. But I think that being punished by Kolkan, and being blessed by him, they may be more or less the same thing.'

Shara remembers Efrem reading from Olvos's *Book of the Red Lotus*, and commenting aloud. *The Divine did not understand themselves — in the same way we do not understand ourselves – and their unintentional effects often say more about them than their intentional ones.*

Sigrud is staring into the palm of his hand. His eye glitters through its swollen lids like the soft back of a beetle between its wings. He blinks – she can tell he is drunk – and says, 'Do you know how I got this?'

'Somewhat,' she says. 'I know it is the mark of the Finger of Kolkan.'

He nods. Silence stretches on.

'I knew you had it,' she says. 'I knew what it was. But I never felt I should ask.'

'Wise. Scars are windows to bitterness – it is best to leave them untouched.' He kneads his palm, and says, 'I don't know *how* they got it in Slondheim. Such a rare and powerful instrument, though it looked like no more than a marble – a grey marble with a little sign of a scale on it. They had to carry it in a box, with a certain kind of lining in it.'

'Grey wool, probably,' says Shara. 'It held a special significance, for Kolkashtanis.'

'If you say so. There were nine of us. They'd kept us in a cell, all together. We drank rusty water from a leaking pipe, shat in the corner, starved. Starved for so long. I don't know how long they starved us. But one day our jailers came to us with this little stone in the box and a plate of chicken – a *whole chicken* – and they said, "If one of you can hold this little, tiny stone for a full minute, we will let you eat." And everyone rushed to volunteer, to do what the jailers said, but I held back because I knew these men. In Slondheim, they played with us. Tricked us into fighting each other, killing each other.' He flexes his left fist; the pink-scarred wastelands of his knuckles flare white. 'So I knew this was not right. The first man tried to hold the pebble, and the second he picked it up, he started screaming. His hand bled like he had been stabbed. He dropped it – it sounded like a *boulder* had struck the floor, when it fell – and the jailers laughed, and said, "Pick it up, pick it up," and the man couldn't. It was like it weighed a thousand tons. The jailers could only pick it up with the grey cloth. We didn't understand what it was, but we knew we were starving, so we wanted to try again, to eat, just a little.

'And none of them could. Some got to twenty seconds. Some to thirty.

Bleeding rivers from their hands. It wounded them so horribly. And they all dropped this little stone. This tiny little Finger of Kolkan.' He takes another sip of wine. 'And then, I tried. But before I picked it up, I thought . . . I thought about what I had lost. I did not know then, as you would tell me later, that my family had survived the coup. I thought they were dead. And I felt I was dead, too. The thing in my heart that made me wish to keep living, that fire, it had gone out. It is *still* out, even now.

'And . . . and I *wished* this stone to crush me. Do you see? I *wished* for this pain. So I picked it up. And I held it.' He turns over his scarred hand as if the stone is still there. 'I feel it still. I feel like I am holding it now. I saw their faces: my father's, my children's, my wife's. And I held it. Not to eat, but to *die*.' The hand turns into a fist. 'But eat I did. I bore the Finger of Kolkan for not one, but three minutes. And then they took the stone from me, unhappy, and said, "You can eat, for you have won. But before you do, you must decide – will you eat all the chicken, or will you share it with your fellow inmates?" And they all stared at me – ghosts of men, thin and pale and starving, like they were fading before my eyes.'

Sigrud begins rewrapping his hand. 'I didn't think about it,' he says softly, 'for even a second. The jailers put me in a different cell from the rest of them, and I ate it all, and I slept. And it was not even a week before they started hauling out the bodies from my old jail cell.' He ties the bandage, massaging his palm. 'The Divine may have created many hells,' he says, 'but I think they pale beside what men create for themselves.'

'You're positive you won't reconsider?' says a voice.

'I'm positive I haven't been *allowed* to consider it,' Mulaghesh's voice says back. 'Your damn council didn't even give me the chance.'

'They can't even *vote*, though!' says the voice. 'The assembly was incomplete! You only have to exert some influence, Turyin!'

'Oh, for the seas' sakes,' mutters Mulaghesh, weary, intoxicated. 'Have I not exerted enough tonight? I will do as I am told, thank you, and they told me very clearly to *fuck off*.'

Shara enters the kitchen to see Vohannes Votrov, now clad in his usual white fur coat, standing before Mulaghesh, who eyes him sourly over a brimming glass of whisky. Votrov's cane beats an impatient *tap, tap* against the heel of his boot.

'I thought we were locking down the embassy and admitting no visitors,' says Shara. '*Especially* this one.'

Vohannes turns and grins at her. 'So! Here is the triumphant warrior, fresh from her conquest. What an epic night you've had!'

'Vo, I honestly do not have time for your *supposed* charms. How did you get in?'

'By liberally applying my supposed charms, of course,' says Vohannes. 'Please, help me. We must convince Governor Mulaghesh here to *get up*. You're all letting a phenomenal opportunity float by!'

'I will not,' says Mulaghesh, 'lift my ass one inch off this chair. Not tonight.'

'But the city's in a mad shambles!' says Vohannes. 'One half can only get to the other by walking all the way round the walls! I know that Bulikov does not have the resources to begin to reconstruct the Solda Bridge with any speed.'

'Don't you *own* most of the construction companies in the city?' asks Shara.

'Well, true. But while my own companies *could* begin to make headway, it'd be nothing compared to the exertion of the Polis Governor's office, or the Regional Governor's office.'

'And why would we want to do this?'

'Do you think you'd have nothing to gain,' asks Vohannes, 'by rendering all of Bulikov dependent on your planners and developers?'

'And we'd have to work with all of *his* companies, too,' says Mulaghesh.

'Merely a pleasant bonus,' says Vohannes.

'Literally, a bonus,' says Mulaghesh.

'Dozens of people are dead tonight, Vo,' says Shara. 'I know you have your mission, your agenda, but can't you show some modicum of decency? Shouldn't you be mourning for your people?'

Vohannes' grin sours until it's a vicious rictus. 'I hate to be the one to tell you this, *Ambassador*,' he says acidly, 'but this is far from the first disaster to befall Bulikov. What about when Oshkev Street, destabilised by a random cavity from the Blink, abruptly *collapsed*, bringing down two apartment buildings and a school with it? We wept and mourned then, but what good did that do us? What about when the Continental Gas Company fumblingly tried to install a line in the Solda Quarter, and started a fire that couldn't be put out for *six days*? We wept and mourned then, but what good did that do us?'

Shara glances at Mulaghesh, who reluctantly shrugs – *No, he's not making this up.*

'Disaster is our constant companion in Bulikov, Ambassador,' says Vohannes. 'Grief and decency are mere decorations that hang upon the real problem: Bulikov desperately needs help and reconstruction. *Real* reconstruction, which we cannot do ourselves!'

'I'm sorry,' says Shara. 'I should not have said that.' She sits – her legs sing out in praise – and rubs her eyes again. 'But the bridge has just fallen,' she moans, 'and already we must begin scheming again. What is this about a council?'

'The City Fathers called an emergency meeting to discuss what to do,' says Vohannes. 'After deciding basic search and rescue matters, I wanted them to ask Saypur for help in recovery. They eventually voted against me, though they offered no alternative plan. But the vote isn't really legitimate, as Wiclov was nowhere to be found.'

Shara's fingers drum against the table top. 'Was he . . .'

'Yes, funny, isn't it? No one's seen him for nearly a week, not since he stood at the embassy gates and hurled invective at you, in fact.'

Though Sigrud saw him deliver Torskeny to the mhovost *before disappearing down an alley,* she thinks, then blearily looks at Mulaghesh for help.

'Please don't make me stand up,' Mulaghesh begs.

'I won't,' says Shara. 'Not tonight. This . . . Vo, this *must* wait until the morning.'

'You must strike,' says Vohannes, 'while the iron is hot!'

'I don't decide public policy!'

'But you do have many friends in high places, don't you?'

'Whose friendship is already tested, or *will* be, by what's happened tonight.' She sighs. 'Vo, you've no idea what's happened in the past few hours. I say this in strictest confidence, but we have suffered *considerable* losses. And we are still nowhere near figuring out who our enemies are, or what they're doing! This is not the time for huge plans. We will leave Bulikov to Bulikov, for tonight.'

'That policy,' says Vohannes, 'is almost certainly what created the Restorationists in the first place, and it will be the father of every consequence thereafter. This city pickles in its own jar. Every disaster is an opportunity, Shara! Make the most of this one.'

'I have suffered so many disasters tonight.' She laughs hollowly. 'You don't want me in your corner, Vo. By sunrise, I might not have a career.'

'I very much doubt that. *Especially* since right now every man, woman and child in Bulikov thinks you all to be glorious, glorious heroes.'

Mulaghesh and Shara are both nodding in their chairs, but they blink awake at this claim.

'Wh . . . *What?*' says Mulaghesh.

'What do you mean, what?' asks Vohannes.

'I mean, what did you just say?'

'Oh? Did you *really* not realise? That crowd out there.' He points north, towards the door. 'Did you think they're angry? Seeking to throw down the gates? No, they're *amazed*! You all slaughtered a monster in front of a terrified city! It's the . . . well, it's the stuff legends are made of.'

Shara says, 'But it was a holy creature. This country used to *worship* that thing!'

'The operative word being *used* to. That was over three hundred years ago! It was trying to *kill* us all!'

'But . . . but it was Sigrud who did almost all of it!'

He shrugs. 'The credit spreads. The City Fathers were confounded about what to do. You may just be the first Saypuri ever to have won the commendation of Bulikov in the city's history. And if you or anyone in Ghaladesh tried, Saypur could sail into this city, rebuild the bridge and be considered a saviour ever after!'

Shara and Mulaghesh both sit dumbfounded.

Vohannes produces a cigarette from a tiny silver box, and fits it into his holder. 'But let's just hope,' he says, 'they don't find out who you *really* are. Knowing your family history, it would create some nasty parallels, would it not?'

*

Shara drinks. It feels appropriate to do so: she is a soldier among soldiers, celebrating their survival when so many perished. The wine mixes with the fatigue, and Vohannes joins her and Mulaghesh, and the whole evening transmutes from one of frayed nerves and horrible trauma to one of their old school nights, sitting up in their common room with their classmates, sharing gossip and determinedly ignoring the mad world outside.

What a wonderful thing it was, Shara thinks, *to feel common.*

Mulaghesh is snoring in her chair in the violet hours just before dawn. Vohannes has to help Shara up the stairs. She stops for breath beside the wide stairway windows. The stars rest on a blanket of soft purple clouds, supported by the walls and cityscape of Bulikov; it is scenic to the degree that it could be the work of a tactless and sentimental painter.

Vohannes slowly limps up behind her, suddenly quite frail.

'I'm . . .' Shara knows she is about to say something she shouldn't, but she's too inebriated to stop herself. 'I'm sorry about your accident, Vo.'

'It's the way things are,' he says softly. If he knows she knows how he really got hurt, he does not show it. 'I only ask your help in changing them.'

When they finally make it to her room, she sits on her bed, holding her forehead. The room spins and sways like the deck of a ship.

'It's been a while,' says Vohannes' voice in the dark, 'since I've been in a woman's bedroom.'

'You and Ivanya?'

He shakes his head. 'It's . . . not quite like that.'

She falls back on to the bed. Vohannes smirks, sits beside her and leans back on one hand so he's hovering just over her, the sides of their hips kissing.

Shara blinks, surprised. 'I didn't think,' she says, 'that this was something you were interested in.'

'Well, it's . . . not quite like *that*, either.'

She smiles a little sadly. *Poor Vo*, she thinks. *Always torn between two worlds.*

'Don't I disgust you?' she asks.

'Why would you do that?'

'I'm not doing anything you want. I'm not helping you, or Bulikov, or the Continent. I'm your enemy, your obstacle.'

'Your *policies* are my enemy.' He sighs. 'One day I will change your mind. Maybe I will tonight.'

'Don't be ridiculous. Do tycoons such as yourself often take advantage of drunken women?'

'Mm. Do you know,' says Vohannes, 'that when I returned, there had been rumours that I'd found myself a Saypuri mistress? I was reviled, you know. And, I think, envied as well. But none of it meant anything to me.' His eyes are lacquered: could he be crying? 'I was not drawn to you for some exotic fling – I was drawn to you because you were you.'

What right does he have, thinks Shara, *to be so pretty?*

'If you don't want me here,' he says, 'say *no*, and I'll leave.'

She thinks on it, and sighs dramatically. 'You always do cause such difficult conundrums.'

He kisses her neck. His beard tickles the corner of her jaw.

'Hm,' she says. 'Well . . . well.' She reaches up, grabs the corner of the bedspread and flips it back. 'I suppose' – she suppresses a laugh as he kisses her collarbone – 'you had better get in.'

'Who am I to deny an ambassador what she wants?' He shrugs off his white fur coat.

Was his council meeting so important, Shara wonders, *that he had to change?*

She must have said it aloud, because Vohannes looks back and says, 'I didn't change. I've been wearing this all night.'

Shara tries to hold on to a thought – *That's not right* – but then he starts unbuttoning his shirt, and she begins to think about many different things at once.

'How would you like me to lie?'

'How would you *like* to?'

'Well, I mean . . . because of your hip.'

'Oh. Oh, yes . . . right.'

'Here . . . is here good?'

'There is good. There is very good. Mmm.'

This is a bad idea, Shara thinks, but she tries to ignore it and lose herself in this small joy.

But she can't. 'Vo . . .'

'Yes?'

'Are . . . are you enjoying yourself?'

'Yes.'

'Are you sure?'

'Yes.'

'I only ask because—'

'I know! I know . . . it's . . . too much wine.'

'Are you *sure* I'm not hurting you?'

'No! You're fine! You're absolutely . . . you're fine.'

'Well, maybe let me shift to . . . there. Is that better?'

'It is.' He sounds more determined than amorous. 'This is . . .'

'Yes?'

'This . . .'

'. . . yes?'

'This should not be so . . . so difficult.'

'Vo . . . If you don't *want* to.'

'I *do* want to!'

'I know, but . . . but you shouldn't feel like you have to—'

'I'm just . . . I'm just . . . *Gods*.' He collapses next to her.

Seconds tick away in the dark room. She wonders if he's asleep.

'I'm sorry,' he says softly.

'Don't be.'

'I suppose I am not,' he whispers, 'the man I was.'

'No one's asking you to be.'

He breathes heavily for a moment; she suspects he is weeping.

'The world is our crucible,' he murmurs. 'And with each burn, we are shaped.'

Shara knows the line. 'The *Kolkashavska?*'

He laughs bitterly. 'Maybe Volka was right. Once a Kolkashtani . . .'

Then he is silent.

Shara wonders what kind of man thinks of his brother when naked in a woman's bed. Then they both find troubled sleep.

Shara's consciousness churns awake, kicking against the dark, oily waters of a hangover. The pillowcase against her face is sandpaper; her arms, exposed, are frigidly cold, while her feet, deep in the quilt, are sweltering.

A voice barks. 'Get up! Get *up*!'

The pillow covering her head rises up, and cruel daylight stabs in.

'Roll over,' says Mulaghesh's voice, 'and get *up*!'

Shara turns in the sheets. Mulaghesh is standing at her bed, holding up the morning paper like it's the severed head of an enemy.

'What?' says Shara. '*What*?' She is, thankfully, still wearing her slip; Vohannes, however, is long gone. She wonders if he fled in shame, and feels hurt that he might think so poorly of her.

'Read this,' says Mulaghesh. She points to a blurry article.

'You want me to wh—'

'Read! Just read.'

Shara digs in the pillows for her glasses. Shoving them on her nose, she encounters her own face, rendered in black and white on the front page of the newspaper. The picture shows her standing by the Solda: behind her is the dead form of Urav, and at her feet, covered in blood, is Sigrud, whose face is hidden by a veil of oily hair. It is, she thinks, the best photo of her she has ever seen in her life: she is caught in regal profile, the wind catching her hair *just* so, making it a soft river of ebony trailing out from behind her head.

Her bemusement is dashed when she reads the article below:

BULIKOV SAVED!

The central quarters of Bulikov were terrorised last night by a sudden, inexplicable and horrifying attack from the Solda River. It has been confirmed that an enormous creature of an aquatic nature (the nature of the creature obligates this paper to refer to it only as 'the creature', for to be any more precise could incur legal consequences) swam upstream against the Solda, broke through the ice, and begin pulling passers-by off the celebrated river walks and into the freezing water.

The size and mass of this creature were so great that it managed to level several riverside buildings before any municipal forces were able to react. A stunning twenty-seven citizens lost their lives, and as of 4.00 a.m. this morning, more reports are still coming in. Few bodies have been recovered.

The Bulikov Police Department quickly mounted an attack to capture or kill the creature, but this provoked it into damaging the Solda Bridge to the point that it collapsed, killing six officers and injuring nine more, including the celebrated officer Captain Miklav Nesrhev. As of this morning, Captain Nesrhev is now stable and recovering at the House of Seven Sisters infirmary.

The resolution of this threat may be the most amazing element, as the creature was finally felled by a highly unlikely hero, for Bulikov: it has been revealed that the recent appointment to the Saypuri Embassy, Ashara Thivani, is in truth Ashara *Komayd*, niece of the Saypuri Minister of Foreign Affairs Vinya Komayd, and great-granddaughter of the controversial general Avshakta si Komayd, the infamous last Kaj of Saypur. Sources confirm that it was through her efforts and planning that the creature was successfully stopped, and killed.

'The ambassador and her associates identified the nature of the creature, and prescribed a method for containing and killing it,' said a source in the city government, who preferred to go unnamed. 'Without her help, dozens if not hundreds more of Bulikov's citizens would have been lost.'

Several police officers have also commended the ambassador's behaviour during the attack: 'We were trying to evacuate the embassy, but she insisted on coming to help,' said Viktor Povroy, a sergeant in the Bulikov Police Department. 'She and her colleagues set to it right away. I've never seen a more audacious plan put together so quickly.'

The ambassador and the Polis Governor of Bulikov, Turyin Mulaghesh, are also credited with saving Captain Nesrhev's life. 'Without them,' testified Povroy, 'he would have drowned or frozen to death.'

However, many questions remain: why did the ambassador hide her identity? Why was she so singularly adept at combating such a creature? And what does it mean for Bulikov, to have a member of the Komayd family in a position of power in the city once again?

At the time of this paper's publication, the embassy has yet to make an official comment.

Shara stares at the paper, feverishly hoping that the words will dance and rearrange themselves until it tells another story entirely.

'Oh, no,' she whispers.

To have one's cover blown. To be known to an enemy, to have a dossier on you compiled in some distant and lethal department, *that* is one thing: all operatives are prepared for *that*.

But to have your name and story splashed across the newspaper, to be known not in the secret annals of government but in the front rooms and dining rooms and public houses across the world. *That* is horror beyond horror.

'No,' says Shara again. 'No. That . . . that can't be.'

'Yeah,' says Mulaghesh.

'And this is the . . . the . . .'

'*The Continental Herald.*'

'So it doesn't just go to Bulikov, but—'

'To the entire Continent,' says Mulaghesh. 'Yeah.'

The reality of it all comes crashing down on her. 'Ohh . . . oh no, oh no, oh *no!*'

'Who knew who you are?' asks Mulaghesh.

'You,' says Shara. 'Sigrud, Vo . . . A few employees here suspect I'm more than I say I am, but there's a leap between that and being—'

'The great-granddaughter of the Kaj,' says Mulaghesh. 'Yeah. No shit. I know *I* didn't say anything. I never talk to the press.'

'And Sigrud wouldn't,' says Shara. 'So . . .'

She runs through the ideas, the possibilities.

Vinya, maybe? Shara is no longer sure what to think of her aunt. She feels almost certain Vinya has been compromised somehow but, for Vinya, it seems overwhelmingly likely that her compromise would be *political*, ceding power only for the opportunity to gain more. *And this would be very, very damaging, politically.*

She keeps boiling down her options, down and down, hoping to avoid what she increasingly feels is an inevitable conclusion.

'It could only be Vohannes,' says Shara finally.

'Okay, but . . . *why?*'

'I'm not sure yet,' says Shara. 'But it seems like the only possibility, simply by default.' Would this be some petty revenge over last night? It seems unlikely. Or could he be punishing her for her refusal to intervene in Bulikov? Or, 'Could he be trying to use me to get the attention of Ghaladesh?' she asks aloud.

'How would blowing your cover possibly do that?' asks Mulaghesh.

'Well . . . It makes for a great story, doesn't it? The great-granddaughter of the Kaj, swooping in and saving Bulikov. It gets people talking . . . and talk is as good as action in the geopolitical realm. It would focus all the world's attention on Bulikov – and then he could make his pitch. I mean, you've met him. All Vo ever needs is a spotlight.'

'Yeah, but . . . but that has *got* to be,' says Mulaghesh, 'the stupidest possible way to spur Ghaladesh into doing anything! Right?'

Shara doesn't entirely disagree, but she doesn't entirely agree, either. And she remembers what Vo mumbled last night. *Once a Kolkashtani . . .*

She can't help but feel that she's missing something. But whatever the cause, she knows she cannot trust Vo any longer, and she thinks it was foolish to have done so in the first place: to collaborate with such a passionate, broken, divided creature was always a poor decision.

From nearby, there's the sound of a throat being cleared.

Mulaghesh looks to the window, and asks, 'What was that?'

But Shara knows that sound quite well, having heard it throughout her childhood: two parts impatience, one part condescension.

'Nothing outside,' Mulaghesh says, peeking through the curtained window, 'except for the crowd, of course. I didn't imagine that sound, did I?'

Shara glances at the shuttered window next to her desk. The bottom left pane is shimmering strangely, and the reflection in the glass is slightly warped.

'Governor,' Shara says, 'could you please excuse me for a moment?'

'Are you going to be sick?'

'Possibly. I just need to . . . to gather myself.'

'I'll be downstairs,' Mulaghesh says, 'but I won't have long to wait around. There's so much to clean up, I'll have to return to my quarters very shortly.'

'I understand.'

The office door clicks closed. Shara arrives at the window just as her aunt's face appears.

'I believe that I am almost as much to blame as you,' says Vinya.

Shara says nothing. She does not move, she does not speak: she only watches. Vinya, for her part, is just as reserved and removed as Shara. The two look at one another through the glass with expressions slightly suspicious, slightly hurt and slightly aggrieved all at once.

'I should have stopped you when you were younger,' says Vinya. 'Your interest in the Continent was always quite unhealthy. And I have trusted you more and more, letting you go out on your own without my supervision. But now I regret that. Perhaps I should have brought you home more. Maybe you were right. I wish you could have come here and seen exactly how things are changing here in Parliament, shifting, and . . . and how delicate and precarious everything is.'

Ah. I have endangered her political career. Having faced fire and Urav last night, Shara finds it difficult to muster sympathy for someone grappling with parliamentary squabbles. In fact, Shara finds it difficult to bother to do anything in this conversation. She is content to let her aunt keep talking, allowing Shara to watch as Vinya's intents and motives crystallise in the glass pane like autumn's first frost.

'The discourse has changed considerably, almost overnight. For so long, no one ever even *thought* of engaging the Continent, but now . . . now we are open to the idea. Now, suddenly, we are *curious*. Despite all my efforts of the past decade, the Ministers are now reconsidering their stance on the Continent. And all their aides, all their assistants, are reviewing all their personal correspondence from the Continent, and they are finding one name on hundreds and hundreds of petitions: Votrov, Votrov, Votrov.'

A tremor in her stomach. This Shara did not expect. Could she have been right? Could blowing her cover really be a wild gambit on Vo's part? And – even more insane – could it have *worked*? Right before the City Father elections, too.

'I suppose you are waiting,' says Vinya, 'for me to get to the part where I tell you what action I will be taking.'

Shara purses her lips, blinks; beyond that, she gives Vinya nothing.

Vinya shakes her head. 'I should have told you never to enter the Warehouse,' she says. 'It should have been an order. You *listen* to orders. I should have known right away that you, as obsessed with the Continent as you are, would have found the Warehouse totally irresistible.'

Shara cocks an eyebrow. 'Wait . . . what are you—'

'But, of course, the second you learned it existed, you'd try and find a way in,' continues Vinya. 'You'd break in, poke your nose into it, and riffle its shelves one way or another.'

'What! Auntie Vinya, I didn't *want* to go into the Warehouse! I *had* to!'

'Oh? Oh, really? Last I heard, you were interviewing a University maid about the death of Dr Pangyui. Next, you've penetrated the Warehouse, the most classified building currently in existence in this world, *burned* it down, and then you're battling Divine river monsters on the front of the paper! *With* your cover blown! I struggle to understand exactly how all that could have evolved organically, Shara! It seems much more likely that you, as obsessed with the musty dead gods as you are, simply broke in to see what was there for yourself, as if it was a damn museum, and you wound up getting quite literally burned *and* freeing some abysmal Divine creature!'

Shara's mouth falls open. She is utterly and completely aghast: all of the mad things and sights that she's experienced in the past forty-eight hours are minuscule in comparison to this. 'I . . . the Warehouse was *mined*!'

'Oh, by the Restorationists?' Vinya pronounces the name as if describing a group of illiterate potato farmers.

'Yes!'

'And how did they get in?'

'They . . . they used a miracle!'

'Ah,' says Vinya. 'A *miracle*. Very convenient, those. Especially when, theoretically, most of them shouldn't work any more. So why would they mine the Warehouse, which was full of things they themselves held sacred?'

'To cover their tracks!'

'And where did their tracks *lead*, dear?'

'There . . . there was something they wanted to steal!'

'Which was?'

'I don't know! It was mined!'

'So *you* set off the mine.'

Shara is so outraged she can hardly speak. 'They had been accessing the Warehouse using an ancient Divine miracle! They had been doing it for months!'

'And what intent would they have for whatever it is they stole from the Warehouse?'

'I don't know!'

'You don't know.'

'No! Not yet! I know it . . . it has something to do with steel!' This sounds pathetic even to Shara's ears. 'I am currently investigating the situation!'

Vinya nods and slowly sits back in her chair, thinking.

'Talk to Mulaghesh! Talk to Sigrud! Talk to *anyone* here!' shouts Shara.

'Mulaghesh's reputation is not quite as sterling as it used to be,' says Vinya, 'as the Warehouse was *her* jurisdiction, and is now a pile of ashes. And I would no sooner listen to your Dreyling's word than I would consult with a rabid dog. But most of all, Shara, my dear, no other operative on the whole of the Continent has reported *any* hint of such a plot.'

'That's because these people are damn good! Unlike us! I arrived in Bulikov to find the walls swarming with rats! These machinations were well under way before I ever got here!'

Vinya rolls her eyes and shakes her head, concerned, dismayed, as if listening to a demented relative at dinner.

'You don't believe me,' says Shara desperately.

'Shara, you went to Bulikov on your own to investigate a disastrous international scandal. And now, you have caused one much, *much* larger. Thank the seas that the Continent doesn't know about the Warehouse. If they knew you'd burned down thousands of years of history, they'd want your head, and mine! Can you imagine the consequences? And apparently somewhere in the midst of all this, you somehow blew your own cover, which really does not surprise me, at this point. You are either vain and stupid, or reckless and stupid, I am not sure which one I prefer. And I notice that you haven't mentioned Pangyui's murder *yet*. Unless I am mistaken, that was the primary reason I allowed you your time in Bulikov, wasn't it? Has your investigation into these grand, dark plots shed any light on who might have killed him, and why?'

Shara glances at Vohannes' white suitcase, which sits underneath her desk. 'Perhaps I would have something,' she says savagely, 'if you would allow me to review his dead drop material!'

Vinya snaps forward. 'And if you did *that*, then you would be directly disobeying a Ministry order! That material is to be reviewed by *me* first! And if I think it could be of use to you, *then* I will allow you access to it! That's how the chain of command works! It's what our entire intelligence agency is predicated on! And I will not allow my arrogant niece to buck the system solely because she believes that reading enough dusty old books gives her more insight than any other intelligence officer! Your fascination with the Divine has always been a fault, *not* a virtue! And I will tell you right now, *right now*, that my first instinct is to rip you out of Bulikov and put you on a ship back here right away!'

Despite the argument, despite the promise of punishment, despite everything, Shara's heart leaps at this idea.

'But,' says Vinya, 'I cannot. Because of what *you* did. You are a glorious hero here in Saypur, Shara. The champion of Bulikov. Hail the conquering hero, grand victor over a threat she herself created! So much talk is swirling throughout the halls of power here right now, and I have no idea what the final resolution will be. I wish I could tell them exactly how terribly you've botched everything, but that would require telling them about the Warehouse – which I expressly cannot do. So, rather than endanger any of my functioning, *productive* policies, I will do nothing. I will do nothing, except give them all what they want – you.'

'Me?'

'Yes. I am *promoting* you, dear. I am fully recognising your status as Chief Diplomat to Bulikov. And I am putting you somewhere where you cannot damage any more intelligence operations.'

Shara blanches. 'Oh, no.'

'Oh, yes. You will be a public creature. I am, for the moment, suspending all your intelligence credentials. You will lose all clearance to all sensitive materials, to all operations. Any requests you make to any other Ministry operatives will not be answered. You will be, in effect, the very prominent and very accessible face of Saypur in Bulikov. And I am sure you will be applauded and celebrated for it,' she says acidly.

Shara feels sick. There is nothing – *nothing* – that could ever be more terrifying to an intelligence operative than being installed in public office, exposed and vulnerable to all the pleas and restrictions they could previously simply sidestep in their shadow life.

'You will, I think, be very busy,' says Vinya. 'Bulikov and Saypur very much wish to talk to one another, it seems. And they will talk through *you*. I don't know if you and that man, Votrov, concocted this scheme together, but if so, you must be *so* proud that it worked – so I am going to make sure you shoulder the majority of the burden, for now.'

So this is her punishment, says Shara. *I would almost prefer to be indicted and imprisoned. But Vinya never had a taste for mercy.*

Shara clears her throat. 'Auntie Vinya . . . listen.'

'Yes?'

'If . . . if I was to tell you that there is a real, credible threat in Bulikov, that I have witnessed, at first hand, evidence indicating one of the original Divinities, in some form or fashion, has *survived* . . . What would you do?'

Vinya looks at her pityingly. 'Is that your great secret? Your terrible suspicion? *That's* why you went into the Warehouse?'

'Yes. I'm sure of it. I really am, Auntie Vinya.'

'Oh, Shara, I would do the same thing I did when I heard it the *last* time, two months ago. And the time before that, *seven* months ago. And the time before that, and the time before that, and the time before that. I receive, on average, nearly ten reports a year telling me that the gods aren't dead, that they're still kicking around somewhere, planning their return. We have received a steady stream of these since the *War*. If we stacked them, the pile of reports would be three storeys tall! And all of them are always completely convinced – because the *Continent* is convinced this will happen. It's their silly fable, their desperate dream, like the Dreylings and their

Dauvkind. Lost kings and queens who will one day sail back. It's nonsense, Shara.'

'But I am the most experienced expert on everything Divine. Doesn't that count for something?'

'You are the operative most *obsessed* with everything Divine,' Vinya says gently. 'And that is something very different. You may have your interests and pet curiosities, Shara, but you are a servant of Saypur first and foremost.'

Shara nearly shouts, *Like you? Who owns you, Auntie? Who has got to you? Why is it that you're suddenly so much more secretive, and so much more irrational, than you've ever been before?* But she does not, of course: to reveal one's hand in such a manner would be unwise.

'Perhaps this will be good for you,' says Vinya. 'Maybe you will finally, finally learn something from this.'

Shara nods, looking crestfallen, but thinking, *I believe I've already learned a lot, Auntie.*

'I hate to say this, but please don't contact me like this again, dear,' says Vinya. 'Not until everything's settled. We must be so careful, in the wake of everything that's happened. We are all being watched very carefully now. And miracles, as you know, are so terribly dangerous.' She smiles sadly. 'Goodbye, my dear.'

With a wipe of her fingers, she's gone.

Shara stands in the empty room, feeling suddenly more alone than she ever has in her life.

Shara slowly closes the window shutters. Her hands are trembling with rage. Never could she have imagined that her aunt could think so poorly of her – breaking into the Warehouse and accidentally freeing Urav as if she was some bumbling, slapstick fool? Like she was some vain little brat, and the world her playground? And smiling so *sadly* at her, as if believing the Divine might still exist was some kind of dispiriting mental deficiency.

Shara wishes she had someone to talk to about this. But the only person she's ever really honestly talked to about the Divine was Efrem Pangyui, for the handful of days they had together.

She looks back at the white suitcase under her desk.

She walks over, pulls out the suitcase, puts it on her desk, and thinks.

Shara Komayd graduated from the Ministry of Foreign Affairs training academy with a record low number of demerits. She graduated from Fadhuri with full marks. And she has always been one of the few high-level operatives in the Ministry to actually, personally do all of her paperwork herself – a virtue she takes pride in.

Always the good soldier. Never a toe out of line. *And look at where it's got me.*

But she still cannot quite bring herself to open the suitcase.

Just remember, she tells herself, *it's not like you have any more of a career to throw away.*

The latches click open with a *snap*, and the top lifts up.

Inside is a stack of papers bound together with string. The papers are covered in spidery handwriting, and she does not need to look for the slumping T or jagged M to identify the hand as Efrem's. The first page is different from the ones below, written hastily, and slapped on the top of the stack.

She will have only today to read it, she thinks. Vinya's people will definitely be at the embassy soon, after Urav.

Shara nestles down in her chair and cuts the string.

Hello,

 If you are reading this, then you have found the safety deposit box belonging to, through a chain of aliases, Dr Efrem Pangyui of Ghaladesh.

 It seems unlikely that you would not know this already, & since the only indication of this deposit box's existence is a message encoded in a mixture of old Gheshati, Chotokan, Dreyling & Avranti, then the probabilities suggest that only a person with great experience in ancient translation would be able to find this box at all.

 I suppose what I am saying is – Hello, Shara.

 If you are reading this, then I am either dead, missing or safely in your protection. I hope it is the latter: I hope, as you read this, I am across from you & we laugh over this histrionic letter, & how needless it was.

But as of right now, I am not at all convinced it is needless.

What follows is my personal journal (or at least what I was able to snatch from my offices) recorded over my time in Bulikov, from the 12th of the Month of the Scorpion to the 14th of the Month of the Rat.

I hope what I am giving you is enough to complete my research. I have touched upon a truth in Bulikov perilous enough that I feel my life is in danger – but I am not certain <u>which</u> truth. Yet you are, in many ways, wiser & worldlier than I ever wished to be, & I hope that you may succeed where I have failed.

I hope to see you again, & if I do not, then I wish you safe studies.

Yours,
Efrem Pangyui
16th of the Month of the Rat

Journal of Efrem Pangyui

12th of the Month of the Scorpion, Bulikov
This is ridiculous.

I am looking at my notes in my office (a dingier & darker place could never be found) as well as the list from Minister Komayd's warehouse, & I am struck both by the marvel of what we have saved, what we have stored, & the enormity of the task before me.

So far I am about three-quarters of the way through just compiling a list strictly of documents: issuance of edicts from Continental priests, Divinities or Divine agents, anything recording significant 'policy changes' (I am obliged to use this execrable term for what I seek). The stack of paper now comes up to about knee height. I once jokingly predicted I would die entombed in documents, yet now that prediction seems much more possible. It is fascinating material, to be sure – I would have killed to grasp but a fraction of it months ago – yet now I feel I shall drown in treasures.

Sketches, sketches . . . I hope I shall find a place to keep all of these sketches.

27th of the Month of the Scorpion
Already, a pattern emerges.

I must allow that I <u>could</u> be biased. I have looked at the most obvious opportunity for correlation – the Night of Convening, & the founding of Bulikov – & though I do perceive <u>much</u> correlation, that doesn't mean I'm right.

But the facts remain:

In 717, while the Divinities & their peoples were still squabbling & fighting for territory, a Taalhavshtani priest wrote a series of essays expounding the benefits of allying with Jukoshtan. These became exceedingly popular throughout all of Taalhavshtan, being read aloud in numerous gathering places.

In 720, on the other side of the Continent, a phalanx of Voortyashtani precepts helped a wandering Olvoshtani monk return to his home, & reflected at length upon how much they had in common with their warring neighbours. This was recorded in several letters sent to the foremost Voortyashtani acolyte, who noted that he approved of the sentiment.

That same year, in Ahanashtan, a county magistrate wrote letters to his sister, describing a town meeting in which much sympathy with the Kolkashtanis was expressed, despite the ongoing six-way war.

So on, & so on . . . I can cite nearly thirty more instances of naked sympathy for other Divine factions, & more continue to creep out of the pile, <u>despite</u> the Divine war being waged at this exact same time.

Then – 'abruptly' – in 723, all six Divinities felt compelled to sit down in the Night of the Convening, in the future spot of Bulikov, hash out their differences, & form what was, more or less, a pantheon of equal Divinities . . . yet all religious texts I have reviewed indicate this was decided with <u>no</u> consultation with their mortal followers whatsoever! This was, reportedly, a 'unilateral' decision among Divinities, as one would expect, for why would a god consult with his or her followers, like a politician among constituents? Yet obviously the shift had been brewing for years, among their mortal flock!

The two groups – mortal & Divine – were not as divided as history would have us believe.

This is an absurdly large example, akin to deciphering the destination of a ship by which way the seabirds are buffeted by the winds . . . yet it sketches the outline of what I expected to see.

I wish I could consult Shara about it. But I am not entirely sure how genuine her interest in me was – how can you ever tell what is & is not an act with such people?

There is a café I find myself frequenting, just adjacent to the Seat of the World. Bulikov is a mixed-up jumble of a city there – the Blink still reverberates in the city's bones – & there I watch children play & fight, wives gossip & laugh, men smoke & drink & play cards &, often ineffectually, court the women.

People fall in love & bicker over silly things, even in a place as mad as this, life goes on, & I must smile.

15th of the Month of the Sloth

It is saying something that I, veteran of libraries, begin to tire of my task. I look forward to finishing this so I can continue on to my <u>next</u> task: researching the Kaj. How ridiculous it is that, though the man's profile emblazons coins, flags & so on, we know almost as little about him as we do the Divinities. Especially with regard to how he actually managed to <u>assassinate</u> them . . . I can understand why the Minister wished me to research this subject first, but I, stupidly, convinced her that the Continentals still derive a sense of legitimacy from the Divinities, so researching their nature would offer more definite geopolitical benefits.

Listen to me. I sound like Shara.

The grass is always greener on the next task, surely, but the Kaj has always been a fascination of mine . . . He just seems to suddenly <u>appear</u>, the son of a wealthy, Continental-collaborator family, poking his head up in history & surging forward . . . I have reviewed numerous family trees, & have found almost nothing about the man.

Some list his father as never even having married! Was the Kaj, possibly, the product of an illegitimate relationship? Was he even the man's son at all?

I no longer sound like Shara. Now I sound like a gossip magazine.

I sometimes go to the sections of the city most disrupted by the Blink. The stairs there look like fields of giant cornstalks, rising into the sky, ending suddenly. The children play a funny game: they run up the stairs, see who is bravest to go the highest, then run back down.

Up the stairs & down the stairs they run, over & over, always hurrying, yet never quite going anywhere.

I sympathise.

I must focus . . . I must examine the threads of history, the calendars & timelines, & see if they align.

If they do not, as I expect, what does this mean for the Continent? What does it mean for Saypur?

29th of the Month of the Sloth

Yesterday I met something I am not sure is legally permitted: an Olvoshtani monk.

I think it was a monk . . . I am not sure. I was taking a break from my work, revelling in sunlight on the Solda, sketching the bridge (it is so much narrower than nearly every bridge I've seen – I forget, of course, that it was meant solely for foot & horse traffic) & the walls behind it when she approached: a short, bald woman in orange robes.

She asked me what I was doing, & I told her. I showed her my work, & she was very appreciative. 'You have captured its essence exactly,' she said. 'And they say there are no more miracles!'

I asked her her name. She said she had none. I asked her the name of her order. She said she had none, only a 'disorder'. (A joke, I presume.) I asked her what she thought of Bulikov these days. She shrugged. 'It is being reinvented.'

I asked her what she meant.

'Forgetting,' she said, 'is a beautiful thing. When you forget, you remake yourself. The Continent must forget. It is trying not to – but it must. For a caterpillar to become a butterfly, it must forget it was ever a caterpillar at all. Then it will be as if the caterpillar never was, & there was only ever the butterfly.'

I was so struck by this I fell into deep thought for some time. She skipped two stones across the Solda, bowed to me, & walked away.

2nd of the Month of the Turtle

<u>Amazing</u> discoveries, & terrifying ones. The discussions I have found taking place just before the Great Expansion have shed so much more light on the strange relationship between Divinities & mortals.

Between 768 and 769:

In Ahanashtan, a priest stood on the shore & daily preached his reflections of foreign lands; in Voortyavashtan, a sparring master pointed to mountain canyons headed east, below (then) the Dreyling lands, & commented on the way the rain must fall on the other side of the mountains, inspiring numerous exploration parties; later, in Jukoshtan, a starling-singer (must research this term later) sang a three-day poem of the currents in the ocean, & how they carry one so far away to distant places, & perhaps distant peoples . . . & so on, & so on.

One can see, then, that the Continentals were thinking about lands besides theirs. I have discovered a <u>wealth</u> of text that noses at the boundaries of their geographic knowledge.

Yet I have trudged through Divine decrees of all kinds during this <u>same</u> period, & have found <u>no</u> Divine mention of anything beyond the Continent's boundaries & shores!

It is odd that the Divinities remained silent on a conversation surging through their mortal flock.

But look how the discourse changes among the Continentals between 771 & 774:

In Kolkashtan, a town magistrate claimed that, since the Continent is blessed by the Divinities, there is nothing they do *not* own – they own the stars, the clouds & the waves in the ocean; in Voortyavashtan, a 'gallows-priestess' asked why they make blades that will shed no blood, for there are no more wars to fight in, & debated whether this was a sin; in Ahanashtan, a 'mossling' (some kind of nun?) wrote a poetic epic about what will happen when Ahanashtan grows so large (was the city alive? I must research further) that it begins to harm itself, bringing disharmony, starvation & exhaustion. This epic was terribly successful, & caused many debates & much anxiety, with some even demanding the mossling's imprisonment.

The Continentals were thinking, however peripherally, about expansion. It is patently obvious to anyone that they feared exhaustion, starvation, & moreover they began to feel that they deserved to expand, & take ownership of new places.

The Divinities, however, were not thinking about expansion – Kolkan was starting down the train of thought that would begin with his period of open judgement, & Taalhavras, always the most distant of Divinities, was adding to the walls of Bulikov – and, I believe, altering the nature of Bulikov in many more profound, invisible ways . . . All of them were engaged in their own concerns, while the people of the Continent fretted over the future.

Yet then, in 772, all six Divinities met in Bulikov, & elected – in what we previously thought to be an inscrutable, spontaneous gesture – to begin the Great Expansion, the conquering & domination of all nearby nations & countries, including Saypur.

Even the Continentals themselves recorded some surprise at this decision – but why, if they were already thinking about it themselves?

The argument I pose may be tenuous, but it compensates in quantity of evidence – in my studies, I have found nearly six hundred other instances of similar phenomena, on a much smaller scale: edicts that were proclaimed well after public opinion had been formed, laws that were passed after everyone was already following them, persecutions & prejudices that were in place well before the Divine, or their institutions, announced them.

The list goes on & on.

The pattern is undeniable: the timelines do not align. It is as if there was a delay! The Continentals made their decisions, formed their attitudes . . . & the Divinities followed, making them official.

Who was leading whom? Is this evidence of some kind of unconscious <u>vote</u>, which the Divinities then enacted?

I wonder, sometimes, if the Continentals were like shoals of fish, & the slightest flick of one fish caused dozens of others to follow suit, until the entire shimmering cloud had changed course.

And were the Divinities the sum of this cloud? An embodiment, perhaps, of a national subconscious? Or were they empowered by the thoughts & praises of millions of people, yet also yoked to every one of those thoughts – giant, terrible puppets forced to dance by the strings of millions of puppeteers.

This knowledge, I think, is incredibly dangerous. The Continentals derive so much pride & so much power from having Divine approval . . . but were they merely hearing the echoes of their own voices, magnified through strange caverns & tunnels? When they spoke to the Divinities, were they speaking to giant reflections of themselves?

And if I am right, then it means that the Continentals were never <u>ordered</u> to invade Saypur, never <u>ordered</u> to enslave us, never <u>ordered</u> to force their brutal regime on to the known world: the gods merely enforced it, because the Continentals wished it.

Everything we know is a lie.

Where did the gods come from? What <u>were</u> they?

I find it hard to sleep, knowing this. I relax at night with a game of cards, played on the embassy rooftop. You can see the scarring in the city. It is like a road map of clashing realities.

So much forgotten. If this city is a chrysalis, it is an ugly one.

24th of the Month of the Turtle

The Minister is pleased with my progress, but asks for more verification. I have compiled a tower of contradictions in Continental history – & this, for me, would suffice – yet I will find more for her.

Yet something absurd has happened: I have discovered among the piles in my office some crumbling letters written by a soldier close to the Lieutenant Sagresha . . . & thus close to the Kaj himself! How could I have forgotten or missed <u>this</u>? Perhaps I never even looked at them . . . Though sometimes I worry my office at the University is being tampered with. Yet this may be silly paranoia.

But what the soldier writes is eye-opening to say the least:

We have suspected for some time that the Kaj used some sort of projectile weapon: a cannon, gun or bolt that fired a special kind of fire or lightning against which the Divinities had no defence.

Yet I believe we have been thinking about this the wrong way: we think about the gun, the cannon itself, rather than what it fired. But this soldier records stories of a 'hard metal' or a 'black lead' that the Kaj produced & stored & protected! Here, upon the Kaj's execution of the Divinity Jukov:

'We followed the Kaj to a place in the city – a temple of white & silver, its walls patterned like the stars with purple glass. I could not see the god in the temple, & worried it was a trap, but our general did not worry, & loaded his black lead within his hand-cannon, & entered. Time passed, & we grew concerned, yet then there was a shot, & our general – weeping! – slowly came out.'

A valuable piece of history, certainly, but also a revolutionary one! What if it was not the cannon at all that was important? What if it was simply the metal that was used in the shot? It seems mundane, even silly . . . But we know the Kaj was something of an alchemist: we have records of his experiments. What if he produced a material that the Divine could not affect, just as we cannot affect an arrow through our hearts?

Even stranger, the soldier writes of the Kaj mentioning a 'djinnifrit' that was kept in his father's manor house back in Saypur . . . We do know that certain Continental collaborators were given Divine servants as a reward, but it would be scandalous for anyone to discover that the Kaj had such close contact with any agent of the Divine! Djinnifrit servants prepared their masters' beds, served them food, wine . . . I cannot imagine what everyone would say if it was revealed that the Kaj had been pampered in such a way.

I will wait to send this information back to the Minister until I know more.

20th of the Month of the Cat

I am not sure if what I have found helps the case of the Kaj . . . I have discovered more letters from the Kaj's inner circle during his time on the Continent, immediately after the capture of Bulikov, when he sank into a depression so severe he spoke to no one at all.

I have confirmed that the Kaj's mysterious weapon was, indeed, 'black lead' or 'hard metal' – a metal whose reality could not be altered by Divine means. Both the Divinities & their servants were helpless against it: the Kaj merely needed to decipher a way to propel it forward, much as one would a common firearm.

But how he created it . . . that I did not anticipate.

After the brutal Massacre of Mahlideshi, when Saypuris revolted after the horrific execution of that simple girl, it seems the Kaj was so horrified & so furious that he did conduct experiments, as we thought . . . but he conducted them on his family's djinnifrit servant! From what I have read, it sounds very much like torture, even monstrous torture: the djinnifrit was bound to serve the Komayd family's will, so the Kaj forced it to comply with his efforts, burning & wounding the djinnifrit until he had created a material that worked not only on the djinnifrit, but on all Divine creatures, including the Divinities themselves . . . & upon succeeding, he executed his childhood servant.

Will this endear him to the more nationalistic factions in Saypur? Or will they, like myself, be horrified by what I have learned? I have still not found any account of the Kaj's maternal lineage . . . Did he, like the Divinities, simply manifest, with no explanation, coughed up on the shore of Saypur from the seas of history?

19th of the Month of the Bear

I no longer believe myself to be safe.

I am spied upon – I am sure of it. The cab driver in the street, the maid at the University, the newspaper seller who never seems to leave my street, nor to sell any newspapers . . . I am being watched.

I performed a test today – I sent my report to the Minister via our telecommunications device, & kept an eye on the street. The

newspaper seller was still there, still watching me, yet a young man
came running up, whispered something in his ear, & sprinted away . . .
The newspaper seller remained there for a few minutes more, then
crept away.

Is he reading my reports? Are our transmissions being intercepted?

How can I tell the Minister? Could I perhaps get word to Shara?
The Governor?

Could I even move without their knowing?

6th of the Month of the Lark

I am sure of it now: some of my sketches have been stolen, & some of
the Governor's warehouse list is missing too . . . Yet I am not sure if I
can trust the Governor. Perhaps she has informants in her staff!

The City Fathers rail against me. They wish me lynched, assassi-
nated . . . There are protests at the University, & the embassy is no
help, either, as the Chief Diplomat is a blithering toad . . . What a
fool I was to come here!

I have begun sending the Minister messages that I hope will arouse
her suspicion, if not anger: delays, excuses, etc. She <u>must</u> realise that
something is wrong.

Yet I begin to suspect even her. I think all day about the Blessed, &
what this could mean not just for Saypur, but for the Continent.

Is everything we believe a lie?

29th of the Month of the L

Should I even write in this honesltly

   Honestly honestly

   Can't even spell

   Blessed

   Watch the windows, watch

14th of the Month of the Rat

History will not let us forget: it wears disguises, reintroduces itself to
us, claims it is someone new & wonderful . . . But it will not let us
forget.

I shall die in Bulikov, I believe.

And perhaps then, the chrysalis will open.

Shara takes the last piece of paper, gently turns it over, and places it with the others.

Someone downstairs calls for more coffee; there is an answering cry that it's coming.

Pigeons coo and mutter on the embassy rooftop, sharing gossip in their own language.

Shara is faint. She nearly falls out of her chair.

A world view is a series of assumptions, of perceived certainties, a way things must be because they have always been that way, and they cannot be otherwise: any other way, any other world, is completely inconceivable to that world view.

Shara has always felt that certain world views are more flexible than others: some are myopic and strict, while others are quite broad, with permeable borders and edges, ideas and events floating through without any resistance. And for so long, Shara thought she possessed the latter.

Yet now . . . Now it feels like all the assumptions and certainties that made up her world are dissolving under her feet, and she will plummet down, down, down.

What a brittle, tiny thing the world is.

All the mysteries and murders and intrigue of the past days shrink until they are meaningless to her.

It's a lie. All of it is a lie. Everything we've ever learned is a lie.

She ties up the stack of paper with new string, replaces the papers in the white suitcase, and shuts it.

> *I sing and caper*
> *Dance and twirl*
> *And many a merry pattern I weave.*
>
> *But cross me not, children*
> *For there is no burning coal in all the fires of Bulikov*
> *No raging storm in all the Southern Seas*

No element on this earth or in this world
That could match my fury.

My name is Jukov
And I do not forget.

The Jukoshtava, *Book Six*

The Divine City

The days tumble by.

Appointments, appointments. Shara is no longer a person: she is a personage, the physical representation of an office, yet ironically being such a thing renders her powerless. She is shuffled from meeting room to meeting room, listening to the pleas of Bulikov, the pleas of the Continent, the pleas of taxpayers, merchants, the wealthy, the impoverished. She lives on a diet of agendas, each stuffed in her hand as she walks through the door, and a parade of bland and vapid names: 'Today is the Legislative Co-Action Association of the Kivrey Quarters,' someone tells her, or, 'Now is the Cultural Charities of Promise Committee,' or, 'After this is the Urban Planning and Redistricting Task Force of Central Bulikov.'

There is no crueller hell than committee work, she decides, and Vinya must have taken great pleasure in knowing this. Shara now sits on committees that decide who shall be nominated as committee chairs to other committees; then, after these meetings, she sits on committee meetings to formulate agendas for future meetings; and after these, she attends committee meetings deciding who shall be appointed to appoint appointees to committees.

Shara smiles through these, which she thinks is quite a feat: for inside she is filled with boiling, thrashing, groaning secrets. She feels at times as if the city is filled with ticking bombs that could go off at any moment, and only she is aware of them, yet she cannot open her mouth to warn anyone. Every morning she awakes in a sweat and dashes to check the papers, sure to discover some lethal plot unfolding only blocks away.

But the world is quiet, and still. Saypuri cranes reconstruct the Solda Bridge, segment by segment. Vohannes has not contacted her since their clumsy night together (and Shara has not yet decided if this is damning evidence or not – even if she *didn't* suspect he was the one who blew her cover, she still isn't sure she'd be able to look him in the eye). Ernst Wiclov's leave of absence grows longer and longer and longer. Mulaghesh has, after receiving some biting telegrams from the Regional Governor's Office, reluctantly returned to her regular duties. Shara does not have to look hard to see Auntie Vinya's hand in that.

But in Shara's head, the pages of Pangyui's journal flit in and out of her thoughts, and she must force a smile on to her face as she listens to the worries of Bulikov and the Continent, thinking all the while, *These are lies. This is all a lie. Everything these people believe, everything* Saypur *believes, is built upon lies. And I am the only person alive in this world who knows it.*

She has not seen Sigrud for more than a week. But this is actually good – she has assigned him to watch all of Wiclov's loomworks. The man himself might have disappeared, but he can't take whole factories with him, and the loomworks form one leg of the Restorationists' triune – the other two legs being the steel, and whatever was stolen from the Warehouse. And Vinya might have warned Shara against attempting any sort of covert work, but standing in a street and watching a building isn't *inherently* covert, is it?

So for now, she watches, and she waits.

Specifically, she waits for nightfall. Because tonight she can actually get some real work done.

Sigrud looks up from where he kneels in the alley. It's so dark out, it's hard to see which eye of his is missing. 'You're late,' he says.

'Shut up,' snaps Shara as she jogs up. 'I've been trying to escape all evening. These meetings, they're like thieves – they follow you around, wait until you're not looking, then pounce.' She stops and leans against the wall, breathing hard. Just beyond Sigrud, on the floor of the alley, is a single line of chalk – the same chalk line Shara herself drew weeks ago, when she first tried to deduce exactly how someone could vanish in the middle of a city. 'Did you bring them?'

Sigrud holds up a canvas bag. It tinkles slightly. 'Wasn't cheap.'

'Oh, I wouldn't expect old money to be cheap. Let's take a look.'

She sits on the alley floor and sifts through the bag, which contains about six pounds of coins, all of many different types and denominations. They all have two things in common, however: they are all very old, and they are all Continental.

'It looks like we have all the polises covered,' mutters Shara. 'Taalhavshtan, Voortyavashtan, Kolkashtan, Ahanashtan, Ol . . . Wait. *Olvoshtan?*'

Sigrud shrugs.

'This is a priceless artefact!'

'You asked me to be thorough. Just don't ask *how* I managed to be so thorough.'

Shara studies the coins. 'Right . . . So. Many different markings, many different meanings. The question is: which of the meanings has *meaning?*'

Sigrud stares at her blankly. 'What?'

'Never mind,' says Shara. 'There's only one way to find out.' She turns and flings the coins down the alley, past the chalk line. They go ringing on the concrete, clattering and bouncing and rolling away to lie among the refuse.

Sigrud and Shara wait for them to settle, then pace down the alley to examine them. 'Silver, silver,' mutters Sigrud. 'Silver . . . ah, here. Lead.' Shara extends a hand. He places the coin in her palm, and they continue looking. 'Silver, silver, silver . . . silver . . . lead. And silver . . . two leads . . .'

Shara and Sigrud meet in this alley two nights out of every week. Shara would like to manage three, but her schedule won't allow it – there are so many evening events which demand the presence of Bulikov's Chief Diplomat, receptions and dinners and the like. But it is this alley, and its invisible door, that occupies every moment of Shara's waking life.

Does this alley function by calendar? By time? By the phase of the moon? Must it be approached from a certain angle? Sigrud has seen people both run and fall through these invisible doors, so the latter is unlikely. Does someone need to be on the other side of the door, to allow them through? Does it only work for men, not women? No, of course not, don't be absurd.

Trial and error, trial and error. Boil down all the possibilities until only one remains.

After picking up lead coins for nearly ten minutes, Shara has a brimming handful. She sits back to study them, one by one.

'Well?' says Sigrud.

Shara continues counting under her breath.

'Well?'

'Yes! Yes. It's as I thought – all of the lead ones are either Jukoshtani, Kolkashtani or Olvoshtani. The others remain silver.'

Sigrud lights his pipe. The scarred brick walls glint with orange, and his one eye glows. 'So?'

'So, whatever is happening in this alley, it happens to specific items with specific markings. A reaction – like a chemical. It waits for the right thing. It's not looking for an incantation, or some gesture, it's looking for . . . I don't know. For things to *look* right.'

'Like a soldier,' says Sigrud.

'Like what?'

'Like a soldier, trying to get through the gate of a fortress. Does he have his badge? Are his colours right? Does he carry the right flag?'

'Yes, I suppose, like a unif—' Shara stops. She slowly sits back to stare down the alley.

'What?' says Sigrud.

'A uniform. Sigrud, what's the last thing to have disappeared down this alley?' she asks softly.

'Umm . . . the man who drove the car.'

'Yes. But think of this alley like the gate of a fortress, and there is something invisible here, acting as a guard.'

'Checking his uniform,' says Sigurd. 'So you are saying . . .'

'I am asking,' she looks up at him, her glasses glinting in the moonlight, 'how easy would it be for you to get hold of the Kolkashtani wraps that were worn by the men you killed?'

Sigrud sighs. 'Oh, boy.'

Another cold night, another sky smoked with thin clouds, another moon weak and formless like a coffee stain. Shara stands as Sigrud comes pacing down the pavement towards her, a heavy satchel swinging from his shoulder. 'Now *you're* late. What took you so long? Was it so hard to get the wraps?'

'The wraps,' he says slowly, 'were not the problem. But I have them.' He reaches inside his satchel and hands one to Shara.

It is a hard, lumpy, dense ball of grey wool. The fabric is so tightly woven, it's almost like sealskin. *But of course it would be*, thinks Shara. *Kolkashtanis wouldn't want to entertain even the* chance *of having something show through.* 'Excellent . . . excellent!' she says. 'Do I want to know how you got this?'

He shrugs. 'I took some police officers whoring. Frequently the easiest solution is best, I find.'

Shara feels the edges of the fabric, her small fingers parsing the threads. 'Come on, come on . . . there has to be . . . wait!' The fabric around the neck is stiff and scratchy, like it has dried paint on it, or, 'Wait, is this . . . is this *blood*?'

'You think I had time to wash them?'

'Oh, my goodness . . . well.' She takes a breath. 'Anything for the job, I suppose. Now . . . hm. Yes. Here.' She feels something hard in the collar of the wrap, turns the collar inside out, and pulls apart the woollen strands. It's a small copper necklace engraved with the symbol of Kolkan. She feels the rest of the clothing and finds lumps in the wrists, the ankles, the waist – all of them trinkets and jewellery bearing Kolkan's scale.

She laughs. 'Yes,' she says. 'Finally! It's what I expected! They're not coins, per se, but they definitely have similar sigils and markings. This is a breakthrough! It was *so* obvious! I don't know why I didn't—' She looks up at Sigrud, grinning, but she sees he's dolefully watching her. 'What's wrong?'

'I am wondering how to tell you something,' he says.

'How to tell me something? Plainly and quickly, I would hope.'

He rubs his chin. 'Well. The loomworks – the ones you have had me watching,'

'Yes?'

'For a long while, it has been business as usual. Just . . . wool. Thread. Workers. Rugs. Boring.'

'Yes, and?'

'But today, and yesterday, at two of the loomworks . . . I saw someone. The same person at both places. Visiting.'

Shara slowly lowers the wrap. 'Who?'

Sigrud rubs his chin a little harder. 'Votrov.'

'*What*?'

'I know.'

Shara stares at him. '*Vohannes Votrov* is visiting these loomworks?'

He nods, wincing. 'Yes.'

'But *why* would he do that?'

'I have no idea. But I saw him. Vohannes Votrov himself. It was a very secretive visit. He was trying to sneak in the back way. But I caught him. I thought, maybe he wants to buy these loomworks. You know, maybe to rub salt in Wiclov's wounds, but no, I checked – all are owned by Wiclov, and so far there is no record of anyone trying to change that. That is why I was late.'

'You're . . . you're sure.'

'I'm sure. Vohannes Votrov. As plain as day. He did not look well, though. He looked quite sickly. And not at all happy. He looked, I thought, like a dying man. He wasn't even dressed the same, he was dressed like a sad little monk.'

This confuses Shara so much that she stops thinking about the alley entirely. 'Are you suggesting that *Vohannes Votrov* is acting like he's complicit with the *Restorationists*?'

Sigrud raises his hands, as if defending himself. 'I am telling you what I saw. He snuck into a factory owned by Wiclov, did business, then moved on to the next factory. The people there seemed to recognise him. Were I to guess, I'd say those were far from his first visits.'

'Then why . . . why would he *tell* us about the loomworks, and make us suspicious of them, if he's doing whatever it is he's doing there himself?'

Sigrud shrugged. 'He looked sick. I think he is a sick man, frankly.'

And with those words, he cuts straight to the heart of a suspicion Shara has harboured for a while: that Vohannes Votrov is not himself. His actions are too inexplicable. Why would he leak her identity? Why would he, having now extracted exactly what he wanted out of the Saypuri government, not talk to *her*, now the figurehead of Saypur's presence in Bulikov? Why would he, a man whose whole life was marred and damaged by his Kolkashtani upbringing, mutter lines from the *Kolkashavska* in the drunken depths of sleep?

The only answer is that Vohannes, a man already divided, is even more divided than she imagined. Perhaps divided enough that he is unwell, that he does not truly know what he is doing.

'There's nothing we can do about that here,' says Shara finally. 'We . . . we have to soldier on.'

'Fine,' says Sigrud. 'Then what were you saying?'

Shara tries to refocus. 'These wraps: they're seeded with tiny charms. Little medallions and bracelets and pieces of metal bearing the mark of Kolkan — just like the coins were, in a way. So these wraps, whenever they encounter that space in the alley, will evoke a reaction of some kind, just like the coins.'

'Meaning?'

'Meaning . . .' Shara bunches up the wrap until it's a tight ball, turns, and throws it towards the chalked line in the alley . . .

. . . yet it never crosses.

Sigrud blinks.

The ball of grey cloth has gone.

'Good,' says Shara. 'To be completely honest, I was not entirely sure that would work.'

'What . . . ?'

'I do feel a bit bad, I suppose — I hope you have more than one or two of those.'

'What just . . . what just happened?'

'I think I was right,' says Shara. 'This alley is damaged by the Blink in a very deep way. Not just the alley. *Reality*.' She brushes off her hands, and turns to face the chalk line. 'That is the first spot of reality static witnessed since the end of the Great War.'

'After the War, after the Divinities were killed, it took a long time for reality to figure out what it was supposed to be,' says Shara. 'In one city, one tenet was absolutely and completely true; then, in another, the opposite.

When the Divinities were killed, these two areas had to reconcile with one another, and decide what their true state was. While that was getting resolved, you had—'

'Static,' says Sigrud.

'Exactly. Places where the rules were suspended. A deep marring to the fundamental nature of reality, caused by the Blink.'

'How could reality still be broken here, and never have anyone notice?'

'I think part of it' – Shara waves at the street – 'is that it blends in so well.' The area is like much of Bulikov: twisted, warped, pockmarked, with buildings trapped inside buildings, streets ending in tangles of stairs. 'As anyone can plainly see, Bulikov has never really recovered from the Blink.'

'And on the other side of that' – he points at the invisible spot in space, wondering what to call it – 'that *static*, is another *reality*?'

'I believe so,' says Shara. 'Specifically, it's a reality that pays attention to what sort of Divinity you worship, whose markings and sigils and signs you bear.'

'I suppose it's true, then. The clothes make the man.'

'How many more wraps do you have?'

He looks in his satchel. 'Three.'

'Then please give me your smallest one, if you can. We're going over.'

Shara and Sigrud each pull on a set of clothes: for Shara, the clothes are absurdly large, and for Sigrud, absurdly small. 'I really do wish you'd washed these,' says Shara. 'This one is still stiff on the inside.'

'You're *sure* this will work?' asks Sigrud.

'Yes. Because once, *you* almost went there.'

Sigrud frowns. 'I did?'

'Yes. When you saw the first disappearance, the man jumping down into the alley, you said you glimpsed, just for a moment, tall, thin buildings of white and gold. And I believe the only reason you *did* see that' – she points at his right hand in its grey glove – 'is because of *that*.'

'Because I had been touched,' says Sigrud, 'by the Finger of Kolkan.'

'You bore a Divinity's mark, so it was willing to accept you. Halfway, at least.'

Shara pulls on the Kolkashtani hood and steps towards the chalk line.

'You should let me go first,' says Sigrud. 'Over there, it is enemy territory. Only our attackers have ever gone there.'

Shara grins for the first time in what feels like weeks. 'I have spent half my life reading about other realities. I'd never refuse the opportunity of stepping into one for the very first time, even with my life at stake.'

She walks forward.

There is no change, unlike when she passed through to the Unmentionable Warehouse. She is not even sure if anything has happened at all: she is still in the alley, standing on the stone floor, facing a street that looks almost exactly like it did before.

She looks down. At her feet is a Kolkashtani wrap, tied up in a tight bundle.

She turns round to see Sigrud manifest – there is no other word for it – in the middle of the alleyway. His one eye blinks behind the Kolkashtani hood, and he asks, 'Are we through?'

'I think so,' says Shara. 'But where we are doesn't seem that diff . . .'

She trails off and stares over Sigrud's shoulder.

'What?' he says. He turns to look, and says only, 'Oh.'

The first really noticeable difference is that, beyond the next building, it is day. Not just day, but a *beautiful* day, a day with a cloudless, piercingly beautiful blue sky. Shara looks back in the other direction, and sees that over those buildings the sky is an inky, smoky purple, the night sky she just came from. *Even time is in disagreement, in this place.*

But that doesn't come close to the other *real* difference: beyond the end of the alley, where the beautiful day begins, are huge, splendid, beautiful white skyscrapers, lined and tipped with gold, covered in ribbons of scrolling and interlacing vegetal ceramics, penetrated with fragile white arches and decorative window shafts, layered with pearl and glass.

'What,' says Sigrud, 'is *that*?'

Shara, breathless, totters out to the street, and finds that the entire block is lined with gorgeous, lily-white buildings, each bearing their own frieze. The walls are covered in calligraphic facades, resembling twisting vines or lines of text: one building, she sees, is covered in giant lines from the Voortyavan *Book of Spears*. Shara's brain begins overheating as it tries to identify their many depictions: *Saint Varchek's loss at the Green Dawn . . . Taalhavras repairs the arch under the world . . . Ahanas recovers the seed of the sun.*

'Oh, my goodness.' She is trembling. She falls to her knees. 'Oh, oh my goodness.'

'Where are we?' asks Sigrud as he walks out.

She remembers what Saint Kivrey said: *It was like living in a city made of flower petals.*

'Bulikov,' says Shara. 'But the Bulikov of old. The Divine City.'

'I thought all this was destroyed,' says Sigrud.

'No – it *vanished*!' says Shara. 'Bulikov shrank by huge amounts during the Blink. Whole sections of the city just abruptly disappeared. *Some* of it was destroyed, certainly – but not all of it, it seems. This section of Bulikov must have been saved but cut adrift, tethered to our reality by a handful of connections.'

Moths caper and twirl in sunbeams. A courtyard's crystal windows send golden prisms dancing in the street.

'So this is what they fight to return to?' He casts his one eye over a half-mile-high tower tipped with a wide, golden bell dome. 'I can see why.'

'This is just a piece of what it was like,' says Shara. 'Much more was genuinely lost, along with anyone else in the buildings.'

A fountain carved to resemble stacks of jasmine blossoms percolates happily. Dragonflies flit from edge to edge, their green eyes sparkling.

'Thousands, then,' says Sigrud.

She shakes her head. 'Millions.' Then she thinks. 'Here. I want to try something.'

She holds her hands out and begins murmuring things. Her first three attempts fail – 'What are you doing?' asks Sigrud – but on the fourth . . .

A glass sphere the size of an apple appears in her hands. She laughs gaily. 'It works! It *works*! Let me see if I can . . .' She manoeuvres it so it catches a ray of sunlight: instantly, the sphere lights up, glowing a clear, bright gold. Shara cackles again, puts the sphere on the ground, and rolls it towards Sigrud. He stops it with his boot: its glow persists, lighting him from below.

'A miracle,' says Shara. 'From the *Book of the Red Lotus*, of Olvos. One that *never* works on . . . well, in *our* Bulikov, I suppose. But here . . .'

'It works quite well.'

'Because this reality obeys different rules. Watch – roll it back to me.' Shara picks it up, tosses it high, and cries, 'Stay and show!' The glowing sphere hangs ten feet over them, bathing the streets around them in soft light. 'They had these throughout Bulikov, rather than street lights. Much more convenient.'

'And a good way to tell people where we are,' says Sigrud disapprovingly. 'Take it down, please.'

'Well, actually, I don't know how to do that, exactly.'

Sigrud, grumbling, picks up a stone and hurls it at the sphere. Shara shouts and covers her head. The shot is dead centre, and the sphere pops and bursts into a cloud of dust, which blows away down the street.

'It is good to know that stones still work here,' says Sigrud.

They wander Old Bulikov – as Shara has termed it – not sure what they are looking for. The city is completely abandoned: the gardens are barren, the courtyards empty, the ornamental ponds all scummed over. Everything is very clean and white, though: Shara is happy to have the Kolkashtani wrap, as it helps reduce the glare. But though it is beautiful, she cannot absorb it without thinking of Efrem's theory: *Did the gods make this place*, she wonders, *or did they simply make what the Continentals wished them to make?*

Sometimes when they glance into windows or alleys of this empty city they do not see what they expect: instead of more alleys, or the inside of a building, they see muddled, filthy streets packed with frowning Continentals, or a drainage ditch leading to the Solda, or just a blank brick wall.

'More reality static,' says Shara. 'A connection to New Bulikov – *our* Bulikov.'

Sigrud stops and looks into one window, which gazes in on an old woman's kitchen. He watches as she cuts the heads off four trout. 'They do not see us at all?'

'Excuse me,' says Shara into the window. '*Excuse me!*'

The old woman mutters, 'How I hate trout. By the gods, how I hate trout.'

'I suppose not,' says Shara. 'Come on.'

After a few blocks they come to a sprawling estate with a white-walled mansion, horseshoe arches, grass-floored courtyards (which are now clotted with weeds), and dozens of reflecting pools, each of which is positioned to reflect the flower-shaped citadel.

'I wonder what esteemed person lived here,' says Shara. 'A high priest, or perhaps one of the Blessed.'

Sigrud points to one of the horseshoe arches. 'Someone we know, actually.'

On the top of the arch are the words: The House Of Votrov.

'Ah,' says Shara softly. 'I should have guessed. Vohannes did say the original house had vanished during the Blink. But I did not realise it was quite *this* nice.'

'What did you mean, one of the Blessed?' asks Sigrud.

'People who had interbred with the Divine,' says Shara. 'Their progeny were heroes, saints, unusually fortunate and legendary sorts of people. The world rearranged itself around the Blessed to give them what they wanted.'

Shara remembers one of the last entries in Efrem's journey, and the single word: *Blessed*.

'That must be nice,' says Sigrud. 'And you think the Votrov family was one of these?'

'Oh, no, not at *all*. Those sorts of lineages were always well documented. If he was, I'm sure his family would never have let anyone forget about it. Wait . . . look.' She points at a spot where the weeds of one courtyard have been parted. 'Someone's been here. Quite recently.'

Sigrud walks to the disturbance, squats and reviews the markings on the ground. 'Many people. *Many*. Men, I think. And recent, as you said.' He carefully steps forward into the weeds. 'Most of them burdened. Carrying . . . heavy things.' He points ahead, towards another horseshoe arch that exits on to a descending hillside. 'That is where they went.' He points to the citadel of the house of Votrov. 'And that is where they came from.'

'Can you follow the trail?'

He looks at her as if to say – *Did you really just ask that?*

Shara debates splitting up, but decides against it *If we get lost in here, how will we ever get out?* 'We'll follow the trail where they *went*,' she says. 'And if we have time, we'll examine where they came from.'

They stalk along white streets, through courtyards, around gardens.

The silence gnaws at Shara's sense of ease until she mistakes every glimmer for a lowering bolt-shot.

All the Continentals conspire against us. I should have never allowed Vohannes into my bed.

'Why do you not dance?' asks Sigrud.

'What? Dance?'

'I would think,' he explains, 'that you would be dancing to see Old Bulikov. Running back and forth, trying to sketch things.'

'Like Efrem did.' She considers it. 'I do wish to. I would gladly spend the rest of my life here, if I could. But here, in Bulikov, every piece of history feels lined with razors, and the closer I try and look at it, the more I wound myself.'

A curving house, designed to resemble a volcano, perches over a babbling brook of white stones.

'I do not think that is history's nature,' says Sigrud.

'Oh? Then what is it?'

'That,' he says, 'is the nature of *life*.'

'You believe so? A depressing perspective, I feel.'

'Life is full of beautiful dangers, dangerous beauties,' says Sigrud. He stares into the sky, and the white sunlight glints off his many scars. 'They wound us in ways we cannot see: an injury ripples out, like a stone dropped in water, touching moments years into the future.'

Shara nods. 'I suppose that's true.'

'Yes. We think we move, we run, we push forward but, I think, in many ways we are still trapped in a moment that happened to us long ago, always running on the same spot.'

'Then what are we to do?'

He shrugs. 'We must learn to live with it.'

The wind pulls a tiny dust devil to its feet and sends it tottering along a white stone lane.

'Does this place make you contemplative?' asks Shara.

'No,' he says. 'This is something I think I have believed for a long time.'

A bulging crystal window at the top of a rounded house captures the blue sky, stretches it, and makes a perfect azure bubble.

'You are not,' says Shara, 'the man I freed from prison.'

He shrugs again. 'Maybe not.'

'You are wiser than he was.'

'I look back at what happened to me,' he says, 'through a lens of many years.'

'You are wiser than *I* am, I feel. Do you ever think about going home?'

Sigrud briefly halts on his trail; his eyes dance over the cream-white cobblestones. Then, 'No.'

'No? Never?'

'They do not know me any more. It was a long time ago. They are different people now. Like I am. And they would not wish to see this thing I am.'

They follow the trail for a few moments of silence.

'I think you're wrong,' says Shara.

Sigrud says, 'Think what you like.'

The trail leads on and on and on. 'Of course, they couldn't bring cars, could they?' Shara muses aloud. 'The reality static wouldn't allow them through, being so modern.'

'I would have preferred it if they could have brought a horse or two.'

'And they would simply leave them here for us? We should be so luc—' Shara stops and stares at a tall, rounded building on her left.

'What?' asks Sigrud

Shara's eyes study the walls, which have windows in the pattern of eight-pointed stars, filled with bright violet glass.

'What now?' asks Sigrud.

Shara's eyes study the facade: at its top is an abridged quote from the *Jukoshtava*:

Those who come upon a choice, a chance, and tremble and fear – why should I allow them in my shadow?

'I have read about this place,' murmurs Shara.

'I expect you have read about every place in this city.'

'No! No, I read about this place just . . . just recently.'

She walks forward and touches the white walls. She remembers the lines from Efrem's journal, quoting the letters of a Saypuri soldier about the death of Jukov: '*We followed the Kaj to a place in the city – a temple of white and* silver, its walls patterned like the stars with purple glass. I could not see the god in the temple, and worried it was a trap, but our general did not worry, and loaded his black lead within his hand-cannon, and entered . . . '

Shara feels numb. She approaches the door of the temple – white-painted wood, carved in a pattern of stars – and pushes it open.

The door opens on to a large empty courtyard. The walls are high and frame a piercing bright blue sky above. In the centre of the courtyard is a dry fountain, around which are four small benches.

Shara slowly walks towards the benches. These she also touches, as if to confirm they are really there.

Is this, she thinks, *where a god once sat?*

And did my great-grandfather sit next to him, or stand over him?

She slowly sits on a bench. The wood softly creaks.

Could this really be the place where Jukov himself died? Could I have found it?

She believes so. It seems unreal to see this place, trapped in a fragment of reality long since faded from the real world: but she knows it is perfectly possible. The period after the Blink was chaotic, with pieces of reality flashing into existence, then away.

She looks to the right. A low gallery circles the courtyard, with heavy square roofs supported by white wooden columns.

In one column there is a small black hole. It is just at shoulder height, if you are seated.

Seated and, perhaps, holding out a pistol, maybe to someone's head.

She walks to it, and gets the uncanny sense that something is inside it, watching her. *I have been waiting here for you*, the little hole seems to say, *for so long!*

'Sigrud,' she says hoarsely. 'Bring me your knife.'

He places the handle of the heavy black knife in her palm. She takes a breath, and shoves the blade into the hole in the wood.

A *tink* as it strikes something metal. She begins hacking at the column, carving the wood away, until the thing inside begins to shake loose.

Something small and black clatters to the floor of the courtyard. Shara stoops and picks it up.

A piece of dark, dark metal, half flattened from where it struck the wood, about the size of a fat fig.

She rolls it around in the palm of her hand, feeling its weight.

Jukov must *be dead*, thinks Shara. *He must be. Otherwise, how could this be here?*

'What is that?' asks Sigrud.

'This little thing,' says Shara softly, 'is what brought down the gods.'

They continue following the trail, twisting and turning across the streets, until it unexpectedly ends in the middle of what seems to have been someone's living room.

'Where are they?' asks Sigrud. 'The footsteps end here.'

Shara kneels and examines the floor, but she can see nothing. 'I can never figure out exactly *what* you are using to track people. Where do the footsteps end?'

Sigrud points at a spot on the floor, not quite in the corner, nor quite in the centre of the room.

'More static, I would imagine,' says Shara. 'Just a very subtle spot, one that's very hard to notice.'

'And you think we can pass back through?'

'I don't think our reality – the *actual* reality – rejects anyone. Unlike this one. The question is: *where* will we come back through?'

'I think it would be wise to allow me to go first this time,' says Sigrud. 'We know our enemies are over there, somewhere, doing . . . something. It would be stupid to allow you through. All right?'

'All right.'

Sigrud steps towards the spot. He gradually disappears, his leading foot dissolving, followed by his waist and shoulders, but it all happens too quickly for her eyes to really understand.

She waits. Then she is treated to the bizarre sight of Sigrud's head and hand appearing in mid-air.

He gestures to her to follow, but holds a finger to his lips.

She walks towards the spot, bracing herself.

Last time her surroundings did not seem to change at all, but this time the change is absolute: the white city fades away, and a blue-purple dawn sky comes spilling in above, framed by harsh, sandy mountains. Short, scraggly trees rise out of the chalky soil around them and bend back down to graze the earth.

'So,' says Sigrud, 'where are we *now*?'

Shara's mind races. 'Not in Bulikov, that's for sure. Interesting . . . it seems there is no fixed geographical relationship between Old Bulikov and the *real* Bulikov.'

Sigrud impatiently rolls his index finger – *Get on with it.*

'I *think* that we are outside Jukoshtan.' Shara reaches up, grabs the slender branch of a tree and examines its leaves. 'I think so. This sort of juniper only grows near Jukoshtan. They used to perfume wine with the berries.'

'So is Jukoshtan behind this in any way?'

'I genuinely have no idea,' says Shara. She turns round and examines the spot they just passed through. It bears some minor effects from the Blink – the sand appears molten together, and many of the trees appear bent and mutated – but otherwise you'd never be able to tell this spot had any trace of reality static to it.

She breaks off a branch from a nearby tree, peels back the bark so its green inner core is revealed in a slender stripe, and stabs it into the ground. 'To mark our entry point,' she says. 'Now – lead on.'

The trail leads down a valley, then up the hills, up and up, until they come to the crest, and then . . .

'Down,' whispers Sigrud. '*Down!*' He grabs her shoulder and rips her forward, crashing into the soft sand hills.

Shara lies still, and listens. Then she hears it: voices and hammers.

Sigrud peers through the undergrowth.

'Have we been spotted?' Shara whispers.

He shakes his head. 'No. But I am not sure what I am looking at.'

'Is it safe for me to move?'

'I think so,' he says. 'They are very far down in the valley. And they are very busy.'

She lifts her head and crawls to a spot where she can see. The bottom of the valley is dotted with fires, as if the people there are preparing to work well into the night. But what they are working on is hard to discern: there are six long, wide shapes of gleaming metal that Shara first thinks are giant shoes – pointed at the front and square at the back, like the clogs they wear in Voortyavashtan – but there are doors and windows in the giant metal shoes, and stairs and trapdoors. And in the middle is something that looks like a mast with no sail.

Shara says, 'They almost look like—'

'Ships,' says Sigrud. 'Boats. Giant boats of metal, with no ocean, and no sails.'

She squints to see the figures scurrying around the ships, screwing in screws, welding plates together. All the workers are dressed in traditional Kolkashtani wraps.

'They're definitely Restorationists, I think,' she murmurs. 'But why the hells would they build boats of metal out here in the country? We're hundreds of miles from the ocean! I suppose that's what they needed the steel for.'

'That is not a terribly large fleet,' says Sigrud with some contempt. 'Only six ships? If they *were* going to sail anywhere, there's not much you could do with that.'

Shara considers it. 'Unless you were getting the materials to build the ships in very small quantities. Like the steel. A thousand pounds of steel a month, for a little over a year – that doesn't make very many ships. But this must have been what they were using the steel for!'

'And then what?'

'I'm not sure. Perhaps they found something in the Warehouse that could create ocean wherever you wanted it.'

Eight men are pushing something up a ramp into one of the metal boats. Even though the light is faint, Shara's heart almost stops at the sight of it.

'Oh my,' she says.

'Is that what I think it is?' says Sigrud.

'Yes,' she says. 'A six-inch cannon. I've only ever seen those on a Saypuri dreadnought.'

'And they plan to do what with it? Bombard the hills? Fight a war with the squirrels?'

'I don't know,' says Shara. 'But you're going to find out.'

A pause.

Sigrud says, 'What?'

'I'm going back to Bulikov' – Shara looks over her shoulder, and is discomfited to see that the actual Bulikov is nowhere in sight – 'to the *actual* Bulikov, to telegraph Mulaghesh. But we can't just leave the Restorationists here to do . . . well . . . whatever it is they're going to do.'

'So your plan,' says Sigrud, 'is to leave me here to fight six metal ships loaded with cannons?'

'I'm asking you to watch. Only do something if *they* do something.'

'This something I should do being . . . ?'

'Infiltration, if you can. You must have dealt with a few stowaways in your time, right? Hopefully you learned something from them. If I get back to Bulikov in time, we can return with a small army within days.'

'Days *plural*?'

Shara squeezes his shoulder, says, 'Good luck,' and crawls back down the hillside.

The journey back through the white city of Old Bulikov is a strange and heavy one for Shara. She tries to put her mind to addressing the dozens of mysteries before her: landlocked ships preparing an invasion; Vohannes collaborating with Wiclov and, possibly, arranging passage for the Restorationists in and out of Old Bulikov; yet her thoughts keep returning to the lump in her pocket, jostling with each step.

I have on my person something that has tasted the blood of the Divine.

It takes her a moment to realise that this grants her a profound technological advantage: no matter what Wiclov, Vohannes and the Restorationists are plotting, none of them could imagine she possesses a piece of the Kaj's weaponry, however small. But how to use something that's hardly bigger than a marble?

When she returns to Bulikov – the real, current Bulikov – she sheds the Kolkashtani wrap right away and goes straight to a metalworker's shop.

'Can I help—' The clerk does a double take as he realises he faces the famed Conqueror of Urav.

'I need you to make something for me,' she says before he can comment.

'Oh, ah . . . certainly. What would it be?'

She places the little ball of metal on the counter. 'A bolt tip,' she says. 'Or a small knife.'

'Well, which would you like? A bolt tip or a knife?'

'Something that could be both, if required. I will need this to be quite versatile.'

The clerk picks up the ball of black metal. 'And what would you be hunting, if you don't mind my asking?'

Shara smiles and says, 'Deer?'

CD KOMAYD TO GHS512

EMERGENCY SITUATION \<STOP\>

RESTORATIONISTS PLAN FULL-SCALE ASSAULT \<STOP\>

REQUEST RELOCATION AND FORTIFICATION OF ALL

POLIS TROOPS IN BULIKOV \<STOP\>

CES512

PG MULAGHESH TO CES512

ARE YOU OUT OF YOUR DAMN MIND \<STOP\>

ARE YOU EVEN SUPPOSED TO BE INVESTIGATING

THIS ANY MORE \<STOP\>

MUST PROVIDE MORE DETAILS \<STOP\>

GHS512

CD KOMAYD TO GHS512

CANNOT PROVIDE DETAILS \<STOP\>

NOT DUE TO UNCERTAINTY DUE TO LENGTH \<STOP\>

QUESTION OF JURISDICTION IMMATERIAL DUE

TO THREAT LEVEL \<STOP\>

PLEASE MOBILISE FORCES IMMEDIATELY \<STOP\>

CES512

PG MULAGHESH TO CES512

PLEASE PROVIDE SOME INDICATION OF

THREAT LEVEL \<STOP\>

ANYTHING \<STOP\>
MOVING FIVE HUNDRED ARMED TROOPS TO
AN URBAN AREA NOT LIKE BACKING UP A WAGON
FULL OF POTATOES \<STOP\>
GHS512

CD KOMAYD TO GHS512
RESTORATIONISTS CONFIRMED TO POSSESS
30 PLUS SIX-INCH CANNONS NORMALLY SUITED
FOR DREADNOUGHTS \<STOP\>
TARGETS CURRENTLY UNKNOWN \<STOP\>
GES512

PG MULAGHESH TO CES512
IF I COMPLY WILL YOU TAKE THE HEAT
FOR THIS \<STOP\>
ALSO WHATEVER HAPPENED TO JAVRAT \<STOP\>
GHS512

CD KOMAYD TO GHS512
IF MILITARY REACTION IS NOT IMMEDIATE THEN
LIKELIHOOD OF THERE BEING A MINISTRY TO
APPLY HEAT VERY LOW \<STOP\>
LET ALONE A JAVRAT \<STOP\>
CES512

PG MULAGHESH TO CES512
WILL BEGIN MOBILISATION IMMEDIATELY \<STOP\>
IF YOU MAKE ME START ANOTHER WAR
WILL NEVER FORGIVE \<STOP\>
GHS512

CD KOMAYD TO GHS512
WAR ALREADY STARTED \<STOP\>
CES512

Just once I would like to get eight hours' sleep, thinks Shara. *I would pay for them. Steal them. Anything.*

But Shara cannot sleep. She is working on a deadline — Mulaghesh's forces will arrive in a matter of hours — but knows she is missing something. Yet she feels she is drowning in information: Efrem's journal, the lists from the Warehouse, financial transactions, Continental history, forbidden lists, Votrov subsidiaries, possessors of loomworks . . . All of it dances before her eyes until she cannot hold a single thought besides, *Please, just calm down, stop thinking and calm down, just stop, stop, stop.*

A tap at the door. Shara shouts, 'No!'

A pause. Pitry's voice, 'Well, I think you—'

'No! No appointments. None! I told you that!'

'I know, but—'

'All meetings are off! *All* of them. Tell them I'm . . . tell them I'm sick! Tell them I'm *dying*, I don't care.'

'All right, but . . . but this is a little different.' He slowly enters the room. 'It's a letter.'

'Oh, Pitry.' She rubs her eyes. 'Why do you do this to me? Is it from Mulaghesh?'

'No. It's from Votrov. A boy brought it on a silver plate. And it's . . . very odd.'

Shara takes the message. It reads:

In a game of Tovos Va, one play can end the game, but it can take your opponent some time to realise it's already over.

I know when I've lost.

Come to the New Solda Bridge, but please come alone.

I don't wish the press to know. I don't wish to harm all the good I tried to do.

V.

Shara reads this several times. 'He can't be serious.'

'What's he talking about?'

'To be honest, I've no earthly idea,' says Shara. Could Votrov actually have been involved with the Restorationists? It seems absurd but, if so, could calling in the military have cut off their plans at the knees? And, what is more, how could he have heard?

None of this makes any sense. Either Vohannes has gone insane — something she isn't ready to rule out yet — or she's missing a very big piece of the puzzle.

'What are you going to do?' asks Pitry.

'Well,' she says, 'if he asked me to meet him at his home, somewhere private, I'd never go. But the New Solda Bridge is both public and terribly popular. I think he'd be mad to try something there.'

But that still doesn't answer the question: what is she going to do? *An operative takes care of their sources personally*, she tells herself. *And though he's not a source, he is mine.* But, deep down, she does not want any other Ministry official to deal with Vo. So many insurgents and enemy agents wind up disappearing to meet horrible ends.

If someone needs to talk Vo down off whatever ledge he's climbed up on, she thinks, *it should be me.*

'If you could, Pitry, please get my coat and a thermos of tea,' says Shara. 'And if I'm not back in two hours, I want you to tell Mulaghesh the *moment* she gets here to raid Votrov's estate. There is something terribly strange going on with that man, and I'd hate to personally fall victim to it.'

As Pitry hurries away, Shara rereads the note. *I could never really tell exactly which game I was ever playing with Vo.*

But perhaps now she will find out.

The walk does good things for Shara's mind: the screaming, jabbering questions fade, scraped away by each turning staircase or twisting street, until she is just another person walking along the Solda.

Just imagine, she tells herself, *behind this crumbling city is a hidden, mythic paradise, and one only has to scrape at reality with one's fingernail to find it.*

Gulls and ducks wheel and honk, chasing one another for scraps of bread.

But whatever beautiful miracles the Divinities made, she reminds herself, *they might have been slaves to the Continent almost in the same way Saypur was.*

A crowd of homeless people fry fish in makeshift skillets on the riverbanks; one, quite obviously drunk, claims each of his fish is a piece of Urav, and is met with loud calls to sit down.

Shara suddenly decides that, when all this business with Wiclov and Votrov is finished – and how this will wind up, she has no idea – she'll quit the Ministry, return to Old Bulikov and continue Efrem's work. Two months ago she would have thought the idea of quitting insane, but with Auntie Vinya at the wheel for what might as well be for ever, Ghaladesh and all its powers are now bitter ground to her, and all her discoveries have rejuvenated her interest in the Continental past. The entirety of her Ministry career pales beside her handful of minutes in Old Bulikov, like escaping choking fumes to capture one lungful of mountain air.

And, secretly, she looks forward to the wicked glee of performing another miracle. She wonders what other miracles will work in Old Bulikov: could one walk through walls, or summon food from the sky or earth, or even fly, or . . .

Or even . . .

Shara slows to a stop.

Two gulls dip and snap at one another in mid-air for a scrap of potato peel.

'Fly,' she whispers.

She remembers an entry in the list from the Unmentionable Warehouse:

Kolkan's carpet: Small rug that MOST DEFINITELY possesses the ability to fly. VERY difficult to control. Records indicate Kolkan blessed each thread of the rug with the miracle of flight, so theoretically each thread could lift several tons into the air . . .

A carpet, with every thread blessed.

A loomworks that could take the carpet apart with great ease.

And a small armada of steel ships in the hills with no ocean.

The boy in the police cell, whispering: *We can't fly through the air on boats of wood.*

But perhaps they wouldn't need the ocean at all.

'Oh, my goodness,' whispers Shara.

*

Sigrud lifts his head when he hears the clanking. He turns his attention from the roads in and out of the valley to the six ships still marooned on the ground. The sails are being raised on the masts, and something is being extended from their port and starboard sides.

The sails being raised on the steel masts are unusual: Sigrud has seen many types of sails, but these look to be made for unbelievably brutal winds. But the objects being extended on the *sides* of each ship are something he has never, ever seen before in his life. These adornments are long, wide and thin, with many pivoting parts to them. They remind Sigrud of fins on a fish, and if he didn't know any better he'd suspect they were . . .

'Wings,' he says quietly.

He watches the men ready the ships.

Don't do something, Shara said, *unless* they *do something*.

This definitely counts as something.

He checks that his knife is still in its sheath and begins to creep down the hill.

The New Solda Bridge is a tangle of scaffolding and framing. Huge cement plinths are being laid in the cold waters, guided into place by Saypuri cranes and Saypuri engineers. Continentals watch from the banks or the roofs of homes, grudgingly awed by this show of force.

Shara's brain is still rattling with her last realisation: *You can build the ships anywhere, moor them anywhere, and no one could ever, ever be prepared for an assault from the sky.*

Yet another niggling question comes worming out of her mind: *But if Vohannes is behind it, why would the Restorationists attack his own house to try and get the steel to build them in the first place?*

She sees she'll have the chance to ask him: he sits on a park bench just ahead, legs dandily crossed, hands in his lap as he stares down the river walk, away from her. He is not wearing his usual flamboyant clothing: he has returned, Shara sees, to the dark brown coat and black shirt buttoned up to the neck, like he was wearing on the night of Urav.

She remembers Sigrud saying: *He wasn't even dressed the same, he was dressed like a sad little monk.*

She surveys the crowd. Vohannes is very much alone. Yet he seems to see her, and he looks away, so she can only see the back of his head.

'What's the matter with you, Vo?' she asks as she nears. 'Are you sick? Are you *insane*? Or have you really been working at this all along?'

He turns to her and smiles. She sees he carries no cane. 'The latter, I'm very happy to say,' he says cheerily.

Shara freezes, and immediately sees why he kept his face turned away from her until now.

It's the same as the face she knows . . . almost: the same strong, square jaw, the same glittering smile. But this is not Vohannes simply suffering from some affliction. This man's eyes are darker – and they are sunken, deep in the back of his head.

Shara doesn't wait; she turns and runs.

Someone – a rather short, non-threatening young man – ambles by, sticks his leg out and trips her. She crashes to the ground.

The stranger stands and walks towards her with a pleasant air. 'I did wonder if you'd come,' he says, 'but I guessed the line about Tovos Va would seal it. After all, I taught that game to him. How pleasant to see that it worked!'

She tries to stand back up. The stranger gestures to her and mutters something. There is a sound like a whip crack. She looks down and realises she is now totally transparent: she can see the stone cobbles through her legs – or rather, where her legs *should* be.

Parnesi's Cupboard, thinks Shara, right before someone behind her clamps a rag over her mouth: her nostrils fill with fumes, her eyes film over, and suddenly it's very hard to stand.

She falls back into their arms: two men, maybe three. The stranger – Vohannes, yet not Vohannes – wipes his nose. 'Very good,' he says. 'Come along.'

They carry her down the river walk. The fumes force their way deeper into her brain. She thinks, *Why isn't someone helping me?* But the bystanders merely watch them curiously, wondering why these men appear to be miming carrying something heavy between them.

She gives up; the fumes coil around her; she sleeps.

Across the snowy hills
Down a frozen river
Through the copse of trees
I will wait for you.

I will always wait for you there.

My fire will be burning
A light in the cold
A light for you and me
For I love you so.

Though sometimes I may seem absent
Know that my fire will always be ready
For those with love in their hearts
And the willingness to share it.

Book of the Red Lotus,
Part II, *9.12 − 9.23*

Family ties

Shara wakes facing a blank grey wall. A trickle of air unwinds in her lungs before her body is overtaken with coughs.

'Oh hoh!' says a merry voice. 'Goodness! She's awake.'

She rolls over, her brain fuzzy and hazy, and sees she's in a barren, windowless room that is somehow familiar.

There are two doors to the room, one closed and the other open. The stranger stands at the open doorway, now dressed in a Kolkashtani wrap. He smiles at her, yet his eyes are like wet stones sitting in his skull.

'I really cannot tell,' he says, 'what he could have seen in you.'

Shara blinks languidly. *Chloroform*, she remembers. *It'll be nearly an hour before I'm lucid.*

'You are, as far as I can see, an unremarkable little Saypuri,' he says. 'You are small, dirt brown – perhaps *clay* brown would be a fitting term – with the characteristic weak chin and hooked nose. Your wrists, as is common in your sort, are terribly thin and fragile, and your arms hirsute and unlovely, as is the rest of your body, I imagine. I expect you would have to shave *quite* frequently to even *compare* to the body of any woman of the Holy Lands. Your breasts are not the dangling, ponderous piles I see so often among your breed, but neither are they particularly becoming – in fact, they hardly exist at all. And your eyes, my dear. *Look* at those glasses. Do your eyes function at all? I wonder: what must it be like to be such a runty, unintended little creature? How sad your life must be, to be a creature of the ash-lands, a person made of clay.' He shakes his head, smiling.

It is a horrible perversion of Vohannes's smile: where Vo's is full of boundless, eager charm, this man's smile suggests barely contained rage.

'But the true nature of your crime – the true infraction you commit, as all your kind does – is that you *refuse to acknowledge it*. You refuse to acknowledge your own failings, your miserable, unsightly failings! You know no shame! You do not hide your flesh and body! You do not cower at our feet! You do not recognise that you, untouched by the Divine, bereft of blessings, deprived of enlightenment, are *unneeded*, unintended, superfluous at worst and servile at best! Your kind holds such lofty pretences – and *that* is your true sin, if creatures such as yourself are even capable of sin.'

He is so much like Vohannes, in so many ways: much of his gestures and bearing are Vo's. Yet there is something strangely more decayed and yet delicate about this man, something in the way he cocks his hips, the way he crosses his arms. She remembers the *mhovost*, and its effeminate walk back and forth, mimicking someone she hadn't yet glimpsed.

Shara swallows and asks, 'Who . . . ?'

'If I were to break you open,' says the stranger, 'on the inside, you would be empty. A clay shell of a person, remarkable only in your semblance of self. What *did* you see in her, Vohannes?'

The stranger looks to the corner of the room.

Sitting on the floor in the corner, his arms wrapped around his knees, is Vohannes: his face has been horribly beaten, his one eye swollen and the colour of frog skin, his upper lip rusty from old blood.

'Vo . . .' whispers Shara.

'I had hoped that she would at least offer some temptation of the flesh,' says the stranger. 'Then you could perhaps excuse your dalliance. But there is so little flesh on her to tempt you with. I honestly cannot identify any trait you found desirable in this creature. I really can't, little brother.'

Shara blinks.

Brother?

She says, 'V . . . V . . .'

The stranger slowly turns to her, and cocks an eyebrow.

Vohannes's voice echoes back to her: *He joined up with a group of pilgrims when he was fifteen, and went on a trek to the icy North to try and find some damn temple . . .*

'V . . . *Volka*?' she says. 'Volka *Votrov*?'

He smiles. 'Ah! So. You know my name, little clay-child.'

She tries to corral her drunken thoughts. 'I . . . I thought you were dead.'

He shakes his head, beaming. 'Death,' he says, 'is for the weak.'

'For those who wish to know me,' quotes Volka, *'for those who wish to be seen by my eye, and to be loved, there can be no pain too great, no trial too terrible, no punishment too small for you to pass through. For you are my children, and you must suffer to be great.'*

Volka smiles indulgently at Vohannes, but it's Shara who speaks up: 'The *Kolkashavska*.'

Volka's smile dims, and he watches her coldly.

'Book Two, I believe,' says Shara. 'His writs to Saint Mornvieva, upon why Mornvieva's nephew was crushed in an avalanche.'

'And Mornvieva was so shamed,' says Volka, 'that he had asked Father Kolkan why this had happened, and questioned him in such a manner . . .'

'. . . that he struck off his right hand,' says Shara, 'and his right foot, blinded his right eye, and removed his right testicle.'

Volka grins. 'It is so strange to hear a creature like you say such things! It's like seeing a bird talk.'

'Are you suggesting,' Shara asks, 'that by torturing us, you will better us?'

'I will not torture you. At least, not any more than I've had done to little brother here. But it would better you, yes. You would know shame. It would remove that prideful gleam from your eye. Do you even know what you speak of?'

'I am willing to bet you think Kolkan is alive,' says Shara.

Volka's smile is completely gone now.

'Where have you been, Mr Votrov?' she asks. 'How did you survive? I was told you had died.'

'Oh, but I *did* die, little ash-girl,' says Volka. 'I died upon a mountain, far to the north. And was reborn anew.'

He turns his hand over: the inside of his palm flickers with candlelight, though Shara can see no flame.

'The old miracles still live, in me.' He clutches the invisible flame, and the light dies. 'It was a trial of spirit. Yet that is why we went to the monastery of Kovashta in the first place: to test ourselves. Everyone else died during our pilgrimage. All the men, much older than me. More experienced. Stronger. They starved to death or froze to death or fell ill and perished. Only *I* trudged on. Only *I* was worthy. Only *I* fought through the wind and the snow and the teeth of the mountains to find that place, Kovashta, the last monastery, the forgotten dwelling place of our Father Kolkan, where he dreamt up his holy edicts and set the world to rights. I spent two decades of my life there, alone in those walls, living off scraps, drinking melting snow . . . and reading. I learned many things.'

He reaches out with his index finger and touches something: it is as if there's a pane of glass in the doorway, and he runs his finger down its middle, the tip of his index white and flat, pressed against an invisible barrier.

'The Butterfly's Bell. One of Kolkan's oldest miracles. It was originally used to force people to confess their sins – air, you see, cannot get in or out, and only on the brink of death are we ever really truthful. But don't be concerned. That fate will not befall you.' He looks at Shara. 'You failed, do you know? You and your people.'

Shara is silent.

'Do you *know*?'

'No,' says Shara. 'I don't know what you mean.'

'Of course you wouldn't. Primitive thing. Because there, you see, I found *him*.' He reaches into his wrap, and holds out a charm around his neck: the scale of Kolkan. 'I meditated for years, hearing nothing. And finally, one day, I decided to meditate until I *died*, until I heard his whispering, for death was better than that bitter silence. I almost starved to death. Maybe I *did* starve to death. But then I heard him, whispering in Bulikov. I heard Father Kolkan! He had never died! He had never been gone from this world! He had never been . . . been *touched* by your Kaj!' This last word is a savage growl: Shara glimpses yellow and brown teeth. 'I had a vision: there was a whole part of Bulikov – the true Bulikov, the Divine City – that was free of your influence! Hidden from you, from everyone! And *that* was when I knew there was still hope for my people. There was light amidst the storm, salvation waiting for the holy and the dutiful. I could return, and free us all from captivity. It was just a matter of getting to him, of finding him, and freeing him. Our father. Our lost father.'

'Just like old times,' says Vohannes. 'Running to daddy.'

Volka's beatific joy vanishes. 'Shut up!' he snarls. 'Shut up! Shut your filthy traitor mouth!'

Vohannes is silent.

Volka watches him, trembling. 'Your . . . your *tainted* mouth! What has your mouth touched, you filthy whelp? What flesh has it touched? Women's? Men's? *Children's?*'

Vohannes rolls his eyes. 'How distasteful.'

'You knew you were malformed,' says Volka. 'You always were, little Vo. There was always something wrong with you – a strain of imperfection that should have been weeded out.'

Vohannes, disinterested, sniffs and wipes his nose.

'Have you no excuse for yourself?'

'I was not aware,' says Vohannes, 'that I needed any.'

'Father agreed with me. Did you know that? He once told me he wished you and mother had *died* at your birth! He said it would have unburdened him of a weak-hearted wife and a weakling son.'

Vohannes swallows impassively. 'This revelation,' he says, 'does not surprise me in the least. Such a tender man, daddy was.'

'You slight our father's name just to make me hate you more, as if that could be possible.'

'I *shit*,' snaps Vohannes, 'upon father's name, upon the Votrov name, and upon *Kolkan's* name! And I am glad the Kaj never killed Kolkan, for now when the Saypuris slaughter him like all the other gods, I shall have a chance to climb up on his chin and shit inside his mouth!'

Volka stares at him, briefly taken aback. 'You will not get that chance,' he whispers. 'I will keep you alive, you and her, so Kolkan himself can come and judge you both, and lay down his edicts. You don't even know, do you? He has been here, in Bulikov, tallying the sins of this place. He has been watching you. He has been waiting. He knows what you have done. I will raise the Seat of the World from its tomb. And when he emerges, you will know pain, little brother.'

Shara has decided she definitely knows this room, bereft of furniture and adornment: she remembers how the *mhovost* laughed at her, and how she flicked the candle into its chest, and the stairs of earth leading down.

I know exactly where we are, she thinks, *and where Kolkan is*.

'He's down in the Seat of the World, isn't he?' she says aloud.

Volka looks at her as if she has just slapped him.

Vohannes frowns. 'In *that* rotten old place?'

'No, no. Down underneath, where the real Seat is hidden, yards below us, where we are right now.' She shuts her eyes. The fumes from the rag have wrapped her brain in a fog, but she cannot stop the thought from thrashing up to her. 'And the Divine were fond of using glass as storage space. Ahanas hid prisoners in a window pane, and even kept a small vacation spot in a glass sphere. Jukov stored the body of Saint Kivrey in a glass bead. And when I was down there, in the Seat of the World, I looked for the famous stained glass I had always heard of . . . but all the windows were broken. All except one, in the Kolkashtani atrium. And I thought it was so curious, at the time, that it was whole, unbroken, yet blank.'

She opens her eyes. 'That's where the other gods jailed him, didn't they? That's where Kolkan has been imprisoned for the past three hundred years. A living god, chained within a pane of glass.'

'I don't quite know everything that's going on,' says Vohannes chipperly, 'but this is pretty entertaining, isn't it, Volka?'

'How do you mean to free him?' asks Shara.

Volka stares at her furiously, breath whistling in his nostrils.

'Unless,' says Shara, 'it's a simple Release miracle – one any priest would know.'

'Not any priest,' says Volka hoarsely.

'So it must be much more potent. Perhaps . . .' says Shara slowly, 'perhaps something from a monk in the Kovashta? Something you found written down in their vaults?'

Volka growls like he's been struck.

'Are you so sure, brother,' asks Vohannes, 'that she's your inferior?'

'And Wiclov?' asks Shara. 'Will he participate? It was you who was running him, wasn't it? You were the man who trapped the *mhovost* here, and set it up as a guard dog.'

'What happened to Wiclov will seem like a blessing in comparison to what happens to you,' snaps Volka. 'Wiclov, he was . . . he was a believer. A true Kolkashtani. But once he led you to the Seat of the World, and once you realised how I had found the Warehouse of stolen items, I could not forgive him.'

'What did you do?' asks Shara.

Volka shrugs. 'I had to find out if the Butterfly's Bell really worked some-how. I had never seen it performed. Wiclov made . . . a tolerable subject. I reminded myself – we are but instruments in the hands of the Divine. I did not mind you chasing after Wiclov. You *obviously* had no idea I was even here, for I'd laid all my plans years before you ever arrived.'

'Though I startled you, didn't I?' says Shara. 'When I arrived, you thought you had to hurry, so you attacked Vohannes's house to try and force him to give you what you needed.'

'The arrival of the great-granddaughter of the Kaj would upset any true Continental,' says Volka. 'And I *knew* who you were.' Another flash of teeth as brown as old wood. 'I had stared at portraits of the Kaj for hours, days, thinking of him, hating him, wishing I could have been there to end his life, stop history from bringing us here. And the second I saw you, saw your eyes, your nose, your mouth, I saw the past come to life. I knew you were his kin. From there, it was easy to find out exactly who you were, and a simple thing to tell my countrymen.'

'Wait . . . *you* blew my cover?' She glances at Vohannes, who stares at the two of them, uncomprehending.

'Yet they did not rise up against you, nor did they hang you in the streets as I expected,' says Volka. 'They *praised* you for killing Urav, one of Kol-kan's sacred children. I honestly cannot tell if you are actually talented, or if your inopportune appearances are all coincidence. Like today. Did you *actually* follow us to the *real* Votrov estate, or did you simply stumble into it?'

'Oh,' says Shara. 'You were in the house, weren't you? When Sigrud and I travelled to Old Bulikov, you saw us.'

'I wouldn't even be performing this rite now, if things had gone as I intended,' says Volka. 'But again, your intrusion forces us to make haste. You went to the true Bulikov. You saw the waiting ships. So, rather arbi-trarily, unfortunately, the new age will have to begin today.'

'Will you destroy the city now, with your warships?' asks Shara. 'Why do you need flying warships at all, if you're freeing a Divinity? Can't Kolkan just point a finger at us and turn us into stone?'

'It has been almost three hundred years. Our Father Kolkan may be weak, just as *I* was when I came back down the mountain.'

'Sort of arrogant, comparing oneself to one's god,' remarks Vohannes.

'When Kolkan is restored,' Volka continues, 'our warships will destroy every Saypuri outpost on the Continent. We wished for more ships, but I've no doubt that, even with only six ships, we'll still outmatch any Saypuri weaponry. For all its might Saypur could *never* expect an attack from the air. We will rain down fire from the clouds. We will ravage every fort, every railway station, every ship. We'll return to the old ways, the *right* ways, travelling in the hands of the Divine only . . . and then we will make war upon Saypur. We will shower destruction from the sky like angels.'

Six six-inchers on each ship, probably, thinks Shara rapidly, *thirty-six cannons in total. They could cause devastating damage before any Saypuri force even* imagines *an aerial bombardment*.

'This is good, you know,' says Volka. 'This is *right*. The world is our crucible. And with each burn, we are shaped. You will know pain. Both of you will know pain. You must. And, scourged of flesh, stripped of sin, some part of you, some shred of bone, might just be saved, and found worthy in his eyes.' He takes a breath. 'And he *will* see you both. How pleased with me he'll be – handing over not only one of the most monstrous betrayers of the old ways, but also the child of the very man who killed the gods.'

Volka steps aside. Two thickset men in Kolkashtani wraps join him at the doorway. There's a very faint *pop!* as Volka's Butterfly's Bell dissolves. The two men walk to Shara and Vohannes, violently thrust both of them on to the ground, and tightly bind their hands. Shara is still too sluggish to resist much, and Vohannes is obviously quite badly injured.

Despite this, and despite having his face pressed against the stone floor, Vohannes manages to mutter, 'Taking us to see daddy, Volka?'

Volka attempts a regal pose, and turns away.

Captain Mivsk Ashkovsky of the good ship *Mornvieva* stares through the green lenses of his goggles and into the wild riot of the dawn. Clouds cling to the horizon like newspaper headlines. Down below – miles below, possibly, Mivsk isn't sure – the grey, dark countryside of the Continent speeds by.

Mivsk rummages in his jacket pocket, takes out his pocket watch, and does some estimations. 'Two hours!' he bellows over the raging winds. 'Two hours until Bulikov!'

The crew cheers. All of them are wrapped in thick thermal clothing, all of them wear goggles and masks, and all of them are tied to the deck of the *Mornvieva* by stout cables; Jakoby already fell victim to a sharp starboard wind, and went tumbling off the side, only to be hauled back on deck by his comrades, swearing and spitting and purple in the face.

Two hours, thinks Mivsk. Two hours until he finds out what the good ship *Mornvieva* – and its 23 souls, 6 cannons and 300 six-inch shells – can really do, besides fly very fast in a straight line very high above the ground. He was not even sure it would get *off* the ground, for the experiments with the Carpet of Kolkan had not always gone well: on their first effort they used only one thread of it, and when Volka's priest read the rites to activate the thread, it rose up so fast the priest was unprepared and lost much of his face. 'The miraculous,' Volka observed as the man screamed, 'requires great caution.' It took months to create the design to stabilise the threads – in the case of the *Mornvieva*, 5 threads, each lifting 800 tons – and months after that to acquire the steel the designs required. And all that time, Mivsk – though he was, he felt, truly faithful – had never quite believed it would work.

But now here they are, higher than the highest building in Ahanashtan, hurtling through the atmosphere, pulled along by sword-like sails and giant wings.

Forget not, he reminds himself, *that you have a mission, and a duty. We fly not for your glory, Mivsk Ashkovsky, nor for the crew's, but for the glory of Father Kolkan.* And secretly Mivsk cannot wait to see what Kolkan will think of the destruction the cannons will wreak upon the wretched Saypuris – who, for once, will be outmatched.

Mivsk goes below decks for what must be the seventh time to review the cannonry. No Continental has ever possessed firepower on such a level, and seeing the giant, imposing cannons and their huge shells – longer and thicker than Mivsk's forearm – gives him a sense of power he never felt before.

Mivsk checks the three port cannons: Saint Kivrey, Saint Oshko, Saint Vasily, all in fine shape. Then he checks the three starboard cannons: Saint Shovska, Saint Ghovros, and then Saint . . .

Mivsk stops before Saint Toshkey. There is a tall man in a ripped Kolkashtani wrap leaning against the cannon, staring out of the gunport towards where the good ships *Usina* and *Ukma* cut through the clouds, the starboard portion of their small armada.

Captain Mivsk stares at him, bewildered. 'Who . . . who . . . ?'

'I have never sailed upon a ship of the air,' the man remarks. 'Many things I have sailed upon, but never a ship of the air.'

Mivsk wants to ask him why he is not wearing his goggles, why he is not in uniform, why he does not have on his safety cable; but all these questions are absurd, for Mivsk knows there is *no* one in his crew of this size, is there?

The man looks at Mivsk; one eye in his Kolkashtani wrap is dark. 'Does it sail,' he asks, 'like a regular ship?'

'Well . . .' Mivsk looks behind him, wondering how to deal with this bizarre occurrence. 'Why aren't you above deck, sailor? Why aren't you cabled to the mast? You could fall off i—'

'And the cannons? Could they also function as air-to-air cannons?'

'I . . . why?'

'I believe so. Yes. Yes, I thought so.' The man tilts his head, and thinks aloud. 'Six cannons onboard, and five other ships . . . One shot a ship . . . Then this should be no trouble.' He nods. 'Thank you. That is very good to know.'

Then there is a blur, and Captain Mivsk suddenly feels as if he's swallowed a large chunk of ice.

He looks down and sees the handle of a very large knife sticking out from between his ribs. The ship begins to spin around him.

'It is good for a captain to die,' says the man's voice, 'before seeing the death of his crew. Go quietly, and with gratitude.'

The last thing Mivsk sees is the giant man standing behind Saint Toshkey, using the blade in his hand to imagine lining up the cannon with the good ship *Usina* far away.

They're forced down a familiar path, to Shara: along the little blank hallways, back to the room that held the *mhovost* – the ring of salt still sitting on the floor – and back to the tunnel leading down to the Seat of the World, which, she now sees, has been completely restored.

'You caved in this tunnel, but it was easily fixed,' says Volka. 'I doubt if you can guess at which miracle I used to make it.'

Shara had not imagined that the tunnel's creation was miraculous, but now that she considers it, she jumps to the obvious conclusion. 'Ovski's Candlelight,' she says.

Volka's face tightens, and he waves a hand and leads them down the tunnel, holding his invisible flame. Vohannes chuckles.

He hasn't freed Kolkan yet, thinks Shara. *Maybe Mulaghesh . . . maybe she can . . .* If anything, Shara realises, Mulaghesh is raiding the Votrov estate right now. That, or fortifying the embassy. Neither of which could possibly save either of them. And Sigrud is miles and miles and miles away, outside Jukoshtan.

They are alone.

The tunnel stretches down. Shara imagines Kolkan waiting for them at the bottom, the man of clay seated at the back of a cave, his eyes grey and blank.

'I'm sorry, Vo,' whispers Shara in the dark.

'Nothing to be sorry for,' says Vo. 'I'm embarrassed you had to meet the little shi—'

'Quiet,' says one of their captors, and he jabs Vohannes in the kidney. Vohannes, whimpering, struggles to keep walking.

They enter the Seat of the World. Vohannes gasps in shock. 'My *word*!'

Shara wishes she could feel as amazed as she did when she first discovered this place, but now the temple feels dark and twisted to her, full of black corners and whispers.

Over two dozen Restorationists, all in Kolkashtani wraps, stand in Kolkan's atrium before the blank window. Beside it, Shara sees, is a ladder.

This is really happening.

Volka walks to the stairs leading up to the Seat's defunct bell tower. He raises his hand, which glitters with orange light. 'First to restore the temple to its glory,' he says. He points at Shara and Vohannes, then mutters something. There is a squeaking sound, like fingers being rubbed against glass. Shara's hands are still bound, but she sticks a toe out, testing, and feels an invisible wall. *The Butterfly's Bell, again.*

'Don't breathe too deeply,' says Volka, smiling. 'That one's much smaller.' Grinning like a pompous head boy, he mounts the stairs to the bell tower and begins ascending. Soon he is out of sight.

'He must have found a way to restore the bell tower, too,' says Shara.

'Quiet,' says one of the Restorationists.

'That was just filled with earth a few days ago.'

'Quiet!'

'What are you going to do, punch us through the barrier?' says Vohannes.

The Restorationist makes a threatening gesture at them, then abandons it, as if he has better things to do.

'I should have seen this coming,' says Shara. 'I should have seen this all coming.'

'Shara, shut up,' whispers Vohannes. 'Listen, you . . . you've got something hidden up your sleeve, right? You always have?'

'Well . . . no. No, actually, I really haven't.'

'But you've got the army coming in, right? They'll notice you're missing, right?'

'They might, but they definitely won't look *here*.'

'Okay, but . . . Shara, *please*. Please think!' he hisses. 'You've got to think of something! You've got to, because *I* definitely won't. I don't have a fucking clue what's going on! So please – is there *anything*?'

Shara thinks hard, but she has no idea how to penetrate the Butterfly's Bell, a miracle she never even knew existed until just now. And even if they got out, what could they do? A wounded, limping man and a drugged ninety-pound woman against twenty five Restorationists? *I could blast our way out of here with Ovski's Candlelight . . . if I actually knew Ovski's Candlelight. But I don't. I just know of it, which is not the same thing.* If only there was some other way to hide, or maybe tunnel into the ground, or . . .

. . . or disappear.

'Parnesi's Cupboard,' she says quietly.

'What?' whispers Vohannes.

'Parnesi's Cupboard – it's what your brother used to kidnap me. It puts people into an invisible pocket of air, one that can't be seen through by either mortal *or* Divinity.' *Because it was made by Jukov*, she remembers, *so one of his priests could sneak into Kolkan's nunnery. So it would work excellently here.*

'So even if Kolkan himself shows up—'

'We'd be hidden. We'd be safe.'

'Great! Well . . . why don't you use one of those, then?'

'Because my hands are bound,' whispers Shara. 'There's a line from the *Jukoshtava* I have to read, *and* a gesture.'

'Shit,' says Vohannes. He looks up at the Restorationists. 'Here. Here, let's see if we can shift around.'

Slowly, they rotate so they're facing away from one another. With their hands still tied behind their backs, Vohannes begins to fumble clumsily at her bonds.

'Good luck,' mutters Shara. 'But I think they actually knew what they were doing when they tied these.'

One of the Restorationists laughs. 'My, what an excellent deception! Untie your hands if you want, you depraved little fruit, the only person getting you out of that Bell is Father Kolkan himself.'

'And when he does,' says another, 'you'll wish you'd suffocated to death in there.'

A third man taunts him, 'Is that the first time you've ever touched a woman, Votrov? I would imagine so.'

Vohannes ignores them, and whispers, 'Do you really think my brother can bring back Kolkan?'

Shara glances at the clear glass pane in Kolkan's atrium. 'Well. I will say that I now think *some* Divinity is in there.'

'But . . . not Kolkan?'

'I actually conversed with the Divinity, I think,' says Shara. 'On the night they attacked your house. I saw many scenes from many different Divine texts, but none of them were coherent. What's more, I have seen that many of Jukov's miracles still work – Parnesi's Cupboard being one of them – so I am no longer quite sure that Jukov is truly gone, either.'

Vohannes grunts as he plucks at a knot, which refuses to budge. 'So what you're saying is . . . you don't know.'

'Correct.'

'Great.'

He keeps tugging at her ropes. With some morbid amusement, Shara realises this is the most intimate contact they've had since the night after Urav.

'I'm glad I'm here with you,' says Vohannes. 'Here at the end of all this.'

'When we're free, stay close,' says Shara. 'Parnesi's Cupboard is not large.'

'All right, but I want you to listen . . . I'm *glad*, Shara. Do you understand?'

Shara is silent. Then she says, 'You shouldn't be.'

'Why?'

'Because when my cover was blown, I thought it was you who did it.'

He stops trying to untie her. '*Me?*'

'Yes. You . . . you suddenly got everything you wanted, Vo. Everything. And you were the only other person who knew who I was. And we thought we saw you at the loomworks, but it wasn't really you, it had to be—'

'Volka.' She cannot see him, but Vohannes is quite still. 'But . . . Shara, I would . . . I would *never* do that to you. Never. I *couldn't*.'

'I know! I know that now, Vo. But I, I thought you were sick! I thought something was wrong with you. You seemed so unhappy, so miserable.'

She can feel Vohannes looking around. 'Maybe you weren't wrong there,' he says softly. 'Perhaps there *is* something wrong with me. But maybe I could *never* have been right.'

'What do you mean?'

'I mean . . , I mean, look at these people, these people I grew up with!'

The Restorationists have gathered in Kolkan's atrium, and kneel on the floor to begin a prayer.

'Look at them! They're praying to pain, to punishment! They think that hate is holy, that every part of being human is *wrong*. So of *course* I grew up wrong!'

Somewhere, far in the distance, Shara hears a bell toll.

'What was that?' asks Vo.

'We need to hurry,' says Shara.

Somewhere, softly, another bell tolls.

'Why?'

Another bell tolls. And another. And another.

Shara can tell that they all have different tones, as if some are very large and others are very small. But more than that, each bell has a resonance that seems like it can only be perceived by different parts of the *mind*, pouring in alien experiences: when one bell tolls, she imagines she sees hot, murky swamps, tangles of vines and clutches of flowering orchids; when another bell tolls, she smells flaming pitch, and sawdust and mortar; when the next bell tolls, she can hear the crash of metal, the screaming of crows, the howls of warfare; with the next, she tastes wine, raw meat, sugar, blood, and what she suspects to be semen; on the next, she hears the crushing grind of huge stones being pushed against one another, terrible weight bearing down upon her; and then, when the final bell joins the tolling, she feels a wintry chill in her arms and a flickering fire in her feet and heart.

One bell for each Divinity, thinks Shara. *I don't know how he did it, or even what he's doing, but Volka's found a way to ring all the bells of the Seat of the World.*

'What's going on, Shara?' asks Vohannes.

'Look at the windows,' says Shara, 'and you'll see.'

With each pulse, a faint light appears in the window. Not a holy light: sunlight. Golden sunlight, as if the sun is so bright it is penetrating all the layers of earth to shine into this dark, dreary place.

The sun isn't shining through the earth, she thinks. *We're rising up.*

'He's moving it,' she says. 'He's raising it. He's raising the Seat of the World.'

Mulaghesh's soldiers are doing a half-hearted job of fortifying the embassy courtyard when the light begins to change.

Mulaghesh herself is monitoring their work from the embassy gates: the embassy walls are tall and white with iron railings at the top, and while they're quite pretty they're well short of military defences. The embassy is also very exposed, sitting on an intersection between two major roads: one road runs alongside the walls, and the other runs all the way through Bulikov and straight up to the embassy gates. Mulaghesh can peer through the bars of the gates and see clear to the far side of Bulikov. *If Shara's right about those six inch cannons*, she thinks, *there are about a million angles those things could take to wipe us out.*

Despite this exposed position, Mulaghesh has not prodded her soldiers along much, mostly because she privately hopes Shara is terribly, terribly wrong. But when she begins to hear the bells in the distance, and the shadows of the iron railings begin to dance on the courtyard stone, her mouth falls open enough for her cigarillo to come tumbling out.

She turns round. The sun itself is moving: like a drop of liquid gold, it streaks from where it sat just above the horizon and twirls and dances to the left, twisting through the sky and growing slightly larger until it's on the other horizon, just starting to set.

Mulaghesh wonders, *Is a whole day being lost before our eyes?*

The cacophony of the bells beats at her senses, as if with each toll they are breaking down invisible structures and rebuilding them.

Then yellow-orange sunlight pulses over the rooftops of Bulikov. One sunbeam lances down as if shot through a veil of clouds – yet there are no clouds that she can see – and glances off the bell tower in the centre of the city so it glows brightly.

Mulaghesh and her soldiers are forced to look away; when they look back, they see the sunlight – the *setting* sunlight – glinting off a huge polished roof. Mulaghesh has to shade her eyes to keep from being blinded.

A mammoth, ornate, cream white cathedral sits in the centre of Bulikov, with its bell tower almost half a mile tall.

'What is that?' says one of her lieutenants. 'Where did that come from?

Mulaghesh sighs. *How I hate it*, she thinks, *when the alarmists are proved right*.

'All right!' she bellows. 'Kindly take your eyes *off* the skyline and get your arses back to work! Start installing fortifications and gun batteries behind the embassy walls, and make it quick!'

'*Gun* batteries?' says one of her corporals. A girl barely in her twenties, she wipes her brow, clearly nervous. 'Governor, are you sure?'

'I absolutely am. It looks like the threat we came here to combat is, unfortunately, completely legitimate, so I would personally prefer to bring as much firepower to the table as possible. If I could have brought serious cannonry here, I would have, but we'll have to make do with what we have. So get a move on, and if you need the toe of my boot to speed you on your way, then I will be only too happy to apply it to your dainty backsides! What are you all staring at me for? *Fucking move!*'

> *I am lost among the seas of fate and time*
> *But at least I have love.*
>
> Message scrawled on the common-room
> wall of Fadhuri Academy

What is reaped

Volka descends the stairs in the Seat of the World with a decidedly beatific, satisfied air. 'I have done good works,' he says aloud. 'And I think Father Kolkan shall be pleased.'

Vohannes can't help but scoff in disgust.

'And now' – Volka takes the final step off the stairs – 'to bring him home.' He looks sideways at where Vohannes and Shara are trapped. 'Maybe after this, we shall embrace as true brothers. Perhaps he will cleanse you. Perhaps he will show mercy.'

'If he made you in his image Volka,' says Vohannes, 'then I very much fucking doubt it.'

Volka sniffs, and walks to Kolkan's atrium. The Restorationists are arranged before the clear glass pane, a kneeling congregation awaiting their prophet. Volka calmly drifts through their ranks – Shara is reminded of a debutante at a ball – and stops before one man in particular.

Shara's bonds are growing looser. 'Keep trying,' she says desperately. 'Please, Vo . . .'

Vohannes grunts, pulls harder.

'The hammer,' Volka says softly.

The man produces a long, silver hammer. Volka takes it delicately, then walks to the ladder and slowly climbs up to the glass.

Shara almost has her thumb through one loop of rope, but this has pulled another cord tight around her wrist.

Volka holds the silver hammer to his lips and whispers to it, chanting something.

I don't want to see him, thinks Shara. *I can't. Anyone but him, anyone but Kolkan.*

She twists at the ropes. Something hot drips into her palm. She feels one cord slip over the knuckle of her little finger, then her thumb.

The silver hammer quivers, its edges blurring as if the metal itself trembles, filled with an energy it can barely contain.

Vohannes grabs hold of the ropes; Shara lunges forward, hoping they'll break, but they hold fast.

Volka holds the hammer high. The yellow-orange sunlight blazes off the hammer's head.

The dribbling heat in Shara's palm is now a trickle, thick and wet.

Someone do something, thinks Shara.

Volka cries out, and swings the hammer forward.

With a tinny *snap*, the glass shatters.

Golden sunlight pours through, illuminating the white stone of the temple floor until it flares brightly. It is a sun, a star, a blaze of light that is pure, terrible, heatless.

Both Vohannes and Shara cry out, blinded. The burst of light is so shocking that they twist away and fall over. Something grinds uncomfortably in Shara's wrist: a bad sprain, perhaps.

Then silence. Shara waits, then looks up.

The men in Kolkashtani wraps are staring at something before them.

There is someone standing in front of the broken window, sunlight falling on their shoulders.

It is a man-figure, but he is very tall: nine feet tall at least. He is draped in thick grey robes from head to toe, concealing his face, his hands, his feet, yet his head slowly turns from side to side with a puzzled air, taking in his environs and the kneeling men before him as if awoken from a very peculiar dream.

'No,' whispers Shara.

'He lives,' says Volka. 'He *lives*!'

The robed figure turns its head to look at him.

'Father Kolkan!' cries Volka. 'Father Kolkan, you are brought back to us! We are saved! We are saved!'

Volka scurries down the ladder and joins the men before Kolkan, who still has hardly moved. Volka drops to his knees and presses his face to the floor, hands splayed at the toes of the Divinity.

'Father Kolkan,' Volka says, 'are you all right?'

Kolkan is silent. One would mistake him for a statue, if the breeze did not rustle his robes so.

'You have been away for many, many years,' says Volka. 'I wish I could tell you that all the world is right and good upon your waking. But in your absence, all has gone awry: our colonies have rebelled, they have *murdered* your brothers and sisters, and they have enslaved us all!'

The men around him all nod and peek up at Kolkan, expecting him to react with shock: but Kolkan is still and silent under his grey robes.

'Vo,' whispers Shara.

'Yes?'

'Do what I do,' she whispers. She rolls over on to her front, kneels and bows forward until her forehead kisses the floor.

'What are you—'

'Penitence,' Shara says quietly. 'Kolkan will always recognise penitence.'

'What?'

'Prostrate yourself before him! And do *nothing else*! Anything else will be considered an offence!'

Reluctantly, Vohannes rolls over and bows as well.

And if Kolkan doesn't pay much attention, thinks Shara, *maybe I can finish what Vo started on my knot.*

'Voortya was killed in the colonies,' says Volka. 'Taalhavras and Ahanas were slain when the colonials invaded. And Jukov, cowardly Jukov, surrendered to them, and was executed! The colonials rule over us as if we are dogs, and they have outlawed our love for you, Father Kolkan. We are not allowed to say your name, to worship you as we wish, to hold you in our hearts. But we have waited for you, Father Kolkan! My followers and I have kept the faith, and worked to bring you back! We even rebuilt your atrium in the Seat of the World for you! I laboured to carry the stones from Kovashta itself back to this place, so when you returned you would be met by signs of praise and worship! And we have captured the most heretical betrayer of your ways, *and* the child of the very man who overthrew our Holy Lands!'

Volka points backwards at Shara and Vohannes, and does a brief double take when he sees them bowed forward in penitence.

'Wise cowards, they throw themselves on your mercy. But so do we all! We all throw ourselves upon your mercy, Father Kolkan! We are your devoted servants! We have created an army of the sky to go to war for you, but we fear this will not be enough! We beg of you, please, help us throw off our shackles, rise up, and bring righteousness and glory back to the world!'

The Seat of the World is silent. Shara tilts her head up slightly to see, and begins to quietly work one hand out of her ropes.

Kolkan's head turns back and forth as he surveys his tiny, black-clad flock.

He shifts from one foot to the other, and examines the rest of the Seat of the World.

A voice is then heard somewhere in the temple; not heard with Shara's ears, but somewhere in her mind, a muffled voice that could be the sound of rocks being crushed together, though there is a single word in it:

WHERE?

Volka hesitates and lifts his head. 'Wh . . . Where what, my Father Kolkan?'

Kolkan continues staring around the Seat of the World. The voice sounds again: WHERE IS THE FLAME AND THE SPARROW?

Volka blinks and glances back at his lieutenants, who are just as dumbfounded as he is. 'I . . . I am not sure what you mean, Father Kolkan.'

WHEN I AM MET, says the voice, I AM TO BE MET WITH THE FLAME AND THE SPARROW.

A long pause.

WHY DO YOU NOT BEAR THEM?

'I . . . had never heard of this ritual, Father Kolkan,' says Volka. He rises to kneel, like the rest of his followers. 'I read so much about you, but . . . but you have been gone from this world for many hundreds of years. This must have been a rite that I missed.'

DO YOU, asks the voice, INSULT ME?

'No! No, no! No, Father Kolkan, we would never do such a thing!' Volka's followers fervently shake their heads.

THEN WHY DO YOU NOT BEAR THEM?

'I just . . . I didn't know, Father Kolkan. I am not even sure what they a—'

IGNORANCE, says the voice, IS NO EXCUSE.

Kolkan steps forward and looks at his flock. His head tilts back and forth, as if seeing many things in them.

YOU ARE UNWORTHY.

Volka is mute with shock.

The voice says: YOU HAVE BATHED FRUITS IN THE WATERS OF THE OCEAN. YOU HAVE MIXED LINENS AND COTTONS WITH YOUR GARMENTS. YOU HAVE CREATED GLASS WITH MANY FLAWS. YOU HAVE TASTED THE FLESH OF SONGBIRDS. I SEE THESE WRONGS IN YOU. AND NOW, AS I EMERGE, YOU DO NOT MEET ME WITH THE FLAME AND THE SPARROW.

Volka and his followers glance among themselves, wondering what to do. 'F-Father Kolkan, please,' murmurs Volka. 'Please . . . forgive us. We followed all your edicts that we could find, that we *knew*. But we freed you, Father Kolkan! Please forgive u—'

Kolkan points at him. Volka halts as if frozen.

FORGIVENESS, says Kolkan's voice, IS FOR THE WORTHY.

Kolkan looks at Volka's followers. YOU ARE AS THE DUST AND THE STONE AND THE MUD.

From what Shara can see, there is no change, no flash of light; but in one instant, they are men, and in the next, they are statues of dark stone.

Volka stands before Kolkan, still frozen, but alive: Shara can see his eyes turning in their sockets, trying desperately to move.

AND YOU, says Kolkan's voice, YOU THINK YOU ARE NOT AS THE DUST AND THE STONE AND THE MUD. YOU WILL BE REMINDED OF WHAT YOU ARE.

Volka falls to the ground, gasping. 'I . . . I will,' he says. 'I will, Father Kolkan. I will remem—' He gags, lurches forward, and shrieks with pain. 'Ah! Ah, my stomach, it . . .'

Shara can see his belly bulging, swelling, as if pregnant. Horrified, she turns her head back to face the ground.

Volka's shrieks build and build until finally they are a gurgle. She hears him fall to the ground – there is a *pop!* as the Butterfly's Bell around them vanishes – and Volka is silent, though she can hear him struggling.

YOU WILL KNOW PAIN.

There is a sound like heavy cloth being torn. Helpless to stop herself, Shara glances up. Black round stones come spilling out of Volka's open stomach, hundreds of them, the pile growing and growing even as Shara watches, glistening in a wash of blood.

She gags. Kolkan looks up slightly, and she turns back to face the ground.

HM, says Kolkan's voice.

She and Vohannes are silent. She can hear Vohannes's trembling breath beside her.

THIS IS A SIGHT I KNOW WELL, says his voice. AND A SIGHT I WELCOME. TIME MAY HAVE PASSED, BUT THOSE OF FLESH STILL REQUIRE JUDGEMENT.

Shara feels her limbs stiffen. She wonders if Kolkan is turning them to stone, but apparently not: they are paralysed, just as Volka was.

There is a *crack!* and Vohannes begins to slide towards Kolkan, as if the stone floor of the temple is a conveyor belt. Out of the side of her eye Shara can see Vohannes look back at her, terrified, shocked. *Don't leave me!* he seems to say. *Don't!*

COME BEFORE ME, says Kolkan's voice. AND PLEAD YOUR CASE.

Shara cannot see, but apparently Vohannes is no longer paralysed: 'M-my case?' says his voice.

YES. YOU HAVE ASSUMED THE POSE OF THE SHAMEFUL AND THE PENITENT. PLEAD YOUR CASE, AND I WILL CON-SIDER MY JUDGEMENT.

It's like his judgements before he pronounced his edicts, thinks Shara. *But Vo doesn't know what the hells he's doing.*

A long silence. Then Vohannes's voice says, 'I am . . . I am not an old man, Father Kolkan, but I have seen much life. I have . . . I have lost my family. I have lost my friends. I have lost my home, in many ways. But . . . but I will not *distract* you with these tales.'

Vohannes nearly shouts the word 'distract'. If she had the mind for it, Shara would roll her eyes. *Not a particularly subtle message, Vo.*

'I am penitent, Father Kolkan,' says Vohannes. His voice grows stronger. 'I *am*. I am sorrowful. I am ashamed. Namely, I am ashamed that I was *asked* to be ashamed, that it was *expected* of me.' He swallows. 'And I am ashamed that, to a certain extent, I did as they asked. I did and, and I *do* hate myself. I hated myself because I didn't know another way to live.

'I am sorrowful. I am sorrowful that I happened to be born into a world where being sorrowful for yourself was what you were supposed to be. I am sorrowful that my fellow countrymen feel that being human is something to repress, something ugly, something nasty. It's . . . it's just a fucking shame, it really is.'

If Shara could move, her mouth would drop open in shock.

'I am penitent,' says Vohannes. 'I am penitent for all the relationships this shame has ruined. I am penitent that I've allowed my shame and unhappiness to spread to others. I've fucked men and I've fucked women, Father Kolkan. I have sucked numerous pricks, and I have had my prick sucked by numerous people. I have fucked and been fucked. And it was lovely, really lovely, I had an excellent time doing it, and I would gladly do it again, I really would.' He laughs. 'I have been lucky enough to find and meet and come to hold beautiful people in my arms, honestly, some beautiful, lovely, brilliant people, and I am filled with regret that my awful self-hate drove them away.

'I loved you, Shara. I did. I was very bad at it, but I loved you in my own confused, mixed-up way. I still do.

'I don't know if you made the world, Father Kolkan. And I don't know if you made my people or if they made themselves. But if it was *your* words they taught me as a child, and if it's *your* words that encourage this vile self-disgust, this ridiculous self-flagellation, this incredibly damaging idea that to be human and to love and to risk making mistakes is *wrong*, then . . . well, I guess *fuck you*, Father Kolkan.'

A long, long, long silence.

Then Kolkan's voice, trembling with rage: YOU ARE UNWORTHY. The Seat of the World lights up with screams.

Shara struggles against her paralysis, wishing to rise up and run to Vo's side, but she cannot: whatever miracle Kolkan has used holds her down.

She wants to scream with Vohannes, even as his screams intensify, shrieks of unbearable, inconceivable pain, louder and louder, as Kolkan applies unspeakable tortures to him.

Then the miracle breaks, and she is free.

Shara sits up, and looks: Kolkan stands before Vohannes, one long, rag-wrapped finger pressed against Vohannes's forehead; Vohannes shakes and trembles, his flesh quaking as if the Divinity is pouring endless agony and pain into him and has completely forgotten about her.

Go to him! a part of her thinks.

Another part says, *He baited Kolkan into doing this in order to free you. Kolkan's so angry you've slipped his mind, for now — so what will you do with this chance?*

Weeping, she rips her hands out of the loose ropes, shuts her eyes, remembers the lines from the *Jukoshtava*, and draws a door in the air.

There is the sound of a whip crack. Her arms and legs vanish from her sight.

Kolkan looks up. Vohannes drops to the floor, pale as snow, and does not move.

Shara shuts her eyes, and doesn't dare to breathe: Parnesi's Cupboard does not conceal sound.

Kolkan shuffles forward, his head sweeping the Seat of the World. Shara feels an immense pressure exerting itself on her, as if she is sinking deeper and deeper into the ocean. *He's looking for me, feeling for me.*

THE CUPBOARD, says Kolkan's voice. I REMEMBER THIS.

Shara feels sick with terror. Kolkan is less than four feet away from her now, and she is awed by his size, his filth, the stench of decay leaking from underneath his many cloaks.

I COULD CAVE IN THIS TEMPLE, he says, AND CRUSH YOU. IF YOU ARE STILL HERE.

He looks up, into the ceiling of the Seat of the World.

BUT I HAVE BIGGER THINGS TO DO.

Then, abruptly, Kolkan is gone, as if he had never been there.

Shara still doesn't breathe. She stares about the Seat of the World, wondering if the Divinity could be lurking in some dark corner.

A voice comes booming down out of the skies: THIS CITY HAS GROWN UNWORTHY.

'Oh, no,' says Shara. She looks at Vohannes, wishing to go to him. *Prioritise*, snaps the operative's voice in her head. *Grief is for later*.

She whispers, 'I'm sorry, Vo,' and she stands and sprints out of the temple.

All across Bulikov, in the fishmarkets and the alleys, by the Solda and in the tea shops, the citizens raise their heads as the voice of Kolkan echoes through the streets.

YOU HAVE BROKEN COUNTLESS LAWS, says the voice.

Children at play stop where they are and turn towards the giant white temple in the centre of their city.

YOU HAVE LAIN WITH ONE ANOTHER IN JOY.

A street sweeper stands frozen in shock, hands raised as he tries to shake a sliver of potato peel from his broom.

YOU HAVE BUILT FLOORS OF WHITE STONE.

The elderly men at the Ghoshtok-Solda Dinner Club stare at one another, then at the bottles of wine and whisky.

YOU HAVE EATEN BRIGHT FRUITS, says the voice, AND ALLOWED THEIR SEEDS TO ROT IN DITCHES.

In a barber's shop beside the Solda, the barber, stunned, has removed most of an old man's moustache; the old man, just as stunned, has yet to realise.

AND YOU HAVE WALKED IN THE DAY, says the voice, WITH YOUR FLESH EXPOSED. YOU LIVE WITH FLESH OF OTHER FLESH. YOU HAVE LOOKED UPON THE SECRETS OF YOUR FLESH, AND KNOWN THEM, AND FOR THIS I WEEP FOR YOU.

In the House of Seven Sisters Infirmary, Captain Nesrhev, still bound up in many bandages, sets his pipe aside and calls to the nurses. 'What the *hells* is going on?'

YOU HAVE FORGOTTEN THE WAY YOU SHOULD BE, says the voice.

A pause.

I WILL RESTORE YOU.

Ochre sunlight washes over Bulikov. The citizens shield their eyes, look away from the windows.

And when they look back, they see the view has changed: it is as if all the city blocks have been rearranged, shoved out of the way to make room for . . .

An old woman at the corner of Saint Ghoshtok and Saint Gyieli falls to her knees in awe and says, 'By the gods . . . by the gods.'

. . . splendid, beautiful white skyscrapers, lined and tipped with gold. They look like giant white herons wading among the low, grey swamp of modern Bulikov.

YOU HAVE FORGOTTEN ALL I TAUGHT YOU, says the voice. I HAVE RETURNED TO REMIND YOU. YOU WILL BE SCOURGED OF SIN. YOU WILL BE PURIFIED OF TEMPTATION.

A wind stirs along Saint Vasily Lane. As if in a dream, dozens of pedestrians suddenly walk to the centre of the street, stand together shoulder to shoulder, and face the north. They are mothers, fathers, sons and daughters; none respond to plaintive cries from friends and family, asking what's wrong.

The wind increases. Citizens of Bulikov are forced to raise their hands to shield their eyes, and turn their faces away. There is a clinking and clanking, as if the wind has somehow blown thousands of metal plates down the street. When the people lower their hands and look back, they are shocked by what they see.

In place of the pedestrians, five hundred armoured soldiers now stand in the streets. The armour they wear is huge and thick and gleaming, protecting every inch of their bodies: it is so thick they might not even be soldiers, but animated suits of armour. Their helmets depict the glinting visages of shrieking demons; their swords are immense, nearly six feet in length, and flicker with a cold fire.

Only Shara Komayd, who glances at the soldiers as she sprints to the embassy, recognises them from somewhere: had she not asked Sigrud to tear that painting off CD Troonyi's wall mere weeks ago?

Kolkan's voice says: YOU WILL KNOW PAIN, AND THROUGH IT YOU WILL KNOW RIGHTEOUSNESS.

The soldiers turn to the people on the streets, and raise their swords.

Mulaghesh sees Shara running towards the fortifications, and bellows to her, 'What in hells is that voice talking about?'

'It's Kolkan!' Shara says, panting.

'The *god*?'

'Yes! He's talking about his edicts!'

'White stone floors? Eating bright *fruits*?'

Soldiers help Shara scramble over the fortifications.

'Those are his edicts, yes!'

'And where the hells did these white buildings come from?'

'It's Old Bulikov,' says Shara. 'Parts of Bulikov as it *was*. I suppose he most have pulled it all back in and tossed the buildings in with the normal Bulikov!'

'I have . . .' Mulaghesh searches for words. 'I have *no fucking idea* what you are talking about! Forget all that – what's he going to do now? What do *we* do now?'

The sound of tinny screams echoes through the streets. Mulaghesh shades her eyes to look. 'There are people running towards us,' she says. 'What's going on?'

'Have you ever seen the painting "The Night of the Red Sands"? By Rishna?'

'Yeah?'

'Remember the Continental army the Kaj faces in that painting?'

'Yeah, I—' Mulaghesh lowers her hand from her eyes, and turns to stare at Shara in horror.

'Yes,' says Shara. 'It seems Rishna was quite accurate in her depiction.'

'How . . . how many?'

'Hundreds,' says Shara. 'And Kolkan can make more if he chooses. He *is* a Divinity, after all. But I may have a weapon he doesn't know about.'

Shara races upstairs to her office with Mulaghesh. She opens a drawer in her desk and takes out the piece of black lead she had reworked into the point of a bolt. 'This,' she says softly.

'What's that supposed to be?'

'It's the metal the Kaj used to kill the Divinities,' says Shara. 'It's immune to any Divine influence. He fired this very shot through the skull of Jukov, executing him. All we have to do is lure Kolkan out, and then someone can maybe use it to take a shot at him, just like during the Great War.'

'Okay, assuming everything you're saying is true,' says Mulaghesh, 'during the Great War, wouldn't the Kaj have had hundreds or thousands of those little shots?'

'Well . . . yes.'

'And you've only got the *one*?'

'Yes.'

'Okay. And how do we lure him out?'

'Well . . .'

'And what if that shot *misses*?'

'Well, we'd . . . we'd have to go and get it, I suppose.'

Mulaghesh gapes at Shara with an expression equal parts disbelief and exasperation.

'I didn't have time to plan this out!' says Shara.

'I couldn't tell!'

'I had no idea this'd be happening *now*!'

'Well, it is! And I must admit, Chief Diplomat, I do not have much faith that that plan will work!'

The floor rumbles. Soldiers begin shouting outside. Shara and Mulaghesh reach the window just in time to see a four-storey building further down the street collapsing as if it's been demolished. Glimmering steel shapes come marching out of the dust and debris, holding their giant swords straight up.

'They're strong enough to destroy *buildings*?' says Shara aloud, in disbelief.

'And what is your plan,' asks Mulaghesh, 'for dealing with those?'

She adjusts her glasses. 'How much weaponry do you have?'

'We have the typical bolt-shots, plus five repeat-shot small cannons.' She makes a small 'o' with her forefinger and thumb. 'You crank them and they fire rounds about this big twice every second.'

'No other large cannonry?'

She shakes her head. 'None. The treaties outlawed mobile heavy cannonry on the Continent.'

'And do you think those rounds could pierce the armour of those . . . things?'

'Well, it's Divine armour, right?'

'But perhaps Kolkan,' Shara wonders aloud, 'does not yet know about gunpowder.'

'I'm not really willing to take that chance. My suggestion would be to retreat. But those things appear to move very fast.'

'And even if we did retreat, we'd still have to deal with the flying warships,' says Shara.

Mulaghesh stares at her, incredulous. '*What* flying warships?'

'Never mind. No time to explain now. But I don't think we can retreat, and I don't think we can stay.' Shara rubs her temples. *I always wondered if I'd die for my country*, she thinks, *but I never thought it'd be like this*.

She glances back at her open drawer, wishing – stupidly – that she might find a second bolt tip of black lead to use.

She sees a small leather bag sitting in her drawer, inside which, she knows, are a dozen or so little white pills.

'Hm,' says Shara. She picks up the bag and peers into it.

'If you're starting to think of something,' says Mulaghesh, 'I advise you to think fast.'

She picks out a pill and holds it up. 'Philosopher's stones.'

'The drug you used on the kid in the prison?'

'Yes. They help one commune with the Divine . . . but they also amplify the effects of many miracles.'

'So?'

This is suicide, thinks Shara.

'So?' says Mulaghesh again.

Not to do it is also suicide.

She reluctantly says, '*I* know a lot of miracles.'

'All right!' shouts Mulaghesh. 'Listen up!'

Another building collapses nearby; the Saypuri soldiers glance at one another uneasily.

Mulaghesh continues. 'Ever since you were kids you all wanted to be the Kaj, didn't you? You wanted to fight those wars, to win those victories, to feel that glory? Well, I will remind you, boys and girls, of a history lesson.'

Something explodes beside the Solda; a fireball twenty feet across rises into the air between two tall white skyscrapers.

'Do you remember how The Night of the Red Sands got its name? It's because when the Kaj brought his scrawny army of about a hundred freed slaves to the Desert of Hadesh, they wound up facing not *only* the Divinity Voortya, but also *five thousand* armoured Continental warriors. Warriors a hell of a lot like *those*.'

She points down the street, where silver shapes hack and slash at crowds and wagons and cars and buildings – anything.

'They were outnumbered ten to one, on flat terrain with absolutely *no* strategic advantage! Any decent strategist would have decided they were done for! Hells, *I* would have decided they were done for! But they weren't, because the Kaj brought up a cannon, loaded it with a special shot, and fired it *directly through Voortya's damned face!*' She taps the centre of her forehead. 'And the second Voortya died, all the armour those Continentals were wearing – which was so thick, so heavy, so impenetrable, and so miraculously *light* – suddenly became as heavy as it would normally be. And the army *collapsed* underneath it. These terrifying soldiers, without their Divinity, were helpless, trapped beneath hundreds and hundreds of pounds of iron and steel! And the Kaj's army, a bunch of untrained slaves and farmers who had lived their whole lives being punished and abused by those soldiers, waded among them and used knives and rocks and fucking *gardening tools* to finish them off!'

One of the cranes working on the New Solda Bridge tips back and forth like a metronome, then topples into the icy water. Flocks of brown starlings wheel above the city, shrieking and cheeping.

'They slaughtered a thousand men in one night! They slaughtered them as a winemaker prunes grapes from the vine! The blood was so deep it went up to their ankles! And *that*, boys and girls, is why they call it The Night of the Red Sands!'

Shara is standing in the middle of the courtyard, counting out pills and guessing the right dosage. *Will I go mad? Will Kolkan swoop into my mind and destroy me? Will I simply topple over, dead, and leave my soldiers and my people here to die? Or perhaps it will just be like having too much tea.*

'Now let me remind you of our *current* predicament!' says Mulaghesh.

'We face ridiculous odds, yes! Absurd odds! But we are *trained* soldiers! And we have on our side the great-granddaughter of the Kaj, who just a month ago brought down a Divine horror that was ravaging this very city! You wish to relive history? Are your standards so low? You will *make* it this day! You are heroes that will be sung about for centuries to come! You are legends! And you will be victorious!'

To Shara's utter surprise, a bloodthirsty cheer rises up among the soldiers. They begin to chant *Komayd! Komayd! Komayd!*

Shara turns a furious beetroot red and mutters, 'Oh my goodness.'

'Now man these fortifications,' says Mulaghesh, 'and I want you to aim for those things' fucking *eyes*, do you hear me? They might be armoured, but they're not invincible!'

The soldiers cheer and rush to the fortifications behind the embassy walls. Mulaghesh saunters over to where Shara stands. 'How'd I do?'

'Very good,' says Shara. 'You ought to do this for a living.'

'Funny,' says Mulaghesh. She peers through the gates. 'Those things know we're here. It looks like they break off about a dozen for each building, and we're about to get our fair share. Are you ready?'

Shara hesitates. 'This is five times the dosage I gave the boy in the jail.'

'And?'

'So I have absolutely no idea if potency correlates with quantity.'

'And?'

'So I mean that even if this *does* work, there is a very good chance I may overdose, and die.'

Mulaghesh shrugs. 'Yeah, probably. Welcome to war. Let's see if you can do something before you actually die, though, okay?'

'How can you . . . how can you be so calm about this?'

Mulaghesh watches the advancing armoured soldiers. 'It's like swimming,' she says. 'You think you've forgotten how to do it, but then you jump in, and suddenly it's like you never stopped doing it at all. If you're going to do it, Chief Diplomat' – she points at the pills in Shara's hand – 'do it. Because we're about to find out if our guns are worth a damn against those things.'

The armoured soldiers line up and begin to march towards the embassy with metronomic precision. Teeth-rattling clanks echo across the streets and over the walls. Mulaghesh mounts the foremost gun battery and shouts, 'Focus on the one on the right!' The repeat shooters slowly swivel to aim at the nearest armoured soldier, who does not react at all.

Mulaghesh waits for the armoured soldier to come within range, then drops her hand and bellows, 'Fire!'

The repeat shooters do not sound at all like cannons, Shara finds, but rather huge saws in a sawmill. Rainbows of bronze casings tumble over the edge of the gun batteries and tinkle on the embassy courtyard. Shara watches, hoping the armoured soldier will simply explode: instead, the soldier slows down, small holes and dents appearing in its breastplate, face and legs. It makes a sound like a kitchen cabinet overflowing with an endless stream of pots and pans.

The repeat shooters maintain the stream of bullets; the armoured soldier begins wobbling on its ragged legs; after nearly a full half-minute of shooting, the soldier falls over. Instantly, a flock of brown starlings come fluttering out of the many gaps in the armour, which falls apart as if it had been held together by strings. *Brown starlings*, thinks Shara, surprised. *But that's one of Jukov's tricks.* The soldier behind it implacably steps over the tattered armour, as if the death of its comrade means nothing.

Mulaghesh looks back at Shara and grimly shakes her head – *No good.* 'Keep firing!' she shouts to her men, and they pour a stream of fire into the advancing soldiers, which slows them down but does not come close to stopping them.

Ten of them, thinks Shara. *It'll take five whole minutes to kill them all.*

The soldiers are a hundred yards away now. Their feet clank and rattle with each step.

'Do it, Shara!' shouts Mulaghesh. 'We can't hold them off!'

Shara looks down at the tiny white pills in her hand.

Seventy yards.

'Do it!'

I damn my fate, thinks Shara, *with all my heart.*

She stuffs the pills in her mouth and swallows.

Shara waits. Nothing happens.

The armoured soldiers are fifty yards away.

'Oh dear,' says Shara. 'Oh, no. It's not working at all! It's not—'

Shara gags. Then she jerks forward slightly, gripping her stomach, and touches her mouth.

'I don't feel . . .' She swallows. 'Mm, I don't feel exactly . . .'

She falls to her knees, coughs, and begins to vomit, but what she vomits is rivers and rivers of white snow – as if there is a frozen mountain inside her, sloughing off an avalanche – and it all comes pouring out of her mouth, complete with stones and sticks and flecks of dark mud.

One of the soldiers turns away in disgust. 'By the seas!'

The world ripples around her. Colour bursts in the corner of her eyes. The sky is parchment; the earth is tar; the white skyscrapers of Bulikov burn as if lit by torches.

Ohmygoodnessohmygoodnessohmygoodness.

Her skin is fire and ice. Her eyes burn in their sockets. Her tongue is too big for her mouth. She screams for five seconds before getting control of herself.

'Ambassador?' says Mulaghesh. 'Are you all right?'

These are just the psychedelic effects, she tries to tell herself.

Words appear written in the stones before her: THESE ARE JUST THE PSY-CHEDELIC EFFECTS.

Shara says, 'What a curious drug this is.' But the words come from tiny mouths that have appeared on the backs of her hands. 'How marvellous!'

'If you're going to do something' – Mulaghesh's screamed words make coils of fire in the air – 'then do it now!'

Shara looks up at the advancing soldiers. She counts them and shouts, 'Nine!' for reasons that immediately escape her. She sees that they are walking tangles of many complicated miracles, but inside there are real human beings, people who have been forcefully conscripted into Kolkan's service. *Yet the second the armour is too damaged*, she sees, *the miracle turns them into starlings, and sends them away. Which is definitely something Jukov would do.*

She runs up the fortifications, and cries to the soldiers, 'What armour is it you wear? That of Kolkan, or that of Jukov? Which Divinity do you pay fealty to?' But, of course, they don't answer. Then she laughs madly. 'Oh, wait. Wait! I forgot! I forgot, I forgot, I forgot!'

Twenty yards away.

'Forgot what!' screams Mulaghesh.

'I forgot I *do* know Ovski's Candlelight!' cries Shara happily. 'I read that one long ago!'

She faces the platoon of armoured soldiers – *Scarecrows*, she thinks – and remembers the nature of this miracle: *All hearts are like candles. Focus the light of yours, and it will remove all barriers.*

Shara imagines the soldiers as a metal wall before her.

The soldiers flicker with a golden honey light.

Then it's as if an immense column of burning wind blows through them: the soldiers glow red hot, blur . . .

. . . and suddenly there is an enormous flock of starlings in the street, screeching and cheeping. They flutter up through the canyon of buildings and into the sky, a dark thundercloud raining brown feathers.

The armoured soldiers have collapsed into a sloshing lake of molten metal. Only their shins-down remain, sticking up out of the bright yellow-red tide like two dozen forgotten metal boots.

Shara stares at her hands. Written on the inside of her palms in large type is: I DON'T FUCKING BELIEVE IT.

'I don't fucking believe it!' screams Mulaghesh.

The soldiers shout in triumph and disbelief, banging their bolt-shots on the embassy wall.

Three more armoured soldiers turn and march down the street towards them. The repeat shooters turn and begin to fire, and the metal soldiers quiver as if cold, but do not stop.

Miracles are just formal requests, Shara thinks wildly. *It's like having a form preprinted and filled out and handing it in to get exactly what you want! But you don't always have to do it that way! You can make it up as you go along, so long as you do it right!*

'What is she shouting about?' says Mulaghesh.

'Something about filling out forms?' says a soldier, bewildered.

Shara points at an armoured soldier to her left. *You're a person wearing armour*, she thinks, directing her thoughts at it, *but it's just made of spoons!*

The armoured soldier appears to dissolve like a child's sandcastle struck by a wave, collapsing into a cloud of thousands of tumbling metal spoons that fall clanking on to the cement. Another burst of starlings, which wheel away into the darkening sky.

Shara bursts out laughing and claps like a child at a magic show.

'What the *hells*?' says Mulaghesh.

Shara points at the next two and shouts, 'Spoons! Spoons!' and both of them dissolve as well. More starlings come fluttering out, as if their roosts have collapsed beneath them.

'It's easy!' shouts Shara. 'It's easy once you think about it! I just never thought about it the right way! There are so many muscles you can flex, you just don't know about them!'

Then the sky flickers: it's as if the sky is a paper backdrop, and someone behind it has just touched it . . . someone very big.

There is a pulse in the air that only Shara seems to feel.

She hears Kolkan's voice softly whisper in her ear: OLVOS? IS THAT YOU?

Shara stops smiling.

'Oh,' she says. 'Oh, dear.'

'What is it?' asks Mulaghesh.

The voice inside Shara's head says: OLVOS? WHAT ARE YOU DOING? WHY DID YOU NOT HELP US?

'What's going on?' asks Mulaghesh, impatient.

'He knows I'm here,' says Shara. 'Kolkan knows I'm here.'

'Are you sure you aren't just hallucinating?' asks Mulaghesh.

The voice says: OLVOS? SISTER-WIFE? WHY DO YOU HIDE FROM ME, FROM US?

'I'm positive,' says Shara. 'I don't think I could hallucinate something this strange.'

'What are you going to do?'

Shara rubs her chin. 'I will have to make my own fortifications against this particular assault.' She turns to face the city. *But why do they think*, she wonders, *that I am Olvos?*

She feels something like a hand reach into her mind to try to grasp this thought. OLVOS? says the voice. IS IT REALLY YOU? ARE YOU HURT LIKE WE ARE?

She must clear her mind. She has to clear her mind.

She begins on the physical reality around her: the soldiers are purely physical creations, so she unrolls the street running along the embassy walls (the Saypuri soldiers stare as the stone and asphalt vanishes) and fills it up with freezing water: *Water so cold it will shatter metal.*

A thick ribbon of fog now lies in front of the embassy. Two armoured soldiers advance out of the ruins of a shop. The repeat shooters fire, briefly, before the soldiers step into the lake of swirling, freezing mist; there is the hissing sound of rapidly contracting metal, and the soldiers glaze over with frost. The next burst of shot from the repeat shooters causes them to explode like crashing mirrors, and hundreds of brown starlings take to the sky.

The voice – or is it two voices? – inside her mind asks: WHY DO YOU FIGHT US? HAVE YOU DONE SOMETHING WRONG?

I must construct barriers, thinks Shara. *I must keep it out.*

Information, Shara realises, can be received by so many different channels, and so few speak to one another: just as an antenna cannot receive a telegram, a radio transmitter cannot make sense of a simple document, even though it is all just information, really. The human brain has such a limited number of channels – so few antennae, so few receivers – yet Shara's own brain, she now realises, has just had an untold number of antennae and receivers added, so that all the information she thought was hidden can now course directly into her mind.

Shara looks out at Bulikov, and sees the machinery behind the reality, the many wheels and gears and supports, and she sees how ruined and broken it all is. How phenomenally complicated this city was before the Blink, more than anyone could have guessed! *This is what Taalhavras made*, she thinks, *before he died. A chain of miracles upon miracles forever operating behind the scenes.*

She sets to work building a shelter out of the ruins of the sub-reality that surrounds her. To Mulaghesh and the soldiers around her, it looks as if Shara is conducting an invisible orchestra, but they cannot see the impossibly heavy pieces she is moving into place, the Divine structures hidden to their eyes. *It's like making a lean-to*, thinks Shara, *out of the ruins of a bridge.*

The voice in her head says: WHY DO YOU RUN FROM US? WHY DID YOU ABANDON US, OLVOS?

Shara wonders, *What on Earth is going on?*

She manoeuvres one giant piece to block a gap, and just as she does so the world goes black, and she sees . . .

. . . *Kolkan stands before her on a sea of darkness, his grey robes rippling. 'They imprisoned me,' he whispers. 'They locked me away, stuffed me in a tiny corner of the universe, just for trying to help my people. And then Jukov came to me, he visited me in my cell, and he hurt me, he hurt me so much.'*

. . . *Kolkan vanishes, and in his place is a skinny man dressed in a tricorne hat tipped with bells, and a jester's outfit made of furs. 'I had to!' snarls the man. His voice is like a thousand starlings screaming. 'They were killing us! They killed our children! They piled the bodies of our children to rot in giant graves! I had to do something! I had to hide myself away!'*

The vision fades. Shara is dripping with cold sweat and trembling.

I must block them out, she says to herself. *I must block them out.*

Out of the corner of her eye, she sees another handful of armoured soldiers approach, touch the mist, and freeze.

'Fire!' says Mulaghesh.

The repeat shooters eat the soldiers alive, and the street swirls with starlings.

Shara probes her invisible barrier with her mind. She can almost see the holes, for through the gaps the sky is the colour of yellow parchment. *Outside*, she thinks, *Kolkan is turning the real world into his own – his Divine influence.* She pulls more Divine struts down and uses them to cover the openings, but as she does so . . .

. . . *Kolkan appears, and says, 'You were older than me, the only one older than me. I listened to you, Olvos. When you were gone, I grew frightened, and I asked my flock to tell me what to do. I think I made so many mistakes, Olvos . . .'*

. . . *Kolkan vanishes again. The skinny man in the tricorne hat appears and angrily shouts, 'I looked for you! I searched for you, Olvos! You were the only survivor, besides me! I needed your help! I was forced to resort to faking my own death, pulling down my creations, letting my children die! I was forced to hide with Kolkan in his miserable little jail cell for years and years!'*

Shara tries to focus. *Jukov is alive too*, she thinks in shock as she fills this gap. *But why did only Kolkan appear when the glass broke?*

So many little gaps. So many tiny places he – or they, or it, or whatever it is – could slip in.

I am not stopping him, thinks Shara. *This is just defending, delaying everything, while Bulikov burns and people die.*

Fifteen more armoured soldiers touch the icy mist and freeze. Mulaghesh's repeat shooters tear them apart. Starlings take flight like a cloud of flies.

. . . Kolkan appears before her. 'What am I to do? What are we to do?'

. . . Jukov appears, spitting and snarling. 'Kill them all! Kill them for what they did to us! Incest and matricide and bitterness and horrors! My own progeny, my own Blessed kin, rises up against us and slaughters us like sheep! Let them burn! Let them burn!'

Then she understands. *No . . . no, it's not possible. I saw only one Divinity standing in the Seat of the World, heard only one voice, didn't I?*

The armoured soldiers' footsteps clink and clank. The scream of the repeat shooters. The screech of millions of starlings.

Then the skies ripple like the surface of a dark lake.

Kolkan's voice rings out through Bulikov: STOP.

Instantly, the armies of clanking armoured soldiers halt.

Shara feels a giant eye swivel to look at her.

She looks down the street before the embassy. A tall, robed figure stands watching her, just a short distance away.

Kolkan cocks his head. YOU, says his voice, ARE NOT OLVOS.

Shara frantically fumbles with the Divine machinery surrounding her, trying to pull it together, trying to protect her people, her countrymen.

Kolkan shakes his head. TRICKS AND GAMES, he says.

The air quivers. Rivers of armoured soldiers march out of the alleys, and all line up on the street leading up to the embassy.

IT IS ALL JUST TRICKS AND GAMES.

The sea of armoured soldiers turns to face the embassy, and starts marching.

'No,' whispers Shara. 'No, no, no . . .'

Instantly she feels a huge, terrible pressure on all the defences she's constructed: her river of freezing water begins unravelling, her Divine shelter creaks and groans, her very mind trembles. Madness spills into her skull like water on a sinking ship. She tries to push back. *But it is like an insect,* she thinks, *trying to push back against the lowering foot of a man.*

The freezing water fades. The streets are flooded with gleaming soldiers. Three of them hurl their massive blades at the walls. The swords hack through the white stone, and the Saypuri soldiers tumble black shrieking from a gun post. To Shara's surprise, little Pitry Suturashni, screaming a tinny war cry, mans the abandoned cannon and opens fire. Shara tries to use Ovski's Candlelight, but it feels as if the oxygen has been sucked out of the air, and she cannot even make a spark.

Everything pushes on her, pushes and pushes and pushes, floodwaters piling up against a dam.

I will die as countless Saypuris died, she thinks.

A thousand Divine soldiers push against her invisible walls.

Crushed under the machinery of the Divine.

Then one of the soldiers beside her screams, 'Look! In the sky! Ships! There are ships sailing in the *sky*!'

Shara feels the pressure immediately release. She falls to the ground, gasping and half dead.

She looks over the wall and sees Kolkan staring up: apparently this turn of events is a surprise even to him.

Shara, choking and coughing, thinks, *No, no! Volka's ships are here. After all this work, Volka's ships will be the death of us.*

She tries to peer through the tears in her eyes . . . and sees, to her confusion, that there is only *one* ship in the sky.

Then she hears another soldier's voice. 'Is that a *Dreyling* flag that ship is flying?'

Mulaghesh says, 'I recognise that. That's the flag of King Harkvald. What the hells is going *on*?'

Shara says, 'Sigrud.'

The good ship *Mornvieva*, once occupied by twenty-three souls, now occupied by one sole stowaway, cuts through the clouds and the wind like a dream. Sigrud stands at the wheel, puffing at his pipe, and makes a slight adjustment south-south-west.

Sigrud laughs. He can't remember the last time he laughed. Shipborne for the first time in decades and smoking his pipe . . . it is a blessing he never thought he'd have again.

There is no greater pleasure, he thinks, *than to sail once more.*

On the mast before him is a large steel plate sporting a very large ring; once, twenty-three cables were tied to this ring, anchoring all the crew to the ship. However, now there are only twenty-three severed ends of cables hanging from the ring, and they click and clack in the brutal winds.

To be frank, it might be the easiest time Sigrud has ever had taking a ship: if you just aim a cannon at every other ship in the armada, fire once (in retrospect, Sigrud reflects that this ship was *not* designed to fire that many guns at once, so he is lucky the thing didn't fall apart under the stress), run up to the deck in the confusion, cut all the cables, then grab the wheel and tip the ship over *ever* so slightly.

Sigrud grins wickedly as he remembers all the little black figures tumbling through the clouds, rushing down to the embrace of the Earth.

The Restorationists bet everything on Saypur never expecting air-to-ground combat; but they, similarly, never considered an air-to-air attack.

Sigrud sees the embassy below, with the river of silver soldiers before it, and the giant robed figure standing at its back.

He sets the course and trots below deck. He had expected something like this, so he had all the cannons ready, but some require minor adjustments.

Straight ahead, he reminds himself. *Start at the beginning of that stripe of silver, and work down.*

'Fire!' says Sigrud.

And he begins to pace from cannon to cannon.

The report of the first six-incher is like hearing a whole mountain cave in.

'*Down!*' screams Mulaghesh, but Shara does not listen.

Shara turns to the street, and pulls up a thick, thick wall of soft snow. She tells it to hang in space.

The first block of armoured soldiers explodes. Evidently, though Divine armour was designed to protect its wearer against many things, the Divinities never expected six-inch cannons.

Shara, like everyone else on the fortifications, is blown backwards. Metal ricochets, clanging off building fronts. Shrapnel flies into the veil of snow, slows, then tumbles softly to the ground. The sky is black with starlings.

The next report sounds in the skies . . . and another . . . and another, as if an immense thunderstorm is breaking open above them. Huge explosions reverberate down the street towards Kolkan, who stands with his head at an angle, as if thinking, *This is very unusual. This is all very unusual.*

Sigrud watches, pleased, as the Divine army is progressively decimated by the cannon fire. He adjusts the *Mornvieva* and aims her bow at the robed figure. A *couple of hundred shells going off*, he thinks. *Should make quite a bang.*

He spots a white structure from Old Bulikov with a crystal roof – *What are all these white buildings doing here?* he wonders – as he walks to the side of the ship, and readies himself.

'Probably won't survive this,' he says aloud. Then he shrugs. *Ah, well. I always thought I would die sailing.*

Sigrud jumps.

The crystal roof flies at him much too quickly; he sees the sky in its glittering reflection.

My hand, he realises. *It no longer aches.*

The sky breaks apart.

Shara sits up just in time to see the belly of the steel ship part the smoke above them. A tiny dark shape flies from its side and plummets into one of the white buildings.

Kolkan watches, curious, as the metal ship sails down, down, speeding towards him, the wings cutting through the street facades, stone raining on the streets.

Shara realises what is about to happen. She throws up another layer of snow, then a second, then a third, and screams, 'Off the wall! Everyone off the wall!'

Kolkan watches with a slight air of disbelief as the bow of the ship flies at him, crumples on his brow . . .

The world is turned to fire.

Shara is deaf, dumb, blind.

The world is clanging, ringing, smashing, crashing, cheeping, fluttering.

Shara is sure the massive amounts of psychedelics she took are not help-ing. She hears Mulaghesh groan from nearby.

'My arm, my arm,' the Governor says. 'My fucking *arm*.'

Shara sits up and looks through the gates, which are bent and torn. At first all she can see is smoke and flame. Then the wind slowly, gently scrapes the smoke away.

The building, shops and homes all along the street leading up to the embassy have been halved. Wooden teeth and partial living rooms droop over the exposed foundations. The street itself has been pulverised into a rocky, smoking ditch. Starlings sit on the windowsills, on the street lights, on the pavements, silently watching . . . something.

Kolkan stands in the middle of the street, slightly hunched over, his robes and rags fluttering in the smoke.

No, she thinks. *Not Kolkan.*

Shara stands, takes the bolt tip of black lead from her pocket, and limps down the street to the silent Divinity.

'That hurt, didn't it?' she calls.

The Divinity does not answer.

'You've never experienced the destructive capabilities of our modern age,' she says. 'Perhaps the modern rejects you as much as you reject it.'

The Divinity raises its head to look at her, but otherwise does nothing.

'Maybe you can keep fighting. But I don't think you have it in you. This world doesn't want you any more. And, what is more, *you* don't want *it*.'

The Divinity angrily says: I AM PAIN.

Shara stands before it and says, '*And* you are pleasure.'

The Divinity hesitates, and says: I AM JUDGEMENT.

'You are corruption.'

Then, defiantly: I AM ORDER!

'You are chaos.'

I AM SERENITY!

'You are madness.'

I AM DISCIPLINE!

'You are rebellion.'

Trembling with fury, the Divinity says: I AM KOLKAN!

Shara shakes her head. 'You are Jukov.'

The Divinity is silent. Though she cannot see its eyes, she knows it is staring at her.

'Jukov faked his death, didn't he?' says Shara. 'He saw what was happening to the Continent, so he faked his death, and hid, and sent a copy of himself in his place. He was the Divinity of trickery, after all. The old texts said he hid in a pane of glass, but we never knew what that meant . . . or I didn't, until today. When I saw Kolkan's jail cell – a single pane of clear glass.'

The Divinity bows its head. It seems to tremble, slightly. Then it lifts a hand, and pulls off its robes.

It is Kolkan: the stern man made of clay and stone.

It is Jukov: the skinny, laughing man of fur and bells.

It is both of them: both Divinities twisted together, shoved together, melded into one person. Kolkan's head, with Jukov's warped face appearing at Kolkan's neck; one arm on one side, a forked arm with two clenched fists on the other; two legs, but one leg has two feet.

It stares at her with muddled, mad eyes, a tottering, tortured wreck of a human form. Then its faces wrinkle, and it begins to weep. Its two mouths scream in two voices, 'I am everything! I am nothing! I am the beginning and I am the end! I am the fire and I am the water! I am of the light and I am of the dark! I am chaos and I am order! I am life and I am death!' It turns to the ruined buildings of Bulikov. 'Listen to me! Will you listen to me? I have listened to you! Will you listen to me? Just tell me what I should be for you! Tell me! Please, just tell me! Tell me, please!'

'I see now,' says Shara. 'The prison cell was meant only for Kolkan, wasn't it?'

'For Jukov to hide there, he had to *become* Kolkan,' says the Divinity. It puts its hands over its ears, as if hearing a roaring cacophony. 'Too many things, too many, all in one. Too many things I needed to be. Too many people I needed to serve. Too much, too much, the world is too much.' It looks at Shara pleadingly. 'I don't want to do this any more. I don't wish to be the god of this world any more.'

Shara looks down at the tiny black blade in her fingers.

The Divinity follows her gaze, nods, and says through its two mouths, 'Do it.'

Despite everything, Shara hesitates.

'Do it,' the Divinity says again. 'I never really knew what they wanted. I never really knew what they needed me to be.' The Divinity kneels. 'Do it. Please.'

Shara walks round behind the Divinity, bends low, and places the black blade at its neck.

As she says, 'I'm sorry,' the Divinity whispers, 'Thank you.'

Shara grasps its forehead, and pulls the blade across.

Instantly, the Divinity is gone, as if it had never been.

The air fills with crashes and groans as hundreds of white skyscrapers come tumbling to the Earth, and Shara hears the screaming of many starlings taking flight.

What is sown

A good historian keeps the past in their head and the future in their heart.
Upon History Lost, *Dr Efrem Pangyui, 1682*

Shara lies in the tub of warm water in the dark room, trying not to think. Sheer white undergarments cling and suck at her flesh. Her eyes are wrapped with bandages to keep the light out, yet still she sees bursts of coloured light, and colourful words, and her head still thrums and bangs with a monstrous migraine. She is not so sure she wouldn't have preferred simply dying from the philosopher's stones: having to deal with a hangover this hellish and psychedelic is something she did not anticipate.

She knows she is lucky to receive any care at all. The hospitals of Bulikov are overwhelmed with the injured and the maimed. It is only here, in the hospital at the Governor's quarters, that Shara and her comrades can be looked after.

She hears a door open, and someone enter in soft shoes.

Shara sits up and hoarsely asks, 'How many?'

The person slowly sits in the chair beside the tub.

'How many?' she says again.

Pitry's voice says, 'We're over two thousand now.'

Shara shuts her eyes. She feels hot tears on her cheeks.

'General Noor informs us that this is, despite everything, actually a good thing. So much of Bulikov was destroyed – well, the amount of Bulikov that was there *before* all the buildings from Old Bulikov appeared, I mean – but then, well, almost all of those *new* buildings were destroyed when you killed Kolkan.'

'It wasn't Kolkan,' says Shara hoarsely. 'But kindly get to the point.'

'Well, erm, General Noor says that two thousand casualties is a low figure, considering the amount of destruction. He thinks you distracted Kolk—Ah, he thinks you distracted the *Divinity*, slowed it down, which gave the city time to evacuate. And many of the people, as I understand it, had been transformed into some kind of birds. After the Divinity died, they all suddenly turned back into people – confused, cold and, erm, without clothes.'

'You don't say.'

'Yes. The hills around Bulikov were suddenly filled with hundreds of naked people. Hypothermia became a concern, though we've gathered and clothed and treated them as best we could. Noor has asked if you could possibly explain this.'

'It was a trick that Jukov used to do, worked on a massive scale,' says Shara. 'When he wanted to hide someone, he turned them into a flock of starlings. I expect that, in order to save people from the fate Kolkan had forced them into, Jukov simply extended this protection to them: rather than come to harm, they took to the skies as flocks of birds. How did so many die?'

Pitry coughs. 'Most perished when the buildings collapsed, but many casualties occurred during the evacuation. Apparently it was more of a stampede.'

What a neutered word is 'casualties', thinks Shara. And how pleasant it must be, to sit behind a desk and pare a lost life down to a statistic.

'It's all a tragedy, Pitry,' says Shara. 'A horrible, monstrous tragedy.'

'Well, yes, but . . . it was *their* god, wasn't it? Doing what *they* asked of it?'

'No,' says Shara. Then she adds, 'And yes.'

'General Noor is aware that your recovery might be more, ah, mental than physical . . . but he has asked me to see if I can retrieve clarification on this.'

'You've been promoted, Pitry. Congratulations.'

Pitry coughs again, uncomfortable. 'Somewhat, yes.' I am assisting the Regional Governor's offices now. Mostly because almost all of the Embassy and Polis Governor's staff are . . . indisposed.'

'You behaved quite admirably during the fight. You deserve it. How is Mulaghesh?'

'She's stable. The arm could not be saved. It had been quite crushed. It was, at least, not her good arm.'

Shara groans.

'Mulaghesh takes it in her stride, though. She insists on smoking in the hospital, something that has upset everyone. But she will not listen. Sigrud, however . . .'

Shara tenses up. *Please*, she thinks. *Not him, too.*

'. . . he has managed to stupefy all the doctors.'

'How so?'

'Well, by being *alive*, first of all,' says Pitry. 'And while removing the glass – a full three *pounds* of glass – and shrapnel from his wounds, they discovered' – the crackle of paper as he pulls out a list – 'four bolt tips, one bullet, five *darts* – some kind of exotic, tribal things.'

From Qivos, thinks Shara. *I told him to get a doctor that time.*

'And six teeth which appear to be from some kind of shark. The doctors concluded that most of these were from injuries or altercations that took place, ah, well before this battle.'

'That sounds about right. But he will survive?'

'He will. He will probably have a limp for the rest of his life, they say, and limited mobility in his left arm, but he will survive. And he seems quite merry.'

'Merry? *Sigrud*?'

'Ahm, yes. He asked me how I was, then he gave me some money and told me to procure' – Pitry coughs once more – 'uh, a woman of the evening.'

Shara shakes her head. *My, my. You leave the world for a handful of days and hear rumours of everything changing.*

'I am sorry to ask,' says Pitry, 'but General Noor has been quite insistent with me on the matter of, erm, the issue of the Divinity, or Divinities, or . . .'

She does not answer.

'Even if you have no concrete conclusions. Even if you have only *guesses* about what happened, I'm sure he will be happy to consider those.'

Shara sighs and lets the warm water slosh into her ears. *Let it wash away my memories*, she thinks. *Let it wash away those countless deaths*.

She summarises her conclusions about Jukov hiding in the pane of glass with Kolkan. 'I suspect it was also Jukov himself who sank the Seat of the World through Divine means, to secure his hiding place. But just before he did so, he sent out a familiar – perhaps a *mhovost* disguised as himself – to go to the Kaj, and surrender. This was what the Kaj executed. And when he did, Jukov essentially pulled the strings on many of his Divine creations, allowing all he had built to fall to ruin . . . all so no one would believe he was still alive.'

'Why would he do all this?'

'Revenge, I expect,' says Shara. 'He could be a very merry Divinity, unless you crossed him. Then he was wildly vindictive. Jukov knew that the Kaj had a weapon against which he had no power, so I believe he opted to wait and return once the threat had passed. I am not sure how he planned to do this – perhaps he arranged some sort of method of contacting anyone who looked hard enough for a Divinity – this would explain how he reached Volka Votrov, at least. That is just a guess, as I said. But I doubt if Jukov had expected the side effects of submitting to imprisonment with Kolkan.'

'Being fused together?'

'Yes. The warped thing I met told me the prison was made for *only* Kolkan. To stay there, Jukov was slowly but surely melded with Kolkan, perhaps absorbed by him. They were two diametrically opposed Divinities: chaos and order, lust and discipline. It was Jukov, after all, who convinced the other Divinities to imprison Kolkan in the first place. The end result was the mad, confused thing that begged me to kill it.'

'Noor wishes me to confirm that no more Divinities will be appearing.'

'I can confirm only that no one knows the whereabouts of Olvos, who is now the last surviving Divinity. But no one has seen her for nearly a thousand years, and I doubt if she'd ever be a threat. Olvos has shown no interest in worldly matters since her disappearance, which was well before the Kaj was even born.'

'And we also wish to confirm that the powers you experienced using the philosopher's stones cannot be duplicated.'

'*That* I cannot say for sure . . . but probably. More and more, the Continent is becoming less Divine, which means that the philosopher's stones allow access to fewer and fewer powers.'

'Is that all it took, back in the Continent's heyday? Take a handful of those pills, and attain god-like powers?'

Shara smirks. 'In case you have forgotten, the Divinity almost crushed me like a bug, once I got its attention. My powers were definitively *not* god-like. But it helped that I have been extensively educated in the matters of the Divine, probably more so than some luminaries of the Continent back in the Golden Age. And that *is* how things used to work here: there are records of priests and acolytes taking copious quantities of philosopher's stones and performing astounding miracles – and frequently dying shortly afterwards.' She rubs her head. 'Frankly, I almost envy them.'

Pitry is silent for a few moments. Then, 'The papers in Ghaladesh . . . they think you are a h—'

'Don't,' says Shara.

'But you are being cele—'

'I don't want to hear it. They don't know what it means. They should be *mourning*.' In her mind, Vohannes raises a bruised, trembling finger, and points to the door. 'It might have been mostly Continentals who died, yes. It might have been Continentals who – confused, misled – freed their Continental god, and asked it to attack us. But I was asked many times if we could help the Continent in any way before this catastrophe. I think that was already too late when I heard those pleas. But I was warned that this would happen, and I chose to listen to policy instead.'

'Noor *is* committed to helping the survivors, Chief Diplomat. Saypur will help Bulikov survive.'

'Survive,' says Shara, sinking down. 'Survive and do what?'

Water fills her ears and washes over her face.

Three days later Shara tours the recovery efforts with General Noor's executive committee. The armoured car bustles and bangs over the broken roads of the city, doing nothing to help Shara's headache, which has only faintly receded. She is forced to wear dark glasses, as the sight of sunlight still pains her – doctors have informed her that this damage may be permanent.

She finds this somehow quite easy to accept. *I have looked upon things not meant to be seen, and I have not escaped unscathed.*

'I assure you, this is not necessary,' says General Noor, bristling with disapproval. 'We have matters well in hand. And you should be in recovery, Chief Diplomat Komayd.'

'It is my duty,' she says, 'as Chief Diplomat of Bulikov to concern myself with the welfare of my assigned city. I will go where I wish. And I have some personal matters to attend to.'

What she sees wounds her heart: parents and children covered in bandages; field clinics packed to bursting with patients; shanty houses; rows and rows of wooden coffins, some of them very small.

If I had discovered Volka sooner, thinks Shara, *this might never have happened.*

'It's like the Blink,' she says. 'It's how things were after the Blink.'

'We did tell you,' says Noor quietly at one field tent, 'that you would not like what you saw.'

'I knew I would not like what I saw,' says Shara. 'But knowing that is different from seeing it. And it is my responsibility to see it.'

'It is not all gloom. We have had some local help.' Noor gestures to a section of a field clinic staffed by bald, barefoot Continentals in pale yellow robes. 'These people have swarmed into our offices, and more or less taken over in some cases. They are an invaluable gift, I must say. They relieve us as we await more aid from Ghaladesh.'

One of the Olvoshtani monks – a short, thickset woman – turns to Shara, and bows deeply.

Shara bows back. She finds that she is weeping.

'Chief Diplomat,' says Noor, startled. 'Are you . . . ? Would you like us to take you back?'

'No, no,' says Shara. 'No, it's quite all right.' She walks to the Olvoshtani monk, bows again and says, 'Thank you so much for all you do.'

'It is nothing,' says the monk. She smiles kindly. Her eyes are wide and strangely red-brown, the colour of an ember. 'Please don't weep. Why do you weep so?'

'I just . . . It is so good of you to come unasked for.'

'But we *were* asked,' says the monk. 'Suffering asks for us. We have to come. Please, don't cry so.' She takes Shara's hand.

Something dry and square brushes up against Shara's palm. *A note?*

'Thank you, anyway,' says Shara. 'Thank you so much.'

The monk bows again, and Shara rejoins Noor's staff in her tour. When she is alone, she quickly reaches into her pocket and takes out the note the monk gave her:

I know a friend of Efrem Pangyui. Meet me outside the quarters' gates tonight at 9.00, and I will take you to them.

Shara walks to a fire burning in a campsite and sets the note alight.

The air in the countryside outside Bulikov is cold, but it is not as cold as it was. Shara watches as her breath makes only a small cloud of frost, and realises spring is coming. *The seasons ignore even the death of a Divinity.*

The hills beyond the walls of the Governor's quarters are given soft shape by the stars above. The moon is a white smudge behind the clouds, the road a bone-coloured ribbon.

There is a footfall from the darkness. Shara looks up and confirms no guards are posted. 'Are you there?' she asks.

An answering whisper. 'This way.'

At the edge of the forest, a gleam of candlelight flickers and is quickly hidden.

Shara walks towards the place where she saw the candlelight. Someone throws back a hood, revealing the sheen of a bald pate. As she nears she can make out the face of the female monk from the clinic.

'Who are you?' asks Shara.

'A friend,' the monk says. She gestures to Shara to come closer. 'Thank you for coming. Are you alone?'

'I am.'

'Good. I will take you the rest of the way. Please, follow me closely. Very few have taken this road – it can be somewhat dangerous.'

'Who are you taking me to?'

'To another friend. There are still many questions you have – I could see

it in you. I know someone who might be able to answer some of them.'
She turns and leads Shara into the forest.

Spokes of moonlight slide over the monk's shoulders as they walk.

'Can you tell me anything more?'

'I could tell you *much* more,' says the monk. 'But it would do you no
good.'

Shara, irritated, contents herself to follow.

The road bends and winds and turns. She questions the wisdom of meeting outside the Governor's quarters; then she notes that she never noticed
the forest here was quite so large.

The terrain slopes up. Shara and the monk make a careful passage across
rocky trenches, white stone creek beds, through copses of pines.

Shara thinks, *When did they plant pines out here?*

Her laboured breath creates huge clouds of frost. They crest a stony hill,
and she looks out on a snow-laden, ivory landscape. *But I thought it was getting warmer.*

'What is this place?'

The monk gestures forward without looking back. Her bare feet make
tiny tracks in the snow.

They tread down over the frozen hills, across a frozen river. The world
is alabaster, colourless, with curls and slashes of moonlight and ice on a
background of black. But ahead, a bright red fire flickers in a copse of pine
trees.

I know this, says Shara. *I've read about this.*

They enter the copse of trees. Logs are laid by the bonfire to serve as
seats, and a stone shelf leans against the trunk of a tree, bearing small stone
cups and a crude tin kettle. Shara expects someone to greet them, perhaps
stepping out from behind a tree, but there is no one.

'Where are they?' asks Shara. 'Where is the friend you brought me to
meet?'

The monk walks to the stone shelf and pours two cups.

'Are they not here yet?' asks Shara.

'They are here,' says the monk. She takes off her robe. Her back is naked:
below her robe she wears nothing but a skirt of furs.

She turns and hands Shara one of the cups. The cup is warm, as if it has been sitting on an open flame. *But it was only ever held in her hand*, thinks Shara.

'Drink,' says the monk. 'Warm yourself.'

Shara does not. She stares at the woman suspiciously.

'Do you not trust me?' asks the monk.

'I don't know you.'

The monk smiles. 'Are you so sure?' The firelight catches her eyes, which glint like bright orange jewels. Even when she steps away from the fire, her face appears lit by a warm, fluttering light.

A light in the dark.

No, thinks Shara. *No. No, it couldn't be.*

'Olvos?' she whispers.

'Such a wise girl,' the monk says, and sits.

'How . . . ?' says Shara. 'How . . . ?'

'You still have not drunk,' says Olvos. 'You should try it. It's good.'

Shara, mystified, drinks from the stone cup and finds the Divinity is correct: the concoction is warm and spicy, and feels like it puts a small, soft ember in her belly. Then she realises it's familiar. 'Wait . . . is this *tea*?'

'Yes. Sirlang, from Saypur. I've come to be rather fond of it, myself. Though it can be an utter bitch to get the good stuff.'

Shara gapes at her, the cup, the fire, the woods behind her. She manages, 'But I . . . I thought you were gone.'

'I *am* gone,' says Olvos. 'Look behind you again, around you. Do you see the Continent? Do you see Bulikov? I am gone, and happy to *be* gone. It's pretty pleasant to be here, alone with my thoughts, away from all that noise.'

Shara is silent as she thinks, *After all this – have I walked right into a trap?*

'You're now wondering,' says Olvos, 'if I have brought you here to exact revenge on you.'

Shara cannot hide her alarm.

'Well, I am *gone*, but I am still a Divinity. And this is *my* place.' Olvos pats the log she sits on. 'I can never lose this. And those who join me here, their hearts cannot be hidden from me. You wonder, Shara Komayd, great-granddaughter of Avshakta si Komayd, the last Kaj of Saypur, if I have lured you away from the Continent to get you on your own, and destroy you – to destroy you for your family's crimes, for your crimes, for the countless destruction your wars and laws have incurred.' Olvos's eyes gleam brightly, like rings of fire half hidden below her lids; then the fire in her eyes dims. 'But that, as they say, would be stupid. A very stupid, silly, useless thing to do. And I am a bit disappointed you would expect such things from me. After all, I left the world when the Continent chose to begin its empire. Not just because it was *wrong*, but because it was a very short-sighted decision: time has a way of returning all heedlessness to those who committed it, even if they are Divine.'

Shara is still trying to come to grips with the reality of what is happening, yet Olvos is so profoundly unlike *anything* she expected a god to be that she is not sure what to think: her manner is like that of a fishwife or a seamstress, rather than a Divinity. 'That's why you left the Continent? Because you disagreed with the Great Expansion?'

Olvos produces a long, skinny pipe. She holds its bowl directly into the fire, puffs at it, and watches Shara as if wondering what sort of company she'll be. 'You read Dr Pangyui's notes, didn't you?'

'Y-yes . . . how did y—'

'Then you know he suspected that the minds of the Divine were not always their own, one could say.'

'He thought that . . . that there was some kind of subconscious vote taking place.'

'A crude term for it,' says Olvos, 'but not wholly inaccurate. We are – or *were* – Divinities, Shara Komayd: we draw power from the hearts and minds and beliefs of a people. But that which you draw power from, you are also powerless before.' Olvos uses the end of her pipe to draw a half-circle in the mud. 'A people believe in a god' – she completes the circle – 'and the god tells them what to believe. It's a cycle, like water flowing into the ocean, then up to the skies, and into rain, which falls and flows into the ocean. But it is different in that ideas have *weight*. They have *momentum*. Once an idea starts, it spreads and grows and gets heavier and heavier until it can't be resisted, even by the Divine.' Olvos stares into the fire, rubbing the mud off her pipe with her thumb and forefinger.

'Ideas like what?' asks Shara.

'I first noticed it during the Night of the Convening. I felt ideas and thoughts and compulsions in me that were not my own. I did things not because I wanted to do them, but because I felt I *had* to – as if I was a character in a story someone else was writing. That night I chose, like all the other Divinities, to unite, form Bulikov, and live in what we thought was peace. But I was profoundly troubled by this experience.'

'Then how could you leave?' asks Shara. 'If you were tied or tethered to the wishes of your people, how could they let you abandon the world?'

Olvos gives Shara a scornful look. *Can't you put this together yourself?*

'Unless,' Shara says, 'your people *asked* you to leave.'

'Which they did.'

'Why would they do *that*?'

'Well, I thought I had done a pretty good job with them,' says Olvos, with a touch of pride. She glances at Shara's cup. 'Have you drunk all of that *already*?'

'Erm . . . yes.'

'My goodness.' She shakes her head, tutting, and pours Shara another cup. 'That should have been enough to bring a horse back from the dead. Anyway, if you do these things well – and you, as a bit of a politician, probably understand – they sort of start to perpetuate themselves. I learned very early on not to speak to my folk from on high, but to get down with them, beside them, showing them how to act rather than telling them. And I suggested that they should do the same with one another: that they didn't need a book of rules to tell them what to do and what not to do, but experience and action. But when I started to feel this . . . this *momentum* inside of me, these ideas that pushed and pulled at me, threatening to pull me with them and pull everyone else with me . . . I consulted with my closest followers, and they just' – Olvos is grinning with gleeful incredulity – 'they just said they didn't really need me any more.'

'You're *joking*.'

'No,' says Olvos. 'Man's relationship with the Divine is one of mutual give and take, and we mutually opted to part ways. Honestly, everyone *but* my followers was shocked.'

'Why?'

'Well, I think, in some way, my people saw it coming, and didn't mind.'

Olvos turns serious. 'But this perpetuation – setting up a way of thinking, and just letting it run – it doesn't always yield *good* results.' She shakes her head. 'Poor Kolkan . . . he never really understood himself, or his people.'

'He spoke to me,' says Shara. 'He told me he had depended on you, in a way.'

'Yes,' says Olvos sadly. 'Kolkan and I were the first two Divinities. We were the first to really figure out how it all worked, I suppose. But Kolkan always had a little more trouble running his show. He tended to let his people tell him what to do, and I watched from afar as he sat down and listened to them. Like I told them all when I left, it just wasn't going to end well.'

'So you don't think Kolkan was wholly responsible for what he did?'

Olvos sniffs. 'Humans are strange, Shara Komayd. They value punishment because they think it means their actions are important – that *they* are important. You don't get punished for doing something *un*important, after all. Just look at the Kolkashtanis – they think the whole world was set up to shame and humiliate and punish and tempt them. It's all about them, them, them, them! The world is full of *bad* things, *hurtful* things, but it's still all about them! And Kolkan just gave them what they wanted.'

'That's . . . madness.'

'No, it's *vanity*. And I have watched from the sidelines as this same vanity guided the Divinities on to paths that would bring ruin upon them and their people – vanity I predicted, and warned them about, but they chose to ignore. This vanity is *not* new, Miss Komayd. And it has not stopped because we Divinities are gone. It has simply migrated.'

'Migrated to Saypur, you mean?'

Olvos bobs her head from side to side – not quite a yes, not quite a no. 'But we now find ourselves at a turning point in history, when we can either listen to our vanity, and continue down the path we're on, or choose a new path altogether.'

'So you have come to *me* to try and change this?' asks Shara.

'Well,' says Olvos, 'you weren't exactly my *first* choice.'

Something in the fire pops; sparks go dancing to hiss in the mud.

'You approached Efrem, didn't you?' says Shara.

'I did,' says Olvos.

'You met him on the river while he was sketching, and spoke to him.'

'I did a lot more than *that*,' admits Olvos. 'I do intervene now and again, Shara Komayd. Well, maybe not intervene − "nudge" might be a better term for it. For Efrem, I helped guide his research, prod him in the directions he would find most useful, checked in on him now and again.'

'He would have loved to talk to you as I am now.'

'I've no doubt. He was such a bright, compassionate creature, I hoped he would find a way to divert all the discontent that was building. But it seems I was wrong. Such old rage can only be exorcised through violence, perhaps. Though I still hope we can disprove this, eventually.'

Shara drinks the rest of her tea and remembers something that troubled her when she first read his journal. 'Was it you who placed the journal from the Kaj's soldier on his desk? Because I knew Efrem, and he would never overlook or miss something so important.'

Olvos nods, her face distressed. 'I did. And that might have been my biggest oversight. I had hoped he would understand the grave sensitivity of those letters. But he did not. He felt that information should be shared with *everyone*. He did not adhere to any one specific truth, just the truth as he saw it. It was his greatest virtue, and it was his undoing.'

'But . . . but what could have been so important in those letters?' asks Shara. 'The black lead?'

Olvos sets her pipe down. 'No, no. Well, a little. Let me ask you − do you not wonder, Miss Shara Komayd, how your great-grandfather managed to *produce* the black lead?'

'He experimented on his household's djinnifrit, didn't he?'

'He did,' Olvos says grimly. 'That is true. But even so, the odds that he would ever produce such a material are extremely unlikely, are they not?'

Shara's brain riffles through everything she memorised, but finds nothing.

'Would you not say,' Olvos asks slowly, 'that the creation of the black lead was nothing short of *miraculous*?'

The word dislodges a stone in her mind, which tumbles into her sea of thoughts.

Efrem's writings: *We do not know much about the Kaj. We do not even know who his mother was . . .*

'And not *everyone* was capable of the miraculous.' says Olvos.

A soft wind dances through the copse of trees, and the coals flare brightly.

Efrem's journal: *Djinnifrit servants prepared their masters' beds, served them food, wine . . . I cannot imagine what everyone would say if it was revealed that the Kaj had been pampered in such a way . . .*

A log lazily rolls over in the fire like a whale in the sea.

And when she saw Jukov: *My own progeny, my own Blessed kin, rises up against us and slaughters us like sheep!*

Snowflakes twirl down and die silently as they near the fire.

'The Blessed were legends and heroes, Shara Komayd,' says Olvos quietly. 'Offspring of the Divine and mortals, whom the world went out of its way to accommodate.'

Shara's head spins. 'You . . . you aren't saying that . . .'

'I suppose no one guessed who his mother was,' remarks Olvos thoughtfully, 'because no one would ever have believed it.'

'Her name was Lisha,' says Olvos quietly. 'She was a spirit of the hill trees – the short, bent ones that grow outside Jukoshtan. You've probably seen them, they've survived the change in climate pretty well. She was a sweet creature: soft-hearted, quiet, not terribly bright but eager to help . . . and also very eager to help her father.' She sucks at her pipe. 'Jukov's priests wanted to shore up support among Saypur, for it was Saypur's corn and grapes that kept Jukoshtan afloat. So he offered to *rent*' – the word makes her face wrinkle in disgust – 'his daughter to the Saypuri who would best facilitate their needs, for a time. It was not meant to be anything sexual: it was meant to be purely servitude.

'But then, something happened that Jukov did not expect: she and the man who eventually won her servitude fell in love. They kept it a secret. She stayed on as his . . . his *maid*.'

Shara senses a cold rage surfacing in Olvos.

'And when she bore a child, the nature of its parentage was so dangerous and so terrible that even the child could not know.'

Shara feels ill. 'The Kaj,' she whispers.

'Yes. His father died when he was young. He was never told the Divine servant in the house was his mother. Because, I think, he grew up hating the Divine . . . and his mother, being sweet, soft-hearted, and not too bright, did not wish to upset him. Then Mahlideshi happened.'

Something falls into the snow, and hisses. Shara sees they are hot teardrops, falling from Olvos's cheeks.

'And Avshakta si Komayd decided something must be done . . .' Olvos tries to speak again, but cannot.

'So he tortured his own mother,' Shara says, 'in order to find out what could kill the Divine.'

Olvos manages a nod.

'And though he didn't know it, because he was Blessed, he was able to actually *produce* something, and with it, overthrow the Continent.'

'After killing his despicable little household servant, of course.'

Shara shuts her eyes. The awfulness of it all is almost too much for her.

'I have lived with this burden for so long,' Olvos says. 'I could only ever hint and suggest it to Dr Pangyui – I have never actually told anyone. But it's good, I think, to speak it aloud. It's good to tell someone what happened to my daughter.'

'Your *daughter*? You mean you and Jukov . . .'

'He could be a very charming man,' admits Olvos, 'and though I could tell there was an awful madness in him, still I was drawn in.'

'I sympathise,' says Shara.

'Clever Jukov figured it all out when the Kaj invaded. He understood that he had, through his own pride and arrogance, fathered the death of the Continent, and the other Divinities. Before he hid himself with Kolkan, his last bitter act was to use a familiar to tell this fearsome invader the truth of his parentage.'

'I see,' says Shara. 'The Kaj fell into a deep depression after killing Jukov, and practically drank himself to death.'

'Bitterness begets bitterness,' Olvos says. 'Shame begets shame.'

'*What is reaped is what is sown*,' Shara says. '*What is sown is what is reaped*.'

Olvos smiles. 'You flatter me with my own words.' The smile dissolves. 'I have lived with this knowledge for so long. And for all those years, I knew that the balance of power in this world, this brave new land of politics and machinery, was predicated purely on *lies*. Saypur and the Continent hate one another, completely oblivious that each is now the product of the other. They are not separate, they are entwined. When Efrem came, I decided it was time this secret became public. But you do understand what this means . . . for you.'

Shara is terribly aware of her breathing. She can feel her pulse in her forehead and behind her ears. 'Yes,' she says weakly. 'It means me, and my . . . my family' – the fire is so hot her eyes feel like they simmer – 'we have a trace of the Divine in us.'

'Yes.'

'We are . . . we are the very things our country fears.'

'Yes.'

'And that's why Kolkan and Jukov thought I was you.'

'Probably, yes.'

Shara is weeping – not in sorrow, but in rage. 'And so . . . so is nothing I did true?'

'True?'

'The world shifts to accommodate the Blessed, doesn't it? It helps them achieve great things, not because of how they are doing it, but because of who they are. Did nothing I did really . . . *count*?'

Olvos puffs at her pipe. 'You forget, of course,' she says, 'that the nature of the Blessed becomes diluted through the generations. Often very, very quickly.' She looks Shara up and down, her eyes glimmering. 'Do you feel that you have had an easy life, Miss Komayd?'

Shara wipes her eyes. 'N-no.'

'Have you been given everything you wanted?'

She remembers Vo falling to the ground, pale and still. 'No.'

'Do you think,' asks Olvos, 'that this is about to change?'

Shara shakes her head. *If anything*, she thinks, *I am willing to bet my life is about to get much, much worse.*

'You are not Blessed, Shara Komayd,' says Olvos. 'Though you are distantly related to me, to Jukov, to the Divine, the world treats you as it does anyone else – with utter indifference. Consider yourself fortunate. Your *other* relatives, though . . . that might be different.'

A cold wind tickles Shara's neck. Another snap from the fire, and sparks go dancing.

'I see,' she says.

Olvos is watching her from behind hooded eyes, appraising her. 'I have told you quite a bit, Shara Komayd, information few else know or dream of. I wonder – what do you plan to do with it?'

Rage and pity and grief and sorrow twine around in Shara's mind, looping and curling like fireworks, and somewhere underneath all their chaotic designs, all their frenzied, fruitless spins and chases, an idea comes bubbling up.

Olvos nods. 'Good. Perhaps I was wiser than I thought. The Divine do not always know themselves: maybe we are but tools in the hands of Fate, like any other mortal. And perhaps my selection of Efrem was meant solely to bring *you* here, to me.'

Shara is breathing slowly. 'I think,' she says, 'that I would like to go back to my quarters now.'

'Good,' says Olvos. She uses her pipe to point between two trees. 'If you were to walk through that gap, you would find yourself in your bedroom. You may leave whenever you wish.'

Shara stands and looks down at her, feeling torn. 'Will I ever see you again?'

'Do you *wish* to see me again?'

'I . . . I think I would enjoy that, actually.'

'Well, I think both you and I know that, if you make the choices I expect you will make, and if you are *successful*, your path will take you far away from these shores. And I, being who and what I am, am bound to the Continent.' She taps her pipe against her finger. 'But if you were ever to return, I *might* make myself available for a visit.'

'Good,' says Shara. 'I have just one more question.'

'Yes?'

'Where did you come from?'

'Me?'

'You, and the Divinities . . . all of you. Where did you *come* from? Do you exist simply because people believe you exist? Or are you something . . . else?'

Olvos considers the question, grave and sad. 'That is . . . complicated.' She sucks her teeth. 'Divinities have the very odd ability to overwrite reality. Did you know that?'

'Of course.'

'But not just *your* reality. Not just the reality of your people – but the reality of the Divine, our own. Each time people believed I came from somewhere new, I came from that place – and it was as if I'd never come from any other place, and I never knew what I was before.' She takes a breath. 'I am Olvos. I pulled the burning, golden coal of the world from the fires of my own heart. I fashioned the stars from my own teardrops when I mourned for the sun during the very first night. And I was born when all the darkness of the world became too heavy, and scraped against itself, and made a spark – and that spark was me. This is all I know. I do not know what I was before I knew these things. I have looked, and tried to understand my origins, but history, as you may know, is much like a spiral staircase that gives the illusion of going up, but never quite goes anywhere.'

'But why did Saypur never have a Divinity of our own? Were we simply unlucky?'

'You saw what happened today, Shara,' says Olvos. 'And you know your history. Are you so sure Saypur was *un*lucky to lack a Divinity?' She stands and kisses Shara on the brow. Her lips are so warm they almost burn. 'I would tell you to go with luck, my child,' she says. 'But I think you will choose to make your own.'

Shara steps away from the firelight and through the two trees.

She turns back to say goodbye, but sees only the blank wall of her bedroom over her shoulder. She turns round, confused, and stumbles into furniture.

She sits down upon the bed, and thinks.

'Turyin,' whispers Shara. 'Turyin!'

Mulaghesh grunts and opens one eye a crack. 'By the seas,' she says croakily. 'I'm happy you've visited, but did it have to be at two in the morning?'

Mulaghesh is not the hale and hearty woman Shara knew mere days ago: she has lost a lot of weight during her stay in the hospital, and both of her eyes are still blackened. Her left arm ends just below the elbow in rings of tight, white bandages. She sees Shara staring. 'I hope this' – she raises her wounded arm – 'won't keep me from swimming in Javrat. But at least I still have my drinking hand.'

'You're all right?'

'I'm all right. How are you, girl? You look . . . alive. That's good. The black glasses are, uh, interesting looking, I guess.'

'I am alive,' says Shara. 'And, Turyin, I wish that . . . that for you, this had never—'

'Save it,' says Mulaghesh. 'I've given the very speech you're giving. But when I gave it, it was to boys and girls I knew weren't going to live. I'm alive. And I'm grateful for it. And you are not to blame. But it does give me a damn good excuse to transfer out.'

Shara smiles weakly.

'I *am* still getting transferred, right? Javrat's still happening, right?'

'There is a good chance, yes,' says Shara.

'That sounds like the out clause of a contract. And I don't remember signing a contract. I remember saying, "If I do this, I get stationed in Javrat," and I remember you saying, "Okay." Do *you* remember differently?'

'I have called in some favours with some middle managers in the Ministry,' says Shara.

'There's an "and" or a "but" coming.'

'True.' Shara pushes her glasses up her nose. 'And I am taking a train to Ahanashtan in two hours, then sailing home to Ghaladesh tomorrow.'

'Okay?' says Mulaghesh, sounding suspicious.

'If I disappear during that trip, or when I arrive in Saypur – I will be blunt here, and say that if I am secretly *murdered* – then you will be stationed in Javrat within a matter of months.'

Mulaghesh frowns. 'If you're *what*?'

'If, however, I survive my trip,' continues Shara, 'then much about the current predicament will change.'

'Like what?'

'Like the Ministry of Foreign Affairs.'

'How will that change?'

'Well, for starters, it will probably cease to exist.'

Someone coughs somewhere in the hospital.

'Are you sure that you didn't catch a bump on the head during—'

'I think you and I had the same job, Turyin,' says Shara. 'You weren't to intervene in Bulikovian affairs – things were supposed to stay the same. I constantly intervened in Continental affairs , but always to keep things the way they are – with the Continent desperately poor, and all commerce directed to Saypur. *To leave the Continent to the Continent,*' Shara says from memory, 'which is to say: poor, savage and irrelevant.'

'You don't have to quote the policy to me. I wasted two decades of my life enforcing it. So what are you saying you want to do?'

'I wish to change this. And if I am to change this,' Shara says, 'then I will need allies on the Continent.'

'Aw, shit.'

'Especially here in Bulikov.'

'Aw, *shit*.'

'Because if I need anyone backing me up,' says Shara, 'I want it to be General Turyin Mulaghesh.'

'I'm a Governor first and foremost, but my military rank is Colonel.'

'If I survive, and do what I plan,' says Shara, 'it won't be.'

Mulaghesh blinks and laughs hollowly. 'You want me to play Sagresha to your Kaj? I told you, I'm not interested in promotion. I'm *out* of the game.'

'And I'm going to change the game entirely,' says Shara.

'Oh, by the seas . . . are you *serious* about this?'

Shara takes a deep breath. 'I am, actually. I am not sure how many radical changes I can make, but I plan to try and make as many as I can. The Ministry failed Bulikov last week. It failed you, Turyin. It failed, and thousands are dead.'

'You . . . you really think you can? Do you really think you aren't being, well . . .' Mulaghesh laughs, 'wildly fucking naive about this?'

Shara shrugs. 'I killed a god last week. A ministry should be a small task, shouldn't it?'

'That's a pretty good point, I suppose.'

'Will you help me, Turyin? You and I were meant to be servants, and for years we chiefly served policy. I am offering what I think is our first real chance to serve.'

'Aw, shit.' Mulaghesh strokes the scars on her jaw with her right hand and contemplates the situation. 'Well, I must admit all this is somewhat interesting.'

'I hoped you would think so.'

'And last time I checked, the pay scale for a general is almost twice that of a colonel.'

Shara smiles. 'Enough to afford frequent vacations in Javrat.'

Shara creeps down the hospital hallway towards Sigrud's room.

Is this how governments are made? Forcing decisions on wounded people in the middle of the night?

She halts when she enters the ward and looks out on the sea of beds, each with a pale white burden, some with arms and legs propped up, others eclipsed in bandages, and she wonders which of her choices put them in those beds, and how things could have been different.

Sigrud's voice seeps through the wall beside her. 'I can hear you, Shara. If you want to come in, come in.'

Shara opens the door and steps inside. Sigrud is a mountain of stitches, bandages, tubes; liquids pour into him, and out of him, draining into various sacks; a thick set of stitches march from his left eyebrow up into his scalp; his left nostril has been split, and his left cheek is a red mass. Otherwise, he is still most definitely Sigrud.

'How did you know it was me?' she asks.

'Your footfall,' he says, 'is so light, like a little cat's.'

'I will take that as a compliment.' She sits down beside his bed. 'How are you?'

'Why haven't you visited?'

'Why, do you care?'

'You think I wouldn't?'

'The Sigrud I knew and employed for eight years was never one for caring about much. Don't tell me your brush with death has given you a new perspective on life. You've brushed it many times, often right in front of me, and it never seemed to affect you before.'

'Someone,' says Sigrud, 'has been telling you tales about me.' He thinks. 'You know, I'm not sure what it is. When I jumped off that ship, I didn't think I would have a future at all. I thought I would be dead. But for the first time, I felt . . . good. I felt that the world I was leaving was good. Not *great*, but good. And now I am alive in what could be a good world.' He shrugs. 'Perhaps I only wish to sail again.'

She smiles. 'How has this affected any plans for your future?'

'Why do you ask?'

'The reason I ask is that, if my plans go well, I will no longer be a ground-level operative. I will return to Ghaladesh, and take up a desk job. And I will no longer need your services.'

'Am I to be abandoned? You intend to leave me here to rot, in this bed?'

'No. This desk job in particular will be very, very important. There is no title for it yet – if all this works out, I shall probably have to make one up. But I will need all the overseas support I can get. I believe I will have a strong ally in Bulikov, but I will need more.'

'More being . . . ?'

'If, say, the North Sea is suddenly tamed.'

Sigrud's look of confusion contorts to one of considerable alarm. 'No.'

'If, say, a personage most Dreylings thought to be dead suddenly returned.'

'No!'

'If the legitimacy of the coup that killed King Harkvald was utterly undermined, and the rampant piracy brought to an end.'

Sigrud drums his fingers on his arms, and fumes in silence.

Something drains out of one of his tubes with a quiet *ploink*.

'You won't even consider it?' asks Shara.

'Even when my father was alive,' says Sigrud, 'I did not relish the idea of . . . governing.'

'Well, I'm not asking you to. I have never really approved of monarchies, anyway. What I am asking,' says Shara, sternly and slowly, 'is that if you, *Dauvkind*, lost prince of the Dreyling shores . . .'

Sigrud rolls his eyes.

'. . . were to return to the pirate states of the Dreyling Republics, and had the *full and total* support of Saypur' – she can tell that Sigrud is now listening – 'could that not begin *some* kind of reform? Would that not offer *some* promise for the Dreyling people?'

Sigrud is silent for a long time. 'I know' – he digs deep in the bandages on his arm, and scratches – 'that you would never ask me such a thing in jest.'

'I'm not. It may never even happen. I am returning to Saypur, but . . . there is a chance I might not survive.'

'Then you will need me with you, of course!'

'No,' says Shara. 'I won't. Partially because I am confident I will succeed. But I also wish for your life to be your *own*, Sigrud. I want you to wait here, and get healthy, no matter what happens. And if nothing at the Ministry of Foreign Affairs changes, then you should know that I am dead.'

'Shara—'

'And if that is the case' – she takes out a small slip of paper and places it in his hand – 'then here is the village where your wife and daughters are hidden.'

Sigrud blinks, astonished.

'If I am dead, I want you to go home to them, Sigrud,' says Shara. 'You said the father and the husband they knew was dead, that the fire of life in you had gone out. But I think that is a foolish and vain thing to think. I think that you, Sigrud je Harkvaldsson, are *afraid*. You are afraid that your children have grown, that your family will not know you, or want you.'

'Shara . . .'

'If there was anything I've wanted throughout my life, Sigrud, it was to know my parents. It was to know the people I wished so hard to live up to. I will never have that chance, but your children might. And I think they will be overjoyed with the father who comes home.'

Sigrud stares at the slip of paper in his hands. 'I was not at all prepared,' he grumbles, 'for such an assault.'

'I have never really had to persuade you before,' says Shara. 'Now you know why I'm good at what I do.'

'This nonsense with the *Dauvkind*,' says Sigrud, 'it is all just a children's tale! They believe the son of King Harkvald to be a . . . a fairy prince! They say he will come riding out of the sea on a wave, playing the flute. A flute! Can you *imagine?* They will not expect . . . *me*.'

'After all the battles you've fought, this one gives you pause?'

'Killing is one thing,' says Sigrud. '*Politics* is quite another.'

Shara pats his hand. 'I will make sure you have someone to help you.' She checks her watch. 'I'm late. My train leaves in an hour, and I must prepare for my final interview.'

'Who else must you browbeat into doing your bidding?'

'Oh, this won't be *browbeating*,' says Shara grimly as she stands. 'This will just be simple *threats*.'

Sigrud carefully stows away the slip of paper. 'Will I see you again soon?'

'Probably.' She smiles, takes his hand, and kisses one scarred knuckle. 'If we do a good job, we may meet as equals on the world stage.'

'No matter what happens, to either of us,' says Sigrud, 'you have always been a very good friend to me, Shara Komayd. I have known very few good people. But I think that you are one of them.'

'Even if sometimes I almost got you killed?'

'Being killed . . . pah!' His one eye glitters in the gaslight. 'What is that to good friends?'

The walls of Bulikov are peach coloured with the light of the dawn. They swell before her, rising out of the violet countryside as the train speeds by. *Are the walls alabaster in daylight?* she thinks. *Bone? What word best describes them? What shall I write? What shall I tell everyone?*

The train wheels squall and sputter. She touches the window, the ghost of her face caught in its glass.

I must not forget. I must not forget.

She will not go into Bulikov: the train takes a straight track from the Governor's quarters to Ahanashtan. She will not see the collapsing temple of the Seat of the World. She will not see the cranes around the New Solda Bridge. She will not get to see the construction teams hauling the ancient white stone out of the rubble – the stone of the Divine City, stone older than history itself – nor will she get to see what they will do with it. She will not get to see the armadas of pigeons wheeling through the spokes of smoke as the day begins. She will not get to watch as the mats in the market are rolled out, as the wares are put on show, as merchants wade through the streets crying prices, carrying on as if nothing had ever happened.

I will not see you, she tells the city, *but I will remember you.*

The walls continue to swell; then, as she passes, they shrink behind her.

When I come back to you, she thinks, *if I come back to you, will I know you? Will you be the city of my memory? Or will you be a stranger?*

She could ask the same of Ghaladesh: the city of her birth, of her life, a city she has not seen in sixteen years. *Will I know it? Will it know me?*

The walls have shrunk to a tiny cylinder of peach-white, a can floating on black waves.

The past may be the past, she tells them, *but I will remember.*

Shara waits for over two hours. So far the movements of the ship are smooth and easy, but very shortly they'll enter the deep sea, where the waves will be much less kind.

Shara's cabin is as spacious as the merchant's vessel could allow, and she has promised a worthy fee from the Ministry when she finally returns to Ghaladesh. *Penny for pound*, she muses, *I am probably the most profitable cargo this ship has ever carried.*

She stares into the porthole in her cabin wall. On the other side is the South Sea, but in the window's reflection is a large, dark office and a big teak desk.

Aunt Vinya finally arrives, looking harried and harassed. She violently rifles through her desk, tearing open drawers, slamming cupboards. 'Where is it?' she mutters. 'Where *is* it? These questions, these damn *questions!*' She picks up a stack of papers, flips through them and angrily throws them in her waste-paper basket.

'It looks,' Shara says, 'like you've had a few rough meetings.'

Vinya's head snaps up, and she stares at Shara in the window. 'You . . .'

'Me.'

'What are you doing?' Vinya snaps. 'I should have you arrested for this! Performing a miracle on the Continent is a treasonous act!'

'Well, then, it's probably a very good thing that I'm not on the Continent any more.'

'You *what?*'

'This is obviously not my office.' She gestures to the room behind her. 'You look at me in the cabin of a vessel in the South Sea, bound, of course, for Ghaladesh.'

Vinya's mouth opens and shuts, but no words escape.

'I am coming home, Auntie Vinya,' says Shara. 'You cannot keep me away any longer.'

'I . . . I damn well can! If you come home I'll have you imprisoned! I can have you *exiled*! You are disobeying the orders of the Ministry of Foreign Affairs, and in essence you are committing *treason*! I don't . . . I don't care *how* damn famous you are now, you've no idea what sort of powers I'm allowed, with no questions asked!'

'What sort of powers would those be, Auntie?'

'Powers to eliminate threats to the Ministry of Foreign Affairs, without question, without disclosure, without testimony to any damnable oversight committees!'

'And would this be,' Shara asks slowly, 'what happened to Dr Pangyui?'

Vinya's righteous fury evaporates. Her shoulders sink as if her spine has vanished. 'Wh-what?'

'You may wish,' says Shara, 'to take a seat.'

But Vinya is too shocked to move.

'As you wish,' says Shara. 'I will keep this short. Let's say I have a feeling that somewhere in all the cables and transmissions and orders that have come out of the Ministry – in all the inscrutable, impenetrable, classified, technically *non-existent* communications – there is a message to some unquestioning thug on the Continent informing him or her of a national threat, that threat being Dr Efrem Pangyui at Bulikov University, and that he or she is authorised to eliminate this threat with utmost discretion, and to search for and destroy any sensitive material in his office and library.' Shara adjusts her glasses. 'Would that be right?'

Vinya has gone terribly pale.

'You want to shut down this conversation altogether, don't you, Auntie?' says Shara. 'But you want to know what I know and how I know it. You want to know if I know, for example, that the reason Dr Efrem Pangyui was labelled a threat was one very personal to you.'

Shara waits, but Vinya does not move or speak. Shara thinks she can see something trembling in her aunt's cheek.

'I do,' says Shara. 'I do know, Auntie. I know that you are Blessed,

Vinya. I know that you are a descendant of the very thing that haunts Saypur's nightmares.'

Vinya blinks. Teardrops spill down her cheeks.

'Efrem Pangyui deduced the Kaj's parentage in Bulikov,' says Shara. 'And he, being the dutiful and honourable historian of Saypur, sent back a report, without realising he was signing his own death warrant – for him, the truth was the truth, and hiding it never occurred to him.'

Vinya, who has resisted upper-middle age for nearly fifteen years, sits in her chair with the slow movements of an old woman.

'And you hated hearing this, of course,' says Shara. 'Just as the Kaj hated it when he learned it himself. Efrem, obviously, had no plans to keep quiet about it – he was a historian, not a spy. So you reacted as you would to any national threat, and had him, as you say, eliminated.'

Vinya swallows.

'That's right, isn't it, Auntie Vinya?'

Vinya struggles for nearly half a minute. Then a quiet, 'I . . . I just wanted it to be gone. I wanted to believe . . . to believe I had never *heard* it.'

Sea spray bursts against the hull outside. Someone on deck above makes a joke, which is followed by wicked laughter.

'Why?' says Shara. 'Why did you let me stay in Bulikov at all? You knew there was a chance I'd find out. Why didn't you pull rank and reassign me straight away?'

'Because . . . I was afraid.'

'Afraid of what?'

'Of you,' Vinya confesses.

'Of *me*?'

'Yes,' she says. 'I've always been afraid of you, Shara. Ever since you were a child. Saypur has always been inclined to like you more than me, because of who your parents were. And I have many enemies. It would be an easy thing, to oust me simply by supporting you.'

'And *that* is why you let me stay in Bulikov?'

'I knew that if I made you leave, you would become suspicious!' says Vinya. 'You get so attached to people – by denying you what you wanted, I feared you'd become more determined. And I thought we had destroyed all of Efrem's notes. One week to mourn your friend, then you'd leave Bulikov, move on to the next little case, and all of this would go away.'

'But then Volka's men attacked the Votrov estate,' says Shara, 'and everything changed.'

Vinya shakes her head. 'You don't know what it was like, hearing his report,' she says. 'Hearing that not only am I descended from . . . from *monsters*, but that everything I had ever accomplished was suddenly, just . . . suddenly *illegitimate*! It was as if I'd been given everything, rather than *earning* it! It was sickening, infuriating, insulting. Don't you understand what that's like? That I – that *we* – have some trace of the Divine in us?'

Shara shrugs. 'I was raised to think of the Kaj more or less as a god,' she says. 'A saviour whose memory I spent years trying to please. Honestly, it changes little for me, personally.'

'But nothing that has been made is real! There is nothing but *lies*. The Kaj is a lie, Saypur is a lie, the Ministry—'

'Yes,' says Shara. 'The Ministry as well.'

Vinya wipes her eyes. 'How I detest weeping. There is nothing so undignified.' She glares at Shara through the porthole. 'What will you do?'

Shara wonders how to phrase this. 'The Blessed do seem to meet such tragic ends,' she says. 'The Kaj killed almost all of them during the Great War. Then the Kaj himself died alone and miserable on the Continent. And now you . . .'

'You wouldn't,' whispers Vinya.

'I wouldn't,' admits Shara. 'And I can't. You possess much more lethal force than I do, Auntie. Killing me, of course, during the height of my public profile, would naturally earn much scrutiny – scrutiny I doubt even you could afford. So I will give you a choice. Step down, and give the reins to me.'

'To . . . to *you*?'

'Yes.'

'Give . . . give *you* control over all the Generals across all the nations? Give *you* control over all our intelligence, all of our operations!'

'Yes,' says Shara mildly. 'I will have it, or neither of us will. Because if you do not step down, Auntie, I will leak our awful family secret.'

Vinya looks like she is about to be sick.

'I understand my stock has risen in Ghaladesh these days,' Shara says, with a quaint pout of modesty. 'I am, after all, the only person since the Kaj to have killed a Divinity – *two* Divinities, technically, to the Kaj's three. This, after Urav. They haven't ever crowned another Kaj since Avshakta, but I don't doubt that a few people in Saypur are discussing it. I believe that when I speak, I will be listened to. And as such, I believe your time in the Ministry is over, Auntie.'

Vinya is rubbing her face and rocking back and forth in her chair. 'Why?'

'Why what?'

'Why are you doing this? Why are you doing this to me?'

'I do not do it to *you*, Auntie Vinya. You flatter yourself by imagining so. Things are changing. History itself was resurrected in Bulikov four days ago, and it rejected the present just as the present rejected it in turn. And we now have a new path we could take. We can keep the world as it is – unbalanced, with one nation holding all the power.'

'Or?'

'Or, we can begin to work with the Continent,' says Shara, 'and create an equal balance to keep us in check.'

Vinya is aghast. 'You wish to . . . to *elevate* the Continent?'

'Yes.' Shara adjusts her glasses. 'In fact, I plan to spend billions on rebuilding their nation.'

'But . . . but they are *Continentals*!'

'They are people,' says Shara. 'They have asked me for help. And I will give it.'

Vinya massages her temples. 'You . . . you . . .'

'I also intend,' Shara continues, 'to dissolve the WR, and declassify all the Continent's history.'

Auntie Vinya slumps forward and turns as white as milk.

'I don't think we can build much of a future,' says Shara, 'without knowing the truth of the past. It's time to be honest about what the world really was, and what it is now.'

'I am going to be sick,' says Vinya. 'You would give them the knowledge of their gods *back*?'

'Their gods are dead,' says Shara. 'Those days are gone. That I know. It is time for all of us to move forward. In time, I hope to even reveal the nature of the Kaj's parentage – though that might be decades away.'

'Shara . . . dear . . .'

'Here is how the narrative will go, Auntie,' says Shara. 'It will be said that things are different now – true enough – and the old ways and the old warriors who keep to them must adapt, or go. You can go graciously and quietly, ceding authority to the new generation, after I've returned from an incomparable victory. You might even be lauded for your foresight, as it was you who chose to keep me in Bulikov – that would be a nice touch. And I can make sure that you land on your feet, winding up the head of a research institute or prominent school that can take good care of you. Or, I can *dislodge* you. You've said before you have enemies in Ghaladesh, Auntie. I now have a very big dagger I can give them, which they will then promptly plant in your back.'

Vinya gapes at her. 'You . . . you really . . .'

'I will arrive in two days, Auntie,' says Shara. 'Think about it.'

She wipes the porthole glass with two fingers, and her aunt vanishes.

Sunlight bounds out of the clouds, across the waves, ripples over the deck. Far above the ship, gulls float and dip gracefully from current to current, dodging through the air. Shara grips the ceramic canister a little more tightly as the ship bobs to the port side: she has never been an accomplished sailor – something the crew quickly deduced, and are wary of – and she is thankful the sea is calm today.

'Any time soon, captain?' she asks.

The captain breaks away from a conversation with his midshipman. 'I could give you an exact time,' he says, 'if you were to give me an exact point.'

'I have given you that, captain.'

'The – and I quote – "point equidistant between Saypur and the Contin-ent" ain't exactly as exact as you think, if you pardon my saying so, Chief Diplomat.'

'I don't need for it to be too exact,' Shara says. 'Just how long until we're close?'

The captain tips his head from side to side. 'An hour or so. On such calm waters, and with such a benevolent wind, maybe less. Why do you want to know, anyway?'

Shara turns away and walks to the stern of the ship with the canister under her arm. She watches the churning ocean behind them and the wake of their passage. The stripe of curiously smooth water stretches out for miles: after that, the rise and bob of the waves devour it until it is gone.

She stares at the sea for a long time. The wind caresses her hair and her coat. Her glasses are bedecked with crystalline jewels of sea spray. The air alternates between a pleasant warmth and a pleasant coolness.

'It has been a very long journey, hasn't it, Vo?' she says to the ceramic canister. 'But looking back, it seems like it was all over in only a moment.'

A gull dips low and calls to her, perhaps asking for something.

They did not want to cremate him, of course: cremation was heretical on the Continent. But she refused to let him be buried in the Votrov tomb, to lie among the people who made his life a hell, so she took him with her, the contents of his self baked and burned and funnelled into a little canister, freed of all pain, of all memory, of all the tortures his country and his god had put him through.

She will not cry. She decided this. There is nothing to cry over: there is simply what happened.

'Birthing pains,' she says aloud. 'That's what our lives were, weren't they? The wheels of time shift and clank against one another, and birth a new age.'

Cold wind slaps against her cheeks.

'But there are pains before, violent contractions. Unfortunate that it had to be us, but . . .'

The captain calls that they are near, or near enough.

'. . . a butterfly must emerge from its chrysalis sometime . . .'

She begins to unscrew the top of the canister. Her heart beats faster.

'. . . and forget it ever was a caterpillar.'

Another plaintive cry from the gulls.

She turns over the canister; a cloud of delicate ash comes twisting out, twirling through the winds to settle over the stripe of calm seas behind the ship.

She drops the canister overboard. It sinks almost instantly beneath the dark waves.

She watches the waves, wondering what they know, what they remember.

Time renders all people and all things silent, she thinks. *But I will speak of you, of all of you, for all the time I have.*

Then she turns and walks to the bow of the ship, to look ahead into the sun and the wind and the bright new waves, and to wait for sight of home.

Turn over for a sneak peak at

CITY OF BLADES

Coming August 2015

He said to them:

'Life is death and death is life.

To shed blood is to behold this holiest of transitions, the interwoven mesh of the world, the flow from shrieking life to rot and ash.

For those who wage her wars, who become her swords, she will deem you shriven and holiest of holies, and you shall forever reside beside her in the city of blades.'

And he sang:

'Come across the waters, children,
To whitest shores and quiet pilgrims,
Long dark awaits
In Voortya's shadow.'

Excerpt from Of the Great Mother Voortya atop the Teeth of the World

ca. 556

Make it Matter

Somewhere around mile three on the trek up the hill, Pitry Suturashni decides he would not describe the Javrati sun as 'warm and relaxing', as all the travel advertisements say. Nor would he opt to call the breezes here 'a cool caress upon the neck'. And he certainly would not call the forests 'fragrant and exotic'. Rather, Pitry thinks as he uselessly mops his brow for the twentieth time, he would describe the sun as 'a hellish inferno', the breezes as 'absolutely nonexistent' and the forests as 'full of things with far too many teeth and a great desire to apply them to the human body'.

He almost cries with relief when he sees the little tavern at the top of the hill. He hitches up his satchel, totters over to the building, and is not surprised to see it is almost deserted, save for the owner and two of his friends, because life is quiet and slow here on the island of Javrat. They are all Saypuris, just like Pitry, but Pitry has learned that Saypuris on this tiny resort island are about as foreign as the rest of the world seems to be: the further one gets from the beach resorts, the more one seems to venture back in time.

Pitry begs them for a glass of water, and the owner, exuding contempt, slowly complies. Pitry gives him a few drekels, which somehow makes the man even more contemptuous.

'I was wondering,' Pitry says, 'if you could help me.'

'I've already helped you,' the owner says, gesturing to the water.

'Well, yes, you did do that, and I thank you for it. But I am trying to find someone. A friend.'

The owner and his two comrades watch him, their expressions stony and inscrutable.

'I am looking for my aunt,' says Pitry. 'She moved here after an accident in Ghaladesh, and I am here to give her the dispensation from the settlement, which took some time.'

One of the owner's friends – a young man with a formidable unibrow – casts his eye over Pitry's satchel. 'You're up here carrying money?'

'Ah, well, no,' says Pitry, trying wildly to think up more of his improvised cover story. *Of all the things Shara taught me*, he wonders, *why did she never teach me how to lie?* 'Only the chequing account and instructions for the dispensation.'

'So a *way* to get money,' says the other friend, whose mouth is lost in an abundance of ill-kept beard.

'Anyway, my *aunt*,' says Pitry, 'is about so high' – he holds out a hand – 'about fifty or so, and is very . . . how shall I put this? . . . solid.'

'Fat?' suggests the owner.

'No, no! No, no, no, not really. She is' – he curls his arm, suggesting a formidable bicep that is, in his case, absent – 'solid. She, ah, is also one-handed.'

All three of them say, '*Aaah*,' and glance at one another, as if to say, *Ugh. Her.*

'I take it you are familiar with her,' says Pitry.

The mood among the three men blackens so much the air almost grows opaque.

'I understand she might have purchased property around here,' Pitry says.

'She bought the beach cottage on the other side of the hill,' says the owner.

'Oh, how lovely,' says Pitry.

'And now she won't let us hunt on her property any more,' says the bearded man.

'Oh, how sad,' says Pitry.

'She won't let us try to find seagull eggs on the cliffs there any more. She won't let us shoot the wild pigs. She acts as if she *owns* the place.'

'But it sounds, a bit, like she does,' Pitry says. 'If she bought it and everything, I mean.'

'That is beside the point,' says the man with the beard. 'It was my Uncle Ramesh's before it was ever hers.'

'Well, I . . . I will have to have a talk with her about that,' Pitry says. 'I'll do that now, I think. Right now. I believe you said she was on the other side of the hill, ah, that way . . . ?' He points in a westerly direction. The men do not nod, but he feels a flicker in their surliness that makes him think he's right.

'Thank you,' Pitry repeats. 'Thank you again.' He shuffles backwards, smiling nervously. The men keep glaring at him, though he notices the unibrow is staring at his satchel. 'Th— Thank you,' he mutters as he slips out the door.

Pitry regrets not defining the phrase 'other side of the hill' more precisely. As he marches along the wandering paths, it feels increasingly like this hill keeps producing other sides out of nowhere for him, none of which are bearing any sign of civilisation.

At last he hears the dull roar of the ocean and he spies a small, crumbling white cottage nestled up against the rocks along the beach. 'Finally,' he sighs, and he trots off towards it.

The forest pushes him down, down, until he's wandering a narrow thread of path with the forest brooding over his left shoulder and a rambling, intimidating drop off on his right. He wanders along this stretch of road for a few yards before he hears something over the waves: a rustling in the forest.

About twenty yards in front of him, the man with the unibrow from the tavern steps out of the forest and onto the path. He's holding a pitchfork, which he keeps pointed directly at Pitry.

'Oh, ah . . . Hello again,' says Pitry.

More rustling behind him. Pitry turns and sees the man with the beard has stepped out of the forest and onto the path about twenty yards behind him, brandishing an axe.

'Oh . . . well,' says Pitry. He glances down the ravine on his right, which ends in what looks like a very angry patch of sea. 'Well. Here all are again. Um.'

'The money,' says the unibrow.

'The what?'

'The *money*!' barks the unibrow. 'Give us the money!'

'Right.' Pitry nods, pulls out his wallet and takes out about seventy drekels. 'Right. I know how this goes. H-Here you go.' Pitry holds out the handful of money.

'No!' says the unibrow.

'No?'

'No! Give us the *real* money!'

'The bag,' says the bearded man. 'The bag!'

'Give us the bag!'

'Give us the bag of money!' shouts the bearded man.

Pitry looks back and forth between the two of them, feeling as if he's in an echo chamber. 'B-b-but it doesn't have any money,' he says, smiling madly. 'Look! Look!' He fumbles to open it and shows them it is full of files.

'But you know how to *get* it,' says the unibrow.

'I do?'

'You have a bank account,' says the unibrow. 'You have an account number. That account is full of money.'

'Full of it!' shouts the bearded man.

Pitry now quite regrets the flimsy cover story he made up on the spot. 'Well . . . You . . . I don't . . . I don't . . . '

'You *know* how to—'

But then the man with the unibrow stops speaking and instead makes a very high-pitched, ear-rattling sound, a sound so strange Pitry almost wonders if it's a bird call of some kind.

'I know how to what?' says Pitry.

The unibrow collapses, still making that odd sound, and Pitry sees that there is something shining redly just above his knee that was definitely not there before: the tip of a bolt. The man rolls over and Pitry sees the rest of a bolt protruding from the back of his leg.

There is someone behind him.

A woman stands on the path about ten feet beyond the shrieking man with the unibrow. Pitry sees one dark, thin eye glaring at him along the sights of an absolutely massive bolt-shot, which is pointed directly at his chest. Her hair is dark grey, silver at the temples, and her brown, scarred shoulders gleam in the sun. The hand she uses to steady the bolt-shot – her left – is a prosthetic, dark oak wood from mid-forearm down.

'Pitry,' she says, 'get the fuck down.'

'Right, right,' Pitry says mildly, and stoops to lie down on the path.

'It hurts!' cries the man with the unibrow. 'Oh, by the seas, it hurts!'

'Pain's a good sign, really,' she says. 'It means you still have a brain to feel it with. Count your blessings, Ranjesha.'

The unibrow shrieks again in response. The man with the beard is now shining with sweat. He stares at the woman, then at Pitry, and glances at the forest to his left.

'No,' says the woman. 'Drop the axe, Gurudas.'

The axe falls to the ground with a thud. The woman takes a few steps forward, the point of the loaded bolt hardly moving an inch. 'This is kind of a sticky situation, isn't it, Gurudas?' she says. 'I told you two that if I caught either of you on my property again, I'd expose a goodly amount of your innards to the fresh sea air. And I hate breaking promises. That's what the whole of civilised society is founded upon, isn't it – promises?'

The bearded man says, 'I— I—'

'And I have to wonder,' she says, taking another step forward, 'if young Pitry there isn't the first traveller you've pulled this trick on. I do like to walk, and just the other day I found a few paths through the forest, ones that led almost directly to where you're standing now. You wouldn't even notice those paths unless you knew they were there. And I found some other things out in the woods, too – old clothes, old purses, belts . . . Things a thief might toss away once they found what they wanted, or so it looks to me. Maybe your filthy uncle who owned my house before me helped draw people out here for you, eh?'

Despite the layer of sweat, the bearded man is now sheet-white.

'Now, I don't think Ranjesha there is going to be walking those paths anytime soon,' she says, 'not unless he's got a litter to bear him up that hillside. But you, you're still pretty hale and hearty. Am I going to have to put a few inches of bolt in you, Gurudas? Will that guarantee us a happy ending here?'

The bearded man just stares.

'I asked you a damn question,' says the woman. 'Where do I need to shoot you to free up your tongue, son?'

'N-No!' says the bearded man. 'No, I don't . . . I don't want to get shot.'

'Well, you do have a funny way of following that dream,' says the woman, 'since the second your foot falls on my property, the opposite is most likely to happen.'

There's a pause. The man with the unibrow whimpers again.

'Pitry,' says the woman.

'Yes?' says Pitry. As he's still face-down on the path, the word generates a lot of dust.

'Do you think you can get up and step over that idiot bleeding all over my property?'

Pitry stands, dusts himself off and gingerly steps over the man with the unibrow. He pauses to whisper, 'Excuse me.'

'Gurudas?' asks the woman.

'Y-Yes?' says the bearded man.

'Are you competent enough to come down here and pick up your friend and get his dumb ass back to your brother's shitshack of a tavern?'

The bearded man thinks about it. 'Yes.'

'Good. Do it. Now. And if I ever see either of you again, I won't be so generous with where I stick you.'

The bearded man, careful to keep his hands visible, slowly walks down the path and gathers up his friend. The two of them hobble back down the path, though once they're about fifty yards away the man with the unibrow turns his head and bellows, 'Fuck you, Mulaghesh! Fuck you and your mon—'

He shrieks as a bolt goes skittering across the rocks inches beside his feet, making him jump, which must be very painful considering the first bolt is still lodged above his knee. She reloads and keeps the bolt-shot on them until the bearded man has dragged his screaming friend out of sight.

Pitry says, 'Gener—'

'Shut up,' she says.

She waits a little longer, not moving. After two minutes or so she relaxes, checks her bolt-shot and sighs. She turns and looks him up and down.

'Damn it all, Pitry . . . ' says General Turyin Mulaghesh. 'What in the *hells* are you doing here?'

Pitry was not sure what to expect of Turyin Mulaghesh's living quarters, but he hardly expects the graveyard of wine bottles and filthy plates he meets when he steps through the door. There is also an abundance of threatening things: bolts, bolt-shots, swords, knives, and in one corner, a massive rifling – a firearm with a rifled barrel. It's a new innovation that's only just become commercially affordable, thanks to the recent increased production of gunpowder. The military, Pitry knows, possess far more advanced versions.

The worst of it all though, is the smell: it appears General Turyin Mulaghesh has taken up fishing, but has yet to work out how to adequately dispose of the bones.

'Yeah, the smell,' says Mulaghesh. 'I know about the smell. I just get used to it. Between the ocean and the house, it all smells alike.'

Pitry fervently disagrees, but is smart enough to not say so. 'Thank you for rescuing me.'

'Don't mention it. It's a symbiotic relationship: those two excel at being idiots, and I excel at shooting idiots. Everyone gets what they want.'

'How did you know to be there?'

'I heard a rumour some Ghaladeshi was walking around the beaches asking for me, claiming he had a lot money to hand off. One vendor at the market likes me, so he ran up and let me know.' She shakes her head as she sets a bottle of wine on the kitchen counter. '*Money*, Pitry? You should have just hung a "Please rob my stupid ass" sign on your forehead.'

'Yes, I realise now it was not . . . wise.'

'I thought I'd keep a lookout, and saw you walking up the hill to Haque's bar. Then I saw you leave, and Gurudas and his friend follow. It didn't take me long to work out what was about to happen. You *are* welcome, though. That was the most fun I've had in a while.' She produces a bottle of tea and a bottle of weak wine and to Pitry's amusement, goes about arranging a drink tray, a traditional gesture of welcoming in Saypur with its own subtle messages: taking the tea would be an indication of business and social distance, and taking the wine would be an indication of intimacy and relaxation. Pitry watches her motions: she's become quite used to doing everything more or less one-handed.

She places the tray in front of Pitry. He bows slightly and selects the open bottle of tea. 'My apologies,' he says. 'Though I would be most grateful for the wine, General, I'm afraid I am here on business from the Prime Minister.'

'Yes,' says Mulaghesh, who opts for the wine, 'I figured as much. There's only one thing could possibly put Pitry Suturashni in my backyard, and that's Shara Komayd's say-so. So what's the Prime Minister want? Does she want to drag me back into the military council? I quit about as loudly as anyone could ever quit. I thought it was pretty final.'

'This is true,' Pitry says. 'The sound of your resignation still echoes through Ghaladesh.'

'Shit, Pitry. That was downright poetic.'

'Thank you. I stole the line from Shara.'

'Of course you did.'

'I am, actually, *not* here to convince you to return back to the military council. Chief of Armed Forces General Noor made some recommendations, and we have found a, ah, substitute for your position.'

'Mm. Gawali?'

Pitry nods.

'I thought as much. By the seas, that woman kisses so much ass it's a miracle she can find the breath to talk. How the hells she made general in the first place, I'll never know.'

'A solid point,' says Pitry. 'But the real purpose of my visit is to share some information with you about your . . . pension.'

Mulaghesh chokes on her wine and bends double, coughing. 'My *what*?' she says, standing back up. 'My *pension*?'

Pitry nods, cringeing.

'What the hell's wrong with it?' she asks.

'Well . . . You have heard, perhaps, of what is called the "duration of servitude"?'

'It sounds familiar . . .'

'The basic gist of it is that, when an officer of the Saypuri military is promoted to a new rank,' Pitry says as he begins digging in his satchel, 'their pay is automatically increased, but they must serve in that rank for a set duration of time before receiving the pension level associated with that rank. This was because twenty or some-odd years ago we had a series of officers get to a rank, and then promptly quit so they could live off the enhanced pension.'

'Yeah, I know all this. The rank of general requires two years' servitude, right? I was almost positive I was well past that . . .'

'You *have* served as a general for more than two years,' says Pitry, 'but the duration of servitude begins when your paperwork is *processed*. And as you were stationed in the polis of Bulikov at the time of your promotion, the paperwork would have been processed there – but a good deal of Bulikov was destroyed as, um, you are well aware.'

'Okay. So. How long did it take Bulikov to process my paperwork?'

'There was a delay of a little under two months.'

'Meaning my duration of servitude was . . .'

Pitry produces a piece of paper and runs a finger down it as he searches for the precise number. 'Three years, eight months, and seventeen days.'

'Shit.'

'Yes.'

'*Shit!*'

'Yes. As your duration of servitude is not completed, when the fiscal year ends, your pension will revert to that of your previous rank – that of colonel.'

'And how much is that?'

Pitry puts the piece of paper on the desk, slides it over to her and points to one figure.

'*Shit!*'

'Yes.'

'Damn . . . I was going to buy a boat.' She shakes her head. 'Now I'm not even sure if I'll be able to afford all this!' She waves her hand at her cottage.

Pitry glances around at the dark, crumbling cottage, which in some places is absolutely swarming with flies. 'Ah, yes. Such a pity.'

'So what? Are you just here to tell me I'm getting the rug pulled out from under me, I'm off, see you later?'

'No,' says Pitry. 'This is actually a common occurrence. Some officers are forced to retire due to their health, family, and so on. Sometimes they retire earlier than the duration of servitude requires. In these instances, the Military Council has the option of voting to ignore the remaining time and award the pension anyway. Being as you, ah, did not leave on the best of terms, they have not opted to do that.'

'Those fuckers,' snarls Mulaghesh.

'But we do have an option of recourse. When the officer in question has given exemplary service to Saypur, they are often assigned to go on what I believe is called the "touring shuffle".'

'Aw, *hells*. I remember this. I serve out the remainder of my time wandering around the Continent "reviewing fortifications". Is that it?'

'That is it exactly,' says Pitry. 'Administrative responsibilities only. No active or combat duty whatsoever. The Prime Minister has arranged it so that this opportunity is now being extended to you.'

Mulaghesh taps her wooden hand against the tabletop. While her attention's elsewhere, Pitry glances at the prosthetic limb: it is strapped to a hinge at her elbow, which then buckles around her still-considerable bicep. She's wrapped her upper arm with a cotton sleeve, presumably to avoid chafing, and he can see more of what looks like a harness wrapped around her torso. It's clearly an extensive and complicated mechanism, and probably none too comfortable, which can't help General Mulaghesh's famously choleric moods.

'Eyes, Pitry,' says Mulaghesh calmly. 'Or have you not been in a woman's presence for a while?'

Startled, Pitry resumes staring into the piece of paper on the table.

Mulaghesh is still for a long time. 'Pitry, can I ask you something?'

'Certainly.'

'You are aware that I just shot a man?'

'I . . . am aware.'

'And you are aware that I shot him because he was on my property, and he was being an idiot.'

'I believe so, yes.'

'So why should I not do the same to you?'

'I . . . I beg your pa—'

'Pitry, you are a member of the Prime Minister's personal staff,' says Mulaghesh. 'I'm not saying that you're her chief of staff or anything like that, but you're not just some damn clerk. And Shara Komayd would not send a member of her personal damn staff all the way out to Javrat to tell me my pension's getting re-evaluated. That's why they invented the mail. So why don't you stop dancing around and tell me what's *really* going on?'

Pitry takes a slow breath and nods. 'It is quite possible that . . . that if you were to do this touring shuffle, it would provide an excellent cover story for another operation.'

'Ah. I see.' Mulaghesh loudly sucks her teeth. 'And *who* would be performing this operation?'

Pitry stares very hard at the paper on the counter, as if somewhere in its figures he might stumble upon instructions on how to escape this awkward situation.

'Pitry?'

'You, general,' he says. 'This operation would be performed by you.'

'Yeah,' says Mulaghesh. 'Shit.'

'I mean, damn it all, Pitry,' snarls Mulaghesh. Her wooden hand makes a *thunk* as she brings both hands down on the countertop. 'That's some dirty pool right there, holding an officer's pension hostage to make them go off and get themselves shot.'

Pitry nods. 'I am sympathetic to your position, general. But the nature of the oper—'

'I *retired*, damn it. I *resigned*. I said I was done, that I'd done what I needed to do, thanks, leave me alone. Can't I just be left alone? Please? Mm? Is that so much to ask?'

'Well, the Prime Minister did suggest,' says Pitry slowly, 'that this might be just the thing you need.'

'I *need*? What the hells does Shara know about what I *need*? What could I possibly *need* here?'

Again, she waves her hand at her cottage, and again, Pitry looks at the reeking, filthy home, with carpets tacked up against the windows and one kitchen cabinet door askew, the counters littered with wine bottles and fishbones and tangled dirty clothes. Finally he looks at Mulaghesh herself and thinks only one thing:

General Turyin Mulaghesh looks like shit. She's obviously still in tremendous shape for a woman her age, but it's been a long while since she showered, there are rings under her eyes and the clothes she's been wearing are in desperate need of a wash. This is a far cry from the officer he once knew, the woman whose uniform was so starched you could almost carve wood with the cuffs, the woman whose glance was so bright and piercing you almost wanted to check yourself for bruises after she'd looked at you.

Pitry has seen someone in such a state before: when a friend of his went through a rough divorce. But he can't imagine what Mulaghesh divorced herself from, except, of course, the Saypuri military.

But though this explains *some* of what he's witnessing, Mulaghesh's complete and utter fall from grace is still confusing to him: because no one – not the press, not the military council, not Parliament itself – has *any idea* why Mulaghesh resigned in the first place. As with so many of Mulaghesh's actions, what she did is inconceivable to any ambitious, motivated Saypuri: how could someone just *walk away* from the position of Vice-Chairman of the Saypuri Military Council? The Vice-Chairman almost always becomes Chief of Armed Forces, the second most powerful person in the world after the Prime Minister. People poured through her interactions in the weeks before her resignation, but no one could find any hint of what could have pushed her over the edge.

'So this is what Shara's become?' Mulaghesh says. 'She's a blackmailer? She's blackmailing me into doing this?'

'Not at all. You have the option of just doing the touring shuffle and not engaging in the operation at all. Or you could not do it at all and accept a colonel's pay. She simply said that she felt you would be personally suited to this operation. It was too serendipitous not to offer it to you.'

'So what's the operation?'

'I am told we are unable to reveal that until you have fully signed on.'

Mulaghesh laughs lowly. 'So I can't figure out what I'm buying until I've bought it. Great. Why in hells would I want to do this?'

'Well . . . I think she hoped that her personal ask may suffice—'

Mulaghesh gives him a flat, stony stare.

'—but in the eventuality that it did not, she did ask me to give you this.' He reaches into his satchel and holds out an envelope.

Mulaghesh glances at it. 'What's that?'

'I've no idea. The Prime Minister wrote and sealed this herself.'

Mulaghesh takes it, opens it and reads the letter. Pitry can see pen strokes through the paper. Though he can't read the writing, it looks to be no more than three words.

Yet Mulaghesh stares at this letter with large, hollow eyes, and her hand begins to shake. She crumples up the letter, one-handed, and stares into space.

'Damn it,' she says softly. 'How in the hell did she know?'

Pitry watches her. A fly lands on her shoulder, a second on her neck. She doesn't notice.

'You wouldn't have sent that if you hadn't meant it, would you,' she murmurs. She sighs and shakes her head. '*Damn.*'

'I take it,' Pitry says, 'that you are considering the operation?'

Mulaghesh glares at him.

'Just asking,' he says.

'Well. What *can* you tell me about this operation?'

'The first thing I can tell you about this operation is that it's so sensitive there's very, very, *very* little that I even *know* at this point. I know it is on the Continent. I do know that it is about a subject lots of people are paying attention to, including some very powerful people in Ghaladesh, some of whom are not wholly benign toward the prime minister's agendas.'

'Hence my complicated cover story. I remember when we used to do this stuff to dupe *other* nations, not our *own*. Sign of the times, I suppose.'

'Things do continue to worsen in Ghaladesh,' Pitry admits. 'The press likes to describe Shara as 'embattled.' We're still suffering from the last round of elections. Her efforts to reconstruct the Continent continue to be enormously unpopular in Saypur.'

'Imagine that,' Mulaghesh says. 'I still remember the parties when she got elected. They all thought we were about to start our Golden Age.'

'The voting public remains quite fickle. And for some, it's easy to forget that the Battle of Bulikov took place only five years ago.'

Pitry feels like the temperature in the room has just dropped ten degrees. Mulaghesh draws in a breath, her nostrils whistling. She pulls her prosthetic arm in closer, as if it pains her. Suddenly she looks a great deal more like the commander Pitry saw that day when the god spoke from the sky and the buildings burned and Mulaghesh bellowed at her soldiers to man the fortifications.

'*I* haven't forgotten,' she says.

Pitry coughs. 'Ah, no. I don't suppose you would have.'

Mulaghesh stares off into space for a few seconds more, lost in thought. 'All right,' she says, her voice unnervingly calm. 'I'll do it.'

'You'll do the operation?'

'Sure. Why not.' She places the balled-up note on the kitchen counter and smiles at him. His skin crawls: it is the not-quite-sane smile he's seen before, on the faces of soldiers who have witnessed the deaths of many. 'What's the worst that can happen?'

'I . . . I'm sure the Prime Minister will be delighted,' says Pitry.

'So what *is* the operation?'

'Well, like I said, you won't know until you've fully signed on—'

'I just said *yes*, damn it all.'

'—and you won't be considered fully signed on until you're on the boat.'

Mulaghesh shuts her eyes. 'Oh, for the love of . . .'

Pitry slides one file out of the satchel and hands it to her. 'Here are your instructions for your transportation. Please make note of the date and time. I believe I will be rejoining you for at least part of your trip, so I expect I will see you again in three weeks.'

'Hurrah.' Mulaghesh takes the file. Her shoulders slump a little. 'If wisdom comes with age, why do I keep making so many bad decisions, Pitry?'

'I . . . I don't think I feel qualified to answer that question.'

'Well. At least you're honest.'

'Might I ask for a favour, ma'am? I need to return to Ghaladesh for some final preparations, but, considering today's events, I . . .' He glances at her various armaments.

'. . . would like something to defend yourself with on the road back to port?'

'I mistakenly assumed Javrat would be civilised.'

Mulaghesh snorts. 'So did I. Let me dig you up something that'll look scary but you can't hurt yourself with.'

'I did receive *some* basic training when I first joined the Bulikov Embassy.'

'I know,' says Mulaghesh. 'That's what I'm afraid of. You probably learned just enough to be a danger to your own damn self.'

Pitry bows a little as she marches off into the recesses of her home. He realises that he has never seen Mulaghesh walk another way: it's as if her feet know only how to march.

When she's gone he snatches the balled-up piece of paper on the counter. This is, of course, a grievous violation of his position, not to mention a betrayal of Shara's trust in him. *I am such a terrible spy*, he thinks, before remembering that he's not actually a spy at all, which makes him feel a little less guilty.

He reads the words on the letter, and stares at them in confusion. 'Huh?' he says.

'What was that?' says Mulaghesh's voice from the next room.

'N-Nothing!' Pitry balls the letter back up and replaces it.

Mulaghesh returns carrying a very long machete. 'I have no idea what the original owner used this for,' she says. 'Maybe trying to hack up teak. But if it can cut lukewarm butter now, I'll be surprised.'

Mulaghesh hands it over and walks him to her door. 'So, three weeks, huh?'

'That is correct. The file will have more.'

'Then that's three weeks to eat as much decent food as I can,' says Mulaghesh. 'Unless the Continent suddenly figured out how to make dumplings and rice right. And, ugh . . .' Her hand goes to her stomach. 'I thought for so long my stomach would never have to deal with cabbage again . . .'

Pitry bids her goodbye and walks back up the hill. He glances back once, surveying her bland, unhappy little cottage, the sands around it winking with empty bottles and broken glass. Though he's never been involved in an operation – besides Bulikov, which he feels doesn't count – he can't help but be a little concerned about how all this is starting. And he's not sure why a letter containing only the words '*Make it matter*' could have any impact on whether it starts at all.

Robert Jackson Bennett was born in Baton Rouge, Louisiana, but grew up in the half-developed suburbs of Katy, Texas. He spent most of his time playing on construction sites and in drainage ditches, which would explain a lot. His interest in writing came from hearing about the books his older brother was reading and then attempting to mimic them. He attended the University of Texas at Austin and, like a lot of its alumni, was unable to leave the charms of the city and resides there currently. You can find him at www.robertjacksonbennett.com or on Twitter @robertjbennett.

Author photo © Josh Brewster Photography